HIGH STAKES

The bidding was brisk. When Philippe Manigault opened for twenty dollars, one of the miners dropped out. As the bidding doubled and tripled, the second miner folded, leaving only Philippe and Campbell in the game.

I've got the bluffing bastard, Philippe told himself, looking down at his full house—aces over eights.

"I'll see your two hundred," Campbell said after a pause, his voice husky. "And raise it another two hundred."

This was it, Philippe knew. His big win. His bonanza. "Give me a piece of paper," he said. "I'll write you a marker for the two hundred—and for another two hundred besides."

The room hushed and men from the bar crowded around the table.

"I don't play for markers," Campbell said. "But you've got something I want—the woman you brought with you to Virginia City. Bet *her*. Take back your money, I'll stake all I've got on the table against the woman."

Philippe's heart thudded. He had to think; the man wanted him to bet Monique—how could he do that to her? He looked at his hand again. He knew he would win. Campbell was bluffing, counting on him to drop out.

"Done," Philippe said. "I'll call you."

Smiling, Campbell laid his cards face up on the green felt. Philippe paled as he saw the four fives. Desperate, he reached inside his coat. Strong hands grasped his arms, pinning them to his sides.

Campbell stood, smiling. "Don't hurt the gentleman," he said. He took two chips from the table and tossed them on the bar. "Let him have a few drinks on me—while I'm collecting my winnings."

WOMEN WHO WON THE WEST

Flame
of
Virginia City

Lee Davis Willoughby

A DELL/JAMES A. BRYANS BOOK

Published by
Dell Publishing Co., Inc.
1 Dag Hammarskjold Plaza
New York, New York 10017

Copyright © 1982 by John Toombs

All rights reserved. No part of this book
may be reproduced or transmitted in any form
or by any means, electronic or mechanical, including
photocopying, recording or by any information storage
and retrieval system without the written permission
of the Publisher, except where permitted by law.

Dell ® TM 681510, Dell Publishing Co., Inc.

ISBN: 0-440-02709-8

Printed in the United States of America

First printing—June 1982

1

Philippe Manigault
Strikes a Spark

MARY Vere heard horses' hooves and the clatter of wheels on the road. Running to the window, she looked down from her third-floor room to watch as the dark outline of a carriage disappeared in the direction of the Randolph plantation.

It had been the fifth carriage in the last ten minutes. Mary peered toward the Randolph place, seeing the distant glow of lights in the April darkness. Though she listened intently, she heard only the fading hoofbeats of the horses.

For a moment she stood at the window, undecided. Rowena, her long-haired white cat, twined herself about Mary's feet. Lifting the cat, Mary stroked her, feeling the softness of her fur against her face. She laid the cat in her basket and, draping a shawl around her shoulders, she unbolted the door of her tower room and stepped silently into the corridor.

In her bare feet she padded swiftly down the narrow, curving stairway to the second floor, where she

paused on the landing. The old Jarvis house was
silent around her. The Jarvis family and most of the
house slaves had long since left for the Randolph's.
Mary, who was Clara Jarvis' maid, was neither family nor slave.

As she raced down the stairs, the single lamp on
the wall above her threw her shadow across the railing and into the entry hall. At the bottom of the stairs
she made her way into the dim reaches of the rear
of the house, crossed the deserted kitchen, eased open
the back door, and slipped into the mild Alabama evening.

Her heart raced with excitement and anticipation.
There was no moon, but the night was clear and the
stars shone brightly, dimly lighting the path to the
Randolph's. Hooves thudded in the darkness behind
her. Mary drew in her breath, leaving the path to
seek shelter in the shadows as another carriage sped
past. Inside, women in bonnets tied with gay ribbons
laughed as they bantered with men wearing silk cra-
vats and tall gray hats.

Mary sighed with longing and envy.

Hurrying on, she came to the great oak where the
Randolph drive forked to form a loop in front of the
main house. Mary ran to the right, along a path that
led into a grove of trees. The woods were dark as
pitch, forcing her to slow to a fast walk. Despite herself, she glanced warily to her right and left. A man
shouted behind her. She couldn't make out his words,
and Mary stopped, her hand flying to her mouth in
alarm. Esau? Micah? Were they following her?

No, surely not. The shout must have been the wel-
coming of an arriving guest. She listened. No one was
behind her.

Mary ran on, her pace slower now, so she was
more aware of the night sounds from the woods; the
croak of tree frogs, the distant call of an owl. Music

came from the great house; a lively jig, and she heard the shouts of men and the peals of laughter of women. Her pace quickened again as she left the trees. She stopped. Ahead of her, lamplight shone from the windows of two rows of cabins. The Randolph slave quarters. The soft night voices of the slaves murmured around her as she walked quickly to a cabin at the far end of the rows. She listened for a moment before she knocked.

Dillie opened the door. Good, Mary thought, she's alone.

"I might of known," Dillie said when she recognized Mary. "I might of known wild horses couldn't keep you away."

"Come up to the big house with me, Dillie," Mary said.

"You is gonna get us in trouble, Mary Vere, with your sneaking around where you got no business being. You is gonna get me whipped good and proper, Mary, with them wild ways of yours."

"All evening I've been listening to the carriages go by," Mary said, "and hearing the laughing and the singing. What else was I to do? I had to see for myself. Come with me to the house, Dillie."

Dillie stepped outside, her shapeless brown dress making her seem even taller than she was. Her skin was dark, and her hair jet-black.

"Best not let Massa Micah catch sight of you," Dillie said as they walked between the cabins toward the big house. "Massa Esau neither. Them boys got their eyes on you, Mary Vere; they been after you ever since they come home."

"I'm not afeared of them. If I see one of them, I'll spit in his eye."

Dillie laughed. "Now ain't you the feisty one. You oughtn't be so mean to them boys. If they likes you and you's nice to them, they can be sweet as sugar candy. Only last week Massa Micah done brought me a red silk ribbon all the way from Montgomery."

"What did you have to do?" Mary's voice was eager but tremulous. "What did you have to do to get the ribbon, Dillie?"

"Dillie don't *have* to do nothing."

"Don't tease me, Dillie. What did you do?"

"Now wouldn't you like to know?" Dillie started to hum the tune coming from the house. "Just listen to that music," Dillie said. "Don't it just make you feel like dancing?" She stopped and took Mary's hand. "I'm not meaning to tease you, Mary," she said. "You is young and pretty. You is different, not a no-account nigger like me. You is free just like your ma was."

"You're not no-account, Dillie."

"There's a special something waiting for you," Dillie went on, "and it ain't here with no Micah Randolph. Not with no Esau Randolph, neither."

Dillie released Mary's hand and they walked beneath the trees with the music, the talk, the laughter, leading them to the house.

"Tell me about your pa," Dillie said.

"You don't want to hear about him again."

"I truly does. Tell me. It's like one of them stories you read to me out of one of your books."

Mary sighed, but as she began to talk, she smiled.

"My past," she said, "or so my ma told me before she passed on, was nothing like the folks hereabouts. Not like the folks in Montgomery, neither. He was a white gentleman from the North, a traveling man. Not the kind of traveling man who sells needles and pins or pots and pans. He didn't have to travel, not my pa. He went from place to place because it pleased him."

"Can you imagine that?" Dillie asked. "Going from place to place 'cause it pleases you, not 'cause you has to!"

"And he didn't travel by himself, neither, not my pa. He had what they call a 'retinue' with him. Now this 'retinue' was really servants like me who waited on my pa and brought him whatever he wanted. 'I'm feeling mighty hungry,' he'd say, and one of his servants asks him, 'What do you fancy for breakfast this morning, sir?' and my pa would say, 'This morning I fancy steak and eggs and grits and coffee,' and the man would bow and say, 'Yes, sir,' and go fetch whatever it was my pa wanted."

"Just like old Massa Randolph when he's sick a-bed."

"My pa could buy and sell the Randolphs ten times over, so my ma told me. He was handsome, she said, and in a crowd he stood a head taller than the other men. That's where I got my height, she said. Not a young man, not my pa; he had gray in his hair. And he was kind and loving." Mary's voice lowered and became wistful. "Some day . . ." she began.

"Some day?" Dillie echoed as they left the dark of the trees and paused in the shadows beside a veranda, where light from high windows lay in long yellow rectangles on the floor.

"Some day," Mary went on, "my pa's coming back to Alabama to claim me for his own. He'll take me with him, and we'll ride in the cars to New York where we'll live in a splendid mansion with servants to run and fetch for us. I'll dress in beautiful silk crinolined gowns, and I'll have more furs and jewels than I'll rightly know what to do with. A carriage drawn by six white horses will take me wherever I please to go."

"I hope your pa comes for you like you say," Dillie told her. "I hope and pray he does."

"He will. I suspect he's sick and that's why the money stopped coming from the bank in San Francisco. That's why my ma had to hire out before she died, and why I had to go to work for the Jarvis'.

If he's sick, maybe I'll have to go and find him, wherever he is. Some day."

The two girls climbed the steps and crept along the veranda, keeping in the shadows until they were only a few feet from the windows. Inside, elegantly dressed couples danced around and around to the orchestra's lilting music. The women were dazzling, their faces flushed, their eyes sparkling; the men, several in blue officers' uniforms, were proud and handsome.

"There's Micah," Dillie said, nodding toward a stocky, blond young man lounging in a doorway across the ballroom. "Or is it Esau? Lord, I can't tell them twins apart. I should be able to. I knows them well enough."

"What's it like, Dillie?" Mary asked. "What's it like being with a man?"

"How old are you, Mary Vere?"

"Sixteen, almost seventeen."

"You'll find out for yourself soon enough."

"Tell me, Dillie."

Dillie shrugged. "It ain't a thing a body can explain because it's different every time. It all depends. It can be like drinking on a Saturday night, all wild and screaming and scratching mean, or it can be like waking up of a Sunday morning with nothing to do all day 'cept going to meeting, all peaceful and solemn-like. Or it can be like a jubilee, so you wish it would never end. I ain't certain about that. I just be repeating what I been told. It ain't never been like that for me."

"For me it will be," Mary said. "If being with a man can't be a jubilee, always, then I want no part of it."

Dillie threw back her head and laughed.

"Shhh!" Mary warned. "They'll hear you."

Dillie put her hand over her mouth, but a giggle

still escaped. When she quieted, she said, "Mary Vere, you is so smart sometimes I'm plumb amazed. Then other times you is so dumb. I do declare, I don't know what's going to become of you, I truly don't."

"Look," Mary whispered, stepping closer to the windows. "That man talking to old Mr. Randolph. I never saw him around these parts before."

The man was of medium height, slender, with silvering hair, a neatly trimmed moustache, and a short, pointed beard. As he talked his hands moved ceaselessly.

"That must be one of the gentlemen what come over from the Longstreet's today. I hear tell they's going back tonight, and then they's heading on west. Lord, I wish I was going with them. There be two of them, Caesar says."

Caesar, Mary knew, had been the Longstreet coachman for many years and was a distant cousin of Dillie's.

"He acts like a foreign gentleman," Mary said, "the way he flaps his arms around like a bird caught indoors."

"He's a French *monsieur,* Caesar says. Can outtalk the devil hisself while his friend don't say hardly nothing."

All at once the bearded stranger stopped talking and stared directly at the window. He sees me, Mary thought. She ducked back into the shadows.

"You best stay out of sight," Dillie said, "or there's going to be bad trouble. Look there, that must be the *monsieur's* friend, that one dancing with the Jarvis girl."

Mary followed the direction of Dillie's nod. Staring at the stranger, her mouth opened and she drew in her breath, her hands clenched at her sides. "Dillie, oh, Dillie," she whispered.

Dillie took Mary's arm and tried to turn the other

girl to face her but Mary shook her head impatiently as she stared at the tall stranger waltzing with Clara Jarvis.

"What's got into you, girl?" Dillie asked. "You look like you been walking over your own grave. Or worse."

"I know him," Mary said.

"You does?" Dillie peered into the room. The stranger, a head taller than any of the other men, was clean-shaven, with a thin white scar etched on his left cheek. Though big, almost burly, his step was light. Not handsome exactly, Mary thought, though his brown hair had a graceful wave and his brown eyes glinted in the lamplight.

"*I* never set eyes on him before in my life," Dillie said. "Where you know him from, girl?"

"I've never seen him before, either," Mary said. "Yet it's like I've known him all my life."

"You mean . . ." Dillie paused in awe as though expecting to hear of a miracle. "You mean he's your pa, come to fetch you after all these years?"

"No, of course he's not my pa. He's too young. I can't explain, Dillie. It's as though I know him without ever having set eyes on him before." He's like a knight, Mary thought, from one of Sir Walter Scott's books; a gentle knight, yet strong enough to slay dragons with a single blow.

"You is plumb addled," Dillie said. "Let me tell you what's the matter with you, Mary Vere. You been sitting in your room up there in the Jarvis tower reading too many of them books. What you need is a good licking or a good loving, one or the other. Or maybe both. What my mammy—" Dillie's hand went to her mouth, and she glanced warily right and left into the darkness along the sides of the veranda.

"Someone coming," she whispered urgently. Grasping Mary's hand, Dillie tried to pull her away, but Mary shook her off, her gaze still fixed on the stranger dancing inside. Dillie stared wide-eyed at Mary for a moment, then turned and ran from the veranda.

"You're like a Dickens waif, her nose pressed against the lighted windowpane of a candy shop, dreaming of the sweets within."

Slowly, reluctantly, Mary looked away from the ballroom and into the shadows where the voice had come from. The bearded stranger she had seen a few minutes before stepped into the light and bowed elaborately.

"Philippe Manigault at your service, *mademoiselle*," he said.

In spite of herself, Mary smiled.

"You now have an advantage over me," Philippe said. When Mary stared uncomprehendingly at him, he added, "You're privy to my name, though I don't know yours."

"I'm Mary Vere. From the Jarvis place down the road."

"Mary Vere. The bitter truth, perhaps."

"I'm afraid I don't understand."

"The meaning of your name. But ah, what's in a name? 'That which we call a rose, by any other name would smell as sweet.'" Philippe shook his head sadly, then looked up at the panoply of stars overhead. "On such a night as this—" he began. "What comes next? I don't remember. I truly don't remember. It's been so long since last I trod the boards declaiming Shakespeare."

"You're an actor?"

"One man in his time plays many parts. Here you see Philippe Manigault, thespian, lover of the true and the beautiful, a romantic, a man-of-the-world, and also, alas, a gambler. When I saw your pale face through the window, I made a wager with myself, as I'm wont to do when there's no one else willing to cover my bets. Gambling's my one vice. It keeps me from achieving dull perfection. What comes to perfection, perishes, or so the poet claims."

"What was your bet?" Mary asked.

"The one I made with myself? I wagered that you were really a princess in disguise, a Cinderella searching for her fairy godfather. And I won my bet, for you are, you are. Mary Vere, beneath that drab garment that I refuse to dignify with the word gown, is a beautiful woman waiting to be born. Wouldn't it be a triumph of triumphs if I were to serve as midwife at such a birth?"

"I don't understand half of what you're saying."

"And yet, my dear, you're blushing. It becomes you. Here, let me look at you. Come closer, don't be afraid. I spring from a branch of the Charleston Manigaults and, as you may or may not know, their motto, and mine, is 'No lady need fear.' That's a free translation. The motto's in Latin, of course."

"You're making sport of me," Mary said.

"No, I'm not, I assure you. When you know me better you'll realize I'm never more serious than when I appear to jest. My only possessions are my wit, my dreams, and my tongue—and I mean to use all three as best I can, God willing. Now step into the light and let me look at you. Good. As I suspected, your hair's as dark as the blackest night, your eyes the warm brown of topaz, your skin as pale as the quarter-moon."

"More Shakespeare?" she asked.

"No, undistilled Manigault. No poet ever breathed who could do you justice, Mary Vere."

Behind them, the orchestra played a Viennese waltz. Philippe bowed and held out his arms. "May I have the pleasure of this dance, *mademoiselle*?"

Mary smiled up at him, curtsying. "You may," she said.

He took her hand in his, and before she realized

his intent, he was leading her across the veranda to the door opening into the parlor next to the ballroom.

"No, you mustn't." Mary tried to pull away but his grip on her hand only tightened. "I can't go in there. I'm a servant. I'm not dressed." She looked down at her feet. "I have no shoes," she said, not knowing whether to laugh or cry.

"You're lovelier than any of those begowned and bejewelled women inside." Philippe told her. "On the stroke of midnight your nondescript dress will be transformed into a magnificent gown, your feet will be encased in the smallest slippers to be found in all the state of Alabama, and diamonds will appear to crown your magnificent black hair."

"No, no, no. None of that will happen."

"Wait, you'll see. Philippe Manigault is seldom mistaken when it comes to matters of this sort. He may lose at cards, be outshot by duellists, be beaten and robbed by thugs, but—"

He stopped walking so abruptly that Mary ran into him. Looking around Philippe, she saw one of the Randolph twins standing in the doorway with his arms folded.

"I've asked this young lady to dance," Philippe told him. "If you would be so kind as to stand aside, sir."

"She can't come in this house," young Randolph said. Micah? Was it Micah or Esau? Mary couldn't be sure.

"Not even at the invitation of your father's house-guest?"

Micah, if Micah it was, looked from Philippe to Mary, his glance lingering on her, his full lips twisting into a smile as his eyes roved up and down her slim body. She stared back at him, unflinching, and wondered how Dillie could suffer to lie with him.

"No, sir," Micah said, "she may not. Not only is she a hired servant in Cyrus Jarvis' employ, she ain't as white as she looks. If you were a Manigault from Charleston you'd never presume to bring her inside, much less dance with her."

"Are you questioning my veracity as to my antecedents?" Philippe asked. "After all, sir, I might question yours with quite disastrous results."

"No, sir, I ain't. I'm stating a fact."

As the two men glared at one another, Mary expected the charged air to kindle. But no; Philippe looked away.

"As you wish," he said. "This house, after all, is yours."

Mary, relieved yet disappointed, glared at Micah as his gaze lingered on her for a moment before he nodded and went inside, shutting the door behind him.

"The man's a boor," Philippe said. "It's unfortunate and unexplainable that the good Lord saw fit to create him in duplicate." He sighed. "You don't doubt me, do you?" he asked Mary.

Despite his bantering tone, she realized he was serious. Suddenly she felt much older than Philippe, as though he was a child who needed her to reassure him.

"No," she said firmly, "I don't doubt you."

She spoke the truth. Although she hadn't followed much of what he had said, and though his frivolous manner made her suspect that many of his statements were nothing more than flights of fancy, she believed him. She believed *in* him.

"Shall we dance?" Philippe asked.

She came into his arms, and he whirled her around the veranda, dipping and gliding to the rise and fall of the music. Mary, her head back, closed her eyes, forgetting everything except the gay whirl of the dance. All too soon the music stopped. Philippe bowed and she curtsied to him.

She heard clapping and, startled, turned to see the tall stranger watching them from the shadows.

"It's time we were saying our goodbyes," he told Philippe, stepping into the light. The brown of his eyes, Mary noticed, was interspersed with strange wedges of yellow. She stared up at him, fascinated.

"This always happens," Philippe said, looking from Mary to his companion. "It's my fate to discover lovely women and have you snatch them away without raising your hand."

"We'll be late getting back to the Longstreet's as it is," the stranger said. He looked at Mary, seeming to see her for the first time, and his eyebrows raised slightly as he took in her well-worn dress and bare feet.

"This is Mary Vere, a princess in disguise," Philippe said. "At midnight I intend to turn her pumpkin into a coach-and-four." Philippe's voice was dispirited, as though his friend's glare had been the barb of reality that punctured his balloon of fancy and caused it to fall to earth in a limp heap.

"My heartfelt apologies," Philippe said to Mary. "Duty calls and I must answer. The demands of the world are too much with us, I'm afraid."

Mary ignored him, staring at his friend. "You have the advantage," she summoned the courage to say.

Philippe smiled. "You learn quickly," he told her.

"Jeremy Johnston," the stranger said. With a nod, he swung about and made for the house. Philippe followed, looking at Jeremy, back to Mary, and at Jeremy again. In the open doorway he swept off an imaginary hat and bowed.

"*Au revoir*," Philippe said. Glancing after Jeremy, he added, as though explaining his friend to her, "I saved his life once many years ago, so now he's beholden to me."

The door closed behind him, leaving Mary alone

on the veranda. Not only was she alone, she *felt* alone, more so than she ever remembered feeling before, as a street seems especially empty after a parade has passed by.

She ran from the veranda into the night, ignoring the music coming once more from the Randolph house. Uncertain, she paused near the first of the slave cabins, wondering whether to seek out Dillie, but after a moment she turned away, not wanting to talk to Dillie or anyone else. As she walked rapidly from the cabins she savored her meeting with Philippe and Jeremy, repeating every word to herself so she wouldn't forget them.

The sound of low voices roused her from her reverie. Looking up, she saw the glow of a cigar where a group of coachmen stood talking near the stables. She recognized the high-pitched voice of Caesar, the Longstreet's slave, recounting an involved tale of an overnight journey to Montgomery.

Mary hastened away from the shed-like stable buildings, skirted the empty carriages, and ran along the road leading home. Ahead of her she heard a horse, the beat of its hooves receding into the night. Suddenly she stopped. It must be nearing midnight. At midnight, Philippe had said, a pumpkin would turn into a coach-and-four. Retracing her steps, she approached the carriages until their silhouettes were high and dark against the lights of the house. Not that one, nor this. Yes, here, this was the carriage that had brought the two strangers here and would soon return them to the Longstreet's.

Going to the rear of the carriage, Mary ran her hands along the side of the boot. Careful to make no noise, she climbed onto a spoke of the wheel, lifted the cover and felt inside. The boot was empty. Hope surged through her and she smiled. Caesar hadn't yet harnessed the horses so she had time if she hurried.

This was her chance, she told herself, perhaps her only chance. She had seen too many other servants and slave girls become big with child, and watched as they married into a life of drudgery. That wasn't for her; not for Mary Vere. She wasn't meant to be a servant for the rest of her life. The world beckoned to her. Somewhere in that world she would find her father.

Mary hurried down the road away from the Randolph house, heedless of the noise she made as she ran, not caring whether or not she was seen. She passed no-one. Panting as she ran into the Jarvis yard, she looked up at the three-story house looming darkly over her, chimneys thrusting into the sky, a weak light shining through two of the rear windows. Mary was certain that no-one had returned from the ball yet.

Still hurrying, though careful not to disturb any of the house slaves who might be asleep in the west wing, she entered the house through the back door, made her way to the stairs, and climbed to the second floor. At the foot of the narrow steps leading to the tower, she hesitated, shivering slightly without knowing why.

As she climbed the last of the stairs, she murmured reassuringly to herself. She'd retrieve her small savings from its hiding place, pack her carpetbag, take her cat, and be ready to leave this house forever. Mary felt no regrets. She had never been happy here as a servant and, besides, she was no longer a child. She could do as she pleased. No matter what some men might think. Remembering the cursory glance of Jeremy Johnston, she frowned. He'll not look at me like that the next time he sees me, she vowed.

She opened the door and stepped into the darkness, walking to the small table in the center of the room. She slid out the drawer and felt inside for a match to light the candle as the cat curled herself around her legs.

Startled by a sound behind her, she whirled around and heard a click as the door of her room closed. A light flared and she saw Micah Randolph grinning at her. Or was it Esau?

"I've been waiting for you," he said.

2

Midnight

"WHAT do you want?" Mary's hand went to her breast as she backed away. The cat scuttled under the bed.

"You know damn well what I want. I want you—and I mean to have you."

The match went out and Micah swore. Mary suppressed a scream, realizing that there was no one to hear her. On tiptoe, she made her way toward the door in the darkness, skirting the spot where she had last seen Micah, holding her breath, afraid he would realize what she was doing.

I'm past him now, she told herself. She reached out and touched the rough wood of the wall, her fingers gliding to the right. There. The frame of the door. Once she escaped into the darkened house he would never be able to find her.

As she felt for the latch she heard a scratching behind her. Glancing over her shoulder, she saw Micah's back shadowed by the flame from the match in his hand. He lit the candle on the table as she lifted the

latch and pulled. The door refused to open—he had
slid home the bolt. Her fingers grasped the bolt's knob
and she desperately shoved it to one side. Footsteps
pounded behind her, an arm circled her waist and
she felt herself lifted into the air.

After pausing to rebolt the door, Micah carried her
across the room and held her over the bed. Without
warning, he threw her forward so she sprawled face
down on the quilted coverlet. Twisting to look up
at him, she saw him smirking down at her, his brawny
body seeming to fill the room.

"You got a choice," he said. "You can let me pleasure you and we can be friends, or you can fight me
so I'll have to take you forcefully. Tell me which way
it's to be."

Stunned by her predicament, Mary shook her head,
her thoughts racing. She knew the twins feared their
father—he had beaten them unmercifully when they
were expelled from the Citadel. She would have to
discover which of the two boys was threatening her.

"Your pa will whip you when he finds out, Micah."
She watched closely to see his reaction to the name.

"Micah? What makes you reckon I'm Micah? Maybe I'm Esau. Don't I look like Esau?"

"You're Micah," she said with more conviction than
she felt.

"Call me Micah if you like." He smiled. "You're
not finding out which I am. It'd be just like you
to go running to pa with some tale about me, but
he's not going to listen when you don't know who
it was. 'Fair's fair,' my pa always says."

Was it Micah? She wasn't sure. Mary stared up at
him, desperate, weighing her chance of darting past
him to the door. No, he'd be on her before she took
two steps. Wait. The knife. Months ago, after the
twins were sent home in disgrace from the Citadel,

she had heard stories of their wild womanizing in Charleston. When they had begun disrobing her with their eyes, she had taken a knife from the Jarvis kitchen and concealed it behind the books on the shelf under her bedroom window.

"I can be real nice to them that are nice to me," Micah was saying. "Just ask your friend Dillie. Did Dillie tell you about the presents me and my brother brought her from Montgomery?"

Mary nodded. If she could only distract him long enough to get the knife. That would scare him off.

"Well?" Micah asked. "Are we going to be friends, me and you? It makes no never-mind to me, I like the feisty kind as well as the other. Better, maybe."

Mary was suddenly calm. She felt as though she was standing outside of herself, watching herself act a part in a play.

"You won't hurt me?" She looked up at Micah with a tremor in her voice. "You're so big. I'm scared 'cause you're so big."

"I ain't never had no complaints," Micah said. He drew himself to his full height and put his hands on his hips, seeming to swagger even though he was standing still.

Mary pushed herself up until she was sitting on the edge of the bed. "Snuff the candle," she told him.

"No, no." Micah shook his head. "I'm not letting you out of my sight again. Besides, I like to see the merchandise."

With what she hoped sounded like a quavering sigh, Mary stood and faced him. Micah reached for her but she put her hands on his chest to hold him off.

"I thought you wanted to see what you were getting," she whispered.

She brought her hands to her throat and twisted

the top button free. Her dress fell slightly open. "Let me take off my dress first. All right, Micah?" She made her voice as sweet as she could.

He smiled and stepped back, watching raptly as Mary undid the rest of the buttons, her dress falling down to reveal the tops of her full breasts above her camisole.

Mary, noting his wide-eyed stare, had, for the first time in her life, a glimmering of a woman's power over men. Of *her* power over men.

She reached down, crossed her arms, and gathered her skirts. After she raised them a few inches above the floor she glanced at Micah whose eyes were following her every move.

Smiling at him, she drew the dress up over her body until she was free of its folds, raised it over her head and, in one continuous motion, hurled it at Micah. The dress wrapped itself about his head. He swore, wildly reaching for Mary with one hand while trying to pull the dress from his face with the other.

Mary slipped past him to the window, pushed the books aside and grasped the handle of the hidden knife. Whirling, she faced Micah who had freed himself from the clinging dress. Hurling it to the floor, he lunged at her.

"No!" she shouted. The knife blade glittered in the candlelight.

Micah stopped an arm's length from her, staring at the knife.

"I'll kill you," she warned him. "If you touch me, I'll kill you. I swear to God I will."

"Bitch!" he spat at her. "Whore!"

"Get out of my room," she said, her voice breathless.

As he looked from the knife to her face, he appeared to relax. Though his face was shadowed she could tell he was smiling.

"You're not going to kill nobody." He spread his arms as a bear might when he rises onto his hind legs before falling on his prey. "I'm going to have you," Micah said, "and you're not going to do nothing." He took a step toward her.

"I warn you," she told him.

With his gaze fixed on the knife, he stepped forward again. "You ain't—"

She thrust the knife at him, aiming for his belly. Micah twisted to one side but the knife cut into his flesh. He grunted in pain, clutching at his side with one hand. When he drew the hand away and held it up his fingertips were red with blood.

"I'll be Goddamned," he said in surprise.

Mary held the knife in front of her, watching a drop of blood fall from its tip to the floor. Though she trembled, her voice was firm. "I meant it when I told you I'd kill you. Don't touch me, Micah."

"You *would* kill me, you bitch, you really would!" He edged to one side, stalking her, his eyes on the knife. She turned to keep him in front of her. "Wait till I get a-hold of you," he said. "You'll pay for what you done. I'll make you pay." The side of his shirt was dark with blood.

Micah's feet tangled in the dress on the floor. He swore, reaching down to snatch it up. He was about to toss the dress behind him when he hesitated, his fair face flushed with anger. Suddenly he smiled. Holding the dress in both hands in front of him, he advanced on her.

From behind her, through the partly open window, Mary heard the drum of hoofbeats and the creaking clatter of a carriage approaching from the Randolph's. The horses pounded past the house and the sound faded. Despair overwhelmed her. That must have been the Longstreet coach. Jeremy and Philippe were gone, and she had been left behind.

Micah threw the dress at her as she had thrown it at him. Distracted by the carriage, Mary paused before springing aside, but she was quick enough to avoid the folds of cloth. Micah kicked out at her. The toe of his boot struck her hand and sent the knife flying into the air to clatter to the floor halfway across the room. Mary gasped in pain and shock.

She backed away, holding her throbbing hand, searching the floor for the knife and not seeing it. Micah laughed and she shivered with fear. When her back was pressed against the shelf, she felt a breeze from the window on her bare shoulders. Reaching behind her, she grasped a book and hurled it at Micah. He dodged and the book thudded against the wall. A grimace of pain contorted his face and his hand went momentarily to the wound in his side.

"You bitch!" he shouted. "You Goddamned bitch!"

His face was mottled with fury as he sprang forward and grasped her shoulders, shaking her so hard her head bobbed back and forth. With his right hand he gripped the top of her camisole and yanked down, tearing the thin fabric and exposing her breasts. He ripped the garment until the camisole gaped open down the length of her body. Taking the shreds of fabric still clinging to her shoulders, he tore the camisole from her arms, pulling and tearing until she stood naked before him.

He stared at the candlelit curves of her body as though mesmerized.

"My God," he whispered hoarsely, "you're beautiful."

Mary struck out at him, her nails raking his cheeks, bringing blood in two jagged lines from his nose to his chin. Micah grasped her wrists and backed away, pulling her after him, his hands gripping her like twin vises. He threw her down on the bed, face-first. She twisted onto her back, scrambling to the other side of the bed to get as far from him as she could.

Micah feverishly unbuttoned his shirt and hurled it behind him. A three-inch gash bloodied his left side. Micah tore at the buttons of his pants. In his haste he had forgotten to remove his hightop shoes. Reaching down, he unbuckled the shoes, kicked them aside and let his pants fall to the floor. He was naked.

Mary, wide-eyed, stared at him, at his evident arousal. She'd bite him, she'd hurt him, she'd—

He advanced on her, still wary, a once-wounded animal returning to the attack. An animal certain of victory. She realized she couldn't stop him from ravishing her—he was too big, too strong. Yet she wouldn't give in.

I'll fight him, she told herself, until there's no strength left in me. I'll bite him, scratch him, kick him. I'll scar and hurt him, tear at his bloody wound with my fingers. By God, no man will have me against my will. Not as long as there's a breath of life left in me.

Micah knelt on the edge of the bed, looming over Mary as she crouched against the wall. She felt the heat of him, and sensed his rage, his blind fury, his hate.

Someone knocked at the door.

Micah jerked and his head cocked, listening. He turned to stare across the room. A breeze billowed the window curtains, causing the candle on the table to flicker, the flame wavering, then, as the breeze lessened, burning with renewed vigor.

The knocking came again.

"Mary! Mary Vere!"

She thought she recognized the man's voice, but was unable to identify its owner. She let out a high, sharp cry. Micah leaped at her, his large hand clamping down on her mouth. She tried to bite his flesh but he held her jaws apart so she couldn't. His naked body, hot and sweating, pushed down on her. She cringed away.

No sound came from the hallway. The night outside her room was quiet. The house creaked. The candle on the table glowed with a steady flame.

A thud came from the hallway. Whoever had called her name had slammed his shoulder against the door. A pause was followed by another thud and a wrenching as the bolt tore partially free. Again a pause, another assault on the door. The bolt ripped from the wood of the frame, the door flew open, and Philippe Manigault burst into the room, stumbling and almost falling.

He recovered and stared at the naked couple on the bed, his eyes blinking, his silver hair in disarray. He wore a gray topcoat and gray gloves.

"Let her go," he said to Micah.

"Get out," Micah blustered. "This here's none of your concern."

Philippe's hand slid inside his coat, reappearing with a derringer. He pointed the small gun at Micah.

"Retrieve your clothing," Philippe told him, "and go. Now!"

Micah pushed himself from the bed and slowly picked up his pants and shirt from the floor, with Philippe watching his every move. Hearing a sound from across the room, Mary, her hands crossed over her breasts, looked past Philippe. Esau stood in the doorway.

"Philippe," she cried. "Behind you."

Philippe swung around. Seeing his chance, Micah sprang at him, seizing his wrist and twisting. The derringer dropped to the floor and Micah kicked it toward the door. Esau knelt and recovered the gun. As he was straightening, he paused and, still in a crouch, walked a few feet to his right where he picked up the knife in his other hand.

Micah pushed Philippe away from him. Esau tossed his brother the knife. Micah caught it by the handle and, holding the knife in his right hand, he took the candle in his left and advanced on Philippe.

"What do you intend?" Esau asked his brother.

"I aim to find out if that pretty beard of his'll burn." Micah raised the knife until the tip touched Philippe's throat. "Now you just hold still while I conduct my little experiment," he told him. Philippe's eyes widened in terror; his sallow face glistened with sweat.

Mary eased herself from the bed, raced across the room and leaped on Micah's back, grasping his neck in the crook of her arm. He tried to shrug her off but she clung to him, her bare flesh slipping and sliding on his while her knees dug into his sides. She felt the thick wetness of the blood from his wound. Micah grunted in pain.

A hand grasped Mary's hair and pulled her head cruelly back until she released her hold. She fell to the floor and Esau, one hand still gripping her hair, pulled her away from his brother. He held the gun ready in his other hand.

"Go ahead," he told Micah, nodding toward Philippe who was crouched against the wall.

"I might of known you'd stir up a hornet's nest one way or the other." They all stared at the doorway where Jeremy Johnston stood looking across the room at Philippe.

Mary gasped. Philippe straightened and began brushing off his coat. "I was wondering how long it would take you to get here," he said.

Esau swung about, released Mary's hair, and backed to the side wall where he stood with the gun trained on Jeremy's chest. The naked Micah, knife in hand, stepped away from Philippe to face the door.

Jeremy's hands fell to his sides. "Give me the derringer," he told Esau, walking casually toward him with his hand extended as though he meant to shake the other man's hand.

"Stay where you are," Esau warned. "It'll be self-defense if I have to shoot you. Anyone can see I wasn't doing nothing."

Jeremy came on. Esau's hand tensed. His finger tightened on the trigger and the gun's hammer clicked home. Mary screamed. There was no shot.

"The gun's not loaded," Jeremy said. His fist lashed out, the blow striking Esau's chin and snapping the blond man's head back and to one side. Esau crashed into the wall and slumped to the floor, eyes closed.

Jeremy turned and advanced on Micah. He *was* a knight, Mary thought, brave and strong, and unafraid.

"Why don't you hand me the knife, sir?" Philippe asked the naked twin. "Before my friend deals with you as he did your brother."

Backing away, Micah looked from Philippe to Jeremy, then took the knife's blade between his thumb and forefinger and proffered it to Philippe.

"Careful," Philippe said, taking the bloody knife and holding it well away from his body. "I had this coat cleaned only last week."

"Take your brother and clear out," Jeremy told Micah.

Micah picked up his pants and started to put them on.

"The pants can wait," Jeremy said. "Get out."

Holding his pants and shirt in one hand, Micah grasped Esau beneath the shoulders and started dragging him to the door. Jeremy crossed the room, picked Esau up in his arms and deposited him across his brother's shoulders. Micah staggered out of the room, and a few moments later Mary heard him making his way down the narrow stairs.

Mary pulled the quilt from the bed and held it in front of her to cover her nakedness. Looking up, she saw Jeremy watching her. She pulled the quilt closer while Philippe picked up Micah's shoes, holding them gingerly as he crossed the room. He stood in the hall and tossed them down the stairs.

"We left the carriage farther down the road," Jeremy told her," so as not to arouse suspicion."

"How can I ever thank you?" Mary asked.

"Don't thank me. It was Philippe's notion to come here, not mine." Mary felt a rush of disappointment.

"Didn't I tell you she was a beauty?" Philippe asked Jeremy as he returned to the room. "Even undressed she retains a certain fresh piquancy and maidenly charm, but garb her in silks and satins, ah, then she'll be the belle of the ball, the mistress of all she surveys. The young gentlemen of Montgomery will compete to pay her homage." He turned to Mary. "If you'll get dressed and come along with us, I guarantee you'll take Montgomery by storm."

She looked from Philippe to Jeremy, all at once modest with only the quilt shielding her naked body from their eyes.

"You're to travel with us," Philippe told her. "It's my intent to instruct you in the social graces, so I can present you as a lady of fashion at the Gentlemen's Friendly Society's Annual Ball."

She could hardly believe that Philippe wanted her to go with them. And after she had planned to hide in the boot of their carriage!

"And what if I don't choose to go?" she asked.

"Then I'll lose my wager with Jeremy, who maintains that a transformation from rural rustic to gentlewoman in two weeks' time is impossible. And, more importantly, you'll lose the opportunity of a lifetime. Afterwards, if it is your desire, you'll be able to return here and resume your duties. Yet, for as long as you live you'll savor the knowledge that you were once the belle of the ball in Montgomery. How many other young ladies, servants or otherwise, will be able to say that? Well, don't stand there gaping at me. Are you coming with us or not?"

"Yes, yes, I'll come. If you'll only let me get dressed."

"Of course."

Philippe bowed, and he and Jeremy left the room, closing the door. Mary put on a dress, pulled on a pair of shoes, and laced and tied them. She packed her bag, hiding her small cache of coins at the bottom. Standing in front of the mirror, she brushed her hair and hummed a happy tune. She, Mary Vere, was going to Montgomery! And after that? After the ball? Well, the future would just have to take care of itself.

There was a tapping at the door. "Ready?" Philippe asked. With a last glance in the mirror, she picked up her bag. Remembering Rowena, she crossed the room. The cat, her head poking out from under the bed, mewed as Mary lifted her with one hand. She blew out the candle and opened the door.

The two men stood in the hallway, Philippe brushing off his coat, Jeremy holding a lantern. Looking down the dark stairs, Mary thought of the twins.

"Will they come back?" she asked.

"I doubt it," Jeremy said. "If they do, we're ready for them. I had Philippe load his gun."

Philippe removed his coat and draped it around Mary's shoulders.

"Your cloak, my lady," he said with a smile. "You already have your fur." He nodded at Rowena. Reaching into his pocket, he brought forth a magnolia blossom. "And this is your crown, my lady," he said, placing it in her hair.

Jeremy, lantern in hand, started down the stairs.

Mary stood as tall as she could but still Philippe's coat swept across the floor as she started to follow him. She paused at the top of the steps and turned to Philippe with tears in her eyes.

"Thank you, Philippe," she murmured. "For saving me. And for taking me with you."

He held up his hand. "Don't thank me. It's fate." He reached into his vest pocket and brought out a gold watch. Opening the cover, he smiled at her. "Look," he said.

Both of the watch's hands pointed straight up.

"Midnight," Philippe said dramatically. With a sweep of his arm he motioned her to precede him. "My princess," he said, "my Cinderella, your coach awaits you."   ᦉ

3

The Friendly Society Ball

"Now," Philippe said, "try it once more. Not so low this time, if you please."

"I'm so tired, Philippe."

"I'm as exhausted as you are, God knows, but you must do it right or we're lost before we begin. Go ahead. I'm waiting, Mary."

She held her skirts and curtsied, head up and smiling brightly, as he had taught her. Her face was stiff from smiling when she had naught to smile about.

"That's better," Philippe told her. "Now the fan."

Mary fluttered her fan vigorously.

"No, no, no. You're not brushing away flies. Use your fan languorously. Turn your wrist gracefully, like this." He demonstrated.

"Didn't you tell me a lady expresses herself with her fan? That when I was bored I should fan myself slowly and when I was impatient I should do it like this?" She fanned herself with short, swift strokes.

"Well, I am impatient, Philippe. I'll never get it right. Your scheme to make me a lady is hopeless. The ball is tomorrow night and I'm not at all ready. I'll be found out the minute I enter the ballroom—if not before."

"Nonsense. Are you saying that I, Philippe Manigault, was wrong? That I possess no gift of discernment? That I can't tell a purse from a sow's ear? Perhaps I've been too hard on you, too much in a hurry. If we only had a few months in which to prepare you rather than a few days! But, *c'est la vie*. Come, I will permit you to take your ease for a short time."

He offered her his arm and escorted her to a small table near the pergola's railing. They were alone, but the upper stories of Montgomery's Addison House were visible through the trees surrounding the small open-sided building and, when the soft spring breeze blew from the right direction, they heard the rise and fall of voices coming from the hotel's veranda.

"I'm so awkward," Mary said as she drank her lemonade. "I feel as though my hands and feet were twice their usual size."

"Sip the lemonade, don't gulp it," Philippe told her.

"You see," she said, setting down the glass. "I've made another mistake. I should have taken off my glove."

"Not so. That's up to you, my dear, to do or not as you choose. But at supper you must always remember to remove one of your gloves."

"Remove one glove at supper," Mary repeated. "I'll remember, Philippe. Don't despair, I'll do it right. I have to. I've always told myself I can do anything I set my mind to, and I can. I'll show them all. I'll prove I'm as good as they are. I'm tired of these women at the hotel with their superior airs."

"I have every confidence in you, Mary. You'll be

the belle of the ball. All you have to do is believe in Philippe Manigault. Trust him. If you have difficulties, he'll be there to help you."

"I do believe in you, Philippe. You and Jeremy. He'll be at the ball, too, won't he?"

"Jeremy, always Jeremy. Wherever our conversation begins, it ends with Jeremy. Yes, I expect he will."

"I've seen so little of him since we've been in Montgomery. He seems so busy, always meeting with this merchant or that banker."

Philippe took her gloved hand in his. "You like Jeremy a great deal, don't you?" he asked softly.

Mary glanced at him and saw his light brown eyes watching her, but she was unable to read his expression. Sadness? Perhaps. Despair? Surely not. Certainly not jealousy, for Philippe had paid her only the most perfunctory and gentlemanly attentions during their week's stay at the Addison House. She didn't know whether to be complimented or piqued.

"I like him well enough, I suppose," she said, "but I don't know for certain because I hardly ever see him. He goes out of his way to avoid me."

Philippe released her hand and stood up. Walking to the rail of the pergola, he stared into the trees, his back to her.

"Jeremy's an extraordinarily enterprising young man," he said. "I wouldn't be surprised to see him extremely wealthy before he's thirty. That's his goal, money. A great deal of money in a very short time. He has shares in California mines, as well as interests in several mercantile establishments in San Francisco. You might say he has banking interests there as well." Philippe had told her earlier that the two men had journeyed to New York to settle Jeremy's father's estate after the older man's unexpected death.

"But what is he?"

"A miner. Basically, he's a miner."

"You mean a prospector?"

"No, a miner. He develops what the prospector discovers."

"And you, Philippe?"

"I'm afraid I'm like the tail of a comet, a great deal of show without much substance. I'm the one who's noticed, but without Jeremy Johnston . . ." He left the sentence unfinished.

Mary went to him and gently touched his arm. "That's not true, Philippe," she said. "You're every bit as good as he is."

"Ah, what do you know of it, my Cinderella? I'm a fraud, a mountebank who plays on the hopes and fantasies of the gullible. I'm worthless; a scrap of paper blown about by the wind, a leaf that was green in its youth, then gloriously hued as it died, but one that's now dried up and good for nothing except to provide fuel for a bonfire."

"That's just not true, Philippe."

Mary had grown accustomed to Philippe's wide swings of mood, having seen him, in the few days she had known him, alternately exuberant and despondent. She constantly found herself either trying to restrain his wilder fancies or rebuking him when he questioned his own worth.

"You're kind to say I'm not a mountebank," he told her. "Yet you'll eventually discover the truth about me, just as everyone else does. When the likes of Philippe Manigault die, there are no comets seen. The heavens themselves blaze forth the death of princes. One day you'll join in the chorus deriding me. Mark my words."

"I won't turn on you, Philippe. That could never happen."

He shrugged. "Do you have any questions, Mary? About the role you're to play tomorrow night?"

The white cat sprang into her lap and she held Rowena's soft fur against her cheek.

"Pay attention," Philippe said.

Mary pouted, then frowned. "Are you sure it's best for me to pretend to be from Charleston?" she asked.

"You see, already you doubt me. Charleston's the only possible abode for a princess. My God, can you imagine the belle of the ball coming from Moncks Corner? Or from Anniston? Or Durham? No, it has to be Charleston. Besides, I've already let it be known that Mary Vere's from one of the best South Carolina low-country families. There's no one in Montgomery at the moment from Charleston so you'll be perfectly safe."

"I know so little about the city."

"You know enough. Do you recall what I told you about the rivers?"

She clasped her hands in her lap and looked sideways at him. "Charleston is on a peninsula where the Cooper and Ashley Rivers meet to form the Atlantic Ocean. Is that right?"

"Excellent. All you have to remember is that Charlestonians believe their city to be nothing less than the center of the universe. All the men from the Palmetto State are gallant cavaliers and all the ladies are beautiful and incredibly genteel. But don't worry about Charleston; you'll find you'll have to say little or nothing on that or any other subject." He began pacing in front of her, waving his arms. "The men you'll meet expect one thing from a woman; complete agreement, and perhaps a word or two at the proper time to let them know how clever you think they are. You don't have to talk to the men, Mary, you only have to listen to them. You may learn little in the process, but they'll come away thinking they've just met one of the world's wittiest conversationalists.

Just be careful to say nothing of any consequence whatsoever."

"And the women?"

"Ah, you won't have to worry about them, either. You'll be kept so occupied by the attentions of men smitten by your beauty that you'll not have to do more than nod to the women. If worse comes to worst, make a vacuous remark about the heat. That always satisfies women."

"Oh, Philippe," she said, "I hope you're right."

By the following evening, the night of the Annual Ball, Mary's confidence had ebbed rather than strengthened. Even looking at herself in the pier glass in her hotel room failed to ease her doubts.

"I can't imagine a lovelier gown," she said aloud, although she was alone in the room.

Philippe had told her the dress was patterned after a ball gown worn by Elisabeth of Austria on the eve of her wedding to the Hapsburg Emperor. The gown was white organdy, embroidered with green floss and gold thread in a design of flowering honeysuckle. Ten tiers of green-edged ruffles decorated the bottom of a vast skirt held out by crinolines and a whalebone cage. The off-the-shoulder neckline was modest, showing her shoulders but not revealing more than a hint of the curves of her breasts. Green and gold embroidery decorated the bodice, and she wore a pair of jade earrings dangling from gold posts, but no other jewelry. The white organdy highlighted her dark hair, worn madonna-like, a gold net holding her chignon in place.

Mary smiled at her reflection, turning this way and that. Her waist had never looked so small, her skin so fair. Her brown eyes sparkled. I'm pretty, she told herself with something like surprise. I'm not afraid and I won't be afraid at the ball. Everything will be wonderful. I'll remember all that Philippe told me; I'll be the belle of the ball.

There was a tapping at the door.

"Come in," she said. For a moment she hoped it was Jeremy, and that Jeremy, instead of Philippe, would be her escort.

Philippe came into the room and stopped abruptly, clasping his hands in front of him.

"Ah, I was right," he said, "that gown does wonders for you."

She pouted. "It couldn't possibly be the other way around?"

"Of course," he said. "I was distracted by the unimportant accoutrements rather than seeing the beautiful woman herself. You're a jewel, Mary, enhanced by your setting, perhaps, but your luster needs no help. From east to west, there's no jewel to compare to Mary Vere."

"Do I really look all right?" she asked anxiously.

"I assure you that you do. Come, take my arm, Mary. Our cab awaits."

"And Jeremy?"

"He'll be along later, or so he informed me this afternoon. The ball starts at nine, so he'll probably make his entrance at ten or so. He's closeted with a Mr. Bingham of the Alabama Mercantile Bank at the moment."

Mary pulled on her white gloves and arranged her stole—white organdy with gold fringe—over her shoulders. "What time is it? We don't want to arrive too early, do we?"

"Oh, it must be a few minutes after nine," Philippe said. "I'm not certain."

"Why don't you look at your watch?"

"My watch is inoperative at the moment." Philippe shrugged. "A speck of dust in the mechanism, I'll wager."

"Let me see," she said, a sudden suspicion dawning.

He pulled out the watch and, with a sigh, opened the cover. Both hands pointed straight up. "My watch tells the correct time twice each day," he said.

"It wasn't running the other night either, was it? The night you and Jeremy rescued me from the twins."

"No, though I'm certain it was midnight when I escorted you from your humble room to the coach—the air had the feel of midnight. Why all this concern with time? Time's not important. We have a lifetime before us, what do a few minutes here and there matter? Besides, we must be going. Here, take my arm, my dear young lady."

Mary put her hand on his arm and accompanied him down the stairs to the waiting cab. As they rattled over the cobbles on the way to the Wheaton Hotel, her uneasiness returned, increased a hundred-fold. A rush of panic sickened her. They were heading for a catastrophe. Philippe's scheme was doomed and had been doomed from the start. He *was* a mountebank, just as he'd admitted the day before. Why had she ever agreed to play this part? She was a servant girl, not a lady. She didn't belong here in Montgomery. Why had she ever imagined that she did?

As the cab drove between two rows of flaming torches, she gasped, tugging at Philippe's arm.

"What is it?" he asked.

"On the sidewalk. One of the twins. We're past him now."

Philippe looked through the rear window. "I don't see him," he said. "Are you sure?"

"No. Perhaps I'm just jumpy. Hold my hand, Philippe."

The cab pulled up outside a white colonnaded mansion on the outskirts of the city. A footman in livery helped Mary from the cab. Philippe climbed down, bowed to her, and they mounted the steps side by side.

Her mind went blank. She couldn't remember a word he had told her. Even if she was able to mumble a few words, which she doubted, she'd still betray her imposture. She looked desperately from side to side seeking a way to escape. There was none. She was trapped.

Philippe pinched the skin of her arm above her glove. "Have courage." He looked anxiously at her. "Don't prove Jeremy right. Show him you can be a lady along with the best of them."

By God, Mary told herself, I will show him.

The door swung open and a servant ushered them inside. "Ladies to the right," he said as he handed Mary a dance card with a pencil attached, "gentlemen to the left."

Mary nodded, for Philippe had warned her that they would be separated while they removed their coats, cloaks and stoles. She walked, as if in a trance, up a curving staircase. She was only vaguely conscious of the music coming from below and of the flickering lights from the scores of candles in the chandelier over her head.

She entered a high-ceilinged room at the top of the stairway. A black woman approached, holding out her hands.

"What?" Mary asked, confused.

"Please, miss," the servant said, "your wrap."

Mary slipped the stole from her shoulders and handed it to the woman. Turning, she saw a tall older woman in a lilac gown staring at her from the doorway, the woman's nose and mouth curling in distaste as though, Mary thought, she'd just discovered a dead mouse in the pantry. What have I done wrong? Mary wondered. She managed to nod.

The woman said, "Stifling, isn't it?"

"Stifling," Mary agreed.

When the woman smiled, Mary realized her expression was permanent and had nothing to do with her. Relieved, she descended the stairs to find Philippe waiting in the entrance hall, beaming up at her.

"Magnificent," he said. "You're radiant tonight. The reception line's next," he added in a lower voice. "Just smile and agree with whatever's said."

"You look lovely, my dear," a white-haired gentleman murmured as he raised her gloved hand to his lips. Mary smiled.

"Mary Vere of Charleston?" a dowdy woman in a pink gown asked. Mary nodded and smiled. "I'm so glad you could come," the woman told her.

"Miss Mary Vere?" the man next in line, introduced to her as Charles Cartwright, asked. She nodded once more. "From Charleston? Then you must be related to the Veres from New Orleans." Again, without thinking, she nodded. "I thought so," Cartwright went on, "I know the family well. Now as I recall, there was old George Vere, he was in cotton, and his son Timothy, the one who raised a few eyebrows when he married that French woman he met in Nassau. Now what was her name?" He stared at Mary expectantly, waiting for a response.

Her heart sank. "I think . . . I think . . ." she stammered.

"Old George Vere." Philippe was at her side. "The man was slightly mad, I believe. Killed a man in a duel after a dispute over a pig, didn't he?"

"Surely you're mistaken, sir. The George Vere I knew was the most even-tempered gentleman I ever met. Why, I remember the time an inebriated young poltroon was rude to George's wife. George had every reason to call him out, but . . ."

"I must be mistaken," Philippe said. "I no doubt was thinking of James Vere of Atlanta. There are so many Veres it would take a brigade of bookkeepers to sort them out." He glanced behind him where couples waited impatiently to make their way through the line. "Come along, Mary," he said. "Good to have seen you again, sir," he told Cartwright.

"I didn't know what to say," Mary told Philippe once they were out of earshot.

"There's no harm done. Now, let me peruse your card. I'll reserve the next dance and the one just before supper. That's customary." He handed the card back, nodded to Mary, and she preceded him into the ballroom.

She'd never beheld anything so grand. Dancing couples whirled around the immense room on a newly waxed parquet floor that gleamed in the gaslight. Palms and potted plants had been placed along the sides of the room to form shaded nooks. Cut flowers graced both the mantels and the sides of the stairs leading to a balcony where the orchestra was partially concealed by greenery. Through glass doors at the far end of the ballroom she glimpsed still more plants, many in bloom.

"The conservatory," Philippe said, taking her in his arms.

They joined the dancing couples, the men resplendent in black velvet frock coats, white ruffled shirts and matching white gloves, the women in colorful hoopskirts, pastels for the most part; pale blues, yellows, and greens. Corsages flowered on their breasts, jewels glittered above the décolletage of their bodices and from their hair; flashing diamonds and sapphires, glowing rubies and emeralds.

The music stopped and Philippe released her, bowing. Only when she saw the other women curtsying to their partners did Mary remember to do the same.

As they walked from the floor, she glanced at the archway leading into the ballroom. She drew in her breath. Jeremy, tall and scowling, gazed from one couple to the next, his face bronzed even in the pale glow from the gas lamps on either side of him. No, he wasn't handsome, she decided, her heart racing. Why was it then that the mere glimpse of him made her forget all else?

Jeremy caught sight of them and his face broke into a sudden smile. He was smiling at her, Mary was certain. She smiled back. As suddenly as it had come, his smile disappeared and, as though a dark curtain had been drawn across his face, he frowned.

"You haven't heard a word I've said," Philippe complained.

"It's Jeremy. He's coming this way."

Jeremy, after bowing and sidestepping his way across the floor, stopped in front of them, nodding at Mary and then taking Philippe's arm and leading him away. Annoyed, she followed the two men to one of the darker corners of the room.

"There's trouble afoot." Jeremy nodded to a group of men and women on the far side of the ballroom. "Colonel Chesnut's here. He's the short gentleman with the sandy moustache and curly hair."

Though Mary peered at the group of men, she couldn't identify the colonel.

"I'm not acquainted with the gentleman," Philippe said.

"Nor am I," Jeremy told him. "But in the reception line just now I learned that he arrived in Montgomery this afternoon, from Charleston, where he's a member of one of the old tidewater families. He knows everyone there and, it seems, in all the rest of South Carolina as well."

"Mary and I will avoid him like the plague," Philippe promised.

"I hope you can. I'd rather lose my bet now that you've taken the affair this far." Jeremy bowed to Mary. "May I have the pleasure of this dance?" he asked.

She nodded eagerly and he took her in his arms, dancing her onto the floor as the orchestra played a waltz.

"You dance well." He sounded surprised.

He means, she told herself, I dance well for a servant girl.

"Thank you," she told him, resisting the impulse to make a biting reply.

"How the men all stare at you. When I was looking for you I heard them asking one another who Mary Vere of Charleston was and how they might meet you. I'll have to admit you've quite captivated them."

Don't admit anything you don't want to, she thought, but she smiled, whirling around the floor as she followed his strong lead. Why is it, she wondered, that I want to snap at him, yet I'd be willing to go on dancing with him forever? Why must I be so perverse?

As they danced, she became more and more aware of the glances of other women looking enviously at her, admiringly at Jeremy. He's mine, she wanted to tell them. Cant' you see he's mine? The hollowness of her fancy made her let out her breath with a sigh. Someday he will be mine, she vowed.

Then the dance was over—too soon, too soon—and Jeremy was leading her from the floor. A stocky man with a black beard nodded to him.

"I'm late for a meeting with that gentleman," he said. Before she could reply he was introducing her to a tall, redheaded man named Paul Rowe.

"You're quite the most beautiful girl at the ball,"

Paul told her as they danced. "You've won the hearts of all the men, myself included."

She smiled, looking past him as she tried, without success, to find Jeremy. Philippe, his back to her, was far across the room, glass in hand, gesturing as he talked to a portly gentleman.

"There's someone who's been asking to meet you," Paul said as the dance ended. He led her across the floor to a smiling older man.

"May I present Mary Vere?" Paul said. "Miss Vere, this is Colonel Chesnut of Charleston. I'm sure the two of you will find a great deal to talk about." ⳩

4

Tar and Feathers

"So you're Mary Vere," Colonel Chesnut said. "I've looked forward to meeting you." She was surprised to find that the colonel was not in uniform.

"I'm retired," he said, as though reading her thoughts. "I earned my rank in the Mexican War, but if the Yankees persist in trampling on our southern freedoms I may have to don my old uniform again."

Mary didn't know what to say to this pleasant man with the twinkling eyes. This dangerous man. If only Philippe were here to rescue her from him! Paul Rowe, she saw from the corner of her eye, had been greeted by a friend who was leading him unwillingly away.

"I understand you're from Charleston," James Chesnut said. Mary clasped her hands in front of her to stop their trembling. Philippe, where are you? she wondered.

"Yes, Charleston." Did her voice sound as frightened to him as it did to her?

"I know the Charles Veres who live near the Battery," Chesnut said. "A fine old family dating from before the Revolution. Huguenots, if I'm not mistaken. They have three sons but no daughters. None at all."

"We don't live in the city," she told him. "Our house is along the Ashley River."

"Then you must know the Hunters. Hunter Hill is one of the older plantation houses out that way."

Mary shook her head.

"The Vaughans? The Hamptons? Surely you're acquainted with the Hamptons if your place is on the Ashley."

Again Mary shook her head, managing to smile at Colonel Chesnut despite a strong impulse to turn and run. The Colonel eyed her narrowly.

"I expect you attended last year's Cecelia Ball," he said. "The one held at Fort Sumter. It's so convenient having the fort practically in the center of the city."

Philippe had mentioned the annual Cecelia Balls. What had he told her, if anything, of Fort Sumter? She couldn't recall. Well, she thought, in for a penny, in for a pound.

"Yes, I was there," she said, "though I don't remember seeing you, Colonel."

"You probably didn't see me, Miss Vere, if you were at Sumter. The fort's on an island well out in the harbor and has been closed for renovation for some time. Hardly the place to hold the Cecelia Ball. Now tell me the truth, Miss Vere. Who are you?"

She spread her fan in front of her face. Tears came to her eyes as she drew in her breath and let it out with a sob. She turned, intending to flee from the

ballroom, from the Addison House. She'd pack—she
still had her cache of a few dollars—and return to
the Jarvis'. Why had she left in the first place?

She'd been foolish to think she could become what
she was not. I'm not a lady. But I'm not a servant
girl, either. What am I then? Who am I?

She raised her head. Damn Colonel Chesnut! Damn
Philippe for bringing me here! Damn Jeremy and all
other men!

She lowered the fan and hurled it to the floor.
Couples stopped to stare. Colonel Chesnut blinked.

"I am Mary Vere," she told him, "but you're right,
I've never been to Charleston in my life. I'm a nobody. I live not forty miles from here. I always have
and I probably always will. Are you satisfied, Colonel, now that you've found me out?"

A man cleared his throat to attract her attention.
Glancing to her right, she saw Paul Rowe holding
her fan, offering it to her. She glared at him, then
snatched the fan away.

"I didn't mean to interrupt," Paul said, retreating
hastily.

"What's your game?" Chesnut demanded as soon
as Paul was gone. "What are you after, you and the
gentleman who calls himself Philippe Manigault?"

"All I wanted was to be someone I wasn't; a lady,
if only for one night, to help Philippe win a bet. Is
that so wrong? Have you ever been a nobody, Colonel
Chesnut? And a female nobody to boot? Do you
know what it's like not to be able to call your life
your own?"

"I admit I haven't been a nobody, as you call it.
No-one should think of themselves as a nobody. And
it's evident I've not been a female, though my wife
has informed me often enough of the so-called plight
of the fairer sex. According to Mrs. Chesnut, the fe-

male of our species is, next to the slaves, the most oppressed of creatures."

"And so they are." Looking at the colonel shifting uncomfortably from foot to foot, the fight suddenly went out of Mary and she sighed. "I'm sorry, Colonel Chesnut," she said, "it's not your fault. I had no business coming here where I'm not welcome. Where I'm not wanted."

"Tell me precisely how you did come to be here, Miss Vere, you and Manigault. I'm intrigued."

She told him of Philippe's wager with Jeremy, of their lessons in the pergola behind the Addison House, of her fear of being found out, and of Philippe's counsel and support.

"The man should call himself Pygmalion rather than Manigault," Colonel Chesnut said when she finished.

"Pygmalion? I never heard of him. Is he from Charleston, too?"

"No, we South Carolinians can't claim him." Chesnut smiled. "He was a Greek, a sculptor in a Greek myth, as a matter of fact. A very demanding gentleman. So demanding, in fact, that there was not a Greek woman created who possessed the feminine virtues he desired. He solved his problem by carving a statue of the perfect woman. This still left something to be desired, since flesh and blood women have obvious advantages over the marble variety. The gods took pity on him and brought the statue to life."

"What happened then?"

"The myth doesn't say, though I suspect Pygmalion often wished he had his statue back again. Women have much sharper tongues than statues. At least that's been my experience."

"I'm sorry if you think I have a sharp tongue."

"I wasn't referring to you, Miss Vere. I had someone else in mind."

"I'll find Philippe and we'll leave," Mary said. "I never should have thought I could be someone I'm not."

"Wait. You mustn't leave the ball on my account. As long as Manigault makes no attempt to take advantage of his little deception, I'll not expose you."

She stared at him. "You won't?" she asked in disbelief.

"I'd be less than a gentleman if I caused embarrassment to a"—he paused—"a lady. If I were twenty years younger—and not married, of course—you'd find me in the forefront of your admirers. I like a woman with spirit. I have difficulty living with them, but I like them."

"Oh, Colonel Chesnut." Impulsively, Mary leaned forward and kissed him on the cheek. His face reddened.

"Miss Vere," he said, "you've just established my reputation in Montgomery as a ladies' man. Now I'm the one who must leave, before I forget my age and marital responsibilities." He bowed. "There's your friend Manigault hovering about waiting for you. Let me offer a word of advice from a man old enough to be your father. Don't trust that particular gentleman too far."

With another bow, Colonel Chesnut was gone. Philippe strode to her side.

"What happened?" he demanded. "Was Colonel Chesnut suspicious? What did he say?"

"Why, Philippe," Mary said with an exaggerated Southern drawl, "I just fluttered my little old eyes at the colonel and he remembered meeting me in Charleston."

"Are you telling me the truth? Did he really say that?"

Mary laughed. "No, he didn't," she said, serious now. "He found me out within the space of two minutes. Did you know Fort Sumter was on an island? I didn't. But he doesn't intend to expose us." She told him what Colonel Chesnut had said, omitting only his final words of warning.

"Well, I'll be damned," Philippe said when she finished. "Good for him!"

"And not for me, Philippe?"

"Of course, good for you as well. You never cease to amaze me, Mary Vere. You're a credit to my acuity in recognizing a true lady. Come, this is our dance, the last one before supper. When it's over I'll bring you a glass of champagne to celebrate our triumph."

He led her onto the floor, took her in his arms, and they joined the other waltzing couples. Never before had she been so light on her feet. She swooped, she soared, she was flying. Elated, she circled the room in Philippe's arms, as exultant as a bird released from its cage. She didn't need champagne; she was intoxicated with happiness. She could be whatever she wanted to be, whatever she set her mind on becoming. Not only tonight, but for the rest of her life, not only here in Montgomery, but wherever she might go.

The sound of music rose and fell, the gas lights glowed warmly, and the other couples whirled past in a glittering array of colors. She heard laughter and the clink of glasses raised in toasts, and smelled the delicate scents of French cologne and perfume. This is what I want, she thought. This is where I belong. If only Jeremy dances with me again, my happiness will be complete.

Looking about the room to see if he'd returned from his meeting, she noticed that there appeared to be fewer dancers on the floor. Were the others going upstairs to supper already? She glanced at Philippe but he seemed unaware that anything had changed.

Mary closed her eyes, letting the light touch of Philippe's hands guide her around and around. What did it matter when they ate supper? She wanted to dance, not eat. If she only dared, and knew the words, she would sing the tune the orchestra was playing. She hummed the lilting melody to herself.

When she opened her eyes she saw Philippe looking to his right and left. There were even fewer dancers on the floor now and, as she watched, another couple retreated to the side of the room. Young men walked from group to group, murmuring a few words before moving on.

"What is it, Philippe?" she asked. "What's happening? Is anything wrong?"

"I don't know but I don't like it. Surely we aren't such accomplished dancers that they prefer to watch us."

Now there were only two other couples on the floor. The onlookers stood impassively along the sides of the room, watching. The talk and laughter had quieted until the only sounds were the music and the rustle of the skirts of the women who still danced.

Another couple left the floor.

"Could your Colonel Chesnut, your great admirer, have betrayed us?" Philippe asked.

"No, he wouldn't do that." How could she be so positive? Mary wondered. Yet she was. Colonel Chesnut, she told herself, was a gentleman.

The last remaining other couple stopped dancing. The women, Mary saw with dismay, were quietly slipping from the ballroom, leaving the men gathered around the floor. Men with grim, set faces.

"Shall we rest?" Philippe asked. "Perhaps stroll in the gardens?" There was a tremor in his voice she had never heard before. Mary squeezed his hand.

"Not as long as the music plays," she told him. "They want us to stop. We won't, we'll dance. We'll show them we're not afraid."

"Oh, my God," Philippe said. "You were right. It's him."

"Who?"

She followed his gaze to the shadowed entrance to the conservatory where a tall blond man stood watching them. She hesitated in midstep, almost causing Philippe to stumble, before she danced on.

"It's Micah, isn't it?" Philippe asked.

"Or Esau, I can't tell them apart." Her heart raced, and her hands were damp with perspiration. Her thoughts were in a jumble. What should they do?

At that instant the waltz ended and they were left standing alone in the center of the ballroom.

"Bow to me," Mary whispered urgently.

Philippe bowed; she curtsied. They turned to find Micah and a short, stocky, freckled young man advancing toward them. The room, now that the music had stopped, was hushed. The women were gone. All Mary could hear was the soft whisper of her own quickened breath.

"We've found you out," the shorter man told Philippe. "Our friend Micah Randolph here has told us all about you." Micah smiled.

"I don't know what you mean, sir." Philippe nervously brushed a speck of lint from his black coat.

"You know damn well," Micah said. "You brought *her*" —the word was a sneer— "here tonight."

"You've insulted the fair ladies of Montgomery," the other man said, "and you've mocked us."

"I'm sure you'll be satisfied when I explain," Philippe said.

"No more talk," the stocky man said. "We mean to teach you a lesson you'll not soon forget."

The two men stepped to either side of Philippe

and grasped his arms above the elbows. Though he struggled, he couldn't break free. They half-pulled, half-carried him toward the men clustered at the side of the room.

Mary ran after them. "Cowards!" she shouted. "What kind of men are you? Forty against one!"

A hand took her arm. It was Paul Rowe.

"Leave while there's yet time," he said under his breath. "Don't wait till they turn on you, too."

"No, I won't leave Philippe. Help me. You've got to help me."

"I can't. After all, you did deceive us, didn't you? But I have no quarrel with you. You're a woman. He must have put you up to it. We'll see that the Frenchman gets his just desserts."

"You're as bad as the rest of them."

Mary looked to the archway through which Micah and the other men had dragged Philippe. Shaking off Paul Rowe, she left him staring after her as she ran to follow them. When she reached the archway, the room beyond was empty. Turning, she saw that Paul, too, had disappeared, and that except for the musicians on the balcony, the ballroom was deserted.

Impeded by her hooped skirt, she hurried across the entry hall to the front door. The liveried servant was gone. Pulling open the door, she saw the women at the bottom of the steps, some waiting, others entering carriages and driving off. Mary ran down the steps.

"You've got to help me!" she cried. "They'll hurt him. They might kill him."

The women turned from her to stare at the dark buildings across the street as Mary hurried from one group to the next, pleading with them.

At last, Mary held her skirts and ran up the Wheaton Hotel steps. Pausing at the top, she looked down as another carriage stopped and a footman helped two women climb inside.

"God damn you all!" Mary shouted. She smiled in satisfaction at the startled gasp, but none of the women looked her way or replied.

Pushing open the hotel door, she crossed the empty hall. The room seemed darker. Glancing over her head she saw that several of the candles in the great chandelier had guttered out. Jeremy. She had to find Jeremy.

Mary raced down a corridor past a succession of closed doors.

"Jeremy!" she cried. "Jeremy, where are you?"

The only answer was the echo of her own voice.

She pushed open a door and found herself once more in the deserted ballroom. Whirling away, she ran along another corridor. She almost collided with a black slave in red and gold livery, the whites of his eyes huge and staring.

"Where are they?" she demanded. "Where did they take him?"

Fear flickered across the black's face. He hesitated, then nodded at a door farther along the corridor. She pushed open the door and saw, through high windows at the end of a hall, the ghostly white light of torches. Panting, she sped to the windows where she stopped, staring in horror across the lawn sloping away from the hotel.

A double row of men stood outlined in the flare of torches thrust into the ground. At the head of the row Micah and another man held Philippe between them. He was naked. As she watched, Micah shoved him forward between the rows. The men raised their weapons—canes, clubs, the flat sides of swords—and viciously flailed Philippe as he stumbled past them. The knobbed head of a cane hit the side of his head.

Philippe pitched forward onto his knees. The men crowded around him to beat his bared back.

Mary screamed. She darted back along the corridor to a door, opened it, and plunged from the house and across the lawn. She hurled herself at the first man she came to, pummeling his back with her fists. He turned, snarling, recognized her, and gripped her by the shoulders and shoved. She staggered back as he turned away.

Philippe was on his feet again, staggering ahead under a rain of blows.

"Get the tar ready," a voice called. "Bring the feathers."

A hand closed on Mary's arm. She struck out wildly, hitting a man's arm.

"Jeremy!" she gasped as she looked up.

"Find a carriage," he told her. "Bring it here. Hurry."

When she started to question him, Jeremy silenced her with a shake of his head. She watched open-mouthed as he strode toward the crowd of men, the pistol in his hand glinting in the torchlight.

She rushed across the grass toward the rear of the hotel. Her feet left the grass and she was on a gravel road, the stones stinging her feet through the thin soles of her slippers. She saw men ahead of her, blacks, keeping a safe distance from the vengeance-minded mob.

Mary slowed, staying in the shadows as she edged past them. A buggy, the horse tethered to a hitching post, stood in front of a low building. Untying the reins, she found a handhold and pulled herself up into the driver's seat. She yanked the whip from its socket.

"What you doing there?" One of the blacks approached her, his lantern raised in the darkness.

She whipped the horse, called out to him, and the

animal reared and lunged forward, scattering gravel behind him. She guided the horse from the road onto the lawn.

Ahead of her, Jeremy, pistol in hand, supported Philippe as the two men retreated from the angry, shouting mob. Mary reined in behind them.

"Jeremy!" she called.

He looked over his shoulder and saw her. With his arm about Philippe, whose pale skin was bruised and bloodstained, he turned and ran to the buggy. Pushing Philippe ahead of him, he climbed in behind Mary as she wielded the whip, and the horse charged ahead. A man ran beside the buggy, shouting at her. Micah. She lashed at him with the whip, saw his hand go to his face, and then he was gone.

The buggy clattered onto the road. "Where to?" she called back to Jeremy. He didn't hear her as he leaned from the buggy and fired over the heads of their pursuers.

"Bastards," he shouted. "Damn bastards."

The buggy careened from the driveway onto a cobbled street.

"Where are we going?" she asked once more.

"I've had enough of the genteel South," Jeremy said. "Damn them and their money. We're heading west to California."

"I'm going with you," she said. The money her father had sent her mother had come from San Francisco. If she went there herself, perhaps she'd be able to find him.

Jeremy stared at her. At last he nodded. "You can't stay here, that's for damn sure," he said. "The three of us, then. First New Orleans, then California."

She nodded. No longer hearing sounds of pursuit, she slowed the buggy. "The three of us," she repeated under her breath.

5

Captain Nylan Entertains

THE square-rigger *Columbia*, two days out of Panama City, sped north before a freshening breeze. The Central American coast, visible all during the first day, had disappeared below the eastern horizon late in the afternoon of the second.

The sun was down and the sky was darkening when Jeremy came to stand beside Philippe at the rail. Neither spoke as Jeremy lit a cigarillo and Philippe stared across the waters of the Pacific.

"What are your intentions?" Jeremy asked as he leaned on the rail beside Philippe.

"My intentions? I plan to head for the Sierra gold fields as soon as I raise a new stake."

"Don't play the innocent with me," Jeremy said. "I mean as far as the girl is concerned."

"Mary? What do you take me for? I intend to protect her as best I can until we arrive. She'll have no problem finding a husband in California. The proportion of men to women there is on the order of ten-to-one, as you know."

Jeremy gripped the other man's arm. Philippe winced with pain.

"That arm's still sore where one of those Alabama bastards hit me with the head of his cane," he said after Jeremy released him.

"Tell me the unvarnished truth," Jeremy demanded. "We've been together too long for you to lie to me. Why do you do it, Philippe? Why do you take the crooked path even when there's no profit in it?"

"I don't lie, sir, I entertain. Merely because you've twice saved my life doesn't give you the right to try to change my nature. Well, perhaps the right to try, but if you make the attempt you'll find it's too late. Here you have Philippe Manigault, for better or for worse. Take me or leave me, Jeremy. Not that I don't appreciate what you've done for me. I do. I suspect you lecture me on my failings because in some strange way you feel responsible for me. After all, I'd be dead and buried if it wasn't for you."

"They wouldn't have killed you in Montgomery. A coat of tar and a few feathers for decoration was more what those southern gentlemen had in mind. It wasn't like Albany." Jeremy leaned over the rail and stared down at the dark sea. From behind them came the sound of a man singing "Flow Gently, Sweet Afton."

"Albany's over and done with." Philippe's voice softened, almost as though he sought to comfort the younger man. "No-one remembers what happened in Albany. It's forgotten."

"Not by me. I can't forget I killed a man."

"The bastard had it coming to him."

"Thank God it didn't happen all over again in Montgomery. Maybe it was because the girl was there." Jeremy flicked ash from his cigarillo over the side. "You're a crafty one, Philippe. I see you've led me off on a wild goose chase again. But it's the girl I'm worried about, not me. I want no harm to come to her."

"She's an attractive wench. Lively too. With more up here than most men can boast of." Philippe tapped his head with his forefinger. "More on other parts of her anatomy as well, as you've no doubt observed. Perhaps I should ask what your intentions are toward my ward."

"Your ward! My God, now she's your ward."

"You'll wake the ship." Philippe glanced aft along the deck to where two fishermen tended lines thrown over the side.

"I like the girl, nothing more," Jeremy said.

"Ah, if we could recruit one more tale-teller we'd be able to hold a convention of liars. 'I like the girl, nothing more.' Good God, I've seen the way you look at her. I've seen the glint in your eye. Don't try to deceive me; you lust after her."

"No more than any man would. She's all you say and more." He searched for the right word. "She's not like other women. But you're forgetting the difference between men and animals. Men can control their lusts."

Does he mean I can't? Philippe asked himself. At least I've never killed a man, and you have, Jeremy. But he said nothing.

Spray stung their faces, so they turned from the sea, putting their backs to the rail. Overhead the stars winked one by one as clouds from the south overtook the *Columbia*.

"Storm coming," Philippe said after a time. When Jeremy didn't answer, Philippe went on. "Man was never meant to sail the sea," he said. "At least not this particular man."

"The inactivity is maddening," Jeremy said. "You still haven't answered me, Philippe."

One of the ship's crew hurried past them, then another, and climbed the ratlines into the rigging.

"All right," Philippe said, "I'll tell you straight out. I have no interest in the girl, not in the way you mean. With me, she's business—and I never mix my personal and business affairs. Not that I'm not fond of her; I am, and as I said, I'll protect her, just like a banker protects his money by locking it in a vault."

"Is that how you see her? As money in a vault?"

"Don't twist my words. There's more to it than protecting her from men. I have to protect her from herself as well."

"Don't talk in riddles," Jeremy told him. "What are you getting at?"

"Haven't you seen how she behaves? You didn't see her with Colonel Chesnut at the ball, did you? She had him eating out of her hand in a matter of minutes. She's a natural coquette. Worse, she's brazen. We found Micah Randolph or whatever his name is in her room in the middle of the night, didn't we, both of them naked as jaybirds? Don't you suppose she invited him there and then found she'd been presented with more than she'd bargained for? Or else, when we arrived, she decided she'd have better luck casting her lot with us."

Jeremy hurled his cigarillo into the sea and grasped the front of Philippe's shirt. He yanked the bearded man to him.

"If we hadn't been together for so long, I'd kill you for saying that."

Philippe made no attempt to protect himself. "You don't want to hear the truth," he told Jeremy. "I'll say no more."

Jeremy pushed him away. "We've been with Mary

for the last two months," Jeremy said. "She's not that sort. She's saucy, perhaps, but there's little harm in that."

"Ha! I made inquiries at the Randolph's before I sought her out. They knew her well. She plays a part with the best of them. She's sweet and demure if that's what's called for, and brazen if she thinks that will serve her. They understood her. The only thing they didn't understand was why she's never found herself with child."

"You never told me this before."

"Philippe Manigault doesn't believe in shattering illusions or in defaming a woman. Men find comfort in their dreams, their false impressions, fantasies, and fairy tales, though I'm afraid our princess Mary is something less than a Snow White or a Cinderella. She's spent more time in bedrooms than in the vicinity of fireplaces."

"I don't believe it."

"Why else did I bring her with us if she couldn't play a part? I'll tell you what I have in mind, Jeremy. I hope it goes no further. If Mary Vere plays her cards right, she'll marry well. Extremely well. What do men from the diggings know of women? Flush with money, looking for a good time, they're ripe for plucking." He held up his hand. "Wait, hear me out. I'm no fool. I don't intend to have her marry the first sourdough that sashays down the pike with a favorable assay report in his pocket. I've set my sights on bigger game. But the idea's the same."

"I don't like it, Philippe. You have no right to meddle with her life."

"It's for her own good. Left to her own devices she'll end up pregnant by some fly-by-night confidence man who'll leave her without a penny. If she listens to me, on the other hand, she'll have wealth and position. Who knows? She may even be happy to boot."

"And Philippe Manigault. You can't have forgotten him. What does he get from all this?"

"Surely he'll manage to sweep up some crumbs in the process. It's not the money, however; it's the challenge. To make a somebody out of a nobody. To create a lady from a servant girl. It's the game that matters, Jeremy, not the pot I may or may not rake in at the end."

"Spoken like a true gambler."

"This particular gambler," Philippe said, "doesn't much care for one of the gentlemen who looks like he wants to sit in on the game. I'm talking about Captain Nyland."

"Nyland? What's Nyland got to do with Mary?"

"I thought I'd be able to pique your interest."

"I admit I don't care for the sanctimonious son of a bitch. Nyland acts as though he received his rules and regulations from atop Mt. Sinai. No profanity on board, no liquor, no gambling. But the man seems competent enough, I'll give him that."

"His maritime skills aren't what concern me. He's had his eye on Mary ever since we came aboard. Have you noticed how his dour gaze never leaves her?"

"I've noticed, Philippe, but if I took offense at every man who looked at her I'd have to fight the world."

"It's not how he looks at her that has me concerned, it's the way she returns his glances."

"That I haven't noticed. You're foreseeing danger where none exists."

"I've had more experience with the ways of women than you have, Jeremy. The portents all point in the same direction and it distresses me. Not only because Captain Nyland has a wife and daughter in New Bedford, either, though I know he does. It's for Mary's sake. I don't want her to cheapen herself.

Captain Nyland is small game compared to what I have in mind for her."

"I'll kill him if he lays a hand on her."

"I'm sure that won't be necessary. I intend to speak to her this very evening."

When Jeremy shook his head as though disbelieving all he had heard, Philippe put his arm around the bigger man's shoulder. "She's a lovely girl, is Mary Vere. I mean that. The best of us have our failings. Her ancestry's mixed, after all, which is no fault of hers."

"She has a touch of Negro blood in her, I know. What of it?"

"It's a race not noted for the observance of all the so-called civilized proprieties. So she's not to blame. Blood will tell."

Jeremy slammed his fist into his open palm. "I still can't believe what you've told me," he said heatedly.

"We're all better off if we can keep our illusions." Philippe squeezed the other man's arm.

Jeremy shook him off and walked quickly away. Philippe shrugged, looking after him, finally walking to the companionway leading beneath the poop deck. As Philippe reached the narrow corridor below decks, the ship shuddered under the impact of a wave. He stopped, his hand going to his mouth. As the ship steadied, Philippe took a deep breath and went on. He knocked on the door of the first cabin on the port side.

"Who is it?" Mary asked.

"Philippe."

She unbolted the door, stood aside and he entered the small cabin, the swinging lamp over the table throwing their shadows onto the wooden bulkheads. Rowena lay curled on Mary's berth, sleeping.

Mary returned to her chair at the table, putting

aside her pen as Philippe sat across from her. When she saw him trying to read what she had written in the journal in front of her, she closed the book.

"I write in my journal every evening," she told him.

"Were you, perhaps, penning a few words in praise of our friend Mr. Johnston?" He knew she'd been writing about him, for he'd glimpsed Jeremy's name.

She blushed. "I may have been," she admitted.

"I just came from talking to him," Philippe said. "He's quite taken with you, Mary."

"If he is, he has a queer way of showing it. We hardly exchange a word all day."

"Jeremy's like that. I've known him for a long time, ever since I saved his life during an altercation in Albany, New York, years ago. He's quite open with men, but women are another story altogether. The man's hopelessly shy where women are concerned."

"I don't think I care to discuss Jeremy." Mary's forefinger idly traced the letter "J" in the word "Journal" on the cover of the book. "He's taken with me?" she asked.

"There's no question of it."

"Philippe," she said. "Can you keep a secret?"

"When I want to be, I'm as close-lipped as a man holding four aces."

"I've never felt about any other man the way I feel about Jeremy," she said. "When he's near me, I'm tongue-tied. I don't know why—I can talk to other men. Yet I want to be near him. When I'm not, I can't get him out of my thoughts. I find myself remembering the wave in his hair, those strange yellow wedges in his eyes, his gentleness. I'm impatient whenever I'm not talking about him. Is there something wrong with me, Philippe?"

"Nothing that hasn't afflicted womankind for the last ten thousand years. As Shakespeare said, 'Love looks not with the eyes, but with the mind, and therefore is wing'd Cupid painted blind.' You're in love with the man, Mary, it's as simple as that."

"And yet he ignores me. Sometimes I want to shout at him, 'Look at me! This is Mary Vere, pay attention to me.' "

"Do you mind if I make a suggestion?" The ship creaked and Philippe glanced apprehensively from side to side. For a moment she expected him to bolt from the cabin. When the ship steadied, he relaxed. "My God," he said, "I don't know if I can survive five more weeks of this perpetual motion."

"You'll have your sea legs before long." Mary waited for him to go on. When he didn't, she said, "You had a suggestion for me."

"Ah, yes. About Jeremy. Men are a perverse breed. For some reason we don't want what's offered to us, no matter how magnificent the gift may be. We always want what we think we can't have, or what we observe other men coveting. It's been the same ever since Eve lusted after the only fruit in Eden that was forbidden."

"Eve was a woman, not a man."

"The principle's the same." Philippe paused, drumming his fingers on the table. "Captain Nyland's a fine figure of a man, don't you agree? And a courageous seaman to boot, or so I was told in Panama City."

"Captain Nyland?" Mary frowned, not following him. "I suppose you might say he is. I've scarcely noticed the Captain."

"He, however, has noticed you. From the time you set foot on the *Columbia*, he's been casting admiring glances your way. I'm surprised you haven't been aware of them."

Mary's face reddened. "I may have been. What does Captain Nyland have to do with Jeremy?"

"If you were to smile at our good captain, rather than ignoring him, the effect on Jeremy might be dramatic. If our good captain invited you to hold the wheel and you accepted, and Jeremy saw him guiding your hand with his own, who knows what would happen?"

"No." Mary shook her head vigorously. "I couldn't do that. I don't like to be devious."

"They say all's fair in love and war." Philippe shrugged. "But you have it your own way. All I want, Mary, is your happiness. If you're content to long for a man who doesn't deserve you and refuses to notice you, then that's your business. I'm not boasting when I admit to being something of a man of the world. I've lived longer than you, seen more things, and met more people; people that were good and bad, virtuous and wicked, forthright and sly. So perhaps, just perhaps, mind you, I know whereof I speak. What you do, of course, is up to you. I don't intend to try to influence you in any way. After all, you'll have to live with the result, I won't."

Philippe stood up. Bracing himself with one hand on the bulkhead, he leaned down and kissed Mary's forehead. "Sleep well," he told her.

"You too, Philippe."

After he left, Mary bolted the cabin door and turned to stand with her back to it. When the ship rolled beneath her feet and she heard the rush of the ocean, she smiled. During the voyage across the Gulf of Mexico and the Caribbean from New Orleans, she had discovered she loved the sea and ships. She had delighted in standing at the bow with the spray on her face, her hair blowing loose in the wind as the rigging creaked and groaned above her and the deck rose and fell beneath her feet.

She felt free, with the past receding behind her, the future a bright glow on the horizon. Even the isthmus trip had enthralled her as their train rattled across long trestles above tropical swamps and the swift Chagres River before laboring over the mountains to the seaport of Panama. At night she went to bed tired, yet content. The mornings found her eager to discover what the new day might bring.

There was only one cloud—the knowledge that each day brought her closer to California and the end of her journey, closer to the time she might no longer be with Jeremy. She didn't know what his plans were—he never talked of San Francisco—but she sensed that she would not be part of his life there. She must have known from the first that she loved Jeremy. Only now had she admitted the fact to Philippe and to herself.

She opened her journal to the last entry. On the next line she wrote, "Jeremy Johnston." On the line below she wrote, "Mary Vere." On the third line she wrote, "Mary—" When she began to add another name she found her pen dry. She dipped it in the ink bottle and wrote, "Johnston." For a long time she stared at the name before closing the journal and sliding it under the mattress on her berth.

The next day, the *Columbia* ran before the storm from sunup to sundown. Philippe was nowhere to be seen. Jeremy seemed preoccupied. He looked at her, Mary thought, in a different way, as though appraising her in a new light. His gaze, speculative and somehow accusing, made her uncomfortable.

She was acutely aware of Captain Nyland. The master of the *Columbia*, she decided, was a strikingly handsome man. His hair, originally as black as her own, was edged with gray, as were the sideburns he wore from his ears to his chin. His eyebrows, though, remained jet black, and the blueness of his eyes startled her.

She never saw him smile.

He watched her as she walked about the deck during the days after the ship outran the storm, his gaze solemn. The lines at the corners of his mouth, she noticed, turned down rather than up, making him look like a man who has just received tidings of a calamity. His habitual gloominess piqued Mary's curiosity.

Each time she met him on deck or in the corridor outside her cabin, he tipped his visored cap.

"Good morning, Miss Vere," he said, frowning.

"Good morning, Captain." She nodded and walked on.

Still Jeremy kept his distance. So, on the third day after the ship's escape from the storm, she smiled at the captain when she wished him good morning, Captain Nyland paused, the corners of his mouth twitching in what she suspected might be a smile.

"Miss Vere," he said, "I'm a plain-spoken man. I've been meaning to tell you ever since you boarded my ship that I admire you greatly."

"Why, thank you, Captain," she said, flustered.

"I'm planning a small dinner party for this evening," he went on, "in my cabin. As of tomorrow morning we'll be a week out of Panama City."

She waited, expecting him to explain the connection between the dinner party and the ship's progress, but he did not.

"You would honor me greatly, Miss Vere," he said, "if you would be my guest tonight at eight bells. That's eight o'clock. You will honor me with your presence, won't you?"

She hesitated. Looking about, she saw Jeremy walking aft past the mainmast. He glanced up, spied her talking to the captain, and glanced quickly away. Perhaps Philippe was right, she told herself. Every day found them closer to the end of their journey, yet she was no closer to Jeremy.

"I'd love to come, Captain Nyland," she said with a smile.

He saluted her, turned, and climbed the ladder to the poop deck, where she heard him shouting orders a few minutes later. Crewmen scrambled into the rigging to let out more sail, and the ship sped north before a following wind.

That night Mary dressed with care, choosing a gown Philippe had selected in New Orleans. The waist was narrow, the skirt full. "In the French style," he had said. The dress was blue, the color of Captain Nyland's eyes. The neckline was square-cut and modest. Her only jewelry was a gold filigreed breast-pin shaped like a butterfly.

When she heard eight bells ring, she left her cabin and walked along the lamplit corridor to the captain's door. She hesitated, all at once unsure of herself. She had told no-one that she was dining with the captain, and now she wondered who else had been invited. Jeremy? Not Philippe; he was still too ill to eat more than the hot tea and soup she brought him.

She tapped on the door. Captain Nyland, dressed in black, motioned her into the cabin, then offered her his arm and led her to a small dining area. He held her chair before seating himself on the other side of the table.

"Henry!"

Captain Nyland clapped his hands, bringing his messboy running from the galley. The boy placed two sparkling glasses on the table, glancing at the captain, who nodded, before pouring white wine. "To a speedy voyage," the captain said to Mary, raising his glass.

"A speedy voyage," Mary repeated. She felt a warm glow as she sipped her wine. "I see I'm the first to arrive," she said.

"To the prompt and charming Miss Vere." The captain raised his glass again. She smiled, touching her glass to his before sipping more of the wine. The warm glow deepened and spread. The ship rose and fell with a gentle lulling motion.

"What is it called?" she asked. "The wine," she added when she saw his puzzled look.

"It's a Chablis." He raised his glass once more. "To the Chablis," he said.

She had rarely tasted wine before at all, and had never tasted wine that made her feel so . . . . Words eluded her. So free, as though she had left her cares ashore. Jeremy . . . wouldn't she rather be with him? Yet he didn't care a fig about her. A pox on Jeremy, she thought.

"Is Mr. Johnston coming?" She said his name as two distinct words. How odd. And her voice sounded so strange, as if she was listening to a stranger speak. She saw the captain staring at her from a great distance, shaking his head.

"Good," she said, "I'm glad. No," she went on, "not good. Bad. No, I still don't have it right. I don't care whether Mr. Johnston comes to your wonderful dinner or not." The captain still stared at her. Had she spilled wine on her bodice? She looked down. No, she hadn't.

The captain refilled their glasses from the bottle that had been left on the table by the messboy. He started to talk, soberly and unemotionally, describing his many voyages, the sights he had seen, and the foreign lands he had visited.

"I've always wanted to travel," she said, "though I never have until now."

"May you journey to each of the seven seas."

They toasted the pleasures and rewards of travel. Captain Nyland named the foreign ports of call he had visited, and they drank to them each in turn.

Mary had been hungry when she sat down, and had looked time and again to the galley, hoping that Henry would appear with the first course. She found, to her surprise, that she no longer cared whether she ate or not. The cabin seemed to whirl pleasantly about her.

"We're being sucked down into a great whirlpool," she said. "We're going around and around and around and around."

"Would you like to lie down for a moment?" Captain Nyland asked.

She shook her head. "The other guests. They'll see me. What will they think?"

"There are no other guests. I invited no-one but you."

"To the no other guests." As she raised her glass, Mary started to laugh. "Captain—" she began.

"Call me Nehemiah," he told her.

"Nehemiah." She repeated the word with difficulty. She frowned. What was it she had meant to tell him?

"My wife is dead," Captain Nyland said, lowering his head into his hands. Mary heard a ship's bell strike two times. Had she been in the captain's cabin an hour already? How quickly the time had flown.

"My only daughter as well," Nehemiah was saying. "They were both killed in a fire while I was at sea."

"How horrible." That explained his sobriety, she told herself. What a tragedy to lose both wife and daughter! She wanted to comfort him, to help ease his grief.

"Sometimes," he went on, "I despair. Life is so meaningless. What have I to live for?"

He stood up and she had the sudden notion that he meant to harm himself.

"No, you mustn't." She pushed her chair back and went to him. He took her in his arms just as the ship rose bow first and they staggered backward, his lips seeking hers. He kissed her. She drew away from him, stumbled, and fell onto his berth.

He knelt beside the bed, his hands on the shoulders of her gown, pulling the cloth down, his lips following the trail of his fingers across her white skin. She felt a draft of cold air. Looking down she saw that the captain had bared one of her breasts. He pressed his mouth to her flesh, his tongue circling her nipple. Mary closed her eyes, her head going back as she moaned. Her mind was a maelstrom of desire and fear; of an awakening battle with revulsion.

His lips left her breast and his tongue tingled along her flesh to her neck. Finding her lips, he kissed her, his tongue probing in her mouth, touching hers, his hands insistent on her back as he held her to him.

With a sigh, she circled his neck with her arms. She was floating, around and around and around, down, down, down. She kissed him, clinging passionately to him. Her lips left his.

"Jeremy," she murmured.

6

San Francisco!

MARY felt a hand on her leg beneath her skirt, cool
and insistent. She opened her eyes. Captain Nyland
loomed over her. Captain Nyland, she thought, confused. She tried to push him away but he held her
to him with one hand on her back, the other on her
leg.

She squirmed to one side. He followed, lying on
the narrow berth and crowding her against the far
bulkhead. Clear-minded again, she screamed. He
drew back, looking at her in surprise.

"Let me up," she told him.

"Take off your dress," he whispered, breathing
hoarsely. "Here, let me help." His hand went to the
buttons on the front of her torn bodice.

She put both of her hands on his chest and shoved
with all her strength. The captain lost his balance
and tumbled from the berth onto the cabin deck
where he lay staring up at her. He muttered to him-

self, not an oath, she was certain, and rolled over onto his knees.

Mary darted past him to the cabin door, the captain a few feet behind. She threw open the door and fled along the narrow corridor, looking behind her as she ran. She collided with a man blocking her way.

"Jeremy!" she cried.

He shoved her aside and faced the captain as Mary held her torn dress over her breasts.

Captain Nyland stopped short. "Get out of my way," he told Jeremy. "This is my ship."

"I don't give a damn whose ship it is." Jeremy's face was flushed with rage.

"I won't permit blasphemy on board the *Columbia*," the captain told Jeremy. Mary stifled a sudden impulse to laugh.

"You damn hypocrite," Jeremy said. "No blasphemy, no gambling, no liquor. I note you don't include fornication on your list of don'ts."

The two men glared at one another, the air electric between them. Jeremy was the taller of the two, and the younger. Though Captain Nyland was lithe and strong, Mary didn't fear for Jeremy, but for what he might do to the other man. When she saw Jeremy's hand clench into a fist, she leaped forward and grasped his arm.

"No, Jeremy. Don't. It was my fault."

He tried to shake her off but she wrapped her arms about him, pinning his arms to his sides. Turning, he stared down at her and she realized her dress had once more fallen from one of her breasts. Captain Nyland tensed, as though ready to lunge forward, and Mary released her hold and threw herself between the two men with one hand on Jeremy's chest, the other trying to hold her gown to her body.

"Captain!"

A crewman stood at the foot of the companionway looking past Jeremy, unsuccessfully attempting to ignore Mary's deshabille. He cleared his throat. "Captain," he said again.

"What is it, Jenkins?" Captain Nyland asked.

"You're needed forward. A fight. Over cards."

"Gambling? On my ship?" Captain Nyland pushed his way past Mary, glaring at Jeremy before stepping around him. The captain looked relieved at the interruption, she thought. He disappeared up the ladder, with Jenkins a few steps behind him.

Jeremy watched until they were out of sight before turning to Mary.

"Philippe?" she asked.

"Philippe can take care of himself." Jeremy took her arm. "Get to your cabin," he told her. "You're half undressed."

"Let go of me," she whispered.

He pushed her ahead of him. "Slut," he said. "Whore."

Stunned, she drew in her breath as tears filled her eyes. Jeremy unlatched her cabin door and shoved her inside. She stumbled across the cabin, unseeing, with Jeremy following her. She turned to face him, shaking her head, her hands to her bodice.

His hands grasped her wrists and pulled her arms away from her body.

"Why so modest all at once?" he demanded. "Do you save yourself for ships' captains? I never would have believed it. Philippe was right, you *are* a good actress."

"I'm not, I'm not." She covered her face with her hands, feeling the top of her dress drape about her waist. What could she say? She had wanted Captain Nyland, at least for a moment; she couldn't deny it. Perhaps she *was* what Jeremy had called her.

No, she wasn't! She pulled free and crossed her arms over her breasts.

"Get out," she told him.

His gaze left her bared upper body to look into her tear-stained face. She thought she detected a hurt in his eyes, a sadness. Dear God, she thought, what have I done?

"Oh, Jeremy," she said. She recognized more than disillusionment in his eyes, she saw desire there as well. "Jeremy," she whispered.

She took a step toward him. He stepped to her and stopped. With a cry she threw herself at him, pummeling his chest with her fists, angry and hurt, wanting to wound him yet not wanting to, wanting him to kiss her. He grasped her wrists and held her away.

Her anger spent, she went limp and he released her wrists, her arms falling to her sides. He lifted her hair, his hand caressing the nape of her neck before pulling her to him. He kissed her. Mary started to struggle but then a languor spread through her and she lost herself in his kiss, hoping it would never end. A trembling began within her, a feeling she had never experienced before; a radiating warmth, a rising tide of excitement.

The kiss went on and on, his lips bruising hers, her breasts pressed against the cloth of his shirt as her arms circled his neck. For a moment, remembering the captain, remembering kissing him only minutes before, she tried to draw away. But Jeremy's hand brought her mouth back to his and his tongue found her lips, probing between them, his tongue meeting hers. Her heart pounded in her chest.

Jeremy let her go and stepped back.

"Your clothes," he told her. "Get them off."

As though mesmerized, her hand went to the remaining buttons on the front of her gown. She undid them slowly, watching him watch her, then reached down and gathered her skirts in her hands and pulled it over her head, letting the gown fall to the deck. She knelt, unlaced her slippers, and stepped out of them. Now she wore only the torn camisole. A tear revealed one breast, and the thin fabric only partially concealed the other.

"Finish the job," he told her. His breath quickened. She saw his excitement.

Mary felt no shame, no sense of immodesty. She reached down and lifted the camisole with a quick, natural movement, as if she was alone in her cabin, undressing to get ready for bed. She laid the garment over the back of a chair and stood before him, naked. This is right, she told herself. With Jeremy, it's meant to be.

He stared at her bared body, his mouth slightly open, his lips working as if he was about to speak. She saw him draw in his breath, but he said nothing.

She went to him. "Let me undress you," she said. He thought her a wanton. All right, she'd play the role.

Her hands twisted the buttons of his shirt, releasing them. He wore nothing underneath. She spread the shirt apart, her fingers caressing his bared chest, curling the hair around her forefinger. Jeremy tore off his shirt and threw it aside. She gasped as he gripped her beneath her arms and lifted her from the deck, kissing her, the flesh of his chest deliciously warm on her breasts.

He swung her legs up so one of his arms could grip her beneath the knees, the other could cradle her back. Walking to her berth, he pulled down the blanket and laid her gently on the sheet before crossing the room and bolting the door. Returning to the bed, he paused beside the lamp, turned down the wick and blew out the light, throwing the cabin into darkness.

"I don't mind the light." She was afraid to tell him that she wanted him to leave the lamp on, that she wanted to see him and felt no shame that he would also see her. It was as though she had known this would happen since she first met him. Something so fated, so right, didn't need darkness.

Clothing rustled near her. The ship rolled, causing the great timbers to creak. Mary pictured the endless sea all around them, the water heaving up and down as the ship sped northward.

Jeremy lay next to her, his body warm on hers, and she turned to him, opening her arms to enclose him in her embrace. His hand slid between their bodies, trailed up along her leg to her thigh. She stiffened, fearful that he might hurt her, wanting to tell him that she had never been with a man before, but, shy and afraid, she said nothing. She drew in her breath as his fingers found her sex.

She felt nothing.

Slowly his fingers slid over and into her. Still she felt nothing. His lips closed over hers, kissing her, his mouth drawing away to return to her breast, his other hand cupping her breast and holding it to his mouth. A warm glow rose within her, spreading and enveloping her.

Jeremy raised himself until he was over her, their bodies swaying with the rocking of the ship. Mary closed her eyes, imagining the ship thrusting through mounting waves. Then she imagined she was standing on a breakwater gazing across a turbulent sea. There was no ship now, only the waves crashing around her, the spray stinging her face, the taste of salt in her mouth, its tang in her nostrils.

The waves lessened, and the sea receded from the shore to expose the sand and rocks of the ocean floor.

Looking out to sea she saw a great wave whose curling crest rose above the horizon. The wave thundered toward her, mounting higher and higher as it roared down on the breakwater.

The wave crested and broke over her. Mary cried out in shock and pain as she was borne aloft to be carried higher and higher, the water warm around her. She rode the crest of the wave, unresisting as she was swept shoreward.

A trembling rose in her legs, spreading and growing, an excitement that frightened her, carrying her up and up to sensations she had never known before.

The great wave broke on the sand, the waters of the sea sweeping higher and higher onto the beach, rushing farther inland than a wave had ever gone. She let herself be swept along, the foam white and warm around her, until she felt sand beneath her, the water receding to leave her naked body glistening in the sun.

She lay on the warm white sand listening to the waves breaking peacefully on the beach. The sun beat down, drying her, her body languorous and content, her skin glowing. Mary stretched, sighing. She had never felt so at peace.

She turned on her berth and faced Jeremy. Though she couldn't see him, she sensed that he was on his back, staring up into the darkness. Leaning to him, she nuzzled her face against his chest, nipping his flesh with her teeth until he turned to her, his lips kissing her hair and his fingers tingling their way along her upper arm until they found and caressed her cheek. She turned her head to kiss his fingers.

"Don't leave me, Jeremy," she whispered. "Now that we've found each other, never leave me."

He kissed her lips.

"I love you, Jeremy," she said. "I have from the first moment I saw you. You don't have to say anything. I don't need words, I only need you. Just never leave me as long as I live. Promise me you won't."

"Mary," he said, his lips finding hers, kissing her, the kiss going on and on until she felt the trembling begin once more, the trembling that rose and grew.

Her hand slid between their bodies and she touched him, drew away, touched him again to lead him to her and into her, her legs spreading and then meeting behind him to clasp him to her, her arms circling his body as waves of passion engulfed her.

When her body had quieted, she still held him to her, as though fearful he might escape from her embrace and leave her. This is how it will be forever, she thought. A jubilee. I couldn't love him as I do if he didn't love me. We're not two, we're one, we were meant to be one from the beginning. We were meant to meet, to love one another and then go forth not separately but together.

She fell asleep in his arms. When she awakened, she sighed, not remembering at first why she was so happy, why she felt so right. Jeremy. She reached out to him but her hand touched only the bare sheet. Her mind went blank with panic and she sat up.

The ship was rolling and tossing. A wave slammed into the port side and the *Columbia* shuddered, her timbers groaning in protest. The ship dipped into a trough in the waves, listing until Mary had to grasp the sides of her berth. Slowly the ship righted herself.

Mary swung her legs from the bed. The cabin, she sensed, was empty. Lighting the lamp, she looked about her. Jeremy was gone. Not only was he gone but he had left no trace of himself behind. She ran to the door and threw it open. A swaying lamp revealed a deserted passageway.

Mary slowly closed and bolted the door, her heart pounding. How foolish, she told herself, she had no reason to be so fearful. Jeremy had been with her and they had loved one another. Nothing could ever be the same again for her, nor, she was sure, for him. She loved him. Her body ached for his touch. Hugging herself, she smiled at the memory of their love-making.

"He's mine," she whispered aloud.

The *Columbia* sailed through the narrows into San Francisco Bay on a sun-spangled day in early July. Mary saw the spacious harbor open before them, the Marin headlands brown to the left. To the right, two cannon sat guarding a bluff with an American flag blowing in the sea breeze between and above them.

Jeremy had come to her each night for the past four weeks, leaving her cabin before dawn. She had not seen him, though, since they had sighted land.

"Yerba Buena Cove," Philippe told her as the ship sailed around a headland into a crowded anchorage, with the city of San Francisco rising on the hills beyond.

"It's beautiful," she said.

As they drew closer, she noticed several abandoned sailing ships decaying at their moorings. Another ship had been run aground and sat tilting precariously on the beach.

"Relics from the glory days of the gold rush," Philippe said. "The crews all rushed to the diggings and left their ships to rot."

"All clear," Captain Nyland called. "Let go the anchor."

The chain rattled and the anchor struck the water with a splash. Still Jeremy had not appeared.

A small boat approached the ship. When the boat pulled alongside, two men climbed down a ladder from the *Columbia's* deck.

"It's Jeremy," Mary said, recognizing the second man.

Philippe held her arm as she started to go to him. "No," he said, "wait."

Jeremy stepped into the rowboat, the oarsman pushed off, and the boat headed for a nearby pier, with Jeremy looking neither right nor left. Mary felt a rising panic as she watched him climb a ladder onto the dock. A young woman ran to him, her blond hair showing beneath her bonnet. Even from a distance, Mary could tell she was beautiful.

Jeremy opened his arms and embraced her.

"That's Laura McAllister," Philippe said quietly, "of the banking McAllisters. She's Jeremy's fiancée."

7

A Glimpse of the Future?

"You should have told me, Philippe. Why didn't you? How could you have kept it to yourself?"

"You're absolutely right, Mary. I agree I was wrong in not telling you. I thought perhaps . . . well, never mind what I thought."

"I never want to hear Jeremy's name again. Not as long as I live." Mary clenched her fists and stared unseeing from the hired rig taking them from the wharf.

"All this land used to be part of the bay," Philippe said. "Year by year, more and more of the bay is being filled in to let the city grow."

"I want to know what you thought, Philippe. Tell me."

"I'm sorry, but it has to do with Jeremy. Didn't you just say you didn't want to hear his name again?"

"Never mind what I said, tell me."

"To tell you the truth . . ." He paused. "I must warn you, Mary, to beware of men who begin a sentence by saying they're about to tell the truth. It usually means they're not in the habit of truth-telling."

"Philippe! Tell me!" Her eyes gleamed with exasperation.

"My idea was to wean our friend Jeremy away from Miss Laura McAllister. With a long sea voyage, seeing you day after day, liking you as much as he does, well, my hope and expectation was that he'd see the error of his ways. But, alas, it was not to be."

"It's her fault, I know it is. She's a cold and calculating hussy who used her wiles to ensnare Jeremy."

"I'd have to disagree with you, Mary. Laura's none of those things. As a matter of fact, she's a beautiful young woman, quite charming and, I expect, very much in love with Jeremy. The romance, actually, was initiated by Mr. Johnston. He even had to overcome considerable reluctance on the part of the McAllisters. I believe Laura's father, Jonas McAllister of the California Bank, was particularly unhappy with his daughter's choice."

"Then why did you want Jeremy to become interested in me?"

"I could say for your sake, Mary, because I knew how much you liked him. But if I said that, I'd be lying."

Not liked him, Mary told herself. I loved him. I still love him, she added with a wistful smile. I'll love him forever. No matter what he does, no matter who he marries, I'll love him. She narrowed her eyes. But I hate him, too. How could he betray me? She glanced at Philippe.

"You encouraged Jeremy to help yourself, didn't you?" she asked. "For Philippe Manigault's sake."

"I have a confession to make." Philippe tapped his cane on the cab's floorboard. "My motive was altruistic. For at least once in my life I had the good of another human being in mind, not my own."

"If not for me and not for yourself, then who? Who did you do it for?"

"The only other possible person. Jeremy. I believed with all my heart that Jeremy would be happier with you than with Laura McAllister. Not because you love him; love can lead to disaster as easily as to happiness. But with you, he'd be able to pursue his destiny. Be his own man. Marrying into the McAllister clan will make him but another extension of Jonas McAllister and his bank."

"Not Jeremy. He knows his own mind, what's best for him. He'd never knuckle under to anyone."

"Are you sure he knows what's best? After all, he seems to think that Laura McAllister's better for him than you are."

"Stop twisting my words, Philippe."

"You don't understand Jeremy. He's flawed. He lusts for power, for money, for position. This is his chance, as he sees it, his once in a lifetime opportunity to reach the top of the heap in one great bound. No more panning for gold in the Sierras, working from dawn to dusk at a rocker, or a Long Tom for a few dollars a day." Philippe glanced sideways at her. "Besides," he said with a sigh, "he genuinely cares for the young lady."

"No! I don't believe it. You wouldn't say that if you knew . . ." Her hand flew to cover her mouth.

"Though I don't know what went on between you and Jeremy on the *Columbia,* I have my suspicions. After all, I was his cabinmate. Remember, I didn't say he loves Miss McAllister, I said he cares for her. She's an attractive and charming young lady. In fact, she passed the acid test—she's liked by women as well as by men."

No, I refuse to believe him, Mary told herself. Jeremy loves me, not this flaxen-haired San Francisco woman. He's not the kind who puts money above love.

Not Jeremy, not the man who kissed me, who loved me. If he loves me, he can't love Laura McAllister.

Of course he has an obligation to Laura. They must have been engaged before he traveled east. Jeremy will have to find a way to break the engagement without alienating Laura or her father. That's why he hurried away, to rid himself of that blond hussy so he can come back to me.

"I think," she said slowly, "that if I wait a few days things will change."

Philippe smiled sadly. "Hope springs eternal," he said.

The cab stopped in front of the Whaley Hotel, and a doorman helped Mary, who was carrying Rowena in a basket, to the sidewalk. As she and Philippe mounted the carpeted steps, he leaned to her.

"When my love swears that he is made of truth," he said, "I do believe him, though I know he lies."

"I do believe Jeremy," Mary said. "And I know he doesn't lie."

Philippe shrugged and strode to the desk to register. After he left her in her fourth-floor room, Mary went to the window and looked across the bay at the hills rolling away to the east. So different from Alabama! The grass was brown and there were few trees. The pale blue sky was a huge cloudless vault over her head, diminishing her. Why did I leave home? she wondered. Here she was a stranger in a strange land.

What am I to do? she asked herself. She lifted Rowena from her basket, and put the cat on the upholstered seat of a chair, kneeling on the floor to stroke her. Rowena mewed plaintively until Mary laid her face against the cat's white fur.

"Oh, Rowena,' 'she whispered, "Jeremy's gone." A tear rolled down her cheek. The cat turned her head and licked Mary's chin.

How could I have ever thought he'd want to marry me? she asked herself. Who am I? Mary raised her head and wiped away her tears.

"I'm Mary Vere," she said aloud. "I can do anything I want to do and be anybody I want to be." She nodded vigorously to herself.

An hour later she met Philippe, and they descended the stairs to the Whaley House dining room, a spacious hall of chandeliers and draped windows where red-jacketed waiters glided to tables set with sparkling crystal and gleaming silverware.

"I want you to help me," Mary told Philippe as she ate her oyster dinner.

"Your humble servant, *mademoiselle*. It's good to see the spark back in your eyes again."

"Will you teach me to be a lady?" she asked. "I don't mean just to be able to go to a ball in Montgomery. I mean to actually be a lady. Someone like, well, like that Laura McAllister."

"You are a lady, Mary, nothing will ever change that. But, yes, I'll do whatever I can." He held up his hand. "Though if you're thinking to discover a pathway leading to Jeremy's heart, I fear you're in for a disappointment."

"Damn Jeremy! I want to do it for myself."

"There's much more to being a lady than wearing fine clothes and having gracious manners."

"I suppose there is, yet that's what the world sees. That's how a woman's judged."

"At times, I think you've learned too much from me already. You're becoming so cynical that you see base motives in whatever men do."

"You didn't teach me that, Philippe. Jeremy Johnston did. But enough of Jeremy. You will help me, then? I want to change, become a different person, not be Mary Vere for the rest of my life. Mary was a servant. I want to be a new person with a new name. What shall it be, Philippe? Tell me."

He put his hand to his beard and considered. "Monique," he said. "Yes, Monique will be your first name and Vaudreuil your last. Monique Vaudreuil. Does the name appeal to you?"

"I'm not sure. It's so different."

"The initials are the same as yours."

"I think I like the name, Philippe. Monique. I'll have to get used to it."

"You will soon enough. Your transformation to Monique Vaudreuil begins tomorrow with a visit to the couturier's."

"Oh, Philippe, can you afford it?" Impulsively, she put her hand on his. "I'll give you all the money I have, but it will hardly be enough. Can you afford to stay at this hotel, paying for cabs and for dinners like this one?"

"Don't fret about expenses. Despite Captain Nehemiah Nyland's rules and regulations, I was able to raise a modest stake by participating in some games of chance on board the *Columbia*. We can afford to stay in these posh surroundings for several months at least."

"I'll pay you back, Philippe. As soon as I'm able, I'll pay you back. Make a list of everything you spend so I'll know how much I owe you."

"To see you happy, Monique, is recompense enough, though I will keep an accounting in case fortune smiles on you, as I'm sure she will."

The lessons began the next day. Philippe taught her the felicities of social intercourse: the niceties of introductions and salutations; the art of conversation; the etiquette of visiting cards; how to conduct herself at evening parties, receptions and suppers, and at balls, masquerades, soirees, musicales and lawn parties.

Soon the table in her sitting room was piled high with volumes on the social graces. While Monique read, Philippe practiced shuffling and dealing cards. When Monique tired of reading, she joined him, and he taught her how to play monte and faro, and explained the strategies of poker and twenty-one.

"Never admit that you have a knowledge of games of chance," Philippe told her. "Only the most common women play cards."

"I've heard that some women deal in the gambling halls."

"For a woman it's only a small step above a much more ancient profession," he said. "The descent from dealing cards to being a lady of the evening is short and quick."

The first time that Philippe left her alone during the day, she hurried from the Whaley Hotel and made her way to Montgomery Street, uncomfortably aware of the men who stopped in the street to stare after her. At last, she found herself looking up at a yellow-brick building with "Merchants and Miners" lettered across the window.

"It's a private matter," she told the teller. He led her to the mezzanine overlooking the bank lobby, and introduced her to a Mr. VanderMeer.

"How may I help you?" the balding Mr. Vander-Meer asked, adjusting the pince-nez on his nose.

"I'm looking for my father," Monique said. She told him of the checks that had come to her mother month after month from this bank, and how they had stopped without warning or explanation.

"I see," VanderMeer said. "I don't know if I can help. After all, this is most irregular. Will you excuse me, please?"

When he returned a few minutes later he was shaking his head.

"Those records are confidential," he said. "I was afraid I'd be unable to help and I am. I'm sorry."

"But he was my father. Can't you tell me anything?"

He glanced uneasily around him. "Only this, though I'm afraid it won't help. I can tell you that if I revealed all that our records show, you would know precious little more than you do now."

"That doesn't help. Can't you tell me anything else, Mr. VanderMeer?"

"Believe me, I'd like to, but my hands are tied."

Despairing, she left the bank and returned to the hotel. She found Philippe waiting for her.

"I went for a stroll," she said before he had a chance to speak.

"You shouldn't have, not by yourself. A lady doesn't walk the streets of San Francisco alone. Now, are you ready for your lesson on table manners?"

"Yes, yes, whatever you say."

"Good. Today I intend to instruct you on the proper approach to a bowl of soup, on how to partake of grapes, what to do with the cherry-stone left in your mouth after you've consumed the cherry, and when it's permissible to use Adam's knives and forks."

"Adam's knives and forks?"

"The ten fingers, Monique, the ten fingers."

"I don't think I'll ever get used to being called Monique. I still think of myself as Mary."

"Keep repeating the name to yourself. Monique, Monique, Monique. Now, concerning the use of your fingers. You may eat olives with your fingers, or asparagus, celery, or lettuce. Of course, when the meal is over you must use the fingerbowl. You'll find the bowls have a geranium leaf or a slice of lemon floating on top of the water. Dip your fingers in, one hand at a time, rub the lemon between them, and then dry your hand on your napkin."

Monique stood and walked to the window. "Can't we do this another time?" she asked. "I can't concentrate on lessons today."

"Of course." He crossed the room to stand behind her. "Do you want to tell me what happened?"

"Oh, Philippe, it's my father. I went to a bank looking for a clue to where he might be. I was turned away."

"Your father? You've never mentioned a father before. I assumed he was dead."

"No, I don't think he is." She told him all she knew of the father she had never seen, whose name she didn't know, and of the money that had been sent to her mother.

"I'll see what I can discover," Philippe said when she was done. "The bank's records can't be all that confidential. Not if you know the right people."

"Do you mean the McAllisters? I don't want to ask Jeremy for anything."

"He'll never know. Trust me, Monique, I'll be the soul of discretion."

When he came to her room the following day, Philippe answered her questioning look with a shake of his head.

"What VanderMeer told you was quite correct," he said. "The payments to your mother were made at the behest of a Mr. Charles Vere. The bank never saw the gentleman because all the transactions were done by mail. Finally, the deposits stopped coming and the bank stopped making the payments."

"Charles Vere? But Vere was my mother's maiden name. I never knew what my father's name was. She never told me."

"That was the name he gave," Philippe said. "Charles Vere. I suspect he used your mother's name to cloud his trail. I'm afraid you're no closer to finding your father than you were before."

"I'll find him, though, some day, if he's still alive. I know I will."

"You shall if I have anything to do with it. I promise you that."

"Have you seen Jeremy since we landed?"

Philippe hesitated. "Yes, I've seen him."

"And did he say anything?"

"About you? Yes, he asked after you. Wanted to know how you were and what you planned to do."

"Did he give you a message for me?"

"Wouldn't I have told you at once if he had? No, there was no message. Don't look so woebegone, Monique. It's not the end of the world."

"You're right, it's not." She blinked back tears. "I don't need Jeremy or any other man. I don't care a fig what he's doing. Tell me what you've planned for our lesson for today."

"We'll have a vacation from lessons. I'll hire a rig and after supper we'll see a bit of the city."

"Drive to the McAllister house," Monique told him as they left the livery stable that evening.

"I don't think that's wise. In fact, it would be a great mistake."

"Take me to the McAllisters, Philippe. If you don't, I'll go by myself."

Philippe sighed. "How did you become such a willful woman? There's a demon in you, Monique. Perhaps it's best, after all, if we try to purge it. We'll go to the McAllister's first. The house is something of a landmark on Rincon Hill."

Leaving the stores and shops behind, they drove past a parklike square surrounded by new brick houses. Farther on, Philippe drew up in front of an imposing home set amidst shrubs and trees. Looking through the rails of the black iron fence, Monique saw a statue of a naked woman carrying a jug in her arms at the foot of the front steps. The setting sun silvered the water as it poured from the jug into the fountain below.

"Is Jeremy staying here?" she asked.

"No, he's at the International House." Philippe looked quickly at her. "You're not to go there," he told her firmly. "Unchaperoned women do not visit men in their hotel rooms."

"Philippe," she told him truthfully, "the idea of seeking him out never entered my mind."

Until now, she added to herself. She missed Jeremy so, longed to see him, to hear the sound of his voice, to feel the touch of his hands.

"Good." Philippe flicked the reins and they drove down the hill. "There are other men. In fact, we're going to the Chambers' supper party tomorrow. Young Ward Chambers will be there. He's recently returned from Boston."

"When is the wedding?"

"Ward's not getting married." Philippe frowned. "You don't mean Chambers, do you? Jeremy's wedding? No date's been set. Don't let that encourage you. He definitely plans to marry Laura McAllister. They're seen everywhere together."

Philippe's words were like the thrust of a knife. She clenched her hands into fists.

"I didn't think the McAllister house was all that grand," she said. "I'll build a better one someday, with two fountains in front and gargoyles on the chimneys and marble statues of stags on the lawns."

Monique closed her eyes, seeing herself in the parlor of that house dressed in a velvet gown. Jeremy was on his knees before her, asking her to marry him, pleading with her as she shook her head.

"Monique!"

She opened her eyes to find that Philippe had tethered the horse and was waiting for her to get down from the rig. With a self-conscious smile, she let him help her to the ground and lead her out onto the Long Wharf. On both sides of them, buildings perched on piles—commission houses, groceries, saloons, auction houses, cheap-John shops. After leaving the Wharf, Philippe guided her to Sacramento Street. The day was at the edge of night, and the streets were bright with lights. Fourth of July flags snapped above their heads.

They rounded a corner and were in China.

Birds chirped in an aviary, pigtailed Chinese hastened to and fro, and lanterns twinkled outside shops whose long narrow signs were printed, black on red, with gnarled and twisted Chinese letters. Climbing a flight of stairs, they entered the open door of a Joss-House. Mary stared in fascination at the statues of black-bearded and moustached gods; the god of war, the god of medicine, and the god of fortune.

The Chinese have brought something of home with them, she thought. They have their gods, their foods, and their friends. She felt a sympathy for them, for they, too, were aliens in this strange land of California. All she had was Philippe. She held firmly to his arm as they left Chinatown, followed by the thin whine of a fiddle, the tinkle of bells, the clang of gongs and the clash of cymbals from a nearby theater.

"In the diggings," Philippe said, "the first rule the miners make is to forbid the Chinese to file claims."

"Why on earth would they want to stop them?"

"Because the pigtailed Celestials are so different, I suspect. They work hard, keep to themselves and cause little or no trouble, but they're heathens with a penchant for smoking opium. We passed some of their opium dens but I didn't point them out. They're not fit places for a woman."

"I'm different, too," Monique said. "We all are in some way. I don't think it's fair."

"It's the way of the world," Philippe said. He led her back to their rig and they drove through Portsmouth Square, where goats grazed around the base of the flagpole. On all sides of the square shouts and laughter came from the gambling houses and saloons, while roistering men careened along the streets outside.

Monique glanced at Philippe. "Yet we have our whiskey dens, don't we?" she asked.

Philippe smiled. "That's different," he said.

After a few minutes, he turned from the main thoroughfare and they entered a dark district of narrow streets, where their carriage jounced over a succession of holes in the dirt road. Monique wrinkled her nose at the smells. Hearing a scrabbling from an alley, she drew close to Philippe. They passed a pig rooting in garbage strewn on the ground.

Turning another corner, they heard music coming from a dimly lit grogshop. Lights glowed in the windows of mean houses, outlining women standing in doorways and sitting in windows. Men, many staggering, roamed the streets and alleys, while others sat slumped in dark doorways nursing bottles of wine or whiskey. As their carriage passed, women called out to Philippe, only turning away when they saw Monique huddled on the seat beside him.

Who were these women? Monique wondered. What did they want? She gasped. Of course; they must be the women that men called "soiled doves."

"Why do they do it?" she asked. "Those women?"

"What else is there for them? What else can they do to earn their daily bread? If a woman doesn't have a man to care for her, her chances of making a living are slim. She can run a boarding-house, perhaps, or be a seamstress, or teach school if she's qualified."

Monique stared at the shanty-like houses along the way. In one well-lighted window an older woman sat looking at herself in a mirror held in her hand. The woman's hair was an unnatural red, her features sagged, and her cheeks were red with rouge. As the carriage passed, the woman lowered the mirror and stared down at Monique as though she recognized her, an impossibility, Monique knew, because of the growing darkness. The woman smiled, revealing a gap-toothed mouth, and she called out, not to Philippe, but to Monique, the words unintelligible.

Monique looked away, thinking she heard the woman's raucous laughter following them.

"Let's go back to the hotel," she whispered to Philippe.

"I mean to. I must have taken a wrong turning. I didnt' intend to come here." Monique glanced at him. Philippe rarely acted through error or by chance.

As their rig clattered from the narrow street onto a well-lighted avenue, leaving the bagnios behind, Monique turned to look back with mingled horror and fascination. All at once she shivered.

"What's wrong?" Philippe asked.

"Nothing," she said.

"If they're attractive enough," Philippe said, "the women usually start their careers in the parlor houses. From there they may strike out on their own, but age takes its toll and, if they aren't lucky enough to marry, they end up in the cribs you've just seen. Many of the fair but frail ladies commit suicide by taking poison or hanging themselves."

He went on talking, but Monique was no longer listening. Looking behind the rig again, she saw only the glow of the streetlights and the lighted window of a honky-tonk. She pulled her shawl closer around her shoulders.

Monique shivered again. Don't be foolish, she told herself. Foolishness or not, for a moment she had imagined that the red-haired woman was herself, that she had been looking not at an aging harlot, but at Monique Vaudreuil as she would one day be. ❧

8

A Hasty Departure

"How did you like him?" Philippe asked at breakfast the morning after the Chambers' supper party.

"Who do you mean?" Monique held her knife above her steak and flashed a teasing smile at Philippe. "I danced with a Mr. Thomas of Placerville, a Mr. Kravitz of Sacramento, a Captain Bond, and so many others. I can't remember all their names."

"You know very well who I mean. Ward Chambers. Whenever I looked, he seemed to be engrossed in a conversation with you."

"Oh, yes, I liked Mr. Chambers." She touched Philippe's hand. "He's so—so gentle. He knows how to compliment you without being forward. Polished? Is that the right word?"

"Polished will do as well as any other. I'm glad you liked him, Monique. I suspected you would."

"He reminds me of Jeremy." She found she could say his name without her voice quavering.

Philippe frowned. "He's nothing like Jeremy."

"Ward's gentleness reminds me of Jeremy. Oh, don't worry, Philippe, I've quite forgotten Jeremy Johnston. I told myself to put him from my mind and I have. As a matter of fact, Ward is taking me boating on the bay this afternoon."

"Splendid."

"Would you feel the same if the Chambers didn't have so much money?"

"What do you take me for, a fortune hunter?" Philippe asked. When she nodded, he smiled. "I'll admit that although the rich have their faults," he said, "their money somehow makes it easier to overlook them."

"I won't marry a man just because he has money. I'd have to love him."

"Of course, I quite agree."

"Oh, Philippe," she said impulsively, "I owe you so much." She got up and went around the table to kiss him on the forehead. He reddened with embarrassment. "But I'd like you even if I wasn't beholden to you."

"I've grown fond of you, too, Monique," he said. "More than I ever thought I could." He patted his lips with his napkin and changed the subject. "I look forward to hearing all about your boating expedition," he said.

She didn't see Philippe that evening. When she met him at breakfast the next morning his eyes were shadowed and he looked tired.

"We sailed to Alcatraz Island," she said when Philippe asked about Ward Chambers. "The view of the bay and the hills is delightful from there."

"And Mr. Chambers? Was he equally delightful?"

Monique put her napkin to her mouth to stifle her laughter. "Hardly delightful," she gasped.

"What happened?"

"On the way home we ran aground, and when Ward

tried to push the skiff off the rocks he fell into the bay. I had to pull him out."

"Unfortunate, but hardly fatal."

"I wondered why he kept going to where he'd hung his coat on a branch while we were on the island, but it wouldn't have been ladylike to ask. Now I suspect he was drinking."

"Many of our most substantial citizens have a fondness for the fruit of the vine. Even Philippe Manigault is often tempted. I wouldn't judge Mr. Chambers too harshly on the basis of this one occurrence."

"I won't, Philippe. I know men drink."

The next morning Philippe was again late for breakfast. When he arrived, he slumped into his chair and put his hand to his forehead. Finally he managed a smile.

"Are you all right?" Monique asked, concerned.

"I ventured into the El Dorado on Portsmouth Square last night," he said. "Unfortunately, the cards ran against me."

After a few minutes he asked, "Have you heard from Ward Chambers again?"

"In a way," she said stiffly.

"I'm intrigued. In what way?"

"I woke up in the middle of the night thinking I'd heard a sound. It came again, like something hitting the side of the hotel, so I put on my robe and went to the window and looked down. It must have been well after midnight, but in the light from the lobby I saw Ward on the street. He was throwing stones at my window to attract my attention."

"A romantic notion."

"He must not have seen me because he threw another stone while I watched. It broke the window pane."

"You do have to hurl a stone quite hard to reach the fourth floor. You weren't hurt, were you?"

"No, fortunately. I opened the window and called to him to stop. I realized he'd brought a fiddler with him when the man started to play 'Oh, Susanna!' while Ward climbed up the side of the hotel on the fire ladder."

"Ah, shades of Romeo and Juliet. 'Good night, good night! parting is such sweet sorrow, that I shall say goodnight till it be morrow.' Did Ward have elopement in mind?"

"I'm not certain what he had in mind, because when he'd almost reached the second floor he fell from the ladder. I was frightened half to death."

"Oh, my. Was he hurt?"

"I rushed downstairs to find out. Philippe, he was pixilated! He didn't even seem to know he'd cut his arm, though he was bleeding. But no, he wasn't badly hurt."

"You and he are a pair of star-crossed lovers to be sure."

"Lovers! I never want to see him again. I was so frightened when I saw him fall. Then I was embarrassed. Ward and his fiddling friend woke the whole hotel. At least they all seemed to be watching me when I rushed into the street in my nightgown."

"The man showed poor taste from first to last. Philippe Manigault would never have chosen 'Oh, Susanna!' to serenade his lady fair. A ballad would be more appropriate, a haunting melody evoking memories of rose gardens and moonlit nights. Well, I'm afraid I'll have to cross off Mr. Ward Chambers as a suitor for your hand. I'll list him as a victim of one of Fate's broken rungs."

"It wasn't at all amusing, Philippe. He might have killed himself."

"I quite agree. Farce borders so closely on tragedy I often fail to note the line between."

"However . . ." Monique paused.

"There's that devilish glint in your eye again. Tell me."

"Don Fernando Martínez intends to invite me to his *rancho* near Monterey. He'll present the formal invitation to you, my guardian, later today. We're both to go if you accept."

"Don Fernando Martínez! I've heard of him. Isn't he the eldest son of the eldest son of Esteban Martínez, one of the last of the great Spanish landholders? Of course we'll go. What's he like, this Don Fernando?"

"Nothing like Ward Chambers. He's tall and slender and dark. A charming gentleman. So gallant. So masterful."

"I like this Don Fernando already. He may be one of the last of a dying breed, but the Spanish *dons* are dying out so magnificently."

A week later, they left the Whaley House in a carriage escorted by two of Don Fernando's *vaqueros*. When Fernando met them at the gate of the Martínez Rancho, he swept his hat from his head to welcome them.

"My house is your house," he told Monique as he helped her from the carriage in front of his sprawling adobe ranch.

He was as good as his word. She met his sisters and his mother—his father was dead—and enjoyed the spicy evening meal in the company of the other women while the men ate separately. After supper, Don Fernando led her to an orchard, where a white-haired man sat beneath an apple tree as gnarled as himself.

"This is my grandfather, Don Esteban," Fernando told her.

The old man rose and, leaning on his cane, bowed to her. "You have come a great distance," he said. "From New Orleans, my grandson tells me."

She nodded. She could see that Fernando had inherited his grandfather's dark handsomeness.

"Once I journeyed to the City of Mexico," Don Esteban said, "to gather men and arms to fight the *gringos* here in California. I failed. I have never regretted the journey. All of us must make a great journey at least once in our lives, and whether we find what we seek matters little. Mexico. Ah, truly the greatest city in the western world. The splendors. The Cathedral. The multitudes of people. The women." He closed his eyes as though seeing once more the glory of his youth.

"My father once told me," Fernando said when they were alone, "that there was an American girl, the great love of my grandfather's youth. The old gentleman never talks of her but I think she lives in his dreams."

"I like your grandfather." Monique smiled. "He must have been very handsome when he was young. He still is handsome."

"All the Martínez men are well-favored." She glanced at Fernando to see if he was smiling to mock his boastfulness. He wasn't. "We're good horsemen as well. In his day, my grandfather was the best in all of California. They say that I take after him."

"There'll be horse racing at the *fandango*, won't there?" The celebration was to begin the following day.

"Racing and more. You shall see."

All the next day, families rode into the *rancho*, some having journeyed from as far away as Los Angeles. After supper, colored lanterns were lit in a glade behind the house and the singing and dancing began. Monique was dazzled by the brightly-hued dresses of the dark-eyed women, and entranced by the music of the guitars as she danced with a succession of courtly, admiring men.

The following day, the *caballeros* competed in feats of racing and roping. Fernando was right, Monique admitted, he did sit his horse well. He seemed, in fact, to have been born to ride. Late in the afternoon the guests gathered at the edges of a field for the final contest.

"Is this another race?" Philippe asked her somewhat wearily. "If it is, I'll bet on Don Fernando."

"I don't know. But Fernando especially wanted me to watch."

A *vaquero* holding a cock cradled in one arm rode to a hole that had been scooped in the ground. Placing the cock in the hole, he covered the fowl until only his head showed.

"What on earth . . ?" Monique said with a frown.

Don Fernando galloped to the far end of the field, where he swung his horse about. Spurring the animal, he dashed toward the buried cock, at the last moment leaning from the saddle to grasp its neck and pull it squawking from the ground. He paraded in front of the spectators, holding the bird aloft in his hand. The cock's head flopped to one side and Monique could see that its neck was nearly severed from its body.

She covered her eyes with her hands until she heard Fernando ride away. When she uncovered her face she stared at Philippe, who shrugged.

"No doubt an old Spanish custom," he told her. She swallowed but said nothing.

The next day they set out to return to San Francisco with Don Fernando escorting them. As they neared the city, a mule cart blocked their way and Don Fernando rode ahead, shouting at the driver.

"What did he say?" Monique asked.

"I believe he cast doubt on the man's parentage," Philippe told her.

The mule driver shouted back in Spanish. Don

Fernando raised his quirt and struck him across the face, and as the driver raised his arm to defend himself, Fernando struck him again, knocking him from the cart onto the ground. The don shouted orders to a *vaquero*, who rode forward and grasped the mule's reins to lead the animal from the trail.

Don Fernando left them at the Whaley House, sweeping his hat from his head and bowing. "*Vaya con Dios*," he said.

Later, at supper, Monique and Philippe seemed to find little to talk about. Finally, over wine, he asked, "What do you think of Don Fernando?"

"He's gallant and charming," she said, "and a terrible brute. If I married him I'd be a servant all over again, a servant in my own house. I don't intend to serve others ever again. I'm afraid you'll have to cross Don Fernando Martínez from your list of eligible men, Philippe."

"I already have," he said with a sigh. Philippe brightened. "That William Rogerson seems a pleasant fellow," he said.

"I've talked to Mr. Rogerson. Did you know he was one of the first to stake a claim near the original gold strike at Sutter's Mill?"

"No, I didn't."

"Some easterners jumped his claim, or so he told me. Later, he claims to have bought some of the best commercial property in San Francisco. But the bankers, he said, waited until his insurance lapsed and burned his buildings to the ground so he had to sell out at a loss."

"A distressing series of circumstances, if true."

"Now he has a mining claim in Nevada's Washoe country. The mine's rich in gold, according to the assay report. He only needs a thousand dollars to develop it."

"He doesn't have the money, I take it."

"No, he doesn't. He intended to borrow it from me or from you."

Philippe snorted. "I can't abide these fortune hunters. And after all the hopes I had for Mr. Rogerson. After all, he does look like . . ." He stopped suddenly.

"You can say it, Philippe. He resembles Jeremy. He's big like Jeremy and has the same brown hair and brown eyes. That's why . . ." Monique bit her lip. "That's why I thought I might like him."

"There are thousands of other men in San Francisco," Philippe said. "We mustn't despair."

That night, Monique stood in the window of her room holding Rowena as she looked down at the lights of the city.

"I tried, Rowena," she said.

The cat purred contentedly.

"I liked Ward Chambers," she went on, "because he was almost as gentle as Jeremy. I admired Don Fernando because he was manly like Jeremy. I thought I could care for Mr. Rogerson because he looked like Jeremy. But none of them *are* Jeremy. There might be thousands of men in the city, just as Philippe says, but none of them can ever be Jeremy."

She clutched the cat to her until Rowena, mewing in protest, struggled to get away. Monique crossed to sit on the edge of the bed, letting the cat go free. Rowena lay on the coverlet licking her ruffled fur.

"They aren't bad men, Ward and Don Fernando and William Rogerson," Monique said. "I'm even sorry I didn't have any money to give to William. He was still so hopeful after all his misfortunes."

The cat climbed onto her lap and Monique bent over her. "I love only Jeremy," she said. "I love him so." Tears filled her eyes and her body shook with sobs. She pushed Rowena onto the floor and flung herself face down on the bed, weeping.

After a time, Monique became aware of the cat's rough tongue licking her cheek. She dabbed at her eyes with a sodden handkerchief and sat up. There was only one thing she could do.

She stood up and returned Rowena to her basket. Taking off her nightgown, she stood for a moment in front of the mirror, the light behind her shadowing the curves of her body. Hurry, she told herself, before you lose your nerve.

Quickly she went to the wardrobe, took out a gown, and pulled it over her head, buttoning the bodice. After pulling on her shoes and grabbing a Chinese shawl, she went to the door.

"Wish me luck, Rowena," she said softly.

The breeze was warm on her face as she hurried along the sidewalk, ignoring the stares and occasional rude comments of passing men. Only one dared to approach her, and he, luckily, was so drunk that she easily outdistanced him.

She hesitated only a moment in front of the International Hotel before climbing the steps to the lobby. Did she dare to ask for Jeremy by name? Wait; she had a better notion.

Leaving the hotel, she approached a shoeshine boy sitting on the bottom step. Searching through her bag, she found a piece of paper on which Philippe had listed the seven acceptable topics for male-female conversation. Folding the paper, she held it out to the boy in one hand while proffering a twenty-five cent piece in the other.

"Will you leave this message at the desk for Mr. Jeremy Johnston?" she asked. The boy tipped his cap, took paper and coin, and ran up the steps.

Monique followed, passing the desk in time to see

we don't need other people. It will be like it was on the *Columbia,* but it will never end. We love each other, nothing else is important. What does anything else matter when we have each other?"

For a moment he stared over her head as though glimpsing a distant Eden.

"We could," he said softly. "By God, we could."

"Yes. Just the two of us."

So insistent was the rapid beating of her heart that for a moment she didn't hear the knocking.

Jeremy looked at the door as if puzzled. Then he frowned, dropping his hands to his sides.

"Jonas," he said. "It must be Jonas McAllister. My God, he can't find you here."

As Monique stared at the door, the knocking came again. Jeremy looked wildly about him and she followed his gaze. There was only the single room. No place to hide. She saw the doorknob turn.

"Behind the door," Jeremy whispered.

"Why?" she whispered back. "If we . . ."

He grabbed her shoulders and pushed her against the wall just as the door opened.

Jeremy stepped quickly forward in time to stop whoever it was a few feet inside the room. Though Monique could see Jeremy, the newcomer was hidden by the open door.

"Jonas." Jeremy's hand reached out and Monique saw a disembodied hand shake it.

"You're late, Jeremy. It's not like you." Jonas McAllister's voice was deep and gruff.

"I was delayed." Jeremy smiled but couldn't stop himself from glancing at Monique. Why didn't Jeremy acknowledge her? she wondered.

"Laura and I have been waiting in the lobby for the last fifteen minutes." Jonas paused. "Are you all right, my boy?" he asked. "You look a bit peaked."

"No, no, I'm fine," Jeremy said.

"Good, I'll come in and wait for you here."

Monique raised her head, straightening her shoulders as she waited to be discovered.

"No!" Jeremy almost shouted. "You shouldn't leave Laura downstairs by herself," he added quickly.

"Perhaps you're right," Jonas said. "You'll be with us in a few minutes?"

Jeremy nodded.

"Father, have you found him?" A woman's voice from the corridor. Laura!

"He's almost ready," Jonas said.

Monique's hand clutched nervously at the top of her bodice. Now, she silently urged Jeremy. Tell them about us now.

"Jeremy." Laura's voice. As Jeremy stepped forward, Monique caught the scent of lilies-of-the-valley, then heard a kiss. Jeremy reappeared, arms extended as though he was holding Laura as he had held her a few minutes before.

Monique grasped her breast as pain twisted inside her. Jeremy had no intention of acknowledging her presence. Had no intention of eloping with her. He wanted Laura, not her. Did he love Laura?

Rage flared through Monique, almost blinding her. Damn him! She wouldn't let him do this to her. Her hand found the top button of her gown and undid it.

Jeremy glanced at her. She undid the next button and the next. Jeremy stared. She smiled defiantly as she shrugged the top of the gown from her shoulders and let it fall to her waist. She wore nothing underneath. Color suffused Jeremy's face at the sight of her bared breasts.

"Jeremy. What's wrong?" Laura's voice. "You're not well. We'll come in and wait here for you."

Jeremy glanced at Monique. She stared challengingly back at him.

"Laura," he said hurriedly. "Let me talk to your father for a moment. Please. Wait for us down the hall."

Laura started to protest, then her father spoke to her and Monique heard her walk away. Jeremy spoke a few words she couldn't hear to the older man.

"The flux?" Jonas asked. "I suspected something was amiss."

"Will you give my regrets to the Bowers? And will you tell Laura, explain to her?"

"Of course I shall. I'd suggest you take paregoric. Works every time for me."

"I will." Jeremy quickly closed the door.

He gripped Monique's shoulder, shaking her. "Get dressed," he ordered, his voice low and furious. "Get dressed now."

He had changed into a different man. He was no longer the Jeremy of a few moments before. Monique looked away as she slowly put her arms into the sleeves of her dress.

Jeremy opened the door and stepped into the corridor, glancing to the right and left. "It's safe for you to go now," he said.

The anger drained from Monique, leaving her tremulous. "Jeremy," she began, "can't we . . ?"

"No," he said abruptly. "I'll admit you tempted me. You always were a temptress, weren't you?"

Was he thinking of Captain Nyland? "Not with you, Jeremy," she said softly, "never with you."

He crossed his arms. "I intend to marry Miss McAllister as soon as her mother returns from Europe." Although she stared at him, he refused to return her gaze.

Fury stifled Monique's tremors. She raised her hand and slapped him as hard as she could. Jeremy's head jerked to one side but otherwise he didn't move. She ran past him into the corridor and out of the hotel.

When she reached her room, she found Philippe emptying her bureau drawers.

"What are you doing?" she asked, bewildered. "Are you packing?"

"There's been a change of plans," he said. "We leave for the north tonight."

"Tonight? But why, Philippe, why?"

"A slight financial reverse," he said. "If we wait until morning I'm afraid the innkeeper here at the Whaley House will have the local constabulary after us. I'm sorry, Monique."

She had lost Jeremy. There was no longer any reason for her to stay in San Francisco.

"Here, let me help," she said. "I'll be ready to leave in fifteen minutes."   ❧

9

A Washoe Welcome

MONIQUE went to the wardrobe and threw open the door. She stared inside in disbelief.

"My gowns." She turned to Philippe, who looked away. "They're gone," she said. "Have you packed them already?"

Philippe shook his head. "I'm sorry, Monique," he said. "I owed money, quite a great deal of money. The gentleman I was indebted to didn't appear to trust me. He seemed to suspect I might depart from the city without paying him. Why he thought so poorly of me I have no idea. Whatever his reason, he came here and demanded payment. He threatened me with a firearm, as a matter of fact. I had to let him have your dresses."

She gazed at him for a long moment, then touched his arm. "It's all right, Philippe," she said. "You bought them, after all. You're far more important to me than any dress."

"Still, I feel bad about it." He brightened. "Our

luck will turn, Monique. Luck comes in runs that either work for you or against you. The tide is bound to turn, and when it does, Philippe Manigault will be ready to be swept on to fame and fortune."

Monique smiled a little. You could always count on Philippe to bounce back from reverses, she thought. He might be weak, yet he was there when you needed him, unlike Jeremy. Jeremy! She closed her mind to the hurt and anger that the memory of Jeremy's denial brought.

She packed quickly. When she finished, she realized that she possessed little more now than she had when she had first left the Jarvis house months before.

"We have to hurry," Philippe told her, taking her bag. "I packed an hour ago." He opened the door. "We'll descend to the street via the rear stairs. I scouted their location when we first arrived, just in case we were confronted with an emergency."

"Wait." Monique went back into the room. "I almost forgot Rowena."

The cat's basket wasn't in its usual place under the table. She looked around the room without seeing it, then went into her bedroom and searched there. No basket, no Rowena. When she came back to the sitting room, Philippe was standing outside the door, his arms folded, staring at the carpet.

A terrible suspicion stabbed through her. "No, Philippe," she half-whispered. "Oh no. You couldn't have. Not Rowena."

He kicked at the carpeting with the toe of his boot, saying nothing.

"Philippe!" Panic struck her. "Where is she? Where's Rowena?"

He faced her, raising his hands in front of him, palms up. "What was I to do?" he asked. "Cats are in great demand in the city as ratters. They fetch a pretty penny. Didn't I tell you the gentleman threatened me? I had no choice. It was either give him the cat or . . ." He shrugged.

Monique ran to the door. "Quick, take me to him. We must get her back. Hurry!"

"I don't know where he lives. Even if I did, we have no wherewithal to exchange for the fair Rowena."

Monique drew in her breath and let it out with a sob. She bit her lower lip to keep from crying.

"After all," Philippe said, "it's only a cat. You can always get another someday."

"Rowena isn't just a cat, just any cat," Monique cried. "She's mine, she's my friend. I've had her since I was ten years old. I love Rowena. She's all I had." Her voice broke as she thought of Jeremy. "Now I have nothing."

Philippe reached out and brushed a strand of hair from her forehead. His blue eyes had never looked so sad. His shoulders slumped and she noticed that his beard was untrimmed. He looked as lost as she felt.

"You always have Philippe Manigault," he told her. "You have me."

Her anger slowly dissolved, and she put her arms around him and laid her head on his chest as he held her gently to him.

"And you have me," she said as she straightened. "We have each other, Philippe."

He nodded, picking up their bags. "On to the wharf," he said with a show of jauntiness that didn't ring true. "Our ship sails for Sacramento on the morning tide."

She followed him down the back stairs of the Whaley Hotel and along the street leading to the bay.

It's true what I said, she told herself as she trudged along with the first wisps of a cooling fog swirling around her. Philippe and I only have each other.

Bitterness returned, though, like an unpleasant after-taste. Rowena was mine, she thought, not his. He had no right to give her away without asking me first.

She loved Philippe as a sister might love an older brother, but something had changed between them. The bond of their trust, once so strong and resilient, had been tested and found wanting.

Philippe appropriated an abandoned cabin in the foothills of the Sierras north of Placerville, and they settled in for the winter.

"When spring returns," he told Monique one evening after he returned from town, "we'll make our fortune. Until then we can only bide our time."

"Our fortune, Philippe?" she asked. "Where? How?"

"Perhaps here in the gold country. New strikes are being made in California every day. Or perhaps we'll travel across the mountains to the Washoe territory. This afternoon, while I was at the Jenny Lind, I overheard a rumor of a big silver strike there."

"You weren't playing cards again, I hope."

He came to stand behind Monique, who was at the table washing her supper dishes.

"You sound like a shrewish wife," he told her.

"I didn't mean to," she said, rinsing a cup. "But you know what happened in San Francisco."

He took her by the wrist and turned her to face him. Putting his arms around her, he drew her to him and, as she smelled the sour odor of whiskey on his breath, he kissed her. Monique's mouth opened in surprise. She tried to draw away but his body pressed her against the table.

"Philippe, let me go," she told him.

"Do you find me so repulsive?" His arms dropped to his sides and he stepped back.

Without answering, she crossed the cabin, took her

bag, and placed it on top of her cot. She began laying her clothes inside.

"What are you doing?" he asked, alarm in his voice.

"I can't stay here. I can't possibly stay here with you now."

"Monique." He started to come to her, then stopped. "There's nowhere for you to go. Snow's in the air. Besides, I need you."

"You're not giving me any choice."

"Stop being so Goddamned melodramatic." He raised his voice to a shout. "Look at me."

She straightened and faced him.

"Do you take me for a eunuch?" he asked.

"Of course not. I understand that a man needs a woman. But I think of you as family—it's wrong for you to touch me that way."

"Here in Placerville," he said, "I become weary of playing cards despite my penchant for gambling." He looked at her as though wondering whether it was safe to smile. "I give you my pledge," he said solemnly, "that it will never happen again. Do you accept my word?"

"If it ever does happen again," she said, "I'll leave. I'll have to."

He bowed to her before going to sit at the table. He took a pack of cards from the drawer and began shuffling and dealing.

Monique unpacked slowly. She had been shocked by his betrayal. When he kissed her she had felt no leap of passion, only revulsion, as though her own father had turned to her in lust. She didn't want to leave Philippe, for she had no idea of what to do to earn her way. But she knew she would leave if she had to, even though she enjoyed the adventure of keeping house here in the foothills of the Sierras. This cabin was hers, hers and Philippe's, and the duties she had found so onerous when she was a servant—cooking, sweeping, scrubbing, washing clothes—were pleasurable enough when she did them for herself and for someone she cared for.

How much more pleasurable they would be if she were doing them for Jeremy!

The next day Philippe returned from Placerville with a brown bundle tucked under his arm. Brushing snow from his frock coat, he handed her the package.

"A gift of atonement," he said. "I hope you like it."

She unwrapped the package and stared down at a thick dog-eared book.

"*The Complete Works of William Shakespeare,*" Philippe said. "Your education has sadly lacked the flavoring of the bard's language. I intend to rectify that shortcoming forthwith."

"Thank you, Philippe." She wanted to go to him and kiss his cheek but she didn't, afraid of showing her affection.

"This will be our stage." Philippe swept his arm to indicate the interior of the cabin. "And we shall be the players."

As the days passed and winter closed in, they read and acted out the plays: *As You Like It, Henry V, Macbeth, The Taming of the Shrew.* But *Hamlet* was Philippe's favorite and, although she wasn't sure she understood its meaning, the play became Monique's favorite as well.

As Hamlet-Philippe lay dying, tears came to her eyes as she declaimed, " 'Now cracks a noble heart. Good night, sweet prince, and flights of angels sing thee to thy rest!' "

As the winter wore on into January and February, reports of silver strikes in the Washoe country were brought across the Sierras by returning prospectors. The miners in the California gold country, where the once-rich veins were nearing exhaustion, listened intently, their fever for wealth growing from an almost imperceptible heightening of the senses to a disease that raged out of control.

"They say Comstock and the others who struck paydirt are wealthy men already," Philippe told her. "The whole mountain range east of Carson City is one great lode of gold and silver, where men can become rich overnight."

"You're not a miner, Philippe," Monique objected.

"I'm not, that's true. I don't have the patience for that game. If only Jeremy were with us. It's almost as if he has a sixth sense that enables him to smell out gold and silver. At times, when I throw the dice I know a seven will come up and it does. It's the same with Jeremy and gold; he can sense it." Philippe sighed. "He's not with us, however. But where there's gold and silver in the ground there will be men willing to risk their stake in a friendly game of cards. I mean to be there when they do."

"We're going to the Comstock then?"

"As soon as this dreary weather breaks."

In late March they left the cabin on foot, for they were too poor to buy or hire a horse or mule. They found Placerville already crowded with men waiting to cross the mountains, men who, as they said, "practiced for Washoe" by drinking in the saloons and playing faro and monte in the gambling houses. There were no beds at the camp east of town which was their first stop, so Philippe and Monique slept on the floor.

All around them, the talk was of the Nevada diggings, of a man making twenty thousand dollars in a day, and of a canvas hotel in Virginia City worth forty thousand dollars to its owner. Philippe and Monique left the camp early in the morning, with their blankets and provisions strapped on their backs.

As they climbed into the snow-topped mountains,

trains of pack animals struggled from one dry spot in the trail to the next. Mexican muleskinners prodded their teams with cries of *"Carambo! Santa Maria! Diavolo!"*

By nightfall, tired and thirsty, their feet caked with mud, they arrived at Hangtown Mike's, a shanty with a bar next to the common bedroom where they spread their blankets. The furnishings consisted of a piece of a looking-glass on the window frame and a public comb hanging by a string from the doorpost.

The next day, as Monique waited for Philippe in the pre-dawn darkness outside the shanty, a hulking miner pushed open the saloon door. He stopped a few feet from Monique, looking her up and down. She turned away. All at once she felt his fingers close on her wrist. The miner spun her around. She had the impression of a bearded face and the reek of whiskey.

The man pulled her to him. When she beat on his chest with her fist, he laughed, pressing his face down to hers. She twisted her head from side to side as she bent away from him.

"Philippe!" she cried.

The man's hand clutched the neck of her dress and fumbled downward to her breast. She screamed in terror.

A shot rang out.

The bearded stranger released her and she backed away. Philippe stood on the porch with a smoking derringer in his hand. The bearded man staggered along the path away from them. Oh, my God, Monique thought, Philippe's shot him.

"The next time I'll kill you," Philippe shouted.

The drunken miner stopped and drew himself up as though he meant to charge Philippe. His hands probed his own body searching for a wound. When he found none, Monique let out her breath with a sigh of relief.

"I didn't mean no harm, friend," the miner mumbled. "How was I to know she was spoken for?"

Philippe motioned him away with the pistol and the miner lumbered off into the woods like a bear retreating to his cave. As Philippe thrust the small gun under his waistband, the men who had come out of the saloon at the sound of the shot slowly dispersed.

"I've been afraid this might happen," Philippe said.

"I'm all right. He didn't hurt me."

"But the next time? I can't be with you every minute. You saw how unconcerned everyone was about my shooting at him. There's no law here and less where we're going."

"I've only seen one other woman since we left Placerville. I'm not afraid, Philippe, but if I had a gun I could take care of myself."

"Perhaps you should have a gun; we'll see. But I have another notion for now. You're about my size and almost my height. Dressed in some of my less flamboyant clothes, and with your hair cut shorter, you'd pass as a boy."

"If boys could play Shakespeare's women, I can do the reverse. I might enjoy it, Philippe. But do I have to be as arrogant and overbearing as men are?"

"I don't know where you received your warped view of the male of the species."

"From males of the species, where else? But yes, I'll cut my hair and smudge my face. Make me a boy, Philippe."

An hour later, Philippe Manigault and his younger brother Martin set out to continue their trek over the mountains. They passed taverns built from dry-goods boxes and old potato sacks, saw board and lodging signs above tents less than ten feet square, and saloons where the bar was no more than a whiskey barrel set in the shade of a pine tree.

As they crossed the Sierras, they were never out of sight of other travelers heading for the Washoe—Irishmen pushing wheelbarrows, Mexicans leading burros, gamblers on thoroughbred horses, drovers with hogs and cattle, organ grinders, peddlers, men with divining rods and electric silver detectors, old men and young men, some limping and bent with fatigue, some walking beside lumber wagons piled high with household goods, others, young and strong, striding ahead singly or in pairs. All were infected with the mania for silver and gold.

At the end of their second day on the trail they reached Strawberry Flat. Two days later they gazed down on Lake Tahoe, and the next day they stumbled into the Carson Valley at the bottom of the eastern slope of the Sierras. Their feet were sore and blistered, but they followed crudely lettered signs to a hot salt-spring, where they bathed and rested before going on to Carson City.

From Carson, they booked passage on a stage to take them the final eighteen miles into the barren Nevada mountains to Virginia City, arriving there as the sun set behind Mount Davidson.

Monique and Philippe stood on the muddy street, staring at the roughly dressed miners shouting to one another as they pushed their way in and out of the saloons and gambling halls lining both sides of the street. The town sprawled across the valley on their left, climbed the hill to where they stood, climbed a few more streets up the side of the mountain, frame house seemingly piled atop frame house, and then petered out, as though exhausted, in a scattering of shacks and diggings that looked like holes dug by giant gophers.

"We'd best find accommodations," Philippe said.

Monique nodded, still bemused by the hubbub and confusion around her. She was alarmed by the foul-mouthed bonhommie of the men—she saw no women —and aghast at the reeking smell of the town—smoke, sweat, dung and urine—yet at the same time excited and alive, as though a current of electricity ran through Virginia City, making every other town and city, San Francisco included, seem like a sleepy cross-roads.

"Are you coming?" Philippe, who had gone ahead, looked back impatiently.

She picked up her bag and followed him, hunched over, a cap pulled low on her forehead. Since leaving the camp near Placerville, no one had suspected she wasn't the boy she pretended to be.

"You bastard!"

A short squat man, his feet planted apart, stood on the street some thirty feet in front of her. Looking past him she saw a man facing him, a big man with sandy hair and beard.

"I don't reckon I heard you right." There was menace in the sandy-haired man's voice.

"You're a bastard, Alex Campbell," the first man shouted. "You and Reid jumped my claim."

Before Monique realized what was happening, Campbell had brought a pistol from his coat. The gun barked. Philippe pulled her to one side, pushing her into the shelter of a doorway. She heard another gunshot. She looked past Philippe along the now deserted street. Alex Campbell held a smoking pistol. The other man lay sprawled in the dirt, not moving.

Monique scrambled past Philippe and ran to the fallen man.

"Come back," Philippe called after her.

She knelt at the man's side. His hands were empty and she saw no weapon on the street. She looked up at Campbell. He blew on his gun's muzzle before holstering the weapon.

Putting her hand to the fallen man's mouth, she felt no hint of breathing. Her hand slid under his jacket searching for a heartbeat. There was none. When she drew her hand away it was sticky and stained with blood. Stunned, she looked up to see Alex Campbell walking casually toward her, smiling. Hearing Philippe behind her, she glanced at him and shook her head to keep him away.

"You a friend of Daggett's?" Campbell asked.

Lowering her head to hide her face, she said, "No."

Campbell reached down, pulled off her cap and tossed it aside. He grasped her hair, tilting her head up. She stared defiantly at him, seeing the puzzled look on his face. Kneeling beside her, his hand ran down the front of her coat and over her breasts. She jerked away.

"I'll be damned," Campbell said.

He stood up and swaggered off down the street without another word. ◆◄§

10

A Game of Chance

"THERE was nothing to it." Philippe raised his hand, making a circle with his thumb and forefinger. "The uninformed might call it luck but it's not luck at all. It's skill enhanced by my powers of observation and thought."

"You must have won last night," Monique said.

"More than merely won." Philippe Manigault triumphed gloriously, carrying all before him. "Do you want to learn my secret? I look for clues in the behavior of my opponents. I watch for the man who habitually buys pots by bluffing, the stolid plodder who never bluffs at all, the gentleman who always folds early until he has a strong hand and then overbets. I watch their faces, because only the wiliest man can completely mask his emotions. I look for the blink of an eye, the curl of a mouth, the tapping of fingers on the table. They're all clues."

"I thought our luck would turn here in Virginia

City. I felt it from the first moment we got off the stage, even after that terrible shooting."

"What was bad luck for Ross Daggett was good luck for us. There would have been no vacancy at the boarding house if Daggett hadn't cashed in his chips."

"Don't, Philippe. It's bad enough having to live in a dead man's room without making jokes about it."

"I'm sorry, Monique. The indifference to death here is contagious. Why, I'm told there are twenty men buried in the Virginia City cemetery, and not one of them died a natural death. Most of them succumbed to lead poisoning, as they're wont to say here."

"Let's not talk of death. Not today." Monique drew in a deep breath. "The air's so clear this morning, so cool."

As they walked down C Street, the sun rose above the eastern mountains, throwing long shadows across the dirt road ahead of them. The dust of the day before had settled and the saloons and gambling halls were quiet. A horse neighed in a livery stable, and from the valley below them came the pounding of hammers.

Entering the Sacramento Restaurant, they sat at a rear table and ordered ham and eggs. Monique, still wearing Philippe's clothes and masquerading as a boy, excited no interest or curiosity. She had not seen Alex Campbell since their arrival.

After breakfast, they walked slowly along the board sidewalk while the town began to stir around them. A balding man washed the windows of the Virginia House, metal clanged on metal in a blacksmith's shop, and a "whomp, whomp, whomp," reverberated from the mountains.

"That's blasting in the Ophir mine," Philippe said. Miners sauntered along the streets, pushing in and out of the saloons. Muted laughter came from a gambling hall, followed by the plinking of a piano as someone played "The Girl I Left Behind Me" with one finger. The odors of stale whiskey and cigar smoke mingled with the tang of alkali dust rising from the street in the wake of a lumber wagon drawn by four mules.

"I never should have brought you here," Philippe said.

She looked at him quickly, wondering what had dampened his exuberance. "Philippe," she said, "I like Virginia City. I like the Comstock."

"Surely you miss the comforts of San Francisco. I never dreamed a city with Virginia's fair name would be so barren and uncivilized. The Washoe is God's slagheap. There *must* be gold and silver here, because there's surely nothing else."

Monique shook her head. "When I woke up this morning," she said, "I had this wonderful feeling that a change was on the way—that good times are coming. I felt the same way back in Alabama when I went to the Randolph's to watch the dancing—the night I met you and Jeremy."

She saw him frown. "What is it, Philippe? Tell me."

"The banks are beginning to take an interest in the Comstock," he said. "They're buying out the prospectors, the men like Old Virginia, McLaughlin, O'Riley, Penrod; even Old Pancake Comstock himself. The banks pay them a few thousand for their claims and then send experienced mining men into the territory. I heard yesterday that McAllister is having Jeremy come here from San Francisco."

Jeremy! She stifled her sudden excitement. "Is he . . . . Have you heard if he's married?"

Philippe shrugged. "I haven't heard. But he's probably not coming here at all; the story's probably someone's fancy. A 'quaint,' as Dan DeQuille calls his tales in the *Enterprise*. No . . . I doubt that Jeremy's really coming."

"He is, Philippe, I know he is. That's why I felt the way I did this morning. It's Jeremy." She raised her chin. "Not that I care where he goes or what he does."

"Ever since he first became involved with that San Francisco banking crowd he's been a different man," Philippe said. "I don't think I know him any more, nor do I care to."

"It's not him, Philippe. It's that woman—that Laura McAllister. But don't let's talk about either of them." She looked up at the flag flying from Mount Davidson. "Isn't it strange how the Washoe mountains look? Like pieces of purple cardboard cut out and pasted against the sky."

"I shouldn't have brought you here," Philippe said again. "What would become of you if anything happened to me?"

"Nothing will happen to you—you're indestructable. No matter what, Philippe Manigault will manage to survive. Isn't that what you told me a long time ago?"

"I may have. All at once, I'm not so sure it's true."

"What's wrong, Philippe? Is there something you haven't told me? Finding out about Jeremy isn't all that's troubling you."

"No, there's more. There's a scam afoot here that I don't understand. I have a nose for devious operations, and the smell's telling me that something's amiss. It's nothing I've seen or heard, not directly; just bits and pieces of gossip I've picked up here and there during the last few weeks."

"Tell me, Philippe."

"That's just it. I can't tell you because I don't know myself; not exactly. It's probably nothing but smoke." He shook his head. "No, there's more than smoke.

I've seen too many men celebrating, thinking they've hit it big in Gold Hill or here in Virginia, and yet the assays turn up nothing of value. A short time later, men connected with Reid or the banking crowd make big strikes in the same areas. As though they knew something the prospectors didn't."

"I remember you told me it took the old-timers like Comstock years to realize how rich these mountains were."

"True. They were so dead set on finding gold that they kept getting riled at all the 'blue stuff,' as they called it, that kept clogging up their rockers. It was years before they found out that the 'blue stuff' was silver. Even after that, when they discovered surface gold or silver in the ravines and canyons, they never guessed the ore might be coming from larger veins higher in the mountains. The Mexican miners knew right away. They're used to prospecting for silver, but the men of Washoe didn't."

"Well, there you are, Philippe. Those prospectors you're talking about probably weren't looking in the right places."

"I wish it was as simple as that. It's not my concern, thank God for that. I have enough to trouble me as it is."

"You're not worrying about me, are you? I can look after myself, Philippe." When she went on her tone was light and bantering. "I don't need a man, not even you. I'm perfectly capable of taking care of myself. Women spend too much of their lives looking for men to protect them. It's high time they stopped."

"Ah, youth." Philippe said with a smile. "So exuberant, so full of confidence, and so mistaken. What would you do, Monique, without Philippe Manigault? Tell me; I'd like to hear."

"I could be a hurdy-gurdy girl," she said as they passed the El Dorado. "I'm sure there are men in

Virginia City who would pay a dollar to dance with me."

"There are, there are. And some of the hurdy-gurdies manage to keep their virtue intact, or so I'm told. Most of them, though, are soiled doves."

"Or," Monique said, nodding toward the Silver Dollar, "I could deal twenty-one and faro. You did teach me how, you know. In fact, you said I had a knack for cards."

"You'll never deal cards as long as I have anything to say about it. I've gathered a small stake, Monique. I'll increase it. I'm confident I will." A renewed optimism came into his voice. "My stake will grow until I have enough to invest in a mine. A man hears a great deal at the gaming tables, and if he knows his way around the city he can find out a lot more. I'll buy feet in a mine, not when everyone's trying to buy, but when no-one is. That's how fortunes are made, buying what no-one wants and selling it when everyone's wild to buy. Philippe Manigault doesn't get carried away by the enthusiasm of crowds. He's a man apart, a speculator with ice water flowing through his veins."

Monique smiled at him. "You can do it, Philippe, I know you can. This is our lucky day and this is our lucky city."

"Once I make my fortune—I think a hundred thousand dollars will be enough—I'll swear off gambling. No more speculation for Philippe Manigault, except, of course, for sport—the risking of a pittance here and there. I intend to invest my profits from the mine in merchandise. Groceries, clothing, lumber, supplies for the mines, that's where the money's to be made. It was true in '49 and it will be just as true on the Comstock. One forty-niner in a hundred made a living at his diggings, and only one in a thousand struck

"I felt the same last week," the miner said. "Thought I'd found myself a bonanza, the outcropping of a vein leading to the mother lode. Turned out it was nothing, assayed at less than ten dollars a ton. *Barrasca*! I ain't seen nothing but hard times these last five years."

"Let me buy you a drink, friend," Philippe said, "and perhaps my luck will rub off on you." He threw a silver dollar on the bar.

After finishing his second drink, Philippe strolled from the gambling house. Outside, the wind swirled the dust rising from the busy street. Hurrying miners crowded the sidewalks. Philippe paused outside the *Territorial Enterprise* office, bought a paper for a nickel, and took it into the Nevada House, where he sat in the lobby, his feet up, reading the latest mining reports.

Folding the *Enterprise*, he thrust it into an inside pocket of his frock coat and walked into the gambling hall off the hotel lobby. Two tables were in action, one faro, one poker. After watching for a few minutes, he sat in on the game of draw poker.

The stakes were small, but after an hour he was thirty dollars to the good. Be patient, he told himself. The lucky feeling was still with him; he knew his time was coming soon, just as on a hot and humid day a man knows rain, thunder and lightning are in the offing. But not quite yet. He cashed in his chips and left the Nevada House.

The wind had lessened, so he stopped to light a cigarillo. Pausing in front of the telegraph office, he read the latest news of the fighting north of Richmond, Virginia, and then walked on to the post office and asked for his mail. There was none. Not feeling hungry, he ate no lunch, spending the better part of the afternoon at the Silver Dollar, where he won seven dollars at faro and lost five playing monte.

Not yet, he told himself. Be patient. At the Lucky Seven he settled a quarrel over the author of a literary quotation and later, at the California Emporium, another gambling house, he listened to a heated argument about the rights and wrongs of the Mormon practice of polygamy.

The sun had set behind Mount Davidson by the time he returned to the Silver Dollar. Philippe smiled, realizing he kept coming back to this particular gambling hall. There must be a reason. He was clearheaded now, the effects of the two drinks having long since worn off. He was getting hungry but decided to play a few hands of poker before supper.

"Mind if I sit in, gentlemen?" he asked after watching a desultory game for a few minutes.

One of the players used his foot to push out a chair and Philippe sat down. There were four miners in the game. He'd played with three before, poor players all, and a man he didn't recognize.

Philippe won slowly, steadily. The stranger played a competent game but the cards ran against him. The others were weak players, and only their cautious betting and occasional runs of luck kept them in the game. After an hour, Philippe was fifty dollars to the good.

On the next hand Philippe was dealt nothing, drew nothing, and folded. He felt someone watching him. Hunching his shoulders, stacking and restacking the chips on the table in front of him, he refused to look around. He waited.

A man strode around the table and pulled out the chair across from Philippe. He was a big man, muscular, with sandy hair and bushy eyebrows above small brown eyes. Philippe recognized Alex Campbell, the man who had gunned down Daggett on the day of their arrival in Virginia City.

"Deal me in," Campbell said.

The other men eyed the newcomer warily.

"You look like the big winner," Campbell said to Philippe.

Philippe put his hand over his chips, picking them up and letting them click against each other as he dropped them back on the green cloth. "If this is big money to you," he said evenly, "then you might say I am."

Seeing Campbell redden, Philippe smiled. This man could be goaded into making rash bets. Excitement stirred deep inside Philippe. His time was coming, he sensed. The tide was rising and he was ready for it.

Philippe lost two hands, then won a medium-sized pot, and then lost once more. He ignored the other players as he concentrated on Campbell, his only real opponent. He was more than an opponent, Philippe knew. Campbell was his enemy.

Alex Campbell won his share of the pots, betting heavily when he held good cards, folding early when he had nothing. One miner dropped out of the game, followed quickly by another. Now there were only Philippe, Campbell and two others.

"No cards," Campbell said after glancing at his next hand. Philippe saw him look right and left, and heard him clear his throat.

Philippe and one of the miners had folded. Campbell raised twenty dollars, the other miner threw in his cards, and Campbell raked in the pot. Philippe, watching closely, was sure Campbell had been bluffing.

Three hands later, Campbell bet twenty dollars, then looked right and left and cleared his throat. He's bluffing again, Philippe thought. This time one of the miners called him. Campbell held nothing, as Philippe had suspected.

By the end of another hour most of the chips were

stacked in front of Campbell and Philippe. It was Campbell's deal. The piano fell silent, and for a moment there was an unnatural hush in the room. The talking at the bar stopped and the shouts and clatter from the street lessened. It was not because of anything that had happened, Philippe noted, but purely by chance.

The excitement that had been building in him all day swept upward and peaked, and he was suddenly calm. This was the moment he'd been waiting and hoping for. His time had come.

As Campbell shuffled the cards slowly and painstakingly, the deck small in his huge hands, the piano came to life again, the talk and laughter at the bar resumed, and a muleskinner's curses came from the street. The lamps, all lit now, threw a soft glow over the tables, highlighting the players' faces.

Philippe looked across at Campbell. The big man shifted in his chair, seeming to sense that something extraordinary was happening. He picked up the cards after the cut and held them in front of him.

"Deal," Philippe told him with quiet confidence. "Deal the cards."

Campbell dealt, his fingers awkward. Philippe watched intently, alert for chicanery even though Campbell's massive fingers made any sleight-of-hand improbable. And there was none, he'd swear to it.

"Having trouble?" Philippe asked as Campbell fumbled with the cards.

The big man grunted but said nothing.

Philippe fanned his cards, slowly revealing a jack, an ace, a nine, another ace and a three. When he opened with twenty dollars, one of the miners dropped out.

"Two cards." Philippe drew an ace and a jack in exchange for his nine and three. He now held a full house of aces and jacks.

"Two for me." Campbell looked right and left. He cleared his throat.

I've got the bluffing bastard, Philippe told himself, careful to give no sign of the strength of his hand. Only four of a kind, a straight flush, or a royal flush could beat him.

Philippe pushed four ten dollar chips into the pot. The second miner folded, leaving only Philippe and Campbell in the game.

"I'll see your forty," Campbell said, "and raise you eighty."

Philippe hesitated a fraction of a second as though unsure whether to go on. At last he shrugged. "Match the eighty and raise you another eighty."

"Eighty and eighty more." Sweat beaded Campbell's cheeks and forehead.

"I'll match you and—" Philippe counted his piles of remaining chips before pushing them to the center of the table. "And raise you two hundred."

"I'll see your two hundred," Campbell said after a pause, his voice husky. Reaching into his pocket, he brought out a thonged pouch, counted twenty double eagles and piled them on the table. "And jump it another two hundred."

This was it, Philippe knew. His big win. His bonanza.

"Give me a piece of paper," he said. "I'll write you a marker for the two hundred and for another two hundred besides."

The room hushed as the men from the bar gathered around the table.

"I don't play for markers," Campbell said.

"I don't have any more cash."

"You've got something better."

Philippe said nothing, waiting, not knowing what to expect.

"You got the woman."

"The woman?" Philippe frowned.

"You know the woman I mean. The one you brought with you to Virginia. The one you dress like a boy. Bet *her*. Take back your money. I'll stake all I've got on the table against the woman."

Philippe's heart thudded. This was the hand he knew he would win, was destined to win. Campbell was bluffing, expecting him to crawfish. What did the stakes matter if he was bound to win?

"Afraid?" Campbell was suddenly calm. Determined. Philippe hesitated. What if the other man held the cards? No, impossible.

"Done," Philippe said. "I'll call you."

Smiling, Campbell laid his cards face up on the green felt. He held four fives. Philippe paled. Desperate, he reached inside his coat. Strong hands grasped his arms, pinning them to his sides.

Campbell stood, smiling. "Don't hurt the gentleman." He took two chips from the table and tossed them on the bar. "Let him have a few drinks on me while I'm collecting my winnings." ⋴§

11

Alex Campbell
Claims His Winnings

At first, Monique paid no heed to the shouting in
the distance. Virginia City, she had found, was a
place of alarms and excursions, of firebells clanging
in the night, and of bands of revellers singing drunk-
enly as they trekked "cross-lots" to their shanty homes.

When the hubbub grew louder, she crossed to the
window and, mildly curious, looked down at the
street. A crowd of men surged toward the boarding
house, their bearded faces alternately shadowed and
lighted by the glare from their torches and lanterns.

Philippe? A thrill tingled through her. Had Philippe scored a coup at the gaming tables and was
now being escorted to his lodgings in triumph? She
searched the faces of the men in the front rank of
the crowd but didn't see him. One man, a burly giant,
seemed to be the center of attention. Didn't she know
him? Monique frowned, unsure.

As the shouting mob approached the house, men looked up at her window and she drew back into the room. No, it wasn't Philippe. Yet he should be home soon. The sun was down and he'd made it a habit since their arrival in Virginia City to take her to supper each night at the Comstock House.

She returned to the table where, in the light from a kerosene lamp, she sat reading *King Lear*, her finger following the words across the page. She was puzzling over a passage when she heard the front door of the boarding house open and an army of footsteps thud up the stairs.

It must be Philippe after all. As hope surged within her, she left the book open on the table and went to stand by the door, waiting for the sound of Philippe's key in the lock.

The footsteps stopped outside her room. A fist thudded on the door. As Monique stared at the door, puzzled, she heard a rising murmur of talk and laughter from the hall.

"Who is it?" she called out.

"Philippe Manigault, who else?" The voice wasn't Philippe's.

Of course, the miners had escorted Philippe back in triumph from the gambling house after all. She turned the key and drew the door open. Alex Campbell stood in the hallway, flanked by two men holding lanterns. She instinctively started to shut the door, only to have Campbell put his shoulder to it and barge past her into the room.

"Where's Philippe?" she asked, backing away.

"I've come to claim my winnings," Campbell said. In the light from the lanterns his fleshy, clean-shaven face looked unnaturally pale, like that of a man who spends most of his life below ground.

Monique rushed at him, placed both of her hands to his chest and shoved. Taken by surprise, Campbell stepped back as the miners behind him laughed.

"You got yourself a handful there," one shouted.

Alex Campbell grasped Monique by the upper arms, lifted her high off the floor and carried her across the room, slamming her against the far wall. He held her there with his smiling face level with hers. She gasped, shocked and surprised.

"Put me down," she demanded.

He released her at once and she dropped to the floor, stumbling against Campbell. She looked up at him looming over her, the smile seemingly frozen on his face. When she stood erect, he leaned forward and placed his hands on the wall on either side of her, penning her in.

"What have you done to Philippe?" she asked again.

"It ain't so much what I did to Philippe," Campbell said. "It's what he's done to you. He went and raised your station in life. You're not a gambler's woman no more. You belong to me."

"I don't know what you're talking about. Tell me where Philippe is."

"Your gambling friend's at the Silver Dollar, where he's being royally entertained with drinks paid for by yours truly. Thought he'd get the better of me, Frenchy did. He should of known better than to think he could outsmart Alex Campbell." He turned to the miners who had pushed their way into the room behind him. "Ain't that right?" he asked.

The men murmured in agreement.

"Lookee here," a miner's awed voice said. "She's been reading Shakespeare."

They all knew by now that she wasn't a boy, Monique realized. She closed her eyes as her hands slid over her close-cut hair. What was the meaning of this nightmare? Why were these men here? Where was Philippe?

Campbell gripped her chin between his thumb and

forefinger. She opened her eyes, twisting her head to one side. All at once the big man stepped away and bowed.

"There's no cause for you to be a-feared of Alexander Campbell," he said, his tone ingratiating. He held up his huge hands. "Quiet down," he ordered, and the talk and laughter stopped.

"What happened, ma'am," he told Monique with elaborate courtesy, "was this. Me and your friend Frenchy Manigault had us a game of poker. He thought he was going to win big, but it turned out he didn't know who he was up against."

"Alex Campbell's the best poker player in the territory," a miner said.

"So your friend lost. And what he lost wasn't his money. He's still got that. What he lost was you."

Monique stared at him in disbelief. "No." She shook her head. "You're lying."

"It's God's honest truth," Campbell said.

"Philippe would never do such a thing." She raised her chin. "Even if he had the right, which he doesn't. I don't belong to him or to any man."

"Ain't what I said the truth?" Campbell asked the men behind him. There were shouts of assent.

"He won you fair and square," a miner told Monique. "I seen the whole thing and it was just like Alex here says. He outfoxed the Frenchy good and proper. I seen him do it, we all seen him."

"So I've come to claim my prize," Campbell said, smiling at Monique.

She spat in his face.

The room quieted, the men looking from Monique to Campbell. Inwardly quaking, she stared defiantly up at the big man. He reached into his hip pocket and brought out a red bandanna and used it to carefully wipe the saliva from his face.

He folded the bandanna and returned it to his

pocket. With a slashing swing of his palm, he slapped her face, hard, snapping her head to one side. Her hand went to her stinging cheek as tears welled in her eyes.

"You'll find out," Campbell said, "what your friend found out. It don't pay to mess with Alex Campbell." He turned to the men. "You're all probably wondering what I want with this boy." He underlined the "boy" sarcastically. "Look at her in that baggy no-account shirt and those droopy pants. Wouldn't think a man would look at her once, let alone twice, would you? Well, let me show you how wrong you'd be if you thought that."

He took Monique's hand and shoved her in front of him so she faced the crowd of miners. Jerking her hands behind her back, he held both of her wrists in one of his huge hands while he reached around her with the other and began undoing the buttons of her shirt. Though she pulled and twisted, she couldn't free herself. As soon as the shirt was unbuttoned, Campbell pulled it aside.

The men stared at her white skin above and below the cloth binding her breasts. When Campbell hooked his thumb in the top of the cloth, Monique cried out in protest. He yanked the cloth down and her full breasts sprang free. The miners gaped at Monique as their breathing quickened.

"That's all the show you boys are going to get," Campbell said. "Make yourself decent," he said to Monique as he released her. She quickly buttoned the shirt over her bared breasts.

Alex Campbell walked to her and she tensed, ready to fight, her fingers curling, claw-like, at her sides. She saw him staring at her lower body. When she glanced down he bent over, put his shoulder to her mid-section and lifted her as he might lift a sack of grain.

She flailed at his back with her fists and kicked her feet. He laughed.

"Looks like you got yourself a wildcat," a man said.

"All the better," Campbell told him. "Make way for the wildcat tamer," he shouted, and the crowd parted before him as he carried Monique through the door and down the stairs.

By the time they reached the street she had stopped her ineffectual struggling, letting him lift her into a buggy waiting outside the boarding house. He pushed her onto the seat but, as he started to climb up beside her, she scrambled to the buggy's far side and leaped to the ground. She heard his hoarse profane cry.

She ran hard, the night air cool on her face, her bare feet pounding on the packed dirt of the street. Steps sounded behind her, gaining on her. She darted into an alley between two stores, dodging foul-smelling cans. A moment later a clatter came from behind her as though her pursuer had thrown the cans to one side.

She ran into the darkness. A wall loomed ahead of her. She stopped, then dashed to her right. Another wall. She ran back the other way. Again she was brought up short against the side of a building. Realizing she was in a cul-de-sac, she swung about. Alex Campbell stood ten feet away with his hands on his hips, watching her.

"I reckon I got a mite more than I bargained for," he said.

He reached for her, fumbling for her in the dark, and grasped her wrist and pulled her after him as he strode from the alley, giving her no choice but to stumble after him. Men waited at the alley's entrance. When Campbell reached them, dragging Monique, they raised their lanterns and cheered. Falling in behind Campbell and his captive, they paraded back to the boarding house.

After climbing into the buggy and pulling Monique up beside him, Campbell stood and raised one clenched fist above his head. The miners pressed close, their eyes glinting in the torchlight as they cheered. They looked like savages gathered around a campfire, Monique thought. No, more like wild animals closing in for the kill.

She shuddered, hunching into the corner of the seat. Campbell sat beside her, his fingers biting into her wrist, and motioned to one of the men. A bearded miner climbed up in front of them, took the reins, and urged the horse forward. They clattered over the rough streets as they made their way higher along the side of the mountain. At first the crowd followed, laughing, cheering, and shouting profanities.

"Faster," Campbell ordered.

The driver lashed the horse and, as their pace increased, the crowd fell farther and farther back until at last Monique saw no-one behind them.

She looked from side to side at the dark and quiet houses along the street. Above their roofs, stars haloed Mount Davidson's black and jutting peak. The buggy swung to the left and she had to hold to the rail as they plunged downhill, crossing one street after another. When Monique smelled incense and a heavy cloying odor, she remembered the same scents from her visit to Chinatown in San Francisco.

The buggy stopped and Campbell leaped out. Reaching up, he grasped her wrist again and yanked Monique to the ground beside him. He said one word to the driver. "Wait."

He pushed open the door of a two-story frame building. As Monique was forced to climb the stairs beside him, she heard the sing-song voice of a Celestial coming through the wall. They were in Virginia City's Chinatown, she realized.

At the top of the stairs Campbell paused, cursing as he searched through his pockets. Finally he grunted and she heard a key turn in a lock. Campbell pulled her into a room, let go of her wrist and thrust her ahead of him into the darkness. She stumbled, regained her balance, and turned. The room was completely dark. Hearing Campbell a few feet from her, she edged away from the sound, trying to circle around him to the door.

Her groping hand touched cloth. Pulling it aside, her fingertips pressed against the cold smooth surface of a window pane. She crept past the window with her fingers on the surface of the wall. She heard a scratching behind her. A light flared, and she saw the door at the same time she saw Campbell replacing the chimney of the lamp on the table. She dashed past him to the door and raised the latch.

Campbell laughed. She pulled on the latch. It was locked. He came toward her and she drew back against the door, staring at him. His hand lashed out, striking her cheek. Her mouth stung from the blow and, tasting blood, she brought her hand to her lips.

"What are you afraid of, woman?" Campbell demanded. "You got nothing to fear from me. I ain't about to damage the merchandise."

"I'm not merchandise," she flared at him. "I'm a woman, not a bolt of cloth to be bought and sold. Philippe had no right to do what he did. You have no right."

"You're a wildcat, sure enough. I suspect you got some Latin blood in you. It's not likely you'd find a white woman that was a gambler's whore."

She gasped. "I'm not a . . ." She gagged on the word. "I'm not a whore," she said.

"The only thing I got against that Frenchy friend

of yours is him cutting your hair and decking you out like a boy. Figured he wouldn't have to share you till he found the right house for you, I reckon." Campbell shrugged. "Now you just get over there onto that bed."

She glanced across the room at a high bed with headboards and footboards of gleaming brass. Staring at him in horror, she shook her head. "No," she whispered.

This time she was ready for the blow and twisted her head away, but still his open hand stung her cheek.

"Get on the bed," he said again. "I don't want to have to beat you senseless, woman, but I will if you make me. Now move."

She edged around him, eyeing him warily. When she felt the bed press against the back of her thighs, she stopped, looking past Campbell for a way to escape, seeing only the one door and two heavily shrouded windows. He reached for her, put his hand on her shirt between her breasts and pushed her back so she fell on the bed.

"Don't worry," he said, "I don't mean to do nothing. Not now. I got me some celebrating to take care of first."

He smiled as he looked down at her. "I'm just going to tie you here. Put you on ice, so to speak." He pulled one of her hands over her head and used his bandanna to tie it to the metal frame of the bed. Taking a loop of rope from his belt, he raised her other arm and fastened it to the opposite side of the headboard so she lay with her arms spread like the letter Y.

"No need to gag you," he said, smirking. "These Chinamen know what would happen if they interfered with a white man."

Campbell crossed the room, pausing at the door.

"Now you just think about how you're going to behave when I get back. If you decide to act like a civilized woman, all well and good. If not, I'll beat you till you won't be able to show your face for a good month, if then. Either way, the end result'll be the same. Do you understand me, woman?"

"You're an animal," she told him.

"Maybe so. Been my experience that most women like their men that way." Taking the key from his pocket, he unlocked the door and left the room. She heard the key turn in the lock and the sound of his steps descending the stairs.

Monique twisted her arms, trying to loosen her bonds. The rope on her right wrist bit into her flesh until she winced with pain. The bandanna tying her other arm yielded slightly, but not enough for her to free herself. She shifted her head as she tried to reach the knots with her teeth but failed. Desperate, she threw her body from one side of the bed to the other. With a sudden crack, one foot of the bed collapsed, throwing her partly off the mattress so she hung suspended from her bound hands with her feet touching the floor.

Hunching higher onto the bed, she raised her knees and lay curled on the slanting mattress. She shut her eyes, listening to the low murmur of voices below her, the occasional rattle of a cart passing outside, and the distant tinkle of music from the saloons along C Street.

Drawing in her breath, she screamed. Nothing happened. She screamed again and again, sharp frantic cries for help. Panting, she listened. The sound of voices below her had stopped. She waited, hoping against hope to hear footsteps on the stairs. None came. The voices began again, louder than before, as though trying to drown out the unwanted sound of her screams.

All she could do was wait for Campbell's return. And then? She closed her mind to what he meant to do. What should she do when he came back? Did she have a choice? As he had warned her, the result would be same no matter what she did. She'd do nothing, she decided, neither help him—certainly not help him—nor hinder him. Have it over and done with as soon as she could.

Afterwards, while he slept, she would kill him.

She didn't know how—with his own gun or knife, probably—but there was no question in her mind that she'd kill him. He was an animal. All of them were, all the men who had cheered him on the street outside the boarding house. And so were the Chinese in the house below her, afraid to lift a finger to help.

Not only were these men animals, all men were. Hadn't her own father deserted her years ago, quieting his guilt by sending her mother a few dollars each month? And the twins. She tasted the bile rising in her throat to her mouth at the thought of Micah and Esau. If it hadn't been for them, she wouldn't be here now.

Jeremy, too. He'd lain with her night after night aboard the *Columbia* and then, as soon as the ship dropped anchor, had hurried to the arms of another woman, seeking the power of her father's money. Jeremy was worse than all of the others, because he'd led her to believe he cared and then had betrayed her. It was as though he'd plunged a knife into her back in the midst of their lovemaking.

And Philippe. Tears filled her eyes and rolled unchecked down her cheeks. He was so weak, so spineless. She had given Philippe her love, a sister's love, and he had repaid her by giving her to Alex Campbell. The loss of Rowena should have warned her, yet it hadn't. Philippe had sacrificed her. For what? A few pieces of silver?

She bit her lower lip to stifle her sobs. No, she wasn't going to feel sorry for herself. That's what they expected, these men who preyed on women. They expected you to be weak, to continually turn the other cheek. She'd show them! Mary Vere might have forgiven them but Mary Vere was gone. Not even her name remained. Monique Vaudreuil would have her revenge on Alex Campbell; on all of them.

Time passed slowly. She had no idea whether an hour or more had gone by. She no longer heard the voices from below. Somewhere a coyote howled in the night. The lamp burned steadily on the table.

A horse clip-clopped along the street and stopped in front of the house. Suddenly all of Monique's senses were alert. Slow, heavy footsteps climbed the stairs and paused outside the door. A key rattled in the lock and the door swung open. Alex Campbell stood blinking at her from across the room. His face was flushed and, as he turned to relock the door, his movements seemed over-precise.

Taking the lamp from the table, he approached and held the light over her.

"You *are* a hellion," he said when he saw the bed tilted so the straw mattress lay half on the floor.

Returning the lamp to the table, he came to the bed again and, with a grunt, bent over her. She turned her head to escape the stink of the liquor on his breath. He unbuttoned her shirt to the waist, pulled it from her trousers, and undid the last two buttons before flipping the open shirt to either side. She heard him draw in his breath at the sight of her breasts and, looking at him, she saw his excitement.

His hands fumbled awkwardly as he undid the buttons of her pants. Grasping the cuffs, he pulled the pants from her legs. Except for the shirt, she was naked. She saw sweat beading his forehead and his ruddy cheeks.

"I see you've decided not to put up a fight," he said. "You've got some sense after all." He pulled a knife from a sheath on the side of his boot and cut her bonds. She massaged her aching wrists until the blood flowed to her hands again.

"Get off the bed," he told her.

Eyeing him with apprehension, she stood up beside the bed and watched him grab the mattress and pull it and the blanket to the center of the room.

"Take off your shirt."

She slid the shirt from her arms and let it drop to the floor.

"Get on your hands and knees." He nodded to the mattress.

She stared at him, uncomprehending.

"Get down on your Goddamned hands and knees," he ordered.

She walked to the mattress and dropped to her knees. Lowering herself so she crouched on hands and knees, her breasts pendulous beneath her body, she looked up at him.

"All right," he said.

He walked around the mattress until he was behind her. She heard his hoarse breathing. Unable to tell what he was doing, she looked over her shoulder and saw him toss his shirt on the bed, pull off his boots, then undo his pants and begin pushing them down over his legs.

"You think I'm an animal," he said, "well, I'll act like one."

Monique drew in her breath as she realized what he intended. She scrambled to her feet, forgetting her decision to be passive. He cursed and reached for her, only to trip over his pants. As she dashed to the far side of the table, he yanked off the pants and threw them aside.

She grabbed the lamp and held it in her hand.

"What're you meaning to do, woman?" he bellowed.

He grasped the edge of the table with both hands and shoved it at her like a battering ram. She leaped back. Hurling the table to one side, Campbell lunged for her. She threw the lamp at him with all her strength. He ducked, the lamp smashing against the wall in a crash of broken glass and a rushing blast of flame.

Alex Campbell turned and stared at the fire. The flames were already sweeping along a trail of kerosene across the floor toward him, while tongues of fire licked up the wall to the ceiling. With a curse, he grabbed the blanket and, holding it in front of him, tried to smother the flames.

Monique drew away from the searing heat. Flames crackled in front of her and she coughed as smoke filled her nostrils. Campbell's blanket caught fire and he threw it aside. He leaped across the corridor of flame and through the smoke she saw him pull the cloth away from one of the windows. He picked up a chair and threw it at the glass, the window exploding outward with a shattering crash.

"Come on, woman," he called to her across the blazing corridor of fire. "Get over here!"

She started toward the fire, but the scorching heat drove her back and she retreated to the door, separated from Campbell by a wall of flames. She saw him staring at her, heard him calling to her, and then he was gone. She grasped the latch of the door, forgetting it was locked. The room was ablaze behind her, flames cutting off her escape through the windows. The door was locked.

She screamed in terror.   ❧

12

Flame of Virginia City

MONIQUE pounded on the door, calling out for help. She heard shouts from below. The flames crackled higher behind her, the acrid smoke choking her and the heat searing her bare body.

The door swung open. A small woman stared at Monique and past her at the fire. She was a Celestial in a loose-flowing red dress, her black hair coiled on her head. Monique rushed into the hall, the woman pulled the door shut, and Monique stood gulping in the clear air while attempting to cover her breasts with her folded arms. The woman took Monique's hand and led her along the corridor.

"Hurry, hurry."

The woman's voice was so soft that Monique could barely hear her above the roar of the flames.

Still holding Monique's hand, the Oriental woman led her down narrow back stairs. The sound of the fire lessened as they padded along a hallway to the rear of the house, where the woman stopped in front of a closed door. She pressed Monique's hand.

"Miss, wait here," she said. Monique nodded.

The woman disappeared into the room. When she returned she held an emerald green gown in her arms.

"You take," she said.

Monique held the dress in front of her, then quickly slipped it over her head. The dress was small, but loose-fitting, so she managed to pull it down over her breasts and hips. The skirt fell to slightly below her knees.

The Chinese woman raised her hand to her mouth as though to suppress a giggle as she looked at the ill-fitting gown. She didn't laugh, though, but smiled in sympathy.

"Thank you for saving me," Monique said, "and for giving me the dress."

Not looking directly at Monique, the woman steepled her hands and bowed. "Me Chai," she said.

"My name's Monique."

Chai held out her hand and Monique grasped it, letting the other woman lead her along the corridor to another door. When Chai opened it, Monique felt the cold rush of night air on her face and legs. They hurried across the rear yard. Only when they reached the shadow of a shed did Monique turn to look back. A fierce red glow lit the sky above the house's roof and, as she watched, sparks danced skyward and smoke billowed up into the night. Men wearing their hair in long braids called to one another in Chinese as they ran past.

Chai pressed her hand and Monique followed her along an alley to a narrow street, past a lighted building where, through an open door, Monique saw Chinese men gathered around tables. Was this a fantan house? The two women crossed a street and entered an alley. When they reached the next street, Chai stopped and pointed up the hill in front of them.

"You go," she said.

"You saved my life," Monique told her, wondering if the Chinese woman could understand her. "I would have burned to death in that room if you hadn't come for me. How can I thank you?"

"No need thanks. We women. You, me." Chai paused. "Men!" She shook her head as though in disgust. "Chinese men, American men, all men. They afraid. Afraid of Six Companies, afraid Campbell, afraid Reid, afraid sent back China."

"Men are animals," Monique said.

"An-i-mals?" Chai repeated the word syllable by syllable.

"Pigs, jackasses, goats, coyotes. Animals."

"I understand." Monique thought Chai smiled. "Animals," she repeated.

"If I can ever help you," Monique told her, "if you ever need anything, anything at all, come to me. I'm your friend, remember that." She squeezed Chai's hand. "You and I are friends."

"Yes, friends." Monique was positive the Oriental woman smiled this time. Again Chai steepled her hands and bowed. "Chai must hurry." She turned and slipped into the darkness.

A bell clanged. Looking up the street, Monique saw uniformed men running down the hill toward her. She backed into the shadows and watched as they raced by. The men were harnessed to a wagon whose high wheels clattered over the rutted street. As the wagon passed her she saw, in the light from its two lanterns, the red-painted sides and the hose coiled in the back. A pumper.

"Fire!" The volunteer firemen shouted the dread word as they pounded past her.

"Fire!" Lamps and candles came on in houses on

both sides of the street, shades were raised and tousled-haired men in nightcaps leaned from the windows.

Monique trembled. Folding her arms, she hugged herself. Still stunned by the suddenness of the fire, she turned away from the growing blaze and slowly climbed the hill. Firemen ran past her pulling a hose-cart, dogs yelping and snapping at their heels. Stopping on the board walk of a cross-street, Monique looked back over the roofs of the houses clustered below her on the mountainside.

The flames were spreading, sending forked snake-like tongues of fire to lick the sides of wood walls, crawl across rooftops, and dart from building to building and from shed to shanty. Half-dressed men rushed from their homes, their arms laden with belongings. As they tried to return to salvage more they were driven back into the street by the flames. In the eerie white light, she saw firemen unroll hoses, while others manned the pumps, their bodies thrusting up and down in unison as they worked the brakes to send streams of water arching up into the flames.

She watched, horrified yet fascinated. The fire ebbed and she thought it was under control, but then flames shot up again. Carts and wagons rattled up the hill past her, the fleeing soot-streaked drivers calling to one another in alien phrases.

A column of light rocketed skyward far below her, followed by the roar of an explosion. Another blast shook the ground and then another and another. Stored explosives detonated by the flames? Or were the volunteers blowing up buildings to check the fire's spread? She didn't know.

Again the fire receded. Monique felt a feathery touch on her cheek, a touch as light as a snowflake. She rubbed her cheek with her finger, held the finger to the light, and saw the black smudge of a cinder.

"I suspect our volunteers have managed to control the raging inferno."

Startled, she glanced to her right and saw two men standing a few feet from her, one young and redheaded, with a moustache of the same color, the other taller and older, a grizzled, bearded man who reminded her of pictures of Biblical patriarchs.

"Don't be alarmed," the young man told her. "The Unreliable and myself are quite harmless. You see, we're both employed as scribblers for the local newspapers. My friend represents the Gold Hill *Union* and I serve the interests of the *Enterprise*. I'm Sam Clemens and this is The Unreliable, as I call him, though he's known to his mother as Lester Harrington."

"I'm Monique Vaudreuil." When she looked closely at the two men, Sam Clemens bowed and stared past her as though too shy to meet her gaze. The older man shuffled his feet.

"Delighted to make your acquaintance," Sam said.

"The same," Lester Harrington said.

For a few minutes they watched the dying fire without speaking.

"Our firefighters could make use of Dan DeQuille's solar armor," Sam said finally.

Monique stared uncomprehendingly at him. Lester Harrington spat, and a smile twitched the corners of his mouth.

"I expect you'd like to hear more about the solar armor," Sam said to Monique. "You're probably aware that in the middle of summer the temperatures in the Washoe territory reach heights unrecorded elsewhere. June, July, August, and September are four peculiarly unpleasant months here. The others are

January, February, March, April, May, October, November, and December.

"Be that as it may, in August the Forty Mile Desert becomes literally unbearable. Well, ma'am, there happened to be an inventor, Horace Schwartz by name, who decided it was time to stop complaining and do something. So Horace perfected a helmet to shield a man from the merciless rays of the sun. Solar armor he called it. Attached to Horace's helmet was a tank of ammonia, which was carried on the wayfarer's back, since it's a scientific fact that the evaporation of ammonia acts as a powerful cooling agent.

"Well, ma'am, the miners here on the Comstock are a skeptical lot, except when it come to buying salted claims and speculating in worthless stock certificates. The boys laughed at Horace. 'It won't work,' they said. So finally Horace decided he'd show them. He drove a wagon to the Forty Mile Desert hauling his contraption with him, and while all the scoffers hooted and hollered he put the helmet over his head and strapped the tank to his bank. The boys watched him set off into the desert, all the while making bets as to how far he'd get before he collapsed from the heat.

"After downing a few drinks to ward off the effects of the sun, and a few more to celebrate the occasion, and perhaps two or three to toast Uncle Abe Lincoln in the White House, the boys mounted their horses and mules and headed around to the other side of the desert, where they set up camp to wait for Horace. Not that they expected to ever see him again, at least not this side of Hell.

"They passed the time playing cards and drinking and doing a little prospecting along the edges of the desert. A day went by and then another with nary a sign of Horace Schwartz. So on the third day an expedition of volunteers started out onto the Forty

Mile Desert to find him. The heat was something fierce—their only thermometer boiled over at 117°—but after going maybe ten miles they spied a man's body stretched out on the alkali plain.

"They rode up to him, having to go slow because of the heat, and sure enough, it was Horace. And just like they'd expected, he was dead."

"He'd died from the awful heat?" Monique asked.

"Well, that was the most peculiar circumstance of the whole affair. As a matter of fact, he didn't die of the heat. His solar armor had worked just like he'd said it would, but it worked too well, and he'd frozen to death right there in the middle of the desert. Not only was he completely frozen, but—and I have this from the testimony of two of our leading citizens who were with the party that found him—there was an icicle on his chin."

Lester Harrington slapped his thigh. "Ain't he a caution?" he asked no one in particular.

Monique stared at Sam Clemens, not knowing what to make of him. Finally she smiled tentatively.

"The fire seems about done for." Sam turned to Monique. "Why don't you come to the *Enterprise* office with me? I might be able to help you."

"I don't need any help."

"I happen to think you do. In the newspaper business we hear most everything that goes on in Virginia City. I know about the unfortunate result of yesterday's poker game at the Silver Dollar, and I know about Alexander Campbell. I'd like to try to help. Why don't you come with me?"

Monique realized she had been putting off facing her return to the boarding house and her inevitable meeting with Philippe. Could this talkative newspaper reporter help her? Certainly she knew no one else who might. On a sudden impulse, she nodded.

Lester Harrington raised his hat to Monique when they paused at the bottom of the steps leading up to the *Enterprise* office.

"Do you think the fire's worth a paragraph?" he asked Clemens.

"No more. No one really cares what happens in Chinatown unless they happen to own property there."

Lester nodded and trudged off in the direction of Gold Hill. As soon as they were inside the *Enterprise* office, Sam brought Monique a chair and poured her a cup of coffee.

"Did you really mean what you said about Chinatown?" she asked. "That no one cares what happens there? I think that's terrible."

Clemens shrugged. "I like the Chinese," he said. "They're quiet, peaceable, free from drunkenness, and as industrious as the day is long. A disorderly Chinaman is rare and a lazy one doesn't exist. As long as he has the strength to use his hands he needs no help from anyone. White men complain of lack of work, but a Chinaman never complains for he always manages to find something to do."

"Yet they're not treated like men, or even like women," she said, remembering Chai.

"That's true, and it's surprising, because the Chinese are a great convenience for everyone, even for the worst of the white men. The Chinese suffer for the white man's sins. They're fined for the white man's petty thefts, imprisoned for their robberies, and put to death for their murders. In our courts of law, any white man can swear away a Chinaman's life, but no Chinaman can testify against a white. Ours is the land of the free. No one denies that; no one challenges it. Perhaps it's because we won't let other people testify."

"It's not right. Until I came to California, I used

to think the only slaves were the blacks in the South. Here, all foreigners are treated worse than slaves."

"It's the way of the world," Sam said. "But at the moment, I want to help *you*, not a world full of maltreated men and women. Tell me what happened." When she hesitated, he held up his hand. "I guarantee we won't print a word in the *Enterprise* that might bring harm to you."

She told him the whole story, noticing his interest when she mentioned her change of names. When she described her escape from the fire, he ran his hand through his red hair.

"The Flame," Sam Clemens said. When she frowned, he added, "I christen you The Flame of Virginia City."

"I only hope no-one was hurt. I didn't mean to start a fire, I only wanted to get away from Alex Campbell any way I could."

"Surely no one will blame you for what happened. The man's a brute and a bully. To the best of my knowledge there were no deaths or injuries. A great many buildings were burned, but they'll be rebuilt in a few weeks' time. As I say, the Chinese are an industrious people."

"You said you could help me. How, Mr. Clemens?"

"I'll let it be known around town that if Alex Campbell attempts to harm you, the *Enterprise* will expose him. The men of Virginia City will rally behind a woman in peril, Miss Vaudreuil. This Alex Campbell is a desperado, and his employer, Van Allen Reid, is no better. They say a civilization can be judged by its heroes. In Washoe our heroes are desperadoes, saloon keepers, and stagecoach drivers. Make of that fact what you will."

Monique put her cup on the table and rose. "I have to go back to my room," she said, although she made no move to leave.

"I was intrigued when you told me you'd changed your name," Clemens said, "because I've been considering doing the same. I don't intend to spend the rest of my life in Washoe, nor back home in Missouri, either. I think of Sam Clemens as a typical Missouri name."

"I've changed since I became Monique. At least I hope I'm not the same person I was. I think the same would happen to you, Mr. Clemens. What name did you have in mind?"

"Mark Twain."

"Mark Twain," she repeated. "Yes, I like the sound of it. But if you do change, change completely. Bury Sam Clemens. Really *become* Mark Twain."

"I think I shall, Miss Vaudreuil," he said as he walked her to the door. "May I escort you to your lodgings?"

"That won't be necessary," she told him. "It's only a block from here."

"Then I'll wait on the street outside the *Enterprise* until I know that you're safely home."

They walked down the steps to the sidewalk. Seeing a glow in the sky, Monique, thinking the fire had rekindled, felt a sudden rush of panic until she realized that the glow was the first light of dawn.

"Thank you, Mr. Clemens," she said, "for all you've done."

"Thank Mark Twain," he corrected her. She nodded and walked quickly away.

As she neared the boarding house, her pace slowed. Philippe would be there, she was sure, probably sleeping off the effects of the night before. Monique raised her chin. She'd leave Philippe. If she couldn't find work in Virginia City, she'd ask him to lend her the money to pay her fare back to San Francisco. Surely he owed her that much.

All around her the city was awakening. Pans clattered in the kitchen of a café next door, carts rattled as they rolled past, the feet of miners thudded on the board walks. With a quick nod of determination, she entered the boarding house and climbed the stairs.

When she reached the second floor landing, she realized she had lost her key in Campbell's room. Starting to tap on the door, she paused, tried the latch, and the door swung open. Surprised, she stepped into the room and saw, in the dim light of early morning, Philippe sitting at the far side of the table with his head cradled in his arms.

"Philippe," she said. He didn't move. He's drunk, she told herself.

Monique crossed the room, leaned over the table, and shook Philippe's shoulder. His head lolled to one side.

"Philippe!" she cried.

Hurrying around the table, she gasped in horror as she saw a knife protruding from his lower back. She lifted his hand. He had no pulse. His skin was cold with the chill of death.

"Philippe!" she cried again, shaking him as though she thought she could rouse him back to life.

She drew the knife from his back and held it in front of her, staring numbly at the dark blood on the blade. Hearing a sound, she looked up, knife in hand. A boy of fifteen or sixteen stood in the open doorway staring wide-eyed at her.

"You killed him!"

The boy turned, ran from the room, and down the stairs.

13

A Woman Scorned

In a daze, Monique walked to the table and laid the knife beside the lamp. She glanced at Philippe and then looked away. Feeling as if she couldn't breathe, she stumbled to the bed, sat down, and lowered her head into her hands. She couldn't comprehend that Philippe was dead.

She'd known him only for a year, but it seemed as if it had been forever. She had shared his triumphs and defeats, comforted him when he had despaired, laughed with him when he'd been elated. Now he was dead. She wouldn't really have left him, she told herself. She wouldn't have gone back to San Francisco without him. Philippe was her dearest friend.

Dimly, she heard noises coming through the open window. At first she ignored them, but as the sounds grew louder she got up and, refusing to look at Philippe's form huddled over the table, crossed to the window and looked down.

A crowd milled on the street in front of the boarding house, miners mostly, though she saw several frock-coated gamblers who had been friends of Philippe's. The boy who had discovered her standing beside the body with the bloody knife in her hand was the center of attention as, she supposed, he told his tale over and over as newcomers joined the crowd.

Monique watched the men below her, her face expressionless, her senses numbed. Philippe was dead. Nothing else mattered. Footsteps thudded on the stairs, and she turned as a man strode through the open door into her room. She stared at him in disbelief.

"Jeremy!" she gasped.

"I was in Gold Hill when I heard about the poker game. I came as soon as I could. They told me outside that Philippe was dead." With a glance at Philippe's body, he came to Monique and took her in his arms. She rested her head on his chest.

"I can't cry," she said. "I want to but I can't."

She felt his strong hands stroke her back as he held her to him. Jeremy had come for her. He had waited until she needed him most and then he had come, as he always would, as he was fated to do, because he loved her.

His hand slid up to the nape of her neck and his fingers ran through her short hair as he cradled her head against him.

"Tell me what happened," Jeremy said.

"To Philippe? I don't know. A man named Alex Campbell tried to assault me last night."

"I know the bastard. Did Philippe find him here with you?"

"No. Campbell made me go with him to Chinatown. I threw a lamp at him and started a fire. That was last night. I came back here and found Philippe like this."

He squeezed her hand before he left her to go to the table and kneel at Philippe's side.

"Take the blanket off the bed," he told her.

Jeremy lifted Philippe in his arms and carried him to the bed, where he laid him down with his head on the pillow. Monique stood beside the bed, the blanket in her hands, staring down at the dead man's pale face.

"The blanket," Jeremy said.

Monique blinked, then carefully covered Philippe, leaving his face exposed as though he slept.

"I never should have let either of you leave San Francisco without me." Jeremy's voice was husky. "I want you to come with me now. That crowd's working itself into an ugly mood. There's no telling what they might do."

"I don't have to run away."

He grasped Monique by the arms and shook her. "Damn it, do what I say. Philippe's dead. Isn't that enough? I don't want you dead, too."

"All right," she said. "I'll go with you. Turn around while I change. This dress doesn't fit."

"Hurry."

Jeremy walked to the door, put his clenched fist on the frame, and rested his forehead on it.

Avoiding the bed, Monique took a shirt and pants from hooks along the far wall and laid them on the back of a chair. Shouts came from the street outside. She pulled Chai's dress over her head and let it drop to the floor. Hearing a sound behind her, she looked over her shoulder to find Jeremy staring at her.

"Jeremy," she whispered.

She turned slowly to face him, watching his gaze travel slowly down the length of her naked body. She was aware of his arousal. She stepped toward him.

"Damn it," he said, "get dressed."

Monique bit her lip. He had left her for another woman, she reminded herself. How could she have forgotten so soon? She hurriedly put on the shirt and pants, pulled a cap low over her forehead, and crossed the room to his side. Jeremy didn't look at her.

Are you afraid to look at me? she was about to ask when she saw that he was gazing across the room at Philippe's shrouded body. Jeremy raised his hand to his forehead in a last salute.

Tears welled in Monique's eyes. She ran across the room and, kneeling beside Philippe, smoothed the silver hair back from his forehead, leaning over the bed to kiss his cold cheek.

"Good night, sweet prince," she said softly as she drew the blanket over Philippe's face.

When she returned to Jeremy in the doorway, he nodded to her. Though unsure of his exact meaning, she thought he wanted to show his approval, to acknowledge that they had both loved Philippe. Shutting the door behind them, Jeremy walked quickly along the hall to the rear of the house and led the way down the stairs.

He opened the back door and paused, looking right and left.

"It's safe," he said.

He strode along an alley, Monique running to keep up, then crossed a street and followed a path between two buildings. He stopped at the rear of a livery stable.

"Wait here," he told her.

He was back a few minutes later leading two horses.

"This one's yours," he said, nodding to the mare.

She put her foot in his cupped hands and he lifted her into the saddle. After swinging onto the gelding, Jeremy rode from the alley with Monique a few feet behind. The street was deserted. Though she listened,

Monique couldn't hear the crowd, now two blocks behind them.

The air was fresh, the sun was up, and their shadows were long at their sides as they galloped south from Virginia City, their horses' hooves raising puffs of dust behind them.

As soon as they passed the last shack on the city's outskirts, Jeremy slowed. They loped south, the rising sun warming Monique as they rode through Gold Hill. She listened to the steady thud of their horses' hooves, which seemed to repeat over and over: He came for me, he came for me.

Jeremy slowed again and they rode in single file through the narrow canyon between the dark and brooding rocks on either side of Devil's Gate.

"Don't you want to know where we're going?" he asked.

She didn't know what to answer. Still numbed by Philippe's death, she hadn't thought to ask where they might be bound. Am I such a sheep, she wondered, that I'd follow Jeremy anywhere without question? I'm not, she reassured herself.

Yet the thudding hooves said: He came for me, he came for me. The sound echoed the pounding of her heart. Don't trust him, she warned herself. Remember what happened when the *Columbia* anchored in San Francisco, the day he left you for . . . she couldn't say her name. For that woman.

"Well, don't you?" Jeremy asked.

"Don't I what?"

He raised his eyebrows in exasperation. "Don't you want to know where we're headed?"

"Of course. Where?"

"There's an abandoned cabin a few miles south of Gold Hill. I stayed there when I was looking over some claims in the area. We'll go there."

When she remained silent, he glanced at her. "Is that all right?" he asked.

"Where is she?"

"She?" Jeremy frowned. "Don't talk in riddles. Where is who?"

"You know perfectly well who I mean. Your fiancée." Monique felt a moment of panic. "She is your fiancée, isn't she? Not your wife?"

I am a sheep, she told herself. Now I've let him know how I still feel about him. I've told him I still love him and still want him. Now he knows that what happened in San Francisco doesn't make the slightest difference. What's wrong with me?

Jeremy looked away so she couldn't see his face when he answered. "Laura's in San Francisco," he said without inflection. "And, no, we aren't married."

He suddenly swung his horse from the trail onto a track leading into the barren hills.

Monique reined in. He hadn't given warning of his change of direction and he was almost fifty feet ahead. She spurred the mare after him, slowing as she overtook him. She followed him, saying nothing. If I had been the McAllister woman, she thought, he wouldn't have left me in San Francisco when he journeyed to the mines. He can't love that woman; he only thinks he does.

From the top of a rise, they looked down at a rough cabin near the bottom of a dry wash. Jeremy rode down the slope ahead of her and they dismounted in front of the cabin. While he tethered their horses, she walked past him and opened the door.

Inside the cabin it was musty and dim, with only a few slants of light coming through rents in pieces of cloth tacked over the three windows. The single room was some fifteen feet wide and ten deep. The floor was hard-packed dirt, and the only furnishings were a straw mattress on the floor against the far wall, a dry goods box serving as a table, and two kegs used for chairs.

"It's not the International Hotel," Jeremy said as he came to stand behind her. "But you won't be here long. Tomorrow I'll take you to Carson, where I'll put you on the stage for California."

Put her on the stage? He wasn't going with her, then. Don't be a fool, she told herself, of course he wasn't. He never meant to, no matter what you may have hoped.

"I'm going back to Virginia City," she told him. "I'm not afraid of those men. I'm not going to run away from them."

"Whoa," Jeremy said. "No one's talking about running away. That's not the real problem. The problem is there's nothing for you in the Washoe."

You're wrong, she thought. There's you. She went to the window in the rear of the cabin and ripped off the torn cloth, letting the sunlight stream in. Going to the other two windows, she did the same, and a breeze freshened the dry mustiness of the cabin.

"I could even stay here in this cabin," she said, remembering how, when she and Philippe wintered in the Sierra foothills, she had dreamed of keeping house for Jeremy.

"Don't be a fool," he said brusquely.

She stared at him, hurt and angered. She could call herself a fool, but he couldn't. She raised her chin. "I'm going back to Virginia City," she told him. "I'll be damned if I'll run away."

"Simmer down. I'll ride into town and find out how the land lies. All right? There's a spring a quarter-mile east of here, but there's no food. I'll bring back something to eat. Just promise you won't do anything foolish, like trying to follow me to Virginia City."

"I'll stay here, Jeremy."

"Do you promise?"

"Stop treating me like a child." She raised her voice as her anger flared. "I'm not a child. I might have been when you first met me, but I'm not any longer, thanks to you."

"Whatever I say seems to offend you. Maybe I should have left you there in the boarding house. Maybe I shouldn't have dropped everything to be with you when I thought you needed my help."

Why must we always quarrel? Monique wondered. After all, he had come to her, tried to help her, and had brought her to this cabin so she'd be safe. He cared for her. He loved her without knowing it.

"I'm sorry, Jeremy," she said softly as she stepped toward him.

He looked quickly away, then back at her. She thought he was about to take her in his arms to hold her and kiss her, but he only nodded as though to say she was right to be sorry for doubting him.

He turned from her and left the cabin. A moment later she heard the creak of saddle leather and the sound of hooves, and ran to the open door and watched Jeremy ride up the hillside. When he reached the top she waved to him, but he disappeared over the crest without looking back.

Monique sighed. Crossing to the window, she looked from the desolate rock-strewn ground near the cabin to the sagebrush on the hillside. She closed her eyes, imagining she was in the cabin near Placerville waiting for Philippe's return.

Hearing a whisper behind her, she turned, half expecting to see Philippe walk into the room, toss his hat on the table, and bow to her. The sound came again, and she realized it was only the wind blowing through the slits between the cabin's wallboards.

Oh, Philippe, she thought. How much she missed

him! She had loved him; loved his exuberance, his quick smile, his optimism, and his high-flown language. She had loved the way he read to her from Shakespeare, the way he tied his cravat in front of the mirror, and the upward tilt of his cigarillo as he prepared to venture forth to risk all in a game of chance.

He had been weak, it was true, and he had often been morose, but he'd never been mean-spirited. How could she think that? Monique wondered, knowing he'd given Rowena away and used her as his stake in a game of poker. She could think it because she loved him. Love forgives all things, she decided.

I'll find out who killed him, she vowed. I'll not rest until I know and Philippe is avenged.

Taking a broom—which was no more than dried sagebrush tied to a crooked stick—she swept cobwebs from the corners under the roof and cleaned the wooden sill of the door. Going outside to the rear of the house, she found a bucket inside an empty barrel and set off to look for the spring.

She came on it almost at once. After washing her hands and face, she cupped her palms and drank the cold, bitter-tasting water. Filling the bucket, she returned to the cabin and sprinkled water on the floor to lay the dust. There was nothing else she could do until Jeremy returned, so she climbed the hill in front of the cabin and stood on the rise looking back along the trail. There was no sign of him.

For a moment she imagined she and Jeremy were married, and that he had ridden into town while she waited at home for his return. Her hand went to her short black hair and she wished she had a mirror. She must look a fright! Her boy's clothes, though clean, were wrinkled, and soot from the fire might still be smudging her face and neck.

Back in the cabin, she used a dipper of water to

rinse her face and hands a second time. Facing the bare cabin wall, hands on hips, she turned this way and that as though preening in front of a mirror. Her hands followed the curves of her body, over her full breasts, in at her waist, out at her hips. If only I had been with child in San Francisco, she thought. If I had been, Jeremy's baby would be here with me now, sleeping in a bassinet beneath the window. She smiled at the thought.

Hoofbeats jarred Monique from her reverie. Hurrying to the door, she looked up the hill and saw Jeremy riding toward her. He stopped a few feet away, swung off his horse and, carrying a basket, walked past her into the cabin.

"It's a good thing you stayed here," he said, setting the basket on the table. "They're in a surly mood. They think you killed Philippe. God knows what they might have done if they could have laid their hands on you at the boarding house."

"I'm not afraid of them," Monique said as she started to remove food from the basket.

"I don't want you to take this in the wrong way," Jeremy said, "but I have to ask you a question. Promise me you won't get riled."

"I won't promise anything. Why should I get upset? Ask your question."

"Did you kill Philippe?" When she gasped, freezing, a wedge of cheese held in her hand, he went on quickly. "After all, he did gamble you away in a poker game. I'm not saying you didn't have reason enough to kill him."

"How could you think such a thing? How could you ever believe I'd stab Philippe? Kill him?"

"I didn't say I thought anything of the kind. I merely asked the question. Can't I ask you a question without you flying into a rage?"

"Not a question like that."

"I notice you haven't answered."

She was still holding the wedge of cheese. She hurled it at him. He ducked and the cheese hit the cabin wall and dropped to the dirt floor.

"That's my answer," she said, furious.

"And you're the lady whose gentility was supposed to take San Francisco by storm? You're no different than you ever were."

"You seemed to approve of the way I behaved on the *Columbia,* Jeremy. You didn't mind my unlady-like behavior when it suited your purposes, did you? Answer me, did you?"

His face reddened. "Mary," he said soothingly, "forget everything I said. I don't want to quarrel."

"My name's not Mary. It's Monique."

"Monique then, damn it." He took a step toward her. "What the hell does it matter what you call yourself? You're the same hellion you always were."

"You liked me that way once. Remember? Have the McAllisters changed you? Does your father-in-law-to-be object to your ne'er-do-well friends? That must be why you never came to see me in San Francisco. That must be why you never came to see Philippe, who was supposedly your best friend. You were too busy escorting Laura to afternoon teas and evening soirees to pay any attention to us."

"Keep her out of this." His voice was icy. "I don't want you to say her name, ever."

"Is she too good for me, is that what's bothering you? Too good for someone you think murdered Philippe? Your friend's a goody-goody girl, isn't she?"

"I warned you," Jeremy said.

"What do you intend to do? How can you possibly hurt me more than you have already? What more can you do to me? I loved you, Jeremy, and you turned your back on me; spurned me. You can roast

in hell throughout eternity for all I care, and I
wouldn't lift a finger to help you. I wouldn't do so
much as spit on the flames. Both of you can burn in
hell, you and Laura whatever-her-name-is."

"I warned you." He stepped toward her, his eyes
ablaze.

Monique seized the bucket from the table. "Stay
away from me," she said.

When he reached for her, she threw the half-full
bucket as hard as she could and, though he leaped
aside, the bucket struck his chest a glancing blow.
The water cascaded over him.

"You bitch," he said, looking down at his sopping
shirt and pants.

Jeremy stepped to her and bunched the top of
her shirt in his fist, pulling her toward him. Buttons
flew off and the shirt tore open. He stopped, staring
at her exposed breasts. Monique, unmindful of her
nakedness, picked up the broom from beside the door
and, holding it over one shoulder, advanced on him.

Jeremy backed away, his gaze going from the
broom to her breasts and back to the broom again.
She swung. He grabbed the brush end of the broom
and yanked. She held fast as he pulled her toward
him, the pungent smell of sage filling the room. She
stumbled and fell against him, feeling the wetness
of his shirt on the bare flesh of her breasts.

She gasped and drew back. He tried to pull her
to him but she twisted out of his arms and slapped
him. She heard his quick intake of breath. He came
after her, his brown eyes glinting, and she backed
away.

"Don't touch me," she warned. He grabbed her arm
and yanked her to him. "Don't touch me," she said
again, hearing the tremor in her voice. He kissed her.
"Don't," she said, jerking her mouth away from his.

He gripped the cloth of her shirt in both hands and pulled it down over her arms. She felt his arousal pressing against her. She put her hands on his chest and pushed, but he held her to him with one hand, while the other hand sought the buttons of her pants.

Enraged, she fought him, flailing at him. Her nails scraped across his face, drawing blood.

"Explain that to Laura!" she screamed.

He pushed her pants down her legs, then threw her to the floor and yanked them off. Her hands found his hair, pulling and tearing. He kissed her, biting her lips in his frenzy, his desire, his need, his arms locking around her to hold her bared body to him, his hands sliding down her back to her buttocks. She groaned with rage, and also with desire. She hated him, yet she wanted him.

Her hands grasped his shirt, pulling until the buttons came undone. Her hands went to the front of his pants, where his hands joined hers in freeing himself. He carried her to the mattress, falling with her in his arms, her legs parting as he sought her. When he entered her, she clutched him to her, locking her arms and legs about him as the throbbing pulse of her desire rose and exploded in unison with his.

They lay in one another's arms for a long time, sated and at peace. Finally Jeremy released her, shifting away to lay beside her, his hand caressing her hair. When he stopped, she looked at him and saw that his eyes were closed. Was he asleep?

She reached to him, her fingers feather-soft as they lingered on his bared body, touching his sex with the lightest of caresses before moving away. He murmured and opened his eyes.

"Take off your boots," she said.

He raised himself on his elbow and stared down at the pants bunched over his boots. Sitting up, he pulled off both boots and pants.

"Lie down," she told him.

"What do you mean to do?"

"You'll see."

When he was on his back, she kissed his mouth, a long kiss. Still kissing him, she trailed her lips lower on his body.

"I want to kiss all of you," she said.

He put his hands on the back of her head. Kneeling beside him, she bent her head to his chest, then to his stomach, and lower. She was kissing him, nipping him with her teeth. He moaned as her tongue slid from between her lips and circled his sex.

"Will she do this for you?" Monique raised her head and looked at him. "Will she?" She lowered her head to him once more.

When his arousal peaked, she sat up and straddled him. He reached for her breasts as she leaned over him, drawing her down to him, his tongue curling around one of her nipples and then the other. Using her hand, she led his sex inside.

"Will she do this?" Monique asked as she raised and lowered her hips. Jeremy groaned with desire. When she felt him strain toward her, she stopped, waiting, and not until he quieted did she begin again.

"Will she—?" Monique began.

He reached for her, took her in his arms and pulled her roughly down on top of him.

"When you're with her," she said, "you'll think of me. When you take her in your arms you'll remember how it was with me and you'll wish you were with me, not with her. Wait and see, Jeremy, wait and see."

"Damn you." He rolled her over so she was beneath him, then thrust into her again and again until she cried out and trembled against him.

Afterward, Monique waited only a moment before

she pushed him from her and got up. She pulled on her shirt and pants and slid her feet into her shoes.

"What are you doing?" Jeremy opened his eyes to look up at her.

She didn't answer. Putting on her cap, she knelt beside him and kissed him quickly on the mouth. When he saw her walk to the door, he pushed himself from the mattress.

By the time he pulled on his pants and reached the door, she was leading both horses away from the cabin.

"Where do you think you're going?" he demanded.

In answer, she struck the gelding's flank with the flat of her hand, calling out, "Ay-eee!" The horse shied away, and then stood looking at her. Monique picked up a rock and threw it. When the rock struck the horse's flank, the animal bolted.

Jeremy sprinted toward her, holding up his pants with one hand. She picked up another rock and threw it at him. He stopped, catching the rock in one hand. By the time he recovered and ran after her again, Monique was in the saddle spurring her mare up the hill.

"Where are you going?" he shouted after her.

"Virginia City," she called over her shoulder.

When she reached the top of the rise, she reined up and looked back at his sweat-glistening chest and arms. She raised her hand to her cap, then swung the horse around and rode off.

"Damnation!" Jeremy swore.

His own horse had galloped up the wash and was now out of sight. With another curse, Jeremy started trudging after him. As he walked, he glanced idly at the rock in his hand. All at once he stopped and turned the rock over and over, staring at the blue veins. His pants fell to the ground and he felt the warm wind on his bare body, but he didn't reach down to pull them up.

It can't be, he told himself. Yet he knew silver had been discovered in stranger ways than this. ✍§

14

Hurdy-Gurdy

EVEN though Monique rode through Gold Hill with her cap pulled low to shadow her face, she still found herself turning her head to avoid the casual glances of passersby. I'm not afraid of them, she told herself. Why, then, am I trying to hide?

As she neared Virginia City, she saw an old Piute woman hobbling beside the road with a bundle of sticks on her back. Taking off her cap, Monique tossed it to the Indian woman. I won't need it anymore, she told herself. I'm a woman, not a boy. I'm through pretending. From now on I'll be what I am, what I was meant to be. If Virginia City doesn't like it, then to hell with Virginia City.

She held her head high as she rode into the city, ignoring the stares of miners along the way. She had intended to return to the boarding house, but at the last moment changed her mind and rode instead to the *Enterprise*, tethering her horse at the rail in front.

The newspaper office was fly-buzzing quiet, the presses in the basement stilled. A man sat with his back to her, a glass on the desk in front of him, his feet resting on a pulled-out drawer. As she· stood watching him from the doorway, he raised the glass and drank. He belched and patted his stomach.

"I'm looking for Mr. Clemens," she said.

The man swung to his feet, and she recognized him as Lester Harrington of the Gold Hill *Union*. Sweeping off his hat, he bowed awkwardly, looking, with his gray hair tousled and his eyes bloodshot, as though he hadn't slept.

"Miss Vere," he said huskily, "I didn't hear you come in."

"Vaudreuil," Monique corrected him. "My name used to be Vere but I changed it."

"Sam told me. I mean Mark did. Damn, I can't keep track of people anymore what with the way they change their names at the drop of a hat. It's hard enough to remember a man's name in the first place, let alone keeping two or three different ones in mind."

As he talked, Lester Harrington stared at her, as though, she thought, he was seeing her for the first time. Monique pushed a stray strand of hair from her forehead.

"I think a person should be called whatever they want to be called," she said.

"'Course they should." Harrington shifted his hat from one hand to the other in front of him. "I didn't mean to be off-putting," he said. "Don't take offense. A man's name, and a woman's for that matter, is his own to do what he wants with. I'm told the heathen Chinese never tell you their real names. Sometimes their own kids don't know the names of their parents. So I'm told."

A moustachioed man entered the office, bowed in

passing to Monique, and nodded to Lester Harrington. "Clemens around?" he asked the reporter.

Harrington shook his head.

"Tell him I want to see him when he comes by." The newcomer opened a door on the far side of the room and disappeared down a flight of stairs.

"That's Joe Goodman," Harrington said. "Editor of the *Enterprise*. His name describes him well."

"Have you heard where they've taken Philippe?" she asked. "I was on my way to the boarding house when I decided I'd have a better chance of finding out here."

"You mean the Frenchman that got himself stabbed to death?" When Monique nodded, he said, "His body's most likely at Mandell's Mortuary. Clemens probably headed there when he heard the news of the killing. I was thinking of ambling over to Mandell's myself when I was interrupted by some important business."

Monique resisted an impulse to glance at the shot glass on the desk.

"Here comes Mark now," Harrington said, "with old Doc Jamison in tow."

Mark Twain burst into the office, followed by a wheezing older man. The doctor, dressed in black, carried a black bag.

"Miss Vaudreuil," Mark said, stopping to smile at Monique. "You'll be interested to hear what Doc Jamison has to say."

Mark Twain sat on the corner of a desk, poised a pencil above a pad and nodded to the doctor.

"I examined—the body—first thing—this A.M.," Dr. Jamison said, his words interrupted by his gulping intakes of breath. "Before the heat—got to it." He glanced at Monique. "Begging your pardon—ma'am. The man died of—a stab wound—in the heart."

"This is the part you'll be interested in," Mark told

Monique. "How long had the Frenchman been dead, Doc?"

"From the condition—of the body—the state of rigor mortis—and so forth—and so on—I place the time of death—at approximately midnight. Give or take—a half hour—on either side."

"So you see," Mark said, "the suspicions of the crowd that discovered Manigault's body were completely false. They thought you were the murderer," he told Monique, "but now we know that at the time the Frenchman died you were otherwise engaged."

Philippe was murdered while she was Alex Campbell's prisoner in Chinatown! Monique felt the blood rising to her face.

"Mr. Alexander Campbell has come forth," Mark said, "and made a statement declaring you were with him during the time in question, which was most gallant of him—or so it would seem, until you consider that he provided himself with an alibi at the same time that he exonerated you."

"He wasn't with me all the time," Monique said.

"When he wasn't with you he was in a saloon with four men ready to swear he never left their sight. No, Mr. Campbell didn't kill your friend."

"It wasn't what you might think," Monique said, glancing at the doctor, "my being with Campbell. I told Mr. Twain last night . . ."

Dr. Jamison raised his hand. "The denouement's—in this morning's—*Enterprise.*" He smiled. "The Flame of Virginia City—I believe—the story—called you."

The doctor looked at Mark. "I've got to be running along," he said. "As you know—a physician's time—is seldom his own."

"Thank you for your help, Doctor," Mark said. "I'll make sure to feature your name prominently in the story."

Dr. Jamison nodded and bustled from the office.

"Joe wants to see you," Lester Harrington told Mark.

The redheaded Twain nodded absently. He looked at Monique.

"You listened to the doctor almost without batting an eye," he said. "I expected you to be elated when you heard what he had to say."

"I knew I didn't kill Philippe. I'm glad everyone else will know it now." She glanced through the plate glass window of the *Enterprise* at three miners passing on the street, one with a pick on his shoulder. "They do know, don't they?"

"I expect the news will spread in short order, though I wouldn't show myself on the street for the next few days until we can get some idea of how the land lies. I don't know how the boys feel about you burning down part of the city."

"I didn't mean to! I was protecting myself. I'd do the same thing again if I had to."

Mark held up both hands, palms out, as though to ward her off. "I only offered the advice in the spirit of friendship," he said. "I don't want to see you get hurt. Don't make more work for the doc. I wouldn't want to see our portly friend expire before his time in case I have to call on his services myself some day."

"He's a hydropodist," Lester Harrington said.

"A what?" Monique asked.

"A hydropodist," Mark said. "He believes water cures all the ills of the human body. According to his theory, mankind evolved from the fish of the sea. At some point in the dim past, he claims, we crawled up on the shore, or at least our ancestors did, and became land animals. No matter how we've changed in the aeons since our watery birth, we have a strong affinity for the oceans. The waters that nurtured us in our beginnings still have a powerful curative effect—according to Doc Jamison."

"The man's a humbug," Harrington said. "Everyone knows whiskey's the universal cure-all, not water."

"Yours is certainly the prevalent Virginia City point of view," Mark said. "As for myself, I believe hydropody has undeniable merit. If cleanliness is next to godliness, as our mothers told us, then Doc Jamison's patients are among the most godly in the territory. He soaks them in boiling water, immerses them in ice, and purges them with water administered through all of the body's orifices, or so I'm told. His watery system has its detractors, of course, especially among physicians who swear that bleeding is the greatest cure-all known to man. But I maintain there's a great deal to be said for hydropody."

"And I maintain it's humbug," Harrington said.

"Sam!"

Monique turned to see the editor, Joe Goodman, standing in the doorway.

"Yes, sir," Mark said. "I was just on my way down to see you. Have you met Miss Vaudreuil? Monique, may I present Mr. Joseph Goodman, our notorious editor-in-chief."

"Your servant, ma'am." As he bowed, Goodman glanced at her boy's clothing but made no comment. "Sam," he went on, "Van Allen Reid paid me a visit yesterday afternoon. He was extremely unhappy with your story lampooning the Territorial Senate's vote on the tax bill."

"The bill's a fraud."

"That very well may be," Goodman said. "The fact remains that Reid's one of our biggest advertisers, if not the biggest. Can't you decry the bill without making all its supporters appear to be asses?"

"Anyone who'd support the bill is an ass, or else a poltroon who's sold out to Reid and his ilk."

"We'll discuss the matter later," Goodman said with a glance at Lester Harrington and Monique.

"Whenever you wish," Mark said. "But I warn you. I'm not about to be distracted by facts."

Raising his eyes heavenward, Goodman retreated through the door leading down to what Monique guessed was the pressroom.

"Now," Mark said, "is there somewhere I can take you? We need to find a haven where you can lie low for the next few days until this uproar dies down."

Monique raised her chin. "I don't intend to hide. I mean to return to my room at the boarding house."

"That's not wise. I strongly advise you to wait until the dust from this latest series of untoward incidents has a chance to settle. Virginia City will soon be chasing a new sensation, and the stabbing and fire will be forgotten. There's nothing deader than yesterday's news, as Unreliable here will tell you."

"The young fellow's right," Harrington said.

Monique shook her head. She was determined to run no more, and to hide no more.

"If you want to help me," she said, "someone can bring me a dress and the other clothes I'll need from my room. I intend to walk down C Street to the boarding house, right now, in the middle of the day. And I'll go as what I am, a woman, not as someone flying false colors."

"I admire your spunk," Harrington said. "I'll gladly fetch your belongings. Is there any particular dress you want?"

"The pink if it's still there. The other clothes are in a carpetbag."

As soon as Harrington left, Mark went to a desk, removed a key from the top drawer, and unlocked the bottom one. Reaching inside, he brought out a leather pouch.

"As long as you're so bound and determined not

to listen to me," he said, "I'll give this to you now. I found the money in your room this morning. In Manigault's pocket, as a matter of fact. He must have brought it back with him from the Silver Dollar."

Monique weighed the heavy pouch in her hand before putting it in her pocket. "I can't thank you enough for all you've done," she said.

"I wish I could do more. I admire a courageous woman, particularly a beautiful one. The combination's rare. I suppose when a woman has beauty she doesn't usually need courage."

Lester Harrington walked into the office with a carpetbag in his hand and a pink dress over his arm. "Is this the right one?" he asked.

Monique nodded. Taking the dress and bag, she followed Mark Twain to an empty room at the rear of the building. As soon as he left, closing the door behind him, she removed her boy's clothes and pulled on her drawers and camisole. She slipped into her petticoats, then lowered the pink dress over her head.

There was a small mirror on the wall and, by standing at a distance, she was able to see herself from the waist up. The bodice of the gown was high-necked and formfitting and the sleeves were puffed. The skirt needed a hoop, but she had none. She should have a hat as well, she thought, and a parasol and gloves.

Monique closed her eyes as a wave of weariness swept over her. She put her hand to her forehead, realizing she hadn't slept in almost thirty-six hours. She was so tired, so terribly tired. Opening her eyes, she raised her head defiantly. This wasn't the time to think of sleep. She fluffed out her hair to make the most of its short length.

When she swept from the small room into the office, the two men stared admiringly at her.

"You look lovely," Mark said. "Joan of Arc on her way to the stake couldn't have looked better."

"I'm not going to let you frighten me."

"We'll escort you to your lodgings."

"No, I have to face them alone. But thank you for everything."

"You don't have to face them," Harrington said. "You don't have anything to prove. Let us go with you."

"I think I do have something to prove. I have to show I'm not afraid. I have to prove it not just to them, but to—" She was about to say, "to someone else," meaning to Jeremy. Instead she said, "I have to prove it to myself."

She left them at the door and descended the stairs to the street. Disdaining the sidewalk, she stepped into the dirt of the road and began walking down the middle of C Street, her head held high.

Though she looked neither to the right nor left, she was acutely conscious of the stares of the miners. As she walked on, more men left the saloons and gambling houses and stood on the sidewalks, arms folded, watching her slow progress along the street. No one approached her, no one called to her. The men were as quiet as death.

When she passed Hahn's dance hall, the tinkle of the piano stopped and the hurdy-gurdy girls and their dancing partners joined the men clustered on the boardwalk. At the Silver Dollar, the barman came to the swinging doors, where he stood drying his hands on a towel while he glanced back and forth between Monique and the unattended bar behind him.

Virginia City was hushed. Monique trudged on, willing her feet to go forward. I'll show them, she muttered to herself to drown out the pounding of her heart.

A miner stepped into the street ahead of her, a man she thought she recognized as a member of the crowd that had forced its way into her room with Alex Campbell the night before. She hesitated a moment before walking on. The man, hands on hips, blocked her way. She started around him but he stepped in front of her again. Monique stopped a few feet from him.

"Get out of my way," she told him.

The miner raised his hand, took his hat from his head and threw it into the air.

"Three cheers for the Flame of Virginia City!" he shouted as he stepped to one side.

A ragged cheer came from the miners on the sidewalk. Monique's pulses raced. They're cheering me, she told herself as she walked on toward the boarding house, now only a few buildings away.

"I cant' hear you," the man who had blocked her way shouted to the miners.

"Hip, hip," someone behind her shouted.

"Hooray!" the crowd answered.

The cheer was repeated and repeated once again. Monique climbed the stairs to her room with the cheers echoing in her ears. She closed the door, bolted it, and with a sigh of weariness that turned into a smile of elation threw herself on the bed. As she shut her eyes she heard, in the distance, more cheering, the crack of guns fired in celebration, and the clang of a bell.

When she woke it was dark. The street outside was noisy, though no more so than normal for early evening. Monique lay on her back for a long time staring up into the darkness. Her initial joy at being accepted by the miners had faded, and she felt a great emptiness. She was alone. Philippe was dead. Jeremy? She hugged herself to quell her sharp pain of loss. Damn Jeremy, she told herself. I don't need him.

In the weeks that followed, however, Monique began to wonder if Jeremy—who, she heard, had returned to San Francisco—had been right when he told her there was no place for her in Virginia City. She refused to do a servant's work. She'd vowed never to be a servant again, and she also heeded Philippe's warning against working in the hurdy-gurdy palace or the gambling halls.

Yet what else was there for a woman? She was accepted in Virginia City now. She was saluted on the street by passing miners, who treated her with a respect mixed with awe. And yet, as one day followed another, she felt her life narrowing, as though she had passed through a Devil's Gate of her own, leading her into an exitless cul-de-sac.

Several weeks after her return to the rooming house she had a frightening experience. While walking along C Street after depositing the bulk of Philippe's money in a bank, she was suddenly stopped by a man blocking her way.

He raised his hat and smiled down at her. He was not a miner, she was sure, for he was dressed in a new black broadcloth frock coat, a black hat, and a ruffled silk shirt. A tall man, his hair was as black as her own, though edged with gray, and his skin was as pale as hers.

"Allow me to introduce myself," he said. "I'm Van Allen Reid. Perhaps you've heard of me."

She said nothing.

"If you ever need assistance," he said, "you have only to come to me. I've been an admirer of yours since the day you arrived in our city."

"I don't need your help," Monique said coldly, "and I'm sure I won't in the future."

"The time may come when you'll think differently."

Van's dark eyes never left her face. He looked, she thought, as though he was reading her innermost thoughts.

"Thank you, Mr. Reeve." She tried to keep any hint of her unease from her voice as she deliberately mispronounced his name. "But you're quite wrong. I'll never think differently."

"Time will tell," he said as he bowed and stepped to one side. "My name, Miss Vaudreuil, is Reid. R-E-I-D. Reid."

She swept past him without another word. As she walked on to the boarding house, she felt his gaze on her back, but she refused to look behind her.

When she was in her room with the door bolted, she sat in a chair with her hands clasped in her lap. Unexpectedly, she shivered. Not from fear of Van Allen Reid. No, she wasn't afraid of him. Nor did she like him, for she resented his boldness, his insinuating manner, and his cocksureness.

She was afraid not of Reid but of herself. For, even though she didn't like him, there had been something about the man, an intangible quality, a kinship of some sort, that appealed to her. It had struck fire deep within her. A small flame, to be sure, and one that she would never allow to grow, yet fire nonetheless.

The next day she woke to bright sunlight streaming into her room through the two windows overlooking the street. The early morning breeze was cool, bringing with it the refreshing tang of sage. Why then, she wondered, did she feel this overwhelming sense of despair? She felt as though the world was closing in around her; as though life itself was slowly smothering her.

She lay in bed for a long time, staring at nothing, too dispirited to get up and start another empty day. At last she swung her legs from the bed. With growing determination, she dressed in her pink gown, brushed her lengthening hair, and left her room.

Jeremy had returned to San Francisco. She would go to him. The stage was due to arrive from California sometime in the next half-hour. She'd stop at the depot and book her passage on the return trip. What she would do when she found Jeremy she wasn't sure, she only knew she had to be with him. She would accept his terms, whatever they were, as long as they could be together.

Hadn't he come to her when she needed him? She loved him. Her place was at his side. She wouldn't let Laura McAllister have him. She wouldn't let him marry the San Francisco woman. Jeremy was hers; she hadn't the slightest doubt he had always been destined to be hers.

She had put him off with her querulousness when they were together in the cabin near Gold Hill. If he didn't want her the way she was, she'd change for him. There was nothing she wouldn't do for him. Being with him was all that mattered. If he didn't love her as much as she loved him, and he didn't, what did it matter? She had enough love for the two of them. He did care for her, he'd shown that on board the *Columbia* and in the cabin at Gold Hill.

As she walked toward the depot, the incoming stage passed her. Through the billows of dust raised by the horses, she glimpsed a man's face in the stage window.

Jeremy. He'd come back to Virginia City. Had he changed his mind? Was he returning for her? She hurried along the sidewalk, running the last fifty feet to arrive at the depot just as the passengers were starting to descend from the coach.

Jeremy climbed down, glanced around and saw her. He stared.

"Jeremy," she cried, starting to run to him.

He shook his head, turning from her to look to the open door of the stagecoach, where Laura McAllister waited. He held up his hands and Laura let herself fall, laughing as he gripped her around the waist and swung her to the ground.

Monique stopped a few feet away, staring from Jeremy to Laura. Jeremy removed his hat and bowed. "Monique," he said, "I'd like you to meet Mrs. Johnston, my wife. Laura, Monique was a friend of Philippe Manigault's."

Monique mumbled meaningless words while, through misted eyes, she saw Laura smiling at her. She turned and fled along C Street. The door of Hahn's Dance Hall opened, allowing a gust of music and laughter to escape from inside. Monique hurried past Hahn's, hesitated, then stopped and slowly returned.

She climbed the steps and pushed open the dance hall's door. Through a haze of smoke, she saw an upright piano and gaily dressed women in short, ankle-revealing skirts dancing with bearded miners. She heard the scrape of a fiddle, a woman's voice singing off-key, and a man laughing.

Spying Hans Hahn, the owner, standing at the bar with his thumbs hooked beneath his striped suspenders, Monique walked up to him without giving herself time to change her mind.

"I'd like to be a dancer," she said.

"One of our hurdy-gurdy girls?" Hans asked in a gutteral accent. He pulled a bandanna from his pocket to wipe the sweat from his flushed face.

Monique nodded.

"*Gut.*" Hans looked her up and down. "A dollar a dance, fifty cents for you, fifty cents for me. Agreed?"

Again she nodded. "When can I begin?" she asked.

"Now," Hahn said.

15

From the Depths of the Earth

THE Comstock was changing. At first, the riches of
the lode had been taken from the surface by prospectors wielding picks and shovels. The rock was broken
up first by sledgehammers, and then by huge grind-
ing-stones powered by mules plodding in endless
circles.

The veins of silver and gold, though, refused to
stay on the surface. Instead, they plunged deep into
the mountains, sometimes narrowing and petering
out, other times widening into rich bonanzas.

The miners followed the trail of the veins, labori-
ously tunneling into the sides of the hills and sending shafts probing down from the slopes above. Deeper and deeper they burrowed, reaching depths of a
hundred feet, two hundred, five hundred, a thousand,
the air growing hot and foul, the timbers creaking
under the weight of untold tons of dirt and rock.

As they tunneled into the lode, the men, accustomed to surface mining, learned to overcome the

hazards of the depths through trial and error, from textbook engineers, or from experienced miners lured to the Comstock by wages of four dollars a day. Miners came from Mexico, South America, the Cornish mines of England, and from the gold diggings of California.

They built not one great city in the Washoe, but two. Virginia City rose on the flank of Mount Davidson, while below its streets and buildings a second city of stopes and winzes (tunnels and shafts) grew in the bowels of the earth.

Above, a city of searing sun; below, a city of darkness, broken only by the flicker of lamps and candles, though a city as hot as and, at the lower levels, hotter than the one above. On the surface, a city of dwindling water; below, a city of unexpected floods, where the bite of a miner's pick at a tunnel's face could bring a cascade of steaming water flooding into the mine.

To combat the water, Adolph Sutro, who had fought the Piutes at Pyramid Lake, proposed to build a great four-mile-long tunnel two thousand feet below the surface to drain the mines. The miners scoffed. Men can't work at such depths, they said. Sutro, tenacious, vowed to fight on until his dream became reality.

Machine power gradually replaced manpower and horsepower in the mines. Elevators did the work of hand-drawn buckets, blowers were freighted across the Sierras to force air into ventilating shafts, and giant stamping machines at the mills made mule-power obsolete. Ice hauled from the Sierra lakes sustained miners who, bare to the waist, could work only ten or fifteen minutes at a time in the lower depths before they were forced to retreat from the searingly hot faces of the tunnels.

Men died. They fell hundreds of feet down open shafts, had their guts blown out when black powder exploded prematurely, were crushed in cave-ins, scalded by steaming water, burned to death or suffocated in fires far below the surface, or were felled by heat stroke, their temperatures soaring to 108° as their delirium mercifully yielded to death.

In the midst of death, men lived with a fierce intensity. When shifts ended, the miners, released from the darkness of the underground and from the fear that the pressures of the earth would crush the protecting timbers, burst forth into the city in an orgy of drinking, gambling, and whoring.

Most of these men had seen other mining towns grow and prosper as Virginia City was growing and prospering, only to have the veins of ore run out, the mines close and the towns die. Already the mining West was a graveyard of ghost-towns that had once thought, as Virginia City did in the 1860's, that they would be different, that their lodes of silver and gold were inexhaustible. These were towns where now the only sound was the banging of a broken shutter in the wind, the only movements a swirl of dust above a deserted street and the tumbleweeds bouncing over old wagon ruts.

The Virginia City miners, sensing the eventual exhaustion of the Comstock Lode even though refusing to acknowledge their foreboding, roistered in the saloons and gambling halls along C Street, cheered their favorite performers at Maguire's Theatre, and visited the brothels on D Street and in Chinatown. They didn't lack for money. Weren't they the highest paid miners in the world?

They were young, adventurous, prosperous. They were, most of them, without women of their own. Like berserk billiard balls, they caromed from enthusiasm to enthusiasm: Adah Menken, the buxom actress who, in *Mazeppa*, was shackled naked, (or so it seemed from out front), to the back of an untamed stallion, like a sack of flour, carried from town to town to be auctioned off over and over again for the benefit of the Sanitary Fund to buy bandages, medicine and food for Union hospitals, or the hurdy-gurdy girls at Hahn's Dance Hall who would dance with a man, drink with him, talk to him and, perhaps, dally with him later in a small upstairs room.

Although it was common knowledge that Monique Vaudreuil was available for dancing and nothing more, she was the most popular of the hurdy-gurdy girls, because of her beauty, and because her independence attracted men who were fiercely independent themselves. She was sought after, also, because the miners harbored a grudging admiration and respect for the unattainable while, at the same time, they were challenged by it.

To Monique, the night of the first Saturday in September was much like any other night at Hahn's. The dance hall was crowded, the room smoky and smelling of liquor, the music loud and lilting, the men laughing and high-spirited for the most part and, also for the most part, gamey despite liberal applications of bay rum.

Monique noticed the sharp-faced man watching her from the bar. He sipped his drink, never dancing, only watching, but she paid him little heed. She was used to stares, even from men who, like this man, sat for hour after hour drinking and watching.

At midnight she put her earnings, a double eagle and six silver dollars, in the small pocket at the waist of her gown and smiled at the professor at the piano as she passed him on her way to the rear of the hall. She intended to slip out to the street for the short walk to her room. At the door she glanced back at the bar. The sharp-faced man was gone. She paused, uneasy, then shrugged and went out into the night.

Monique hurried along the dark streets. Men who recognized her raised their hats while others, laughing and singing, made way for her, while still others scuttled by, heads down, without a word or gesture. She opened the front door of the boarding house, climbed the stairs and, pausing at the top, took a key from her pocket and unlocked her door.

Sensing that she wasn't alone, she turned. A man's form appeared from the darkness. When she started to call out, a hand clamped over her mouth and she felt herself pushed backwards into the room. The door slammed shut.

"I have a knife," the man warned. "Do as I say and you won't get hurt."

He released his grip on her mouth. A faint glow came from the windows but his face was shadowed. Was it the man who had watched her from the bar? She thought so but couldn't be sure.

"Take off your clothes," he told her.

"Go to hell."

His fist struck the side of her face. Dazed, Monique stumbled away. He charged, bull-like, pushing her back onto the bed and, before she could recover, he was on her, beating her, his fists pummeling first her face and then her breasts.

He stopped and, panting, stood beside the bed. Pain stabbed her breasts and jaw. She raised her arms to shield her face. He grasped the top of her bodice and ripped down. He tore her underclothing aside, exposing her breasts.

She screamed. Knocking her arms aside, he hit her again, the flat of his palm striking her cheek. Her head snapped to one side. Her cry became a whimper of fear and pain.

"Shut up," he ordered, "or I'll kill you."

When she again held up her hands to protect her face, he grabbed one of her arms and yanked her to her feet. She felt him fumbling at his belt, saw light glint from metal in front of her face.

"It's a knife," he said, his voice high and flute-like. Slowly he lowered the weapon. Pain pricked the side of her breast and she gasped.

"Don't," she said. "I'll do what you say."

"Take off your clothes," he told her.

After pulling the torn dress from her arms, she raised it over her head. He grabbed the dress and threw it to one side. Pushing her down on the bed, he pushed her petticoats up around her waist. She cried out, tried to get up. He struck her with his fist, slamming her head against the wall. She slumped back on the bed, dazed.

She felt her legs being forced apart as the man's weight came down on top of her. Groggy, she still struggled, clawing and hitting at his face. Pulling at his own clothes, he ignored her futile blows.

His sex touched the inside of her thighs and she cringed away, closing her eyes. Teeth clenched, she twisted her body from side to side, but he entered her, violated her. Tears welled in her eyes; fury choked her. She'd kill him if she got the chance.

His hands grasped her buttocks and he thrust up and down for a brief moment before groaning and then collapsing on top of her. She had felt nothing other than outrage and hate. She hated this whiskey-reeking man. She hated all men. Her lower body, bruised by his assault, ached. Pain stung her face and breasts.

With a grunt, the man pushed himself from her and she heard him stumble into a chair as he pulled up his pants. Through a fog of pain she was aware of the door opening and closing. She shut her eyes and drifted into unconsciousness.

When she awakened she lightly touched her aching body with her fingers, moaning as she remembered the brutal assault. Forcing herself to get up, Monique lit the lamp and, removing the remainder of her clothes, bathed her bruised face and the rest of her body with water from the pitcher on the commode. She refused to look in the mirror, afraid of what her reflection would reveal. She was alive. She thanked God that, despite her pain, she wasn't seriously hurt.

After putting on a nightgown, she went to the wardrobe and knelt to remove the pouch hidden in the toe of one of her slippers. Her money, she found, was safe. When she returned to stand beside the bed, she saw a silver dollar on the night-stand, a coin that hadn't been there the day before. She snatched up the dollar and hurled it at the door.

"Bastard," she said aloud.

Remembering that the door was unlocked, she shot home the bolt before returning, exhausted, to bed.

She was awakened by an insistent tapping. Opening her eyes, she blinked in the light of mid-morning. The room was in disarray; a chair lay on its side, her clothes were scattered on the floor. The lamp on the table was out.

The tapping came again.

"Who is it?" she managed to ask through swollen lips.

"Jeremy. Open the door. I have to see you."

Jeremy! When she stood up she was acutely conscious of the lingering pain in her jaw and breasts. Snatching a robe from the floor, she pulled it around her as she walked to the door.

"I was sleeping." Speaking even a few words hurt her lips. "Come back later."

As her senses cleared, her first elation on hearing

Jeremy's voice faded. What did he want with her now? Every time she saw him the end result was pain and heartache. For her, not for him. Hadn't he already done enough to hurt her?

"I'm on my way to San Francisco," Jeremy said through the closed door. "I have to see you. It's important."

"Go away. I don't want to see you. I never want to see you again."

For a moment there was silence in the hall outside. Was he taking her at her word and leaving? I hope to God he is, she told herself. He was a man and, like all men, he used women and then discarded them.

Yet she wanted to see him, wanted him to soothe her pain, to comfort her. Despite everything that had happened between them, she knew she still loved him. Hated him and loved him, if that was possible. Monique shook her head, confused by her conflicting emotions.

"Please," Jeremy said softly. "Please open the door, Mary. Please—Monique."

She walked stiffly to her dressing-table, where she paused to powder her face. After righting the chair and gathering her clothes and laying them on the bed, she went to the windows and pulled down the shades. As she returned to the door, she put up the collar of her robe to conceal the lower part of her face.

She unbolted the door and stepped back. "Come in," she told him.

Jeremy pushed open the door and stood peering into the gloom. He wore a new gray frock coat, she noticed. His cravat was also new, a darker gray, and in his hand he held a glossy gray top hat.

"God, it's stuffy in here," he said.

"What do you want?" she asked, her voice steel-tipped.

"I'm leaving for the coast on this morning's stage. I had to see you before I went."

"Are you tired of her already?" Why did she challenge him this way? Monique wondered. Still, unable to stop, she said, "I told you what would happen, that you'd think of me when you were with her. You do, don't you, Jeremy?"

He gripped her upper arm and she cringed with pain. Letting go at once, he asked, "Are you all right? Is something the matter?"

She shook her head. "No, nothing."

Before he could look closely at her she turned away and walked to the window, where she stood staring at the cracks on the drawn yellow shade.

"Say what you came to say," she told him, "and then go. Please, Jeremy."

"You remember the day when Philippe was killed? How we rode to the cabin below Gold Hill?"

How can I forget? she wanted to say. Tears welled in her eyes and coursed down her cheeks. Had he come to torture her with reminders of their hopeless love? Not their hopeless love; hers. He must think of her with disdain to treat her as he did, if he thought of her at all.

When Monique said nothing, Jeremy went on. "You threw a rock at me as you were riding off," he said. "It had the look of silver ore so I had it assayed. I was right, it was silver, and not more than twenty feet from the cabin. I could have kicked myself for not finding it before. Not a big deposit, but a rich one."

"Why are you telling me? Is that why you came here, to gloat?"

"No, not to gloat." She heard him cross the room and, thinking he was coming to stand beside her, she pulled her robe tighter around her. Instead he went to the bed and she heard the clink of coins.

"This is your share," he said.

When she turned, she saw he had placed a pouch on her night-stand on the same spot where her assailant had left the silver dollar.

"I don't want your money," she said.

"This isn't mine, it's yours. A discovery fee. I never would have found the mine if it hadn't been for you."

"I don't want it," she said stubbornly.

"Don't be a fool. The money's yours." He peered into the dimness at her. "Are you sure you're all right?" he asked.

"Do you think I've been pining away because I haven't seen you these last two months? Were you expecting me to die of grief, of a broken heart? If you were, you couldn't have been more wrong. I've never felt better in my life. Never."

When Jeremy said nothing, Monique went on. "Why don't you use the money to buy Laura a sable coat?" she asked.

"Damn you." Anger flared in his voice. "I told you not to say her name to me again. I don't want the damn money. It's yours. And no, I didn't think you were pining away without me, not with all your other men. Don't you think I know about Hahn's Dance Hall? About your hurdy-gurdy dancing and whatever else goes along with it? That's what I meant when I asked if you were all right."

"Get out," she sobbed. "I never want to see you again."

"Philippe warned me long ago. He told me about you and the Randolph twins. I don't think I believed him, not completely, even after finding you with Captain Nyland in his cabin on the *Columbia*. I believe him now."

"Get out!" she screamed.

"A leopard can't change its spots. Once a—" He stopped abruptly and turned on his heel.

"Get out!" she screamed again. "Go back to that blond bitch of yours." She took the pouch from the stand and threw it at him. The pouch struck the wall and dropped to the floor.

Jeremy paused in the doorway and looked back at her. Monique drew in her breath. For a moment she thought he meant to come to her, to kiss her, and she started to protest even while longing for his touch.

"Goodbye, Mary," Jeremy said softly as he pulled the door shut after him.

She threw herself on the bed, pounding the pillow with her fists. But she didn't cry. I'm past crying, she told herself. I'll never cry again. After a time she took a deep breath and then another, finally standing and walking across the room to take the pouch from the uoor. Returning to sit on the bed, she opened the pouch and poured silver and gold coins onto the coverlet. So many of them, she thought.

She stared at the money for a long time. At last, she nodded her head and, with a grim smile, gathered the coins, listening to them clink together as she dropped them one by one back into the pouch.

Jeremy wouldn't be the only one going to San Francisco, she decided. She'd tell Hans Hahn she wouldn't be back to the dance hall, make the other necessary arrangements and, tomorrow, take the stage across the Sierras.

Not to see Jeremy. The idea of throwing herself at Jeremy's feet had been the notion of a romantic young girl. That girl was no more. Jeremy had killed her as surely as if he'd stabbed her through the heart. She never wanted to see Jeremy Johnston again. She'd keep the money—after all, it was rightfully hers—and put it to good use in San Francisco.

As soon as she was ready, after doing all she had to do, she'd return to the Comstock. And when she did, she told herself, Virginia City would never be the same again. ⇜ઙ

16

Van Allen Reid

LOOKING from the window of the stagecoach as it climbed the long hill to Virginia City, Monique remembered another spring when she had made this same journey with Philippe. She sighed, missing him. Although Philippe had been dead almost a year, she had no more idea today who had killed him than she had had then.

After murmuring a prayer for his soul, a gesture Philippe would have scoffed at, Monique looked with growing excitement at the city ahead of her. How it had grown! Today there were more two- and three-story buildings, more miners crowding the board sidewalks and, surprise of surprises, occasional hoop-skirted women. Glancing into the valley to her left toward Chinatown, she saw no trace of last year's fire. She wondered what had become of Chai.

The stage driver, exuberant, snapped his whip as they clattered up C Street. When he reined the six horses to a halt in front of the Wells Fargo office, a few idlers sitting along the street looked up briefly before returning to their whittling and their tales of the old days, while others left their hats tilted over their eyes. No longer was the arrival of the stage a major event in Virginia City.

A wave of panic swept over Monique and she tensed, wondering if she could possibly succeed. Angrily, she raised her head. Of course I can, she told herself. I haven't come this far only to be frightened away. She remembered her mother, long ago, telling her, "Don't be afraid, Mary, of the day you never saw."

"Ladies, we're here," Monique said to the four young women in the coach with her. "This is your new home."

Ah Sing stared straight ahead, her ivory face showing no emotion. Gabrielle nodded, exclaiming excitedly in French. Mariana smiled, her white teeth flashing.

Tall, blond, regal Astrid said, "It sure as hell better be. My ass is getting damn sore."

"Astrid!"

Monique raised her eyebrows, and Astrid's hand flew to her mouth. As long as Astrid remained silent, Monique thought, no one would doubt she was a native, as she claimed, of Stockholm. As soon as she talked, even the most unperceptive miner would realize she was New York born and bred.

Monique climbed from the coach first, standing to one side to watch the other women descend. All were modestly dressed in the latest fashions but still, Monique had to admit, there was an aura about them suggesting lives spent far from hearth and home.

Ah Sing, barely five feet tall, left the coach first, her eyes lowered, the pearl-gray gown falling from her shoulders giving only a hint of the curves beneath. She was followed by Mariana, a dark beauty with high cheekbones, the golden skin of Spaniards intermingled with Indians, and hair as black as Monique's own. Then came Astrid, tall and big-breasted, a Viking queen of a woman. Finally Gabrielle, bird-like, her hands fluttering like wings, climbed to the ground and stood twirling her mauve parasol. The beautiful French girl's lively talk and sudden moods reminded Monique of Philippe.

"We'll walk," Monique told them when they gathered around her. "It's only two blocks from here."

They set off along the sidewalk with Monique leading the way. Miners stopped to stare, sweeping off their hats even as they nudged one another. Men who had been dozing in tilted chairs looked up, blinking their eyes. A woman glanced at the five newcomers, started to smile, then, after looking more closely, sniffed and walked quickly away.

"Monique!" Hans Hahn raised his hat as he walked from his dance hall to greet her.

"I told you I'd be back, Hans," she said.

"*Fräulein*, I never doubted you. Introduce me to your friends, *bitte*."

"We're tired, Hans, from the ride over the mountains. You'll meet them all in good time."

"Do you mean to open a dance hall? A hurdy-gurdy parlor?"

"You'll find out soon enough, Hans," Monique said with a smile.

Hans stepped aside, shaking his head. After the women had gone on, he called after Monique, "Not near my place. Not another hurdy-gurdy parlor. Remember, Hans was your friend when you needed one. He always treated you good."

He's right, Monique thought, he always did.

Though she looked neither right nor left, Monique soon became aware that they were at the head of a small but growing procession of miners, teamsters, gamblers, idlers, and several solemn-faced Piutes. Virginia City hasn't changed as much as I thought, she told herself with growing confidence.

She stopped in front of a vacant two-story building a few doors from the Silver Dollar. Taking a key from her pocket, the key that had been sent to her by stage the month before, she climbed the steps and unlocked the door. As soon as the four women were inside, she turned to face the crowd gathered on the street.

"What're you intending to do, Monique?" one of the miners asked. She remembered dancing with the man at the hurdy-gurdy palace.

"You'll see, Floyd," she said, "as soon as we get the place prettied up a bit."

"Those are mighty beautiful gals you brought with you," a miner at the back of the crowd called out. "I'd sure like to get to know them better."

"Maybe you will, Hank," she called back. "All in good time."

Looking from face to face, Monique recognized a man here, another there. "Slim, Chet," she said, "it's good to see you all again."

"Going back to Hahn's, Monique?" Chet asked. "We had us good times there."

Monique shook her head. Still glancing about the crowd, she suddenly realized that she was searching for one particular face. Jeremy's. Of course he's not here, she thought. Angry with herself, she nevertheless smiled and waved before going inside and closing the door.

A pox on Jeremy Johnston. Didn't I return to Virginia City, in part at least, to spite him? Wait until he hears I'm back. I'd like to see the look on his face when he finds out what I have in mind . . .

Two weeks later, Monique entered the office of the *Territorial Enterprise*. A young man, a stranger, hurried up to her. "Can I help you, ma'am?" he asked.

Glancing past him, she saw Lester Harrington sitting tilted back in his chair reading a newspaper, his feet propped up on an open desk drawer.

"I know Mr. Harrington," she said.

Hearing his name, Harrington brought his feet down and stood. When he walked over to Monique, she noticed the sweet-sour scent of whiskey. "Miss Vere," he said. "I wondered where you'd got to." His glare sent the young man scurrying away.

"I was in San Francisco, Mr. Harrington."

"Yes, I heard you were. I meant where you'd got to since you came back to Virginia City. I kept expecting you'd stop by the office here, for old times' sake. I didn't want to be presumptuous so I didn't call on you."

"I should have come sooner." She glanced quickly around the office. "Can you tell me where I might find Mr. Twain?" she asked.

"Ah, you came to see Mark." Harrington appeared crestfallen, and for a moment Monique wondered why. Can he be jealous? she asked herself. No, don't be foolish.

"I came to see both of you." When she put both of her hands on his, his face reddened.

"Let me tell you what happened to Mark," Harrington said. "He left town just last month. As a matter of fact, he skedaddled after he got himself involved in a darn-fool duel and became a-feared that the law was after him, since dueling's a punishable offense here in the Territory. Mark lit out for parts unknown. Just between you and me, I suspect he was going to San Francisco and then on to the Sandwich Islands."

"I'm sorry I won't be able to see him. I was grateful to him for helping me. And to you, too, of course. Besides, I liked him."

"Old Mark's got a way with words, even if not with dueling pistols, there's no denying that. He was far and away the best writer on the *Enterprise*, except for Dan DeQuille. I'm not ashamed to admit Mark could write circles around yours truly."

"You don't work for the *Enterprise*, do you, Mr. Harrington?"

"I do as of last week. Joe Goodman says that since I take up so much space here in the office, I might as well do some of the work. He hired me away from the *Union*."

"You might be able to help me, then. My place is opening next Friday night, and I wanted the news to get around. Not with a notice in the paper, but by word of mouth."

"I'd be right glad to help, Miss Monique. A word to the reporters here at the paper, and to the boys at a few of the drinking establishments along the street should do the trick. There's but one problem. I don't rightly know the nature of your business, not that I haven't heard all sorts of rumors since you arrived back in Virginia."

"And exactly what have you heard?"

"Well, there's been those who say you're intending to open a hurdy-gurdy palace. A dance hall like Hahn's. And then there's others who say it's, if you'll pardon my language, going to be a whorehouse." He went on quickly. "Now for myself, I don't believe that's what you've got in mind, but you asked me to tell you what I'd heard."

Monique looked at him steadily. "I prefer to call it a parlor house, Mr. Harrington."

Harrington frowned. "I've heard tell," he said, "they call them that in San Francisco, though I've never visited one myself. Since turning fifty I've come to appreciate the fruit of the grape more than I do the daughters of Eve."

"My place won't be like any that you or the other men have ever seen before. Philippe Manigault showed me how to be a lady and, by God, I'll put what he taught me to good use. There'll be no cussing and spitting, and I'll expect the men to dress and behave as though they're going to call on a lady."

"You're expecting a lot. What if the miners don't see eye to eye with you?"

"I've hired Jess Hubbard to make sure they do."

"Jess Hubbard," Harrington mused. "He must be six-foot-six and weigh two-fifty if he weighs a pound. Do you think the boys will take sass from a black man?"

"Jess won't give them any sass. He'll just invite them to take their patronage elsewhere if they misbehave."

"Jess is sure one big son-of-a—" He paused. "Son-of-a-gun," he finished lamely. "Reminds me of a joke. Where does a two-hundred-fifty pound black man sleep?"

"Where, Mr. Harrington?"

"Wherever he wants to." He smiled. When she didn't, he said, "It's the way you tell the story that makes it funny, I suppose." All at once he was serious. "It's not my place to interfere, Miss—" She knew he was about to say Vere but had caught himself. "Miss Vaudreuil. Yet I can't help wondering if this idea of yours is a good one. I don't know if you've noticed, but Virginia City's been changing, slow but sure. There's more women here now, wives of miners for the most part, and we've got us some new churches. The boys are as wild as ever, true enough, but there's going to be trouble if you flaunt your parlor house in the churchwomen's faces."

"They'd be hypocrites if they made trouble for me and no-one else. What about Chinatown and the houses on D Street? No-one's tried to close them down."

"Out of sight, out of mind. Opening a house right smack on C Street's different. I don't know what might happen once Laura Johnston and the likes of her hears about it, and they'll hear soon enough."

"Laura Johnston?" Monique looked up quickly.

"You've heard of her, I take it. She and her husband are the movers and shakers among the local Presbyterians. For a frail little lady, Laura's got a lot of spunk. She won't take this lying down."

"Laura Johnston had best not interfere with me," Monique said fiercely.

Harrington shrugged. "I don't care much what people might think. I do care, though, what happens to you." He shifted his feet uncomfortably. "I grew kind of fond of you when you were here before and I wouldn't want to see you biting off more than you can chew. It can be a dirty business you're getting into."

"I won't allow any drugs, if that's what you're talking about. And I've already seen Doc Jamison and he's promised to stop by real often."

Again the color rose to Lester Harrington's face. "I shouldn't of said what I did. I can see you've thought it all out ahead of time."

"I've tried to, Mr. Harrington. Thank you for helping by passing the word." She leaned forward to kiss his cheek. "And thank you for caring about what happens to me."

"I'm not the only one, Miss Monique," he said with some embarrassment. "Everybody who knows you cares."

A week after Monique Vaudreuil's parlor house opened on C Street, Van Allen Reid climbed from his carriage, slowly mounted the steps and pulled the bell. A giant black man opened the door.

"How-do, Mr. Reid, sir," Jess Hubbard said, stepping aside.

"I do right well, Jess. And you?"

"Can't complain. Been awful busy this last week."

"Heard you had a bit of trouble with some of the boys."

Jess smiled good-naturedly. "First few days there was a feisty one or two. I suspect they didn't think Miss Monique meant what she said about cussing and spitting and the like."

"I understand you made believers out of them."

"That's right, Mr. Reid, you might say I did. You just might say that."

With a nod, Van walked past Jess into the house's front parlor. The walls were draped with red velvet and decorated with gilt-framed canvases of nudes in the French manner. In a room beyond, several well-dressed men, their hair slicked back, were drinking at a long mahogany bar. Over their heads, candles glowed in a five-tiered chandelier, the light glittering from an array of decanters behind the bar. To the right of the bar was a raised platform for an orchestra next to a small dance floor.

Van saw no women in either room.

"Why, Mr. Reid, it's so nice of you to visit us. I'm gratified. And surprised."

He turned as Monique approached him, hand extended. Taking her hand in both of his, he smiled appreciatively. Her jet black hair was coiled in a chignon on top of her head, her cameo-white face was devoid of makeup except for a touch of scarlet on her lips, and a low scoop neckline revealed smooth pale shoulders. The black silk of the gown matched her hair, moulded her high breasts and highlighted her narrow waist before flaring out in a hoop-skirt that swept the floor.

"You look as lovely as I remembered," he said.

Monique met his eyes for a moment before looking away. She hadn't expected to feel this rising excitement. After all, she reminded herself, Van Allen Reid must be all of forty-five.

"You're early," she said. "Let me find out if our young ladies are dressed."

"No, don't bother. I'm not here to see them."

"Why are you here, Mr. Reid?" she asked, afraid she knew what his answer would be.

"I came for you," he said.

"Let me ask the young ladies if they're ready. You'll particularly like Gabrielle." As soon as she mentioned the French girl's name, Monique realized that of all the girls Gabrielle looked most like herself.

"Thank you, but no. They don't interest me. You do. I've heard the sum of five hundred dollars mentioned."

Monique shook her head, while at the same time conscious of the rapid beating of her heart. What was there about this man? she wondered. Why did he attract her? She knew he could be arrogant and overbearing, and yet he struck a spark, aroused her curiosity, kindled a desire no matter how much she might try to deny it.

"You're shaking your head," Van said.

"The amount isn't five hundred dollars," she said.

"Ah?"

"For you, Mr. Reid, it's one thousand."

She watched his sudden frown. Slowly the frown was replaced by a slow smile, a half-smile, really, for only the left side of his face twitched upward.

"You value yourself highly," he said.

She didn't answer, expecting him to swing about

on his heel and leave. I hope he does, she told herself. Yet a part of her hoped just the opposite.

"Done," Van said, hitting the open palm of his hand with his fist. "One thousand dollars."

Monique drew in her breath, all at once afraid and strangely shy. Before Van had a chance to interpret the hesitation on her face, she turned and started up the stairs, expecting him to follow.

"No, not here," he said. "And not just yet. Put on a wrap and come with me."

Looking down at him in surprise, she said, "I can't possibly leave. I'm needed here."

"You can leave and you're going to," he said flatly. "Surely one of the girls can take your place for the evening."

She hesitated a moment, then shrugged. A few minutes later, a paisley shawl over her shoulders, she preceded him from the parlor house to the carriage waiting outside.

"The mill," Van Allen Reid ordered.

The driver cracked his whip and the black gelding trotted up C Street, turning left at the foot of the mountain. After the carriage dipped into a ravine and climbed a hill, the buildings of the mill loomed out of the darkness in front of them. A rhythmic pounding filled the air.

Van helped her from the carriage. With his hand light on her arm as her own hands held up her skirt, they walked to the first of the mill buildings.

"Where do you think you're going?" a voice challenged them from out of the dark. A lantern shone on their faces.

"Sorry, Mr. Reid," the watchman said hurriedly. "I didn't recognize you." Monique frowned when she heard the obsequious fear in the man's voice.

Van ignored him, walked on and opened the door. The pounding roar of the great machines seemed to double and redouble. Monique stood just inside the doorway, hands over her ears, staring at the stampers pistoning up and down, up and down, rising and falling a hundred times a minute as they crushed the wet ore, thrusting up and down, up and down in a never-ending rhythm.

"This all belongs to me," Van Allen Reid told her.

After a minute, he took her arm and led her outside. She thought he intended to return to the carriage but he escorted her to another building instead. Inside she recognized the hoisting engines and the cables of an elevator at the top of a mine shaft.

"There's another entrance to the mine from my office building in town," Van told her.

"Mr. Reid." The engineer on the platform looked up from a large numbered cylinder. "We didn't expect you tonight."

"You should expect me any time of day or night, Mr. Bryant," Van said.

The engineer nodded, his Adam's apple working up and down. "Yes, sir," he said.

"We're going down," Van told him.

"The young lady, too?" The man sounded surprised.

"Of course. I said 'we.'"

"Yes, sir. You did, sir. I'll have the cage up by the time you're ready." He glanced at the cylinder. "She's at the three hundred-foot level now."

"Over here." Van led Monique to a small room opening off the entrance to the shaft. "You'll find a change of clothes on those pegs."

Van left her before she had time to protest. Looking about, she saw formless smocks hanging on pegs. Two small mirrors had been nailed to the wall of this, the changing room. Monique shrugged and undressed quickly, slipped a smock over her head, pushed her feet into stout shoes, and selected a shapeless felt hat from among a great many other shapeless felt hats piled on a shelf.

Walking from the changing room, she found Van waiting for her. He was now dressed in a long-sleeved cotton shirt and breeches and wore a battered hat. Again she was struck by the blackness of his hair, so like her own, and the whiteness of his skin, so like hers.

A short, beetle-browed man met them on the platform.

"This is Mr. Bemis, my shift foreman," Van told her.

Bemis bowed and waved her into the waiting cage. The two men followed, the foreman raised his hand, and they dropped noiselessly into a womb of darkness lit only by the lantern in Bemis' hand. Great timbers seemed to rush up out of the darkness at them, speed past, and disappear over their heads.

The cage slowed, jounced up and down several times, and stopped. Van took her arm and they stepped onto the wooden floor at the eight hundred-foot level. The station, a large, well-lighted room, was like an underground store packed with tools and row after row of barrels containing candles, fuses, powder, and ice water.

Van took the lantern from Bemis and led Monique into the darkness of a tunnel. She was surprised by the heat in the mine, the heat of an August noon. Thinking of the great mass of earth above her, she hugged herself.

Miners passed them, the men naked from the waist up, their bare skin gleaming palely in the gloom. At the tunnel face, men labored with picks and shovels, their bodies glistening with sweat, some breaking away the wall of ore while others loaded the dirt and rock into small trucks.

"This all belongs to me," Van told her.

When they were on the surface, once more dressed in their street clothes, Van Allen Reid ordered the carriage to take them south, away from the city. Stopping at the foot of an isolated height, he helped Monique over rocks to a promontory above Virginia City. She shivered, finding the night breeze cool after the heat of the mine.

"Someday," Van said, indicating the valley below them with its lights, the roaring mills, the gambling halls, "someday all this will belong to me."

Back in Virginia City, they turned not onto C Street as Monique had expected but into the valley. Skirting the edge of Chinatown, they rode several miles to a house standing alone in the desert, a large house, its turrets and towers dark against the night sky.

Inside, they sat across from one another at a table lit by a single candle. An aged Chinaman served them champagne before he bowed his way from the room.

"This house," she said. "This belongs to you, too, I suppose."

"Yes." He raised his glass in a toast. "You can be a part of all this," he said. When she stared at him, unsure of his meaning, he went on. "We can be allies. Partners."

Monique smiled, letting him refill her glass. "For a moment," she said, "I thought you were proposing marriage."

He choked slightly, raising a napkin to touch his lips. "Marriage isn't for me," he said, "at least not for many years. There's too much I have to do. I can't afford to be hindered by a wife. I've seen too many women squander a man's money on high living, trips to Europe, and castles in the Nevada desert."

"I feel the same," she said. "Not about women, but about men. What they don't gamble away, they spend on drink and women."

He looked at her closely, as though wondering whether she was mocking him. Finally he said, "The first time I saw you, I decided you were the kind of woman who would understand me. More?" He nodded to the champagne and she smiled an assent.

When at last the bottle sat empty on the table, Van stood and bowed. "Come with me," he said.

With a tremor, whether of excitement or unease she couldn't be sure, and with a lightheadedness from the champagne, she followed him along a dim corridor and into a darkened room. She heard the door close. Pulse racing, she waited.

His hand touched her cheek. Taking the shawl from her shoulders, he let it fall to the floor. Slowly, deliberately, Van undressed her, removing her gown, camisole and petticoats. He knelt at her feet and slipped off her shoes and rolled her stockings down her legs.

Naked, she peered into the darkness, hearing the rustle of his clothing. Drawing in her breath, she waited. And waited. Then his arms enfolded her, his bare body pressing urgently against hers.

Without a word he swept her into the air and carried her across the room, laying her on a bed she hadn't seen in the darkness. He knelt on the floor beside her, his hands trailing over her body from her breasts to her stomach, on to her hips an dalong her legs. Still he said nothing, though she heard his rapid breathing.

Her own breath quickened as, with his tongue, he breasts to her stomach, on to her hips and along her breasts, his tongue curling around her nipple, making her draw in her breath. His mouth explored her body, kissing her stomach and then her thighs. Despite herself, a trembling began in her legs, a trembling that grew and grew until it shook her entire body.

His mouth left her. Though she felt the weight of him on the bed beside her, felt the heat of his body near hers, he didn't touch her. With a cry, she reached out to him and pulled him to her as her mouth joined with his. When she kissed him, he returned the kiss while his hand, feather-light, slid along her thigh, circled her sex and finally, caressed her there as her legs parted to claim him, to hold him, to draw him to her. When he entered her, she arched to him, the trembling beginning once more as he thrust into her. Monique cried out, her passion mounting and exploding in a red and orange ecstasy.

When she opened her eyes, he was lying beside her with his arm thrown across her breast. A pounding filled her head and she wondered if what she heard was the distant mills, only to realize the sound was the blood drumming in her ears. She sighed, savoring the moment while pushing aside her wish that Jeremy, not Van, was the man at her side.

"Your girls," Van said.

She blinked as she tried to understand the meaning of the first words he'd spoken since bringing her to the bedroom.

"My girls?" she asked.

"They see many men in a week's time," he said. "There's a great deal your girls could find out from the miners that would be helpful to me. I'd be willing to pay for the information, of course, pay generously."

Why you son-of-a-bitch, Monique thought. What had she expected from Van Allen Reid? A romantic interlude, probably. First she smiled at her rude awakening, then began to laugh.

"What do you find so amusing?"

"I'm laughing at myself."

"What do you say to my proposal?" he asked. "Can we help one another?"

"Go to hell," she told him.

She felt him shrug. "I'm in no hurry," he said. "You'll come around."

Again his hand found her body, his lips following his hand, and again, despite herself, Monique responded to his touch. As he knelt astride her, she pushed him away and they rolled to the edge of the bed and tumbled to the carpeted floor. But when he entered her she cried out and arched to him, her arms circling his body to hold him close.

17

Fe Fi Fo Fum

On a Saturday evening in late summer, Monique was reading when she heard three quick taps on her bedroom door. It's Jess, she told herself.

She opened the door and looked up at the black man looming over her.

"You best come downstairs, Miss Monique," he said. "There's a slant-eyed gal saying she just got to see you. Won't take no for an answer."

As Monique started to nod, a diminutive girl slipped around Jess and threw her arms around Monique.

"Chai!" Monique cried.

Jess' huge hands gripped the girl around the waist, pulled her away from Monique, and lifted her into the air.

"It's all right, Jess," Monique said. "Chai's a friend of mine. She saved my life in the fire last year."

Jess set Chai on her feet, and Monique took the

Chinese girl in her arms. Jess' head jerked up at the sound of shouts and jeers from below.

"I go away two minutes," Jess said, "and all hell breaks loose." He strode along the hall and disappeared down the stairs.

"You my friend?" Chai asked.

"Of course I am," Monique told her. "I'll be beholden to you for as long as I live." She saw tears on the Chinese girl's cheeks. "What's wrong, Chai, what happened?"

"Chai run away. Run away before, they catch Chai."

She slipped her loose-fitting gray dress from one shoulder and turned so Monique could see her upper back.

"Good God," Monique gasped. "Who did it?" Chai's back was criss-crossed with red lash marks.

"Master catch Chai. Whip her. So Chai run away again." She looked up at Monique with fear in her eyes. "We friends like you say?" she asked again.

"Of course we're friends. We're both women, just as you said when you saved me from the fire. Remember?"

"They come for Chai, send men, maybe kill her. I need go San Francisco. Maybe safe there. Friends there."

"No one will harm you while you're with me," Monique said. "If they try, they'll have Jess to deal with."

"You no understand. I belong Chinee man."

Monique recalled having heard that many Chinese girls, purchased in their homeland, were shipped to the states as virtual slaves.

"We'll see about sending you to San Francisco," she said. "Perhaps it would be a good idea. But first I'll have Ah Sing put something on your back, some herbs or one of her other remedies. I didn't believe in them until I found out how well they worked."

Taking Chai by the hand, she led the girl along the corridor.

"Miss Monique!"

Looking over her shoulder, she saw Jess at the top of the stairs. "What is it?" she asked.

"You best come down," he told her. "They got devil-try in mind, no two ways about it."

"You know the rules, Jess, and the men do, too."

"I ain't quite sure they be breaking the rules, Miss Monique. That's why you better come. Besides, I needs someone what understands English."

"You understand English as well as I do."

"I always reckoned I did," Jess said, "but I guess it's American I talks. This gent's an Englishman and he be talking English, not American, and I ain't understood hardly a word he's said yet."

A man's shout came from below. His sally—so faint Monique couldn't understand the words—was greeted with raucous laughter.

"I'll be right there," Monique told Jess.

Turning, she found Ah Sing eyeing Chai hostilely from the open doorway of her room, as though she suspected the Chinese girl was a potential rival.

"This is Chai," Monique told her. "She's my friend and needs help. She'll stay here with us." When she saw Ah Sing's quick glance, she added, "Until she's able to travel on to San Francisco."

Ah Sing smiled and spoke a few sing-song words to Chai, who answered in Chinese. Both young women were smiling as they went into Ah Sing's room.

Monique joined Jess at the top of the stairs. The lamps hadn't been lit, and the house was pleasantly cool in the half-light of early evening.

"Now," Monique said, "you say there's an English gentleman downstairs?"

"More than him. There be him and his 'friends.'"

"I take it you mean they're not really his friends."

"If all my friends were like them gents," Jess said, "I wouldn't lack for enemies. No, ma'am, I sure wouldn't."

"You're whetting my curiosity, Jess. Let's go down and see what the commotion's all about."

"That's exactly what I been wanting you to do. These friends of the English gent ain't nasty mean, exactly, more laughing mean. I ain't saying they couldn't turn the other way. They could, real easy."

With Jess beside her, Monique walked slowly down to the hall. At the foot of the stairs she stopped and stared into the parlor, where at least ten guffawing miners stood clustered in the center of the room.

"That be the English gent in the chair," Jess told her.

As she watched, a burly young man she recognized as Hal Stuart held a wine glass to the Englishman's mouth and, despite the other's protests, forced him to drink.

"Hal," Monique said in a loud voice.

The laughter subsided when the men saw Monique. A few smiled sheepishly. Hal looked around at her and, still holding the glass in one hand, removed his hat with the other.

"Miss Monique," Hal said, "it's right good to see you."

Monique, her hands on her hips, frowned. "Hal, what in heaven's name are you up to?"

"Now don't get that scolding schoolmarm look on your face," Hal told her. "You should be glad to see us, even though we're here a mite early tonight. We fetched you a new customer." The men laughed. "A real honest-to-God customer. At least that's what I think he is." Again the men laughed.

Stepping to one side so Monique could see the seated man, Hal said, "Miss Monique, may I present The Right Honorable High and Mighty Sir Georgia—"

He smirked and the men roared, slapping each other on the back. "I beg your pardon, sir," Hal said, mock-polite. "George," he corrected himself. "The Honorable Sir George Guildford."

The Englishman was using a large white handkerchief to dab wine from his lips. His fair skin was flushed and his blond hair was tousled. The boyish look of his face was belied by the lines around his eyes and mouth. His fawn-colored trousers spoke of expert tailoring, as did his pale-yellow coat. The bow of his large lavender cravat had been pulled to the side of his neck.

Blinking up at Monique, George Guildford rose woozily to his feet and bowed. When he stumbled forward, two miners leaped to his side to steady him.

"Charmed," he said. Hearing his accent, Monique understood why Jess had a problem understanding him.

"You boys have gotten him drunk," Monique said.

"Ma'am," Hal protested, "we only finished what he'd already started. He didn't do no protesting till he saw where we'd brought him."

"I had stopped at a pub after departing a late afternoon church social at Mrs. Laura Johnston's," George said, hiccupping.

That woman again, Monique thought angrily. Wasn't it bad enough to have Jeremy's wife trying to turn all of Virginia City against her? Now she'd sent her this drunken Englishman.

"I apologize," George was saying, "for my most unfortunate condition. These men forced liquor on me and brought me here against my will. As you can see."

"Now that just ain't true," one of the miners said. "We asked him if he'd like to meet a nice refined lady and, at least as best we could make out, he said yes. Didn't he, boys?"

"Sure did," one of his companions agreed, while the others nodded solemnly.

Monique felt a twinge of sympathy for the Englishman. He seemed genuinely confused by his situation and, besides, he reminded her of someone. Who? she wondered.

"We told him," Hal said, "that if he don't have a woman, everyone here in Virginia City's going to take him for a nance, and sure as shooting he wouldn't want that."

"There ain't no boy for him here," a miner said. "That's what the English go for, boys. Bonnie Prince Charlie and their other kings and all the rest of them."

George Guildford raised one arm heavenward. " 'How much longer,' " he cried, as though to some unseen deity, " 'must I suffer these slings and arrows of outrageous fortune?' "

"Or should he take up arms against a sea of troubles?" Monique completed the quotation from Hamlet's "To be or not to be" speech to herself. Of course! George Guildford reminded her of Philippe. Even so, he was a friend of Laura Johnston's. Monique hardened her heart against the Englishman.

"What do you say, Miss Monique?" Hal asked. "Ain't we doing his lordship a favor by letting him prove himself? Virginia City's no place for a man what ain't a man, if you know what I mean."

"I think," Monique said slowly, "that he'd like Astrid. She'll find out what kind of a man he is soon enough."

"Astrid, Astrid," the miners chanted. The tall Swedish girl from New York City had become a favorite with the men of the Comstock.

Going to the stairs, Monique called, "Astrid, you have company."

A moment later the tall flaxen-haired girl, who had obviously been listening, started down the stairs. Looking up, the miners saw first her gleaming red slippers, then a red diaphanous skirt revealing the outlines of her long legs, a boldly cut red bodice that barely concealed the nipples of her large breasts, and finally her rouged face, framed by blond hair cascading over her shoulders.

The men cheered appreciatively when Astrid stopped a few steps from the bottom of the stairs and posed with one hand on her hip. Two miners grasped George Guildford's arms and half-led, half-carried him to the stairs. He gazed up at Astrid, who seemed even taller than her five-ten, with what Monique recognized as awe and fear.

"Turn him loose, boys," Astrid said. Reaching out, she ruffled the Englishman's hair. "Don't be afraid of Astrid, honey," she told him.

"I'm not afraid of you, my good woman," George said.

"That's the way to win her," Hal whooped. "To the best of my recollection you're the first hombre that's ever called Astrid a good woman."

"He may need some encouragement." Monique's soft words were unnoticed in the gust of laughter.

"I'll give him all the encouragement he can handle," Astrid told her in a booming voice.

"She sure will," a miner said. "The only question is, will it do any good?"

George reddened, and again Monique pitied him. Yet he had no right coming to Virginia City, she told herself, not if he didn't know how to take care of himself.

"Come on sweetie," Astrid told George. "Come along upstairs with Astrid."

Taking him by the hand, she guided him to the

second floor. Just before disappearing along the upper hall, George looked back with an unspoken plea for help clearly written on his face.

"Let's mosey over to the bar," Hal said, "and wait and hear what Astrid has to say about whether our English friend's a bonanza or a *borrasca*. To my way of thinking, it ain't going to take very long."

The men, laughing and hollering, followed Hal from the parlor to the bar in the next room. With a sigh, Monique started up the stairs. Poor George Guildford, she thought. After tonight the boys would laugh him out of town.

"Miss Monique."

Jess, his hand clasped on a boy's shoulder, came toward her from the front of the house. She looked at the youngster twice before she recognized him as the boy who had found her standing over Philippe on the night the Frenchman was killed.

Poor Philippe. She was doing all she could to find his murderer. Van Allen Reid had suggested using the girls to ferret out information to help him in his mining ventures. Instead, Monique had asked them to discover anything that might lead to the unmasking of Philippe's murderer. So far, though, they had found nothing.

"This young fellow," Jess told her, "saw something you ought to know about."

"Let go of me," the boy said as he tried to twist from Jess' grip.

Monique nodded and Jess released him.

"What is it?" Monique asked.

"Gimme a drink first." The boy drew himself up to his full height. "A whiskey."

"You'll get no liquor here," Monique said. "You ought to know that."

"Ain't no harm in asking, is there? What I come

to tell you about is them Presbyterians. It ought to be worth a dollar to you. At least a dollar."

Monique took a silver coin from her pocket and held it in the glow from the recently lighted lamps. When the boy reached for the glinting coin, she closed her fingers around it.

"Tell me about the Presbyterians first," she said.

"They was holding this big meeting at the Johnston place."

"That ain't news," Jess said. "An English gent told us that more than ten minutes ago."

"Let me finish," the boy said. "It's what they're doing now you'd be interested in. That Reverend McDonough was there, and he made a speech about the evils of fair but frail women. I heard him through the open window. He got them ladies all riled up and when he suggested they march down here they all allowed as how that was a right fine idea. So what I come to tell you is, they're on the way and singing to beat the band to boot."

"The churchwomen are coming here?" Monique asked.

"Swear to God. I ain't got no way of telling what they're up to, but they was sure breathing hellfire and damnation when they left Johnston's. I ran all the way to beat them here so I could warn you."

"I'll be Goddamned," Jess said. "Begging your pardon, Miss Monique."

Monique spun the coin into the air. Catching it in one hand, the boy darted past Jess to the street. Jess followed him as far as the open door.

"Sure enough, the boy's right," he said over his shoulder to Monique. "Sounds like they's headed this way, singing like a flock of hens at feeding time. Reminds me of the Baptist chapel back home, 'cept these women can't hold a candle to the singing there. Back home they sings like they means it."

Monique looked along the street into the dust-muted twilight. Though she couldn't see the singers, she heard voices raised in a hymn, and after a few minutes she made out the words.

"Rock of Ages," the women sang, "cleft for me, let me hide myself in thee."

A flickering light appeared several blocks up the street, followed by another and then still another. Candles, Monique thought, the women were carrying candles. The lights approached in single file, the women's faces pale in the candles' glow, their voices high-pitched and strident.

"If it ain't one damn thing, it's another." Jess ran his hand over his bald pate. "What you want me to do, Miss Monique? Get a broom and shoo them ladies away?"

"No, don't do that," Monique told him. "I'm not afraid of them. I'm not afraid of *her*."

As the marchers neared with their candles held aloft, Monique was reminded of another night when the men of Montgomery, by the light of torches, had beaten Philippe for daring to bring her to a ball.

The women, still singing "Rock of Ages," stopped in the street outside the parlor house. The men who gathered on the sidewalks to watch were strangely quiet, Monique thought, as though not quite sure what side they were on. The times were changing, she told herself. She suspected that only a few years ago the churchwomen would have been the butt of derisive jokes and catcalls.

When the hymn ended, one of the women stepped forward to the foot of the steps leading to the parlor house. Monique drew in a quick breath as she recognized Laura Johnston. The other woman's blond hair curled around the edges of a prim bonnet. Her white muslin gown was decorated with a delicate design of pink tea roses.

Laura looked tired, Monique thought. Her pale face was thinner than she remembered, and there were dark circles beneath her eyes.

"We have come to bear witness," Laura said.

Monique stepped from the shadowed doorway to the top of the steps and stared down at the other woman.

"Amen." It was a man's voice. Glancing past Laura, Monique recognized the cadaverous face of the Reverend August McDonough.

"We ask you," Laura said to Monique, "to turn away from evil, and to ask the Lord to forgive you for your sins."

"The Lord welcomes the return of the prodigal daughter just as he does the return of the prodigal son," the Reverend McDonough intoned. "He seeks the lost ewe to lead her back into the fold."

Flabbergasted, Monique stared first at the preacher and then at Laura, not knowing what to say.

"There's still time," Laura said. Her high-pitched voice betrayed her nervousness, yet she spoke intently, almost fiercely. "It's wrong to lead men into the ways of Satan," she said.

"What? What did you say?" Anger rose in Monique. Was this woman telling her she had led Jeremy into sin? That certainly hadn't been the way of it.

"Enter into the house of the Lord," McDonough said. "Follow the path of righteousness for His namesake."

"There's still time for you to repent, Miss Vaudreuil," Laura told her.

"Repent?" Monique asked. "What have I got to repent?"

"The sin of bringing the evils of Sodom and Gomorrah to Virginia City," the Reverend said. "The sin of leading men along the path of the devil. The sin of being less than a virtuous woman."

Monique, furious, glanced from McDonough to Laura. "A virtuous woman?" she asked. "Is a woman who steals the man you love a virtuous woman? I've seen chaste women, if that's why you mean by virtuous, who were nasty, mean, and cruel, who were bad-tempered and malicious. Were they virtuous women? Answer me. Were they?"

"The Lord forgives all those who repent their sins," McDonough said.

Ignoring McDonough, Laura answered Monique. "No, of course they weren't virtuous," she said.

"And I've known other women," Monique went on, "and men as well, who were kind and good, warmhearted and generous. Some of those women work here." With a wave of her hand she indicated the parlor house. "They work here because men don't give them a chance to earn their living in any other way."

"Surely they do it for other reasons," Laura said.

"They do it for the same reasons any woman might have for working rather than being beholden to a man."

"Sin is an abomination in the eyes of the Lord," McDonough said. "And the wages of sin are death."

"Let Miss Monique have her say," a miner shouted at him. "She makes more sense."

There was a murmur of agreement.

"Let us pray for the sinners among us," McDonough said. Looking around at the crowd, he added, "Let us all pray."

"Not just for the sinners," Laura said in her high, clear voice, "let's pray for every one of us."

In the light from the candles Monique saw a man standing apart from the crowd in the shadow of a feed store across the street. She recognized Jeremy at once. Their eyes met and held. Finally he looked away, folded his arms, and stared at the ground.

Monique's anger slipped away, leaving a great emptiness, as if all feeling had drained from her. She was suddenly tired, as though she had been drifting without sustenance for countless days on a vast ocean under a searing tropic sun.

"Silently pray," she heard Laura add. Monique realized the other woman was talking to the Reverend McDonough.

"As you wish," McDonough said.

The preacher dropped to his knees in the dirt of the street. Laura sank down beside him, and the rest of the churchwomen followed her example until they were all kneeling, the candles in their hands glowing like haloes.

Monique walked down the steps, knelt, and closed her eyes. One by one the miners, looking sheepish, knelt on the sidewalk and in the street. When several remained standing, Jess walked over and stared down at them.

"I reckon Miss Monique would appreciate seeing you kneel," he said.

The men dropped reluctantly to their knees.

"What in hell have I got to pray for?" one asked.

"For your Goddamn immortal soul," Jess told him as he joined the others on the ground.

In the hush they all heard the far-off stamping of the mills, the whinny of a horse, and the tinkle of the piano in Hahn's hurdy-gurdy palace. A deep melodious voice began to sing:

"Mine eyes have seen the glory of the coming of the Lord."

Opening her eyes, Monique saw it was Jess.

"He is trampling out the vintage," the black man sang, "where the grapes of wrath are stored."

The others began singing, men's and women's voices joining in the chorus: "Glory, glory, hallelujah, Glory, glory, hallelujah, His truth goes marching on."

Inexpressibly moved by the soaring exultation of the hymn, by the candles, and, she admitted, by seeing Jeremy again after so long, Monique's throat tightened and tears welled in her eyes. She frowned. Had she heard her name?

"Miss Monique."

Someone *was* calling her. Looking behind her, she saw Astrid motioning from the doorway.

She'd completely forgotten George Guildford. ◆§

18

The Highwayman

"THE boys were right," Astrid told Monique as soon as the two women were inside the parlor house. "If me and Sir George had been in a poker game, he wouldn't have been able to open. He held nothing high. Nothing."

Monique glanced toward the men in the bar. "He'd been drinking," she said. "I sort of feel sorry for him."

"You and me both," Astrid said. "I like the bugger, even if he can't get it up. He's sort of sweet. Treated me like a lady."

Philippe always treated me like a lady, Monique thought. She saw Hal look up from his drink and glance their way.

"This is what we'll do," she told Astrid, lowering her voice so only the other woman could hear.

"Astrid," Hal called out as he led the men into the parlor to gather around the tall blond girl. From outside Monique heard the receding sound of the churchwomen singing "Rock of Ages."

"Astrid," Hal repeated. "That was mighty quick."

"Boys," Astrid said, "I raised the white flag. I've known a few good men in my time, but never one the likes of Sir George. I came downstairs to thank you for bringing him around. He's one of a kind."

"You're funning us," a miner said.

"Come clean." Hal couldn't hide the disappointment in his voice. "What really happened?"

"Boys," Astrid said, "an old prospector once told me it ain't the size of your pick that matters, it's how you swing it. That bloody Englishman sure as hell knows how to use a pick."

"Well, I'll be damned," Hal muttered.

"We must of figured him wrong," another miner put in.

"We sure did," Hal said. "Send him down here, Astrid, so we can make it right with him."

"If I go up there," Astrid said, glancing over her head, "I don't know if me or him will be back again real soon or not. The last I saw of Sir George he was raring to go at it again, but I'll take a look. Maybe he's simmered down a bit."

As she watched Astrid disappear up the stairs, Monique saw Jess trying to catch her eye from the kitchen doorway.

"What is it, Jess?" she asked as soon as they were alone.

"I grabbed two of them Celestials sneaking through the back window while we was singing up front. I sent them packing. First I had to take these away from them." When Jess stood aside she saw two large curve-bladed knives on the kitchen table.

"You weren't hurt?"

"No, ma'am," Jess said, " 'cause I come on them afore they could get them knives to working." He paused. "I dont' like this one bit. I don't mind men coming at me with their fists. Fact is, I sort of enjoys it when they does, and a gun or two don't scare me none, but when them Celestials start crawling around with daggers and hatchets, I draws the line. You can't hear or see the bastards, begging your pardon, Miss Monique, and when you do see them you can't tell one from the other."

"I'll make sure Chai goes to San Francisco," Monique said. "In fact, I'll take her there myself. I'm thinking of branching out, Jess. There's room for another clothing store in Virginia City, but before I open one I'd like to talk to the suppliers face to face. I was planning to travel to San Francisco in a few weeks to do just that, but now I'll go in the next day or two and take Chai with me."

"Suits me just fine," Jess said.

Hearing a discreet cough behind her, Monique turned and found George Guildford watching them from the doorway. He seemed quite sober.

"Pardon me for interrupting," the Englishman said. "Miss Astrid informed me of what you did, of what you and she said to the miners, and I want to thank you. I can't begin to tell you how indebted I am to you, Miss Monique."

She felt herself blushing. "The boys get carried away sometimes," she told him. "They mean no harm. At least most of the time they don't. I'm ashamed of myself for going along with them as far as I did." I wonder if I would have, she asked herself, if the Englishman hadn't mentioned Laura Johnston?

" 'The quality of your mercy,' " George said, " 'droppeth as the gentle rain from heaven.' "

" 'Blessing him that gives and him that takes,' " she completed the quotation.

George raised his eyebrows. "Quite so," he said. "I'm amazed. I never expected to find a lover of Shakespeare in the uncivilized wilds of Nevada."

"What's the gentleman saying?" Jess asked. "I can't

get my ears to latch onto his words 'cause of the way he twists them."

"I think he's trying to say he didn't expect a Virginia City madam to quote Shakespeare."

"My good woman—" George stopped short as Hal burst into the room.

"We been looking all over for you," Hal said as he slapped the Englishman on the back. "Boys," he shouted, "he's in the kitchen."

The miners poured into the room and crowded around George. Two of them lifted him to their shoulders.

"A cheer for the bloody Limey," someone shouted, and the men gave three "Hip-hip-hoorays."

"The drinks are on us," Hal said. "To the Silver Dollar!"

The men formed a column of twos behind Hal and paraded from the room, George having to duck under the top of the door. Monique, shaking her head, stood beside Jess and watched them march down C Street holding George Guildford aloft, the men lustily singing "For he's a jolly good fellow," the Englishman raising his arms high in the air to salute curious passersby.

"That was right nice," Jess told her, "what you did for him."

"I kind of like George Guildford," Monique said. Because of Philippe, she thought. Was that the only reason? she asked herself.

Two days later, Monique and Chai left Virginia City on the morning stage, bound for San Francisco. Monique had disguised the Chinese girl in a modish French gown and a hat with a black veil that concealed her face.

After waiting until just before departure time, Jess had escorted them to the Wells Fargo office and bustled them aboard the stage. Jess had seen no more Celestials lurking near the parlor house, and none were visible at the stage station.

As they rumbled down Geiger Grade, Monique ignored the sharp precipices along the road as she relaxed in her corner seat, lulled by the swaying of the coach. She had told Jess the truth. She did intend to go into the clothing business, but there was another reason for her trip to San Francisco.

She needed time to herself. Time away from the parlor house and the responsibility for the girls. Away from the wild roistering of Virginia City. Away from a city where, at any moment, she might turn a corner and find herself face to face with Jeremy or his wife. And, she admitted, away from Van Allen Reid as well.

A month had passed since Van had first visited the parlor house, a month with no word from him. Then, on a Monday morning, Jess handed her an envelope that had been delivered to the door. She read the note inside:

"Monique. I will call for you at eight tonight. V."

Monique wadded the paper into a ball and threw it across the room. I won't go, she told herself, and all day she remained firm in her resolve to have nothing more to do with Van Allen Reid. That night, when he arrived, she met him at the door and went with him without a word. Money wasn't mentioned. She would have been insulted if he offered any and, sensing this, he didn't.

When he led her into his bedroom she slipped from her clothes, slid between the sheets, and waited for him. They joined fiercely, their naked, sweat-slippery bodies wrapping one about the other as they arched in passionate ecstasy.

Afterwards, Monique felt sated, satisfied; and yet she knew she had somehow been sullied.

"If being with a man can't be a jubilee," she had told Dillie long ago, "I want no part of it."

It hadn't been a jubilee, a celebration, with Van Allen Reid. With Van she had known the pleasures of the flesh. Her need was satisfied, her insistent burning desire appeased. Nothing more.

Laura Johnston, if she had known, would have branded her a sinner, a scarlet woman. Monique sniffed. To her, sin was a word without meaning. If she harmed no one, how could what she had done be wrong?

Yet wasn't she harming someone? Not Jeremy, certainly, nor Van Allen Reid. The person she feared she had harmed was herself, because she had given herself to a man she didn't truly care for, a man she could never love or trust.

As the coach reached the bottom of the Grade, Monique dozed, dreaming fitfully of fires in the night, of beacons flaring on distant peaks, and of horsemen racing down steep slopes to hurtle past her and disappear in the darkness. She awoke with a start as the coach drew to a halt in Carson City.

"Are we almost there?" Chai whispered.

"No, we still have a long way to go," Monique told her. "Don't be afraid. I'll not let anyone harm you."

As long as they were still in Virginia City, Monique had feared that Chai's master might attempt to force her back into bondage in Chinatown. Once they had ridden down Geiger Grade, though, her uneasiness evaporated. Chai was safe, and would soon be leaving her. Monique realized she would miss the Chinese girl.

My whole life, Monique mused as the stage began the long climb from the Carson Valley into the Sierras, has been one goodbye after another. Her father had left her before she had a chance to know him. Later, she had fled from the Jarvis house, leaving Dillie behind. Jeremy had abandoned her for the McAllister money. Philippe had been killed, senselessly. She had even lost Rowena. Now Chai was about to drop from her life forever.

I need something to hold on to, she told herself. Not something, someone. I need someone to talk to, confide in, share the future with. Once it had been easy to say she had only herself, could trust only herself, but now she found the loneliness of her present life, at times, almost unbearable.

The sun circled toward evening as the trail receded behind them in a billow of dust. They left the foothills with their shrubs, sage, and scattered trees, and entered a land of pines and cedars. The air cooled as the sun lowered, and the stagecoach climbed into high mountain country.

A stream rushed by along the trail, the sparkling water foaming and bubbling over a series of rapids in its descent to the Carson Valley. The streams on the eastern slopes of the Sierras, so alive and crystalline as they left their source-springs, flowed swiftly down into the Nevada Territory, where they were doomed to disappear forever in great desert sinks of sand and alkali.

Monique, shivering, pulled her shawl closer. She looked from the coach, wondering if scattered remnants of the winter's snows might still be visible on the north side of the cliffs or deep in the recesses of the murky glens. But the snows of winter had melted long ago.

The coach swayed around a bend in the trail. The driver cried out in alarm, the horses neighed, and the stage came to an abrupt clattering stop that sent bags and valises tumbling. Monique pitched forward onto the man sitting across from her.

Recovering, she looked from the window. Ahead of the team of six horses a tree lay across the trail.

Two masked men rode from the woods, guns drawn. A man shouted on the far side of the stage. Monique couldn't see him, nor could she make out his words.

"Don't shoot," the driver shouted.

One of the masked gunmen swung from his horse and, pistol in hand, strode to the side of the coach. Monique drew back as he yanked the door open and peered inside.

"You," he told Monique. "Outside."

She stared at him in confusion and dismay. She shook her head.

The bandit motioned impatiently with his pistol. "Out of the stage," he said. "Pronto."

"Don't go," Chai pleaded.

Monique pressed the Chinese girl's hand. Had these men been sent to bring Chai back to Virginia City? she wondered.

She climbed to the ground and faced the gunman. Above the red bandanna tied across his face, the man's brown eyes were bloodshot. He'd pulled his wide-brimmed hat low over his forehead.

Hands grasped Monique's arms from behind and she felt a rope bite into her wrists. Someone thrust a twisted cloth in her mouth and tied it behind her head. When she tried to cry out her words were muffled by the gag. Glancing around, she saw the driver and his companion sitting on top of the stage with their hands raised.

In the distance, beyond the fallen tree, a horseman watched from a small knoll among the pines. His hat, jacket, and trousers were gray, Confederate gray, she realized with a shock, and on his broad belt he wore two holstered pistols and a sheathed sword.

"Miss Monique."

She looked behind her to see Chai climbing from the stage. The gunman who had tied her hands picked up the Chinese girl and lifted her back inside the coach, shutting the door after her. A bandit led a horse forward, grasped Monique's slim waist and lifted her into the saddle. A sidesaddle, she noticed with surprise.

The bandits mounted, one holding the reins of Monique's horse, and looked toward their leader. The Confederate cavalier unsheathed his sword, raised it high above his head, and then pointed it in the direction of the setting sun. He spurred his horse ahead, and his three accomplices and Monique followed him into the trees. When she looked back at the stage, the driver and his companion were still holding their hands high above their heads.

Stunned by the suddenness of the raid, Monique looked warily from one bandit to the next. What could they want with her? A shiver of apprehension ran along her spine as she remembered the sharp-faced man watching her at the hurdy-gurdy hall the night an intruder had waited at the rooming house to rape her.

After riding for ten minutes through the pine forest, the small band halted in a sun-dappled forest glade. Monique stared at the masked leader of the band, the hairs on the back of her neck prickling. Strange, she thought, I think I know him. And yet . . . She shook her head, puzzled.

The gray-clad horseman unsheathed his sword once again and swung it in a circle above his head. The bandit leading Monique's horse dismounted and, after tying its reins to a sapling, remounted his own horse. Together with his two companions, he rode into the woods, leaving Monique alone with their leader.

The Confederate urged his horse forward, circling behind Monique until she had to twist her head to see him. She drew in her breath as he came toward her with sword in hand.

Noting her reaction, he reached up and pulled the bandanna from his face.

George Guildford!

"Please don't be frightened," the Englishman said. "The sword's merely to sever your bonds."

George stopped beside her, leaned from his horse, and cut the rope binding her hands. Monique pulled the gag from her mouth.

"George!" she cried. "Why did you hold up the stage? Why did you bring me here?"

Without answering, he dismounted and untied the reins looped around the sapling. "Don't be afraid," he said. "I won't harm you. There's something I want to show you. Something I want to give you."

"You carried me off to show me something? To give me something? You're mad."

"No, I'm not mad. Impulsive perhaps, but not mad. At least I don't think I am."

"They'll come after you. As soon as the stage reaches the next station the driver will telegraph word to Virginia City. There'll be a posse combing the mountains before nightfall."

"No, my good woman, that won't happen." He swung back into his saddle. "You see," he said somewhat sheepishly, "I paid the driver and conductor well to allow our little band to waylay their stage. I succeeded in convincing them it was a grand joke."

"A joke?" All at once she remembered Chai. "What will happen to Chai?" When she saw George's blank look, she said, "The Chinese girl who was with me. I was taking her to San Francisco."

"I'm afraid I didn't know about her. I heard you tell the colored man who works at your establishment that you intended to journey over the mountains. I didn't hear a reference to a Chinese woman."

"You are mad. Why did you do it? Tell me the real reason."

"If you must know, I'm rather fond of you, Miss Monique. After what you did for me, you and Miss Astrid, the least I could do was return the favor. I'll admit this is a somewhat melodramatic way to arrange to be alone with you, and we will be alone, because my hired assistants have left for Virginia City, but then I'm a romantic sort, as you'll discover when you know me better."

"I'll never know you any better than I do now. I don't want to know you any better."

She slapped the reins against her horse's neck, urging him ahead. As George called to her to stop, she galloped from the glade along the trail leading back to the stage road. Hearing the hooves of George's mount behind her, she bent low over her horse's neck, whispering to him to hurry.

She burst through a screen of branches onto an open avenue of needles beneath the majestic pine trees. Far ahead she glimpsed a figure running toward her. As she rode on she realized it was Chai.

"Chai," she called. "Chai," she said again as she reined in and slid to the ground. She ran across the slippery needles and took the Chinese girl in her arms.

"They come," Chai wailed. "They come."

"It's all right," Monique told her. "The men won't come back. You're all right now."

"No, no," Chai said, "they come." She pointed behind her. As Monique watched, two horsemen—not Guildford's hired band—rode from the trees, brandishing rifles.

"They come for me," Chai cried.   ❧

19

Beginning Again

MONIQUE looked behind her. Her horse had trotted away. They'd never be able to reach it in time, and there was no sign of George Guildford.

"Run, Chai, run," she shouted, taking the Chinese girl's hand.

They ran into the trees, the leather soles of their shoes sliding on the needles, and hampered by their long dresses. The pursuing hoofbeats pounded nearer. As the horsemen overtook them, Monique stopped and faced the two men, pushing Chai behind her.

The riders reined up on either side of them, their horses blowing, the animals' flanks glistening with sweat. One of the men was Alex Campbell, and Monique recognized the other as a man called Russ. The two men, seeing that Monique and Chai were alone and unarmed, thrust their rifles into their saddle scabbards.

Alex Campbell smiled at Monique. "We got us some unfinished business, you and me," he said.

She stared defiantly up at him.

"We're after the Chink," Russ said. "We got no quarrel with Miss Monique."

"Maybe you don't," Campbell told him. "That don't mean I don't. This bitch nearly killed me that time she 'most burned down the town."

Monique thought she glimpsed a hint of an approving smile on Russ' face. "I heard tell about that," he said.

"You two," Campbell told Monique and Chai. "Get your—" He suddenly looked to his right.

George Guildford, astride his horse, watched them from the shadows beneath the trees. The Englishman's hands were folded on top of his saddle horn.

Campbell and Russ drew their rifles. George raised his eyebrows but made no move to defend himself.

"I'll be Goddamned." Campbell snorted as he stared at the Confederate uniform. "If it ain't General Robert E. Lee hisself. What're you doing this far west, General?"

Monique shook her head warningly at George. This wasn't the Englishman's quarrel. Why had he come here instead of riding for help?

"George Guildford's the name," the Englishman said. "This is a colonel's uniform, not a general's. I borrowed it for the occasion. I have no real right to wear the Confederate gray, although I admit I admire the bravery of many of those who do."

"I'll be Goddamned," Campbell said again. "General, why don't you just ride off on your horse to someplace where it's safe to play soldier? We got men's work to do here. You're liable to get hurt."

"I intend to count to three," George said. "If I still see either of you two blighters at the end of that time, I'm afraid I won't be able to answer for the consequences."

Monique stared at him open-mouthed. He was

either terribly brave or terribly foolhardy. Perhaps
he was both brave and foolhardy. Whatever he was,
she liked him, and didn't want him hurt.

"Don't, George," she said. "Campbell's a killer. I
saw him shoot down a man in cold blood."

"One," George counted.

"You'd best listen to the lady," Campbell told the
Englishman. "You're going to get yourself killed."

"Two," was George's answer.

"I'll keep his lordship covered," Campbell told his
companion. "You get the women."

As Campbell raised his rifle, Monique gasped in
fear. Chai peeked from behind her.

"Three," George said. He was smiling.

He kicked himself free of his saddle and crouched
behind his horse. A shot rang out. Campbell's rifle
smoked. There was another shot, and another. Russ
spun from his horse and fell face first to the ground.
Campbell, low over his horse's neck, rifle in hand,
rode directly at George.

As George's horse whinnied and bolted, Campbell
fired. Monique couldn't see through the dust and
smoke. Another shot was fired. Campbell fell. He
scrambled along the ground, still holding his rifle,
toward the trunk of a pine. Where was George? Monique seized Chai's hand and, crouching, the two
women ran into the trees.

Still another shot was fired. She turned and saw
Alex Campbell stagger back. The big man dropped
his rifle and sat down, a startled look on his face.
Russ' horse danced sideways, dragging Russ, whose
foot was caught in a stirrup.

George Guildford, a pistol in each hand, stepped
cautiously from behind a pine. Campbell sat staring
up at him, his rifle a yard from his booted foot. When
George circled behind him, Campbell struggled to

rise. Monique drew in her breath, expecting him to lunge for the rifle. George grasped Campbell's shoulder and yanked him to the ground. The big man fell onto his back, staring up at George as the Englishman holstered one pistol and picked up the rifle, holding it in the crook of his arm.

Monique let out her breath.

"Stay here," she told Chai. She ran across the pine needles to George's side. "Are you all right?" she asked.

"A trifle fatigued," he said. "I haven't done this much riding or this much shooting in anger since the Crimea, and that was some years ago. I'd be obliged to you, Miss Monique, if you'd take a look at the gentleman hanging by his foot from his stirrup. I'm sorry, it's not woman's work, I know, but then, this chap here still has a nasty glint in his eye."

Monique nodded. Seeing Chai peering from behind the trunk of a nearby pine, she waved the Chinese girl back. Russ' horse had stopped among the trees, and Russ lay on his back, one leg raised to the stirrup. He didn't move as she approached.

"Steady, steady," Monique murmured to the horse.

The gelding shied away at first, finally letting her come close enough to stroke his neck. Glancing down, she saw Russ' eyes staring skyward with the blank look of death. She tugged his boot out of the stirrup, and Russ' leg dropped to the ground.

After tethering the horse, she returned to George Guildford. Chai was standing a few feet behind the Englishman, watching him intently as he examined Campbell's wound. Monique knelt on the pine needles at George's side.

"So, you know this gentleman?" George asked.

"His name's Alex Campbell."

Campbell moaned. His eyes were closed. His sandy

hair and beard were matted with dirt. He clasped his left side and, between his fingers, Monique saw the dark red of blood.

"Last year," Monique said, "the night my friend Philippe was killed, Campbell took me to Chinatown and tried to assault me. I threw a lamp at him, started a fire, and managed to get away." She paused. "Is he dying?" she asked.

"Not bloody likely. It's a flesh wound from what I can see."

Campbell opened his eyes. "Hurts," he moaned. "Hurts like hell." His face was white. Despite the cool of the early evening, sweat stood in droplets on his cheeks and forehead. All at once he grimaced as though he'd been seized by a spasm of pain.

"Who sent you after the Chinese girl?" George asked him.

Campbell shook his head.

"He works for Van Allen Reid," Monique said. "Van must have sent the two of them to bring Chai back to Virginia. Van probably owed Chai's master a favor."

"She's his," Campbell said. "Han Ku owns her. Damn it, man," he said to George, "do something to stop the bleeding."

"I'll tear up an old shirt for bandages," George said. "Do you know how to use one of these?" He offered Monique a pistol.

"Yes. Philippe showed me."

George handed her the gun, then pushed himself to his feet and walked to his waiting horse. Monique looked from the gun in her hand to the fallen Campbell. Using her thumb, she drew back the hammer. Moving out of his reach, she aimed the pistol at Campbell's left eye.

"Good God, woman, what are you doing?" Campbell cowered away.

She smiled. "You're right," she said. "Not there." She lowered the pistol until it was aimed at his sex. I promised myself I'd kill him, she thought, and, by God, I will.

"I never harmed you." He spoke rapidly and she could hear the fear in his voice.

"You would have." She held the pistol in both hands. Her finger tightened on the trigger.

"The Frenchman," Campbell said desperately. "Your friend—I know who killed him."

She stared at him. His eyes blinked, his mouth opened and closed, but no words came.

"Who?" she demanded. She drew in her breath as a suspicion burgeoned in her mind. "You killed Philippe, didn't you? Those men you were with at the saloon lied to protect you."

"No, that's not the way of it at all. Swear you won't use that gun and I'll tell you."

Monique grimaced with distaste at his cowardice, hesitated, and then said, "All right, I won't. Tell me."

"It was Russ," he said.

"Russ?"

"Him." Campbell jerked his head in the direction of his dead companion.

"He's dead. You're telling me Russ was the one because he's dead."

"I swear to God it was Russ."

"Why then? Why did he kill Philippe?"

"Reid paid him to. I don't know the reason. Something your friend found out. Reid paid Russ a hundred dollars in gold to kill the Frenchy."

"Reid? Van?" Monique shook her head in disbelief. She had always suspected that Van was no better than he might be, but he wouldn't order a man killed in cold blood. Not Van. Not the man she had willingly slept with, the man whose body had joined hers in passion.

"I know you're sweet on him," Campbell said. "That don't change the truth none."

A twig snapped behind her. Monique whirled around to find George standing a few feet away.

"He claims Van Allen Reid had Philippe killed," she said. "That Russ over there was the one who stabbed him."

"Take the damn pistol away from her," Campbell said. "She was going to kill me. Or worse."

George shrugged. "She undoubtedly has her reasons," he said. "You can use these for bandages." He handed strips of cloth to Monique.

"No. I won't touch him." She eased the hammer down as she walked away to a rise, where she stood staring through the trees at the red-tinged clouds in the west.

"I bandage," she heard Chai say.

After a few minutes, Monique realized someone was at her side. She looked up into George's brown eyes.

"You know this Reid?" he asked.

"Yes," she said. "He's a—I thought he was a friend of mine. I can't believe he had Philippe killed, and paid Russ or Campbell a hundred dollars to do it. I just can't believe it."

"This man Campbell's probably lying."

Monique leaned her head against the trunk of a tree. She drew in a deep breath, smelling the aroma of the pines. "No," she sighed, "I'm afraid not. He's telling the truth, more than likely, except about Russ. I think Van sent Alex Campbell to kill Philippe, and he did. He's lying now because Russ is dead."

"That would make sense," George said. "Now, if you'll keep an eye on Mr. Campbell, I'll round up our horses so we can take these two blighters and Miss Chai to the nearest settlement. All right?"

Monique nodded. As she waited, pistol in hand, for George to return, her first stunned reaction to what had happened slowly turned to anger. Anger at Van Allen Reid for having Philippe killed. Anger at Jeremy.

Philippe and I wouldn't have come to Virginia City, she reasoned, if it hadn't been for Jeremy. If Jeremy hadn't abandoned us in San Francisco, everything would have been different. Philippe would be alive today and I'd be with Jeremy.

It wasn't all Jeremy's fault. It was that woman's as well. Laura's. Laura McAllister—she refused to even think of her as Laura Johnston—and her holier-than-thou Presbyterians. Don't be a fool, she told herself, that's not the way it was. If it was anyone's fault, it was my own for believing Jeremy.

I thought I loved him, she defended herself.

That was a long time ago, she answered. Love's a young girl's fancy, nothing more. The sooner I forget Jeremy and make a new beginning, the better off I'll be. Yes, a new beginning, and not with Jeremy. Alone? Or with someone else? If with someone else, who?

Hearing the creak of leather, she looked up to see George returning with the horses. They set off in the twilight with George in the lead, Alex Campbell next, hands bound behind him, Monique and Chai on the third horse and, at the rear, a horse with Russ' body lashed over the saddle.

Monique urged her mare ahead until she and Chai rode beside George.

"I don't know what would have happened if you hadn't come to help us," she told him. "Chai and I both thank you from the bottom of our hearts."

"I had no choice but to help," George said. "After all, my ambuscade was partly responsible, though I expect those two gentlemen intended to stop the stage at some point themselves."

"Chai told me she left the coach to come looking

for me. They must have been riding behind the stage, saw her, and followed her into the woods."

George nodded. "Don't forget," he said, "I owed you a great favor, you and Miss Astrid, because you didn't tell the miners the truth about what happened at the parlor house."

"Whatever your reason, you were magnificent when you stood up to Alex Campbell and Russ. I was afraid for you. I was afraid they'd kill you."

"Did you care whether they did or not?"

She looked steadily at him. "Yes," she said, "I cared. I cared very much."

His face reddened and he dropped his gaze. Monique had spoken spontaneously, but she now realized how true her words were. She did care for George, much as she had cared for Philippe. She suspected, though, that George's feelings toward her were very different from Philippe's.

They rode for a time in silence as the forest darkened around them. Looking up through the branches of the pines, Monique saw the evening's first star.

"When I was a boy in England," George said, "we always wished on the first star. I've made my wish. Have you made yours?"

Remembering her thoughts earlier in the day, Monique nodded. A new beginning, she told herself, was her wish. A new beginning for her business in Virginia City and, more important, a new beginning for her life. Without Van Allen Reid. Without Jeremy.

"I've made my wish," she told George. "What was yours?"

"Ah, I can't say. If you tell your wish to another it has no chance of ever coming true. Even without telling it, I fear the chances are slight that my wish will ever be granted."

His wish, she suspected, involved her. Again they

rode in silence until, to break the growing unease of unspoken thoughts, she asked, "You fought in the Crimean War?"

"I had that honor, though the campaign was a miserable one. We fought in the wrong place at the wrong time under the leadership of incompetents. Well-meaning incompetents, but incompetents nonetheless. Yet it was in the Crimea that I perfected my strategems."

"Your strategems?"

"If I were to have a motto, I believe it would read, 'Persistence and surprise, these two.' You'll find, Miss Monique, that I can be quite persistent. And those two blighters"—he turned his head to indicate Campbell and Russ—"discovered that I'm capable of springing a surprise."

"I'll admit *I* was surprised. When I saw you in that Confederate uniform, I didn't know what to think."

"Admit the truth. You probably put me down for a fool, just as Mr. Campbell and his friend did. They couldn't believe that someone masquerading as a military man might actually possess some of the attributes of one. Of course they were wrong. If I had been rash enough to meet them otherwise, face to face, the result might well have been different."

"Do you know, somehow I don't think so."

"Brave man," Chai said. "Kill dragons."

"Miss Chai," George said, "if ever again you need a champion to slay dragons for you, I insist you call on me."

Chai covered her face with her hand and giggled.

Monique slowed their horse to let George ride on ahead. When she and Chai were again in their place in line, she let the mare resume her normal pace.

"You like?" Chai asked her.

"George Guildford? Yes, I like him." Monique noted that her tone in speaking to Chai was sharper than she'd intended.

"Ahhh," Chai said. Monique looked over her shoulder, but the Chinese girl's face revealed nothing.

An hour after sunset they arrived at Demming's, a small way-station on the coach road across the Sierras. George made arrangements to have Russ' body returned to Virginia City, while Chai changed Alex Campbell's bloodied bandages. After George talked to the gunman, he joined the two women at the supper table.

"Campbell's agreed to seek out a doctor in Placerville," he told them. "I suspect he won't be returning to Virginia City for some time, if at all."

"How did you manage that?" Monique asked. "Did you threaten him?"

"I used a much cruder method. I offered him more money than he gets from Reid."

Was George Guildford a wealthy man? she wondered. He had paid men to help him hold up the stage, and paid the driver and conductor for their cooperation. Now he was paying Campbell to stay clear of Virginia City. She looked speculatively at the Englishman, but said nothing.

In the morning, he met them on the porch of the inn. The Confederate uniform had been replaced by black trousers and a frock coat of the same color.

"I'd like you to come with me," he said to Monique. "I had intended it as a surprise, but now I see I'll have to tell you what I had in mind. I meant to give you the gift of a week's time in the most beautiful spot in the world. A week away from Virginia City, away from the hurly-burly of business, of men, of roistering miners. A week of peace."

Monique smiled up at him. "You tempt me," she said.

"I'll be the perfect host," George said, "no more, no less. I promise you that."

"No strategems? No surprises?"

"None. Persistence, perhaps, but nothing more. And Chai, of course, is free to go wherever she pleases. I'll have her escorted to San Francisco if that's what she wants."

Chai looked from George Guildford to Monique. She lowered her eyes. "I go you," she said.

Monique glanced at the Chinese girl. "You?" she repeated sharply. "Who do you mean by you?"

"You, Miss Monique," Chai said softly.

Monique turned quickly away so neither of them would see the color rising to her face. My God, she thought, I'm jealous of Chai. When she looked at George again he was watching her, his face expressionless.

"We'll both go with you," Monique told him, "if that's all right with you."

"Of course." She was pleased when she detected disappointment in his voice. "I would have been happy if you had come alone. Now I'm doubly happy to have both of you come." He nodded to the inn. "Chai," he said, "bring Miss Monique's bag."

Chai bowed and hurried inside. As soon as they were alone, George raised Monique's hand to his lips. "It's you I want to be with," he said. "No-one else."

"I don't frighten you?"

Am I too bold? she wondered. Chai certainly wasn't In fact, Chai must be one of the least threatening women George had ever known.

"Ah, I've caught you out," George said. "I can tell who you were thinking of when you said that."

"You can?" Am I so obvious? she wondered.

"Of course. Miss Astrid. You suspect she intimidated me at the parlor house and you suspect you might as well. I'll admit Miss Astrid's a heroic figure of a woman. I wouldn't be surprised to learn that she has a Viking warrior queen among her ancestors. But no, Miss Monique, you don't frighten me. At times, I'll admit, you do startle me. I'm unused to women who aren't afraid to enter the business arena with men, or women who consider themselves equal to men."

"I'm as good as anyone," she said, "man or woman."

"And that, I suspect, is what piqued my interest from the first. I wondered if your unique ways were all they seemed. Mightn't they be the same as my Confederate uniform? A strategem of some sort?"

"What do you suspect I really am without my uniform?"

"A young and beautiful woman, certainly. A desirable woman who doesn't know what she wants from life. Perhaps a woman who's convinced herself she dislikes men, when in reality . . ." He left the thought unfinished.

"That's not true. It's the most ridiculous thing I've ever heard. I don't need anyone. I've gotten along all right so far without a man, and I'll keep on getting along without one."

" 'The lady doth protest too much, methinks.' "

She was about to reply when Chai returned. George led two horses from the corral, and they rode along a trail through the pines. A half-hour later they came out of the forest, and the lake burst upon them.

Monique gasped. The lake was a dark blue oval with pine forests rising from its shores to the foot of snow-covered peaks. White clouds drifted above the mountain.

"It's beautiful," she said.

"This is Lake Tahoe," he told her, "the most beautiful place in the world."

They rode along the eastern shore, the early September air clear and cool. Once they heard a shout in the distance followed by the faint chopping sound of an axe, but they saw no one. Jays scolded them from nearby trees, squirrels leaped from limb to limb, and once they spied a deer, his head cocked, watching them from the crest of a hill.

Monique saw a column of smoke drifting skyward ahead of them. They left the trees and came to a log cabin built on the shore of the lake. A skiff lay beached on the sand less than ten feet away. As they approached the cabin they saw a tethered horse. A bearded man with long matted hair appeared in the doorway.

"Captain," he said to George, raising his hand to his hat, "I been expecting you since last night."

"We were delayed and had to stay at Demming's. Is everything tip-top?"

The man nodded as he held the horse for Monique to dismount. A short time later she saw him saddle his own horse and ride off.

Chai busied herself with the pots and pans, shaking her head when Monique offered to help. Restless, Monique walked to the lake's shore, where she stood on the sandy beach looking out over the water. She breathed in the odors of the pines and the woodsmoke. George came from the cabin and stood behind her.

"I have one other present for you," he said.

"Nothing could be better than this." She spread her arms to take in the lake, the trees, and the mountains.

"I knew you'd like it. Perhaps you'll like this as well."

She turned, and saw he had placed an Indian basket on the ground at her feet. Lifting the reed lid, she looked inside. A gray cat, hardly more than a kitten, blinked up at her.

"Oh!" she gasped in delight as she lifted the cat into her arms and held her against her cheek.

"How did you know?" she asked. "How did you know what would please me more than anything else?"

"I guessed, nothing more. If I'd been wrong, there was no harm done."

As she hugged the cat to her, she remembered Rowena, and remembered Philippe's betrayal when he sold the cat to pay his gambling debts. Again she pictured Philippe with his head on the table, his face pale in death. Tears came to her eyes. She tried to smile but she cried instead. She cried because the gift of the cat had made her so happy, because Philippe could never be with her again, because . . .

She shook her head, laughing and crying.

"My dear," George said. "My dear, have I done something I shouldn't have?"

"No, no." She placed the cat on the ground and threw her arms around him, sobbing against his chest. "I'm crying because I'm so happy," she said.

When she looked up, he kissed her. She returned his kiss, her hand going to the nape of his neck to hold him to her.

20

The Storm

ALTHOUGH the night was cold, they slept wrapped in blankets on the shore of the lake, Monique nearest to the dying campfire, George Guildford a few feet from her. Chai slept on a cot in the cabin.

When Monique awoke, she heard the morning calls of birds from the forest, and smelled the tang of woodsmoke and the delicious aroma of bacon cooking. George knelt by the fire holding a black frying pan. Monique threw her blankets aside and stretched, at peace with the world.

After a breakfast of hot bread, bacon, and coffee, George launched the skiff and rowed her out onto the lake as the sun rose above the pine forest to the east.

"The air's so fresh," she said, "so clear. I never realized before just how dirty and dusty Virginia City is."

"Perhaps the air's better here because we're closer to heaven than we were in Virginia City. We're sure-

ly closer to heaven than they are in San Francisco.
A man who works for me told me that he came to
Lake Tahoe two years ago expecting to die, and today he's in robust health. He suffered from consump-
tion."

Monique frowned. "My mother died of consump-
tion. I don't even like to speak of it." After a moment
she asked, "This man worked for you?"

"As a surveyor," George said. "I'm what's known
as a hydraulic engineer. That's engineering having
to do with water. I studied the subject in France,
and now I work wherever I'm needed. I've been in
the Nevada Territory for the last month, and I expect I have at least another month's work here before I'm finished."

He took a fishing pole from the bottom of the boat,
baited the hook, and cast the line into the lake. Monique watched the worm drift down into the crystal-
clear water toward a bottom of gray boulders and
sand. A school of speckled fish darted from between
the rocks.

"Look," she said, "there must be twenty or more."

"Trout. Lake trout."

"So many fish and yet you aren't getting a bite."

"That's either because I'm a poor fisherman, or else
the water's so clear they see the line and the boat
and take warning. I prefer to think it's the latter."

"If you're a hydraulic engineer," she said, "you
must work for Adolph Sutro."

"The man who dreams of a tunnel to drain the
mines? No, I'm not here to get water out of the
mines. Almost the opposite, in fact. I'm trying to get
water *to* the mines. I've been asked to decide whether
it's possible to pipe drinking water from the Sierras
to Virginia City."

"That's such a long way."

"The pipe would go from the lakes and springs here

in the mountains down into the Carson Valley, and then up into the eastern mountains to Virginia City. The more I look into the project, the more I'm convinced it can be done."

"A hydraulic engineer." Monique looked at him with new-found respect.

"Ah," he said. "A bite."

The line tightened and dipped into the water. George let the fish run, the reel whining as it spun. When the line slackened, he reeled in slowly.

"Damn." He pulled the line from the water. A small fragment of worm remained on the hook, but the rest of the bait and the fish were gone.

They drifted and fished, laughing together when Monique landed the first trout. Later in the morning, George beached the boat and they took a walk in the pine forest. There was none of the tension between them, Monique noted, that she had known with Jeremy and Van Allen Reid. Instead she felt a quietness, an acceptance. They could walk in silence, and yet not feel uncomfortable. They could talk and not quarrel.

She saw George watching her when he thought she was unaware, but they had not touched, except casually, since the night of their arrival at the cabin. At times she wanted him to take her hand as they walked, while at other times she wanted to go on just as they were, at peace, demanding nothing of one another, and having to give nothing in return.

"I wish we could stay here forever," Monique told him later in the week.

They looked from their drifting boat at the morning mist rising slowly from the lake. The rays of the sun slanted through the trees; far overhead, the snow-covered peaks gleamed white and cold.

"You'd soon grow bored with all this splendor," he said. "Even Eve wearied of Eden after a time."

"I probably would tire of it," she said, "though I don't like to think so. I'm too restless, I suppose. I always seem to want what I can't have. I know I do, yet I don't like to think of myself as being that way. Am I making any sense at all?"

"You always make sense to me. How do you like to think of yourself, Monique?"

She raised her eyebrows. "Do you know," she said, "that's the first time you haven't called me Miss Monique?"

"I know," he said softly.

"I like to think of myself as a lady." She closed her eyes. "A lady dressed in satins and sables who lives in a great house like those I saw on the hills in San Francisco. A lady who's witty and charming, yet who's admired for her kindness more than for her social graces. I'd like to be known as someone who never hurts another person." She opened her eyes and smiled. "When I was young, I used to picture myself riding through the streets in a carriage drawn by four white horses. I'd imagine little girls seeing me and saying to themselves, "When I grow up, I wish I could be like Mary Vere.'"

He smiled at her.

"You think I'm childish," she said.

"No, I think you're charming."

"*And* childish?" she insisted.

"How could a man who often pictures himself as a dashing Confederate cavalry officer accuse anyone of being childish. We all have a bit of the child left in us. I often think it's the best part of us, since I like to believe children are born with wisps of heaven still clinging to them."

"I suppose I should be satisfied with what I am."

"Never be satisfied. Try to be better than you are."

"Do you always try to be better? To do better?"

"Not nearly often enough." He trailed his hand in

the water beside the boat. "As you can see, I'm much too indolent. It's a disease afflicting my class. I have bursts of activity when I imagine I'm about to conquer the world, but then I tell myself it's not worth the candle, not worth the price, and I shut myself away for a time with my books and my violin."

"Are you really a lord? The miners at the parlor house called you Sir George, but I thought they were mocking you. They were, weren't they?"

"They were mocking me, yes."

"But are you a lord?"

"I'm an earl," he said. "I suppose you could think of me as a middling-lord."

"Middling?"

"A duke and a marquess both rank higher. A viscount and a baron are lower on the scale."

"I've never known a 'sir' before."

"Are you disappointed? I would be if I were meeting myself for the first time. We're such a stuffy lot; too inbred and much too haughty. My father wasn't. He's dead, you know, but my mother . . ." He paused. "I tried to break out of that mold, but I found I couldn't be what I'm not. The whole British peerage needs a breath of fresh air. I suspect that's why so many of them are marrying American women these days. It's a subconscious attempt to re-invigorate the breed."

They drifted for a while in silence. The mist lifted from the lake, a wind came up, and small whitecaps flecked the surface of the water. In the distance, smoke angled from among the trees on the far side of the lake.

For a moment Monique imagined being married to George Guildford. Sir George Guildford, she reminded herself. She pictured stately mansions, ancestral halls hung with somber portraits, and gardeners spading the earth to plant tulips and rosebushes.

She shook her head. Though she could see the great houses, the lawns, the sweeping drives, she couldn't imagine herself taking part in the life they represented.

No, she didn't intend to marry George, or anyone else. Not that she thought Sir George would ask her; she knew he wouldn't. Even if he did, she'd say no. She had her own life to lead—she'd never become a mere appendage of a man.

". . . quiet you hardly know she's around."

"What?" Monique asked. "I'm sorry, I wasn't listening. I was dreaming, I suppose."

"I said Miss Chai's so quiet you don't know she's around. Yet she works hard. She seems to have the knack of anticipating what I want before I know myself."

"She follows you around like a puppy," Monique said. "I have my new cat and you have Chai."

"Are you jealous?"

"Yes." She smiled. "No, not really. I think I was at first, but I'm not any more. I love Chai. How could I ever be really jealous of her?"

"I was thinking of buying her."

"Buying her? You can't buy another person here in Nevada. She's not a slave."

"I meant I intended to pay the man who brought her to Virginia City so she'd be free of him once and for all. Then she could work as my servant or go on to San Francisco. She could do whatever she wants to do. Would you mind if she worked for me?"

"Mind? It's not up to me to mind or not mind. You can do whatever you like." She reached out to put her hand on his sleeve. "I'd be happy for her if you freed her, George," she said.

He raised her hand to his lips. Looking into her eyes, he said, "You're the one I care for, Monique.

And I do care, very much. The more I see of you and the better I get to know you, the more I care."

She withdrew her hand.

"Do I make you uncomfortable?" he asked.

"You make me feel shy, like a young girl. You make me wish I was a young girl again and that I'd just met you. I almost wish I could undo what's happened these last two years."

"Balderdash! It's not a young girl I've grown fond of. It's you, Monique, the way you are now."

She turned and looked once more at the smoke rising above the pines on the far shore of the lake. "Hunters?" she asked.

"A sawmill," he said. "They're cutting timbers to use in the mines."

"Do you realize," she said, "that in all the time we've been here at the lake we haven't seen another person? Not one?"

"Are you lonely?"

"No. At first I thought I would be, but I'm not. We have one more day?"

"Only one. Sutcliffe, he's my caretaker, will be back tomorrow, and the three of us will leave the following morning." He looked at the sky above the western peaks. "It's clouding over," he said. "More than likely we'll have rain for our last day."

On the following morning, the clouds in the east were streaked with red and orange, and whitecaps flecked the surface of the lake, but no rain fell.

Shortly after midday, Monique found George standing on the shore frowning up at the sky.

"Can we take the boat out?" she asked. "For one last time?"

"Well . . ."

"Please, George. We don't have to row far from shore. Besides, I don't think it wil lstorm. After all, this isn't the ocean, it's a lake. I'm not afraid of getting a little wet."

"I can't say no to you." He pushed the skiff into the water and helped her climb aboard. Taking the oars, he rowed along the shore.

"Let me row," she said after a few minutes.

They changed places and Monique rowed with short, quick strokes. She breathed deeply. The air was fresh and cold. The wind slapped water against the sides of the boat.

"I've never felt so alive," Monique said. Looking up, she saw him watching her. As she drew the oars through the water, wisps of hair blew into her face, and her breasts strained against the pale blue fabric of her bodice.

"Stay closer to shore," he told her.

"Are you afraid?" she teased.

She had a wild impulse to defy George Guildford by rowing far out onto the lake, daring the coming storm to do its worst. The week had been so serene, so peaceful. Perhaps it had been too serene, for now a perverse demon seized her, urging her on, making her want to goad George.

"I prefer to think of myself as prudent rather than fearful," he said.

Thunder rumbled in the mountains and, looking up, she saw dark arcs of clouds massing over the peaks. The breeze freshened and sent water spraying over the bow to wet the back of her hair.

"Let me take the oars," he said. "The storm's coming down on us faster than I thought."

"No, I can manage." She held one oar deep in the water as she pulled on the other. "See, I'm bringing us around. We'll run for shore in front of the storm."

George started toward her but she shook her head, clenching the oars with whitened fingers. As the boat came about she looked over his head at the dark sweep of clouds. She could no longer see the far shore through the veil of the approaching rain.

With a shrug, George settled back on the seat. "Pull hard," he told her.

"Which way's the cabin?"

"It's too far. Make straight for shore."

Lightning streaked from the black clouds over the western side of the lake and, a few seconds later, thunder boomed. The first drops of rain struck her face as the boat rose and fell on the mounting waves. Exultant, yet feeling a tingle of apprehension, she rowed as fast as she could. From time to time she glanced at George, expecting him to ask to row, knowing she would let him. But he sat gripping the gunwales, watching her with a steady gaze, and making no move to take the oars.

Her arms and shoulders ached. Was he matching his will against hers? How long did he mean to wait? The boat pitched and tossed. Did he mean to kill them both?

"All right," she gasped, defeated. "You row."

He eased his way past her and grasped the oars. Propelled by his long deep strokes and by the following wind, the boat leaped forward. Rain drove down on them. She could no longer see the near shore. The waves rose, sending water over the stern.

"Bail!" George shouted. She could barely see him in the blur of the rain.

Feeling along the flooded bottom of the boat, she found a bait can and used it to scoop water over the side. Still the cold water rose over the tops of her shoes and up her legs.

Lightning flashed, the jagged bolt followed at once by a deafening clap of thunder. She bailed desperately, her hair loose and plastered to her face, her dress soaked, water squishing in her shoes. The small skiff rose on a wave, tilted crazily on one side, and she held tightly to the seat with one hand to keep from being thrown into the roiling waters of the lake.

George grasped her arm. As she looked up at him, she realized the skiff had foundered.

"We've run aground," he shouted above the howl of the wind.

Holding her hand, he led her over the boat's tilted bow onto dark, slippery rocks. "We'll have to jump," he told her.

Hand in hand, they leaped from the rocks into the water. Her feet touched bottom and they splashed through water up to her knees to the shore. At the top of the beach, Monique stopped and looked back.

"The boat," she shouted.

"Damn the boat."

He pulled her after him under a canopy of trees. The rain slackened so she was able to see the dark trunks of pines on both sides of her. They found shelter beneath a fallen tree.

"I'll get wood for a fire," he told her.

When he walked away, she started after him.

"Stay where you are," he said over his shoulder.

"I'll help. I want to help."

He turned and put his hands on her arms. Suddenly his arms closed around her and he kissed her. When she felt the beating of his heart against her breast, excitement stirred in her.

He picked her up and, still kissing her, carried her to the shelter of the pine where he laid her on the soft needles. Thunder boomed, fainter now. The storm was passing as quickly as it had come.

After kissing her once more, he drew away. "I'll make a fire," he said. "You must be soaked to the skin."

"Damn the fire."

He smiled and took her in his arms. Gently, tenderly, he caressed her, touching her cheeks and eyes as though in wonder. He undressed her slowly and awkwardly, her clothes clinging wetly, and gazed at her bared body almost reverently, closing his eyes as his lips sought and found her breasts while his hands molded her wet body to his.

When he entered her, she moaned and, as he continued to caress her while he kissed her eyelids, her neck, and her mouth, desire rose in her and she arched to meet him. At that moment she thought, without warning, unwillingly, of Jeremy, wishing he was here beside her and that his arms held her, not George's.

When they lay side by side, hearing the thunder rumble over the distant mountains to the south, hearing water drip from the trees in the forest around them, she smiled ruefully, remembering the day she had warned Jeremy that he would hold Laura and think of her . . .

George Guildford accompanied Monique and Chai to San Francisco. As a result, Monique found doors opening for her, doors she never knew existed. When she returned to Virginia City three weeks later, she opened the Manigault Emporium on B Street, a store specializing in "fine clothing for men and women."

George rented a large house on the southern outskirts of the city. Monique and Chai—the Chinese girl had been redeemed from the merchant Han Ku for three hundred dollars in gold—moved in with him, Monique as his hostess, Chai as her maid.

The house, Monique discovered, was only a block from the new Johnston mansion. Jeremy, his mining knowledge backed by McAllister money, had prospered. She wondered if his new wealth had brought him happiness, one moment hoping it had, the next moment wishing the opposite.

Several weeks after her return to Virginia City,

Monique put on her new, pale-yellow taffeta gown to visit the parlor house and go over the books with Astrid. Business had increased in Monique's absence. Two new girls, Bertha and Rosie, had been hired on Monique's return, and now she intended to let Astrid run the house on her own.

As she walked along the dirt sidewalk toward the center of the city, she saw Laura Johnston approaching. Monique hesitated, then walked on, head high. She hadn't seen or heard from Laura since the evening the churchwomen had paraded to the parlor house carrying candles. The other woman's campaign against Monique seemed to be in abeyance.

Monique smiled as Laura drew nearer. Kneeling together in the street to pray, Monique told herself, had forged a bond between them. They were, after all, both women. They could never be friends, but they could at least be friendly enemies. Friendly enemies was what they were, Monique decided.

Laura looked tired, as though she hadn't slept, and Monique wondered what was troubling the other woman. Her heart leapt. Perhaps Laura and Jeremy's marriage wasn't as serene as it seemed. She stifled the thought. No, there was more than that. With a pang of sympathy she realized that Laura must be ill.

Laura looked up, saw Monique, and stopped. What should I call her? Monique wondered. Laura? After all, we have been introduced. No, she decided, I'll be formal.

"Mrs. Johnston," she said. "Did you know we were neighbors?"

Laura closed her eyes and Monique thought the other woman shuddered. Opening her eyes, Laura stared past her. Then, with a flip of her skirt, she left the sidewalk, crossed the street, and continued walking toward her house on the other side.

Color flooded Monique's face. Fuming, she stalked on in the direction of the city. As she walked, her fury gradually lessened as a plan took shape in her mind. She'd teach that woman a lesson she'd never forget, she told herself, and at the same time banish Jeremy from her life once and for all.

By the time she climbed the steps to the parlor house, she was smiling.

21

The Trap

"WE'LL need to lay a fire soon." George stood with his hands clasped behind his back, looking into the empty grate.

"I expect we will," Monique said.

He crossed the room and stared up at the row of books on the shelf above the knick-knacks on the top shelf of the étagère. He clicked his fingernail over the leather spines.

"Have you decided what to name your cat?" he asked.

"I'm going to call her Guinevere, after King Arthur's queen."

"She was unfaithful, wasn't she?"

"Yes, just as cats are unfaithful. They'll only stay as long as you feed them, give them a place to sleep, and treat them well."

He glanced at her, and seemed about to speak, but instead walked to the window where he peered out into the dark night. Monique saw his somber face reflected in the pane. She sighed, then leaned over and scratched the carpet with her fingers. The cat stalked across the room and leaped into her lap.

"Guinevere," she said softly. "Do you like your name?"

George turned from the window. "Are you talking to me?" he asked.

"No, to the cat. You're so ill-at-ease tonight, George. So jumpy."

He smoothed his hair back with his hand. Leaving the window, he came to sit on the edge of an over-stuffed chair. When she finally looked up from the cat she realized he had been staring at her for some time.

"I'm worried about you," he said. "I'm worried about you and this Van Allen Reid business. I think I have good reason to worry. You know how deeply I care for you, Monique, how much I love you. I don't want anything to happen to you."

"I'm not afraid of Van, and there's no reason for you to be worried. I'm completely capable of taking care of myself."

"Do you realize, my dear, that you've never said that to me?" George said.

The cat purred as Monique stroked her. "Said what? The way you leap from one thing to another, I can't follow you."

"That you love me. You've never said you love me in so many words."

"You know how much I care for you, George. Sometimes words aren't needed." She placed the cat on the floor and went to sit on the arm of his chair. George took her hand and raised it to his lips.

"Perhaps I should pay Campbell to come here from San Francisco," he said, "to tell what he knows about

Reid. Perhaps he'd make the people of Virginia City understand Reid's ruthlessness, and force them to do something about it."

She shook her head. "I don't think Campbell would come back for any amount of money. Even if he did, it would only be his word against Van's."

"Please stop going around town making accusations about Van Allen Reid," he said. "You've had your say and nothing's come of it. Now let it be, for my sake if not for yours. I don't want any harm to come to you."

"Oh, George." She leaned over and kissed him on the forehead. "It's so wonderful to have someone who cares." She stood up abruptly and paced to the hearth and back. "They're cowards, all of them. Joe Goodman and Lester Harrington on the *Enterprise*, the miners, all of the men here. They're afraid of Van. They not only refuse to print the truth in the paper, they won't even listen to it any more."

"Men won't listen to what they don't want to hear. The opposite's also true; they believe what they want to believe. Women are the same. Are you sure you didn't accept Campbell's word because you wanted Van to be guilty?"

"That's ridiculous. Why would I want a man that I—" She paused. "—a man I was acquainted with to be the one who killed my best friend?"

"We seem to have changed roles," George said. "A few minutes ago you were accusing *me* of being ill-at-ease."

"Men are such cowards! Oh, they're brave enough if they have a knife or a gun. They're courageous when they're ordering women about, treating them as though they were their property, making virtual slaves of them, like men made a slave of Chai. Men! Fair-weather heroes, all of them."

"Monique," he said soothingly. Rising, he walked

up behind her, put his hands on her waist and drew her back against him, burying his face in her hair.

There was a sharp rapping on the front door.

Monique stiffened. George is right, she told herself. I am on edge tonight.

"It's probably the telegram I've been expecting," he said. "It's about the contract for the pipes for the aqueduct."

"At this hour? It's almost ten o'clock."

"There's a time-tested method of finding out." George released her, walked to the door, and opened it.

A boy stood on the porch. "Sir George Guildford?" he asked. When George nodded, the boy handed him an envelope. After giving the boy a coin, George tore open the envelope as he walked back into the room.

"You see," he told Monique, "it is a telegram."

"When men are right, they boast of it. What do they say when they're wrong? Nothing at all."

"Not only men, all humankind does that." He unfolded the single sheet of paper and held the message under the lamp.

"They'll be able to make your pipe in San Francisco?" she asked.

He didn't reply. As he stared down at the telegram, his hand began to shake. He folded the paper, folded it again, returned it to the envelope, and put the envelope on the desk. His face, she saw, had paled.

"What is it?" She went to his side and put her hand on his arm.

George drew in a long breath and let it out slowly. "It's my mother," he said. She was a widow, he had told her, living in England. "She passed away three weeks ago."

"Oh, George." She put her arms around him and held him close.

"She was a strong-willed woman," he said, "much

as you are. We had some frightful rows, my mother and I. My father never stood up to her, but I did at first, until I learned it was easier to just, well, go away. To the Crimea. To the States." He paused. "This means I'll have to go home, you know."

So soon! Monique had accepted the fact that George would eventually leave Virginia City but, since the time for his going was in the indefinite future, she'd banished all thoughts of it from her mind.

"I loved her. I loved my mother. And she loved me, in her own way. Too much, I thought at times. She tried to hold me too close. Do you know what I thought of when I read that telegram? I remembered a day when I was a small boy. It was in the spring, and my mother and I walked past the pond and up the hill beyond, across the dirt road bordering the estate, through a woods to a stone bridge. We followed a creek into another woods, and there we looked for the first May flowers. That was thirty or more years ago, yet that's what I remembered. I suppose it's because we were so happy together then."

For a time they stood silently with their arms about one another.

"Is there anything I can do?" she asked finally. "Anything I can get you?"

"Monique," he said softly, "there is one thing you can do." She felt his breath on her hair. "You can sail to England with me."

She shook her head almost at once. "No, no," she whispered. "I couldn't do that."

"Don't say no before you've heard me out. I mean as my wife, Monique. We'll be married in San Francisco, and by the time we reach Sussex we'll be looked on as an old married couple."

He wants to marry me! She felt a warm rush of happiness at the thought. He wants me to be his wife. He wants me to go to England with him as his wife. She drew away from him.

"No," she said, "I couldn't. It wouldn't be fair to you."

"I meant to ask you before I had to leave Virginia City," he said, ignoring her words. "This only hastened my speaking out. I love you, Monique, and I want you to be my wife."

"They'd never accept me in England. I'd be a burden to you."

"Let me be the judge of that. Don't you think I know what's best for me? I want you to be with me always, Monique. I can't bear the thought of leaving here without you. It's more than wanting you. I need you. You're real. I've always considered myself as something of a sham, a mountebank. You're not that. Don't you realize how much I need you? How much I love you? Haven't I told you often enough?"

"England's a long way off, George. It's not like Virginia City. Once we were there, you'd think differently than you do now. I wouldn't fit in. Sailing to England wouldn't make me go through a sea-change."

"In England you'd have all you ever dreamed of, a fine house, carriages, silks and satins to wear, and servants to wait on you. What more could you want, Monique?"

"You tempt me."

"The last time you said that, at Lake Tahoe, you let yourself be tempted and you haven't regretted it. Just as you'd never regret becoming my wife."

"I can't, George. I can't marry you. Besides not being fair to you, it wouldn't be fair to me. I care for you so much and yet . . . You said I never told you I loved you. Don't you see, George, I can't tell you because I'm not sure I do. I can't marry you when I'm not sure."

"If you don't love me now as much as I might hope, as much as I love you, you'll learn to. Love will come. Don't shake your head. Think about it, that's all I ask. I won't be able to leave until the day after tomorrow at the earliest. Think about it till then before you make up your mind. Promise me you'll think about it."

"All right," she said, "I'll think about it. Until the day after tomorrow, then you'll have my answer."

The next evening, Monique had herself driven to the parlor house. When Astrid met her at the door, the two women embraced.

"Honey," Astrid said, "that dress of yours will sure as hell knock their eyes out."

"Wish me luck," Monique said.

"I do. I don't know what you've got in mind, but whatever it is, I know it'll come up aces."

Monique smiled as Astrid left to greet an arriving guest. Taking a sealed envelope from her pocket, Monique went in search of Jess. She found him on the back porch sitting in a chair tilted against the building.

"This is the message, Jess." She handed him the envelope. "Are you sure you remember what I want you to do?"

"I remembers just fine." He shook his head. "I plumb don't like the sound of it, Miss Monique. I suspect you're stirring up a hornet's nest."

"Don't tell me what I should and shouldn't do, Jess. Get the buggy and be ready."

He brought his chair to the porch floor with a thump. Rising slowly to his feet, he took off his hat and held it to his chest. "Yes, missy, ole Jess gwine to do just like you tells him. Ole Jess knows his place."

She frowned as she watched him cross the porch with an exaggerated shuffle. Her frown changed to a thin smile. Whether willingly or not, Jess would do as she asked.

As soon as she was in her bedroom on the second floor, she lit the incense in the two bowls on the mantel, breathing in the rich heavy odor of the burning spices. The single lamp on the table glowed steadily, throwing soft shadows on the walls of the room. The covers on the large bed were turned down invitingly.

Hearing the clip-clop of a horse, she went to the window and looked down at the street. Jess halted the buggy in front of the feed store across the way. When he glanced up at her window, she raised her hand. Though she was certain he saw her, he made no sign.

Monique crossed to the looking glass between the draped windows on the far side of the room. Removing the combs and pins from her black hair, she let it fall to her shoulders. Her dress, a pale blue, was the color of a summer sky at midday. Its high-necked bodice of thin silk outlined her breasts and emphasized her narrow waist. The skirt flared over her multiple petticoats in a cascade of rippling color.

She was ready.

Going to the chair nearest the window, she sat staring into the darkness, her hands gripping the arms of the chair. When she heard the fiddler in the parlor below strike up a Viennese waltz, she drew in her breath.

Wait, she thought, I've forgotten something. Hurrying to the dressing table near the bed, she raised a bottle and lightly sprayed cologne behind her ears.

The scent reminded her of the flowers that had bloomed behind her mother's house in the summer days of her childhood.

Someone tapped on the door.

She crossed the room and stopped, waiting until the knock was repeated before raising the latch and opening the door. Jeremy, dressed in black, looked down at her. The lamplight whitened the small scar on his left cheek and his brown eyes glinted, and for a moment Monique remembered the Randolph's ball, the first time she had seen him. Knowing that she would probably never see him again after tonight, she felt a pang of regret, the bleak emptiness of loss.

"You asked me to come," he said. "What is this matter of life and death?"

When she stepped aside he walked past her to the center of the bedroom, where he stood looking around him. He seemed preoccupied, she thought, and older. Yes, he definitely looked older than she remembered. There were lines on his face she hadn't seen before, and she thought she detected a tinge of gray in his brown hair. The passing years had made him handsomer than ever, she decided.

She clenched her hands, steeling herself for what she had to do if she was ever to have a life of her own.

"It's about Philippe," she said.

He frowned and folded his arms. "I've heard what you've been saying these last few weeks, the accusations you've made."

"Van Allen Reid had Philippe killed. Reid hired either Alex Campbell or that fellow Russ to murder him."

"That's only hearsay."

"It's not only hearsay, it's the truth. My mind tells me it's true, my heart tells me it's true."

"Reid's no fool. Why would he have had Philippe killed?"

"I don't know why, Jeremy, I only know he did. Campbell confessed. I heard him. George Guildford heard him."

"Guildford? Your English lover?"

She gasped. "What right have you to say that? You of all people?"

"Do you actually expect him to marry you?" he asked. "That's what you've wanted all along, isn't it, Mary? To land the biggest fish in the pond. Let me tell you something, my dear. Sir George will never ask you to marry him. Never."

"Let me tell *you* something, my dear. He already has."

She smiled with satisfaction when she saw the surprise on his face. Jeremy shrugged and turned away. "Will you invite me to the wedding?" he asked.

"I haven't given George an answer yet. I haven't said yes or no."

He looked at her, eyebrows raised, and again she noticed the strange yellow wedges in his brown eyes.

"What are you waiting for?" he asked. "Hasn't he offered you all you want?"

Tears came to her eyes and she had to bite her lip to keep from crying. "You—you—" she sobbed. Her voice rose. "You bastard," she screamed.

"Now we're seeing the real Monique Vaudreuil. The bitch lurking behind the false front. The foul-mouthed vixen parading in the fine clothes of a lady."

She lowered her head into her hands. "That's not the reason," she half-whispered. "I didn't accept George because I don't love him."

And, with a start, she realized it was true. She didn't love George. She had never loved him. She raised her head. "I asked you here to talk about Philippe," she said, "not about me. Philippe was your best friend. He was murdered. You promised you'd avenge him. Remember? Reid had him killed. What do you intend to do about it?"

"What do you expect me to do? Take a rifle and go gunning for Van Allen Reid? Is that what you want?"

"Yes."

"Then you're a fool." He reached out to her, then hesitated, his hand falling to his side. "Be careful," he said. "You're making enemies in Virginia City. I'm warning you because I care for you. Because of what we once were to each other. Tread lightly."

"I'll say what I please, when I please, to whomever I please."

"Then you are a fool."

"And you're a coward."

He turned on his heel and crossed the room to the door.

"Jeremy," she whispered.

He opened the door.

"Jeremy," she pleaded. "Jeremy, Jeremy." She shut her eyes, saying his name over and over again.

She heard the door close. You're the one I love, she murmured to herself. Only you. I loved you from the beginning. I love you now. I'll love you forever, without reason. Love doesn't need a reason.

"Jeremy," she said once more.

His arms closed around her and his lips met hers as he drew her to him. Monique opened her eyes and looked at him before she really believed he had come back to her. Her arms went around his neck and she surrendered herself to his kiss.

"Oh God," he said.

She covered his mouth with hers, their tongues meeting. All at once he pushed her away.

"Get those clothes off," he told her.

She went to the lamp, turned down the wick, and

blew out the flame so the only light in the room came from the one unshaded window. Jeremy was standing by the bed. She heard the rustle of his clothing as he undressed.

"The window," she said urgently.

He crossed the room and she saw his body outlined against the light. His chest was bare but he still wore his pants. A moment after he drew down the shade, she heard the buggy rattle up C Street and she smiled in the darkness.

Going to her dressing-table, she slowly began to unbutton the front of her bodice. She heard Jeremy take off his boots and the rest of his clothes, then heard the whisper of bedcovers, followed by the creak of the bed.

"Hurry," he said.

She pulled the dress over her head and laid it carefully across a chair. She unfastened and removed her petticoats, then unbuckled and stepped out of her slippers. Taking off her garters, she rolled her stockings down over her legs. Naked, she walked silently to the bed, where she stood listening to his breathing coming from the darkness in front of her.

His hand touched her side and she drew back as though she'd been burned.

"The door," she said. "It's not locked."

She crossed the room and rattled the bolt, but left the door unfastened. Returning to the bed, she knelt on the carpet beside Jeremy, her hand going to his hair to twist his curls around her finger. He grasped her wrist and pulled her onto the bed. He had thrown the blankets and sheets to the floor, so when he drew her to him she gasped as she felt his naked body against hers.

When he kissed her, her heart pounded and her breath came in short gasps. It had been so long since they had been together.

"Wait," she murmured. "Lie on your back."

He rolled over and she knelt astride him, feeling his hardness against her leg. She leaned forward until her nipple touched his chest. Slowly, tantalizingly, she drew her body up over his, her nipples trailing along his chest until one rested on each side of his face. He turned his head, curled his tongue around her now-hard nipple, circling and circling before nipping at it with his teeth.

She drew back.

"God, how I've missed you," he said.

Had she heard the sound of the returning buggy? she wondered. So soon?

"What is it?" he asked.

"I thought I heard something. Outside."

"What does it matter?"

Reluctantly, not wanting to leave him, she slipped from the bed and ran to the window, where she lifted the side of the shade and looked along the street. Yes, a buggy was coming. Jess loomed large on the near side, and next to him Monique caught a glimpse of blond hair.

Laura. She smiled. Laura would find her husband in another woman's arms. She started to laugh.

"What are you laughing at?" Jeremy asked from the bed.

She didn't answer. Finding them together will hurt her, she thought, more than anything else I can do. I'll wound Laura and shame Jeremy. He'll hate me when he realizes the trap I laid for him. I'll never see him again. I'll be free of him forevermore.

The buggy slowed to a stop outside the parlor house. For an instant Monique remembered another street, a street in San Francisco, remembered riding in a buggy with Philippe and looking up to a window where she saw a redheaded woman, a woman who had laughed at her just as she was now laughing at Laura.

Monique let the shade fall shut. Have I become that woman? she asked herself. She walked toward the bed, longing for the touch of Jeremy's hands on her body, longing to feel his lips on hers again.

I can't, she told herself. I can't do this to him. I can't do this to myself. If I hurt him like this, I'll never be able to live with myself.

"She's coming," Monique said urgently. "She was in that buggy outside."

"Who's coming?"

"Laura. I sent Jess for Laura. Hurry, you've got to leave. Take your clothes, you don't have a moment to lose."

22

Laura

MONIQUE lit the lamp as Jeremy swung from the bed and yanked on his pants. He shoved his arms into the sleeves of his shirt and reached for his boots.

"You don't have time," Monique said urgently. "She'll be here any minute."

"I should have known I couldn't trust you. I called you a fool. I was wrong. I'm the fool for not remembering what you're like."

She bit back a reply and, still naked, inched open the door to look along the hall. It was empty.

"Go to the left and down the back stairs," she told him.

Carrying his boots and coat, Jeremy stepped into the corridor. "What will you tell her?" he asked.

"That I lied to bring you here. When you found me out, you left. All right?"

"For God's sake, put some clothes on." He turned and hurried out of sight along the hall.

He might at least have been grateful, she told herself as she bolted the door. After all, I sent him on his way before Laura arrived. A word of thanks would have been too much to expect, she supposed.

Monique put on her undergarments and was fastening her petticoats when three loud taps sounded on the door. Jess? She'd told him to send Laura up alone.

"I'll be there in a minute," she said as she pulled her blue dress over her head and started buttoning the bodice.

"Miss Monique, open the door." It was Jess. I look a fright, she told herself as she glanced in the mirror. She quickly ran a comb through her hair, then gathered the bedclothes from the floor and put them on the bed.

"Miss Monique." Jess' voice was louder, more insistent.

In her bare feet, she crossed the room, slid aside the bolt, and opened the door.

"Jess," she began, "I didn't want you to . . ." She stopped when she saw that Jess was carrying Laura Johnston in his arms.

He strode past her, glancing about the room before going to the bed. Monique ran past him and pulled the rumpled covers up over the pillows before he laid Laura down. The other woman's face was pale, her eyes shadowed. There was a trace of blood in the corner of her mouth. When she looked up at Monique her eyes seemed unnaturally large.

"I'm sorry," Laura said.

"Jess, what happened?"

"She done got sick in the buggy. I says to her, 'Let me take you to Doc Jamison,' and she says, 'No,' and I says, 'Let me take you back home,' and she says, 'No, take me to Miss Vaudreuil's,' so here we is."

"Fetch the doctor," Monique told him.

"No!" Laura's thin hand grasped her wrist. The

blond young woman pushed herself up on one elbow. "See," she said, "I feel better already."

All at once she began to cough. She raised a blood-stained handkerchief to her lips as dry coughs racked her body.

Monique led Jess to the door.

"Find the doctor," she said softly. "Tell him to come here at once."

Jess nodded. As he left the room, Monique walked quickly to the commode, poured a glass of water, and returned with it to the bed. Laura, sitting up, was gasping for air but she was no longer coughing.

"Drink this." Monique held the glass to the other woman's lips and, as Laura drank, her gasping stopped.

Laura looked around the room. "Jeremy?" she asked. "He needs me?"

"I sent the note," Monique admitted, "not Jeremy. I asked him to come here, but when he saw what I had in mind he walked out. He's probably home by now."

"You lured him here? Do you hate me so much?"

Monique carried a chair to the bed and sat at Laura's side. She put her hand on the sick woman's forehead.

"You're burning up. You should have let Jess drive you home."

"The fever comes and goes. I wanted to see you. Because of the other day." She stopped to catch her breath. "The day I crossed the street so I wouldn't have to speak. I'm sorry I was so rude. I apologize."

Monique didn't know what to say. "I was furious," she said finally.

"And that's why you wanted to hurt me?" Laura shook her head. "You had every right to be furious," she said. "I was embarrassed. I didn't know what to say. I think I'm afraid of you."

"Afraid? Why on earth would you be afraid of me?"

"Of what you might do. Do you think I'm blind? Do you think I don't have feelings? Do you imagine I'm so caught up in myself that I don't know what's going on around me?"

Seeing beads of perspiration on Laura's forehead, Monique dampened a handkerchief and wiped off the moisture.

"I sent Jess for the doctor," she said.

Laura smiled slightly. "There was no need. I know what he'll say. Take cough syrup and cod-liver oil. And he'll suggest a change of climate."

"Is there anything I can get you? We have a Chinese girl here who uses herbs for medicine. Sometimes they work wonders."

"There's nothing you can do," Laura said. "Except answer my question. Do you really think I don't know the truth?"

"I'm not sure what you're talking about."

"I'm talking about Jeremy."

Jeremy! I'm not going to discuss Jeremy with this woman. Shaking her head, Monique went to the window and looked out, her arms folded.

"The doctor should be here soon," she said.

She heard a sound behind her and turned to see Laura getting up and starting to walk toward her. Monique ran across the room, took the other woman's hand and led her back to the bed. Fluffing the two pillows, she put one atop the other.

"Now," Laura said as soon as she was sitting with her back to the pillows, "you're the one who seems afraid of me, not vice-versa."

"I don't fear you, I envy you."

"You envy me?" Laura smiled ruefully and closed her eyes. "I wanted to be a schoolteacher," she said.

Monique waited for her to go on.

"My father wouldn't hear of it," Laura said. " 'There's no reason for you to become a teacher,' he told me. 'You don't have to work. You'll have a good dowry, you'll marry well. You'll never want for money.' Still I insisted. My father put his foot down. He said I'd soon have children of my own to teach, that he didn't want to hear any more foolishness from me. So I didn't become a teacher. You envy me? No, I envy you."

"Me?"

"You seem to do whatever you want. You're not afraid of anything or anyone. Not that I approve of what you do. Of this." Laura glanced around the dimly lit room.

"I've always envied you," Monique said. "You have so much, a great house in San Francisco, all the money you need, fine clothes, servants to wait on you." And Jeremy, she added to herself.

"Perhaps we should trade places," Laura said.

"You wouldn't like my life."

"Nor you mine, I suspect. You'd soon grow bored." Again Laura looked about the room. What had seemed so grand to Monique a short time before suddenly appeared tawdry—the dark red drapes, the bowls of smoldering incense on the mantel, the fourposter bed. It was tawdry because it sought to recreate European elegance in the Nevada desert, tried to be what it could never be.

"When Jeremy returned to San Francisco from the East," Laura said, "I offered to release him from his vows. He seemed different, somehow, not the same man who had courted me the year before. I don't mean I didn't love him any more. I did, even more than I had before. I loved him more because he seemed farther away from me. Do you understand?"

Monique smiled sadly. "I understand."

"When I told him he didn't have to marry me, he

claimed nothing had changed. I told him I didn't want him to marry me just because I'd become ill. He denied that my condition had anything to do with it. So we were married, and I put everything else aside to try to make him happy. I made Jeremy my life, my whole life. Making him happy was all I cared about."

"I'd never do that for any man," Monique said.

"That's why I envy you, because you wouldn't. I envy you because you wouldn't change, or at least not much. You'd marry a man on your terms, not his."

"If you once let a man know you're weak, he'll take advantage of you. It's their way."

"I did what I had to do," Laura said. "That's the kind of person I am, I suppose. You can't change overnight."

"You can change, though. I have. I believed men's lies once, their sweet talk, their promises. I don't anymore. Sometimes I wish I could, but I can't. You can change, Laura, if you really want to."

"I don't have the time." She reached out to Monique. "Take my hand. Please." When Monique clasped the other woman's hand in hers she found it damp and clammy.

"I'm going to die," Laura said.

"Hush," Monique told her almost automatically. "Don't talk nonsense."

"I don't intend to die here," Laura said, "not in Virginia City. I've never felt at home in Nevada, and I refuse to die here. Jeremy's taking me back to San Francisco at the end of the week. I want to be where I grew up, in my father's house. Is that so wrong?"

Monique stared at her. Laura meant what she said, she realized. The other woman did expect to die. She felt a surge of pity and of sorrow, while at the same time her heart leaped. Jeremy would be free. She shut the thought away in a remote corner of her mind as soon as it appeared, but she couldn't deny its existence.

"No, not so wrong," she answered. If I wanted to go home, she asked herself, where would I go? I have no home. None at all.

"Do you know what the Reverend McDonough told me?" Laura asked. "He said that I had to guard against being selfish. That sick people often think only of themselves and not of others. At the time, I thought it was just another of his antiquated notions. He has a great many of those, but I soon realized he was right. So I stopped worrying about myself so much, and started wondering how I could help others. It's difficult not to put yourself first."

"Very difficult."

"Yes, even when you see things like I do. It's as though I'm able to stand apart from everyone, as though every day I'm farther away. People seem smaller and smaller, but at the same time I can see them more clearly. I can't explain, not exactly. It's as though everyone else is on a stage and I'm in the audience. Haven't you often seen the hero of a melodrama in danger? You want to cry out to him to take care before it's too late, yet if you did you'd feel foolish because, after all, it's only a play. Now I feel that way, as though life is a play that I'm not a part of, as though I'm in the audience. Yet I still hesitate to speak up, because I don't think people will pay any attention to me. I have this eerie feeling, too, that the curtain will come down before the play's over, and I'll still be watching, knowing the actors and actresses are playing their roles behind the curtain where I can't see them. I'll never know how it all comes out."

Laura drew in a series of short, sharp breaths. As

she stared into Monique's eyes, tears started down her cheeks.

"Oh, Monique," she whispered. "I'm so afraid."

Monique leaned forward and hugged her, holding her close, wishing there was something she could do for her. After a moment, Laura drew back.

"I'm all right now," she said. "At times I forget that God will look after me, and that I'm going to a better place than this. I forget that I'll dwell in the house of the Lord forever."

"I wish I had your faith."

"I understand why he likes you," Laura said. "I thought at first you must be a bold woman who had brazenly tempted him. When I organized the church-women's march, I told myself it was because you were an agent of the devil, just as the Reverend Mc-Donough said." Laura tried to smile. "I knew, though, why I singled you out. I was afraid that this was where Jeremy spent those evenings he wasn't home, those evenings he claimed to be working."

Monique shook her head. "No," she said. "Oh, no, you misjudge him. I've heard from others about the long hours Jeremy works."

Laura sighed. "He's driven, I know. Why?" Her large eyes questioned Monique.

"He wants—Jeremy wants—" Monique paused and flung her arms wide. "He wants to be the best," she said.

"You do care for him, don't you? You truly care for him."

"I love him," Monique said. "I love him more than I've ever loved another man and more than I'll ever love anyone else."

She felt tears welling in her eyes. There is something I can do for Laura, she realized. There was a gift she could offer. Laura was watching her intently.

"He never loved me," Monique said. "I tried to

make him love me on the ship sailing north from Panama, and here in Virginia City. I failed. You're the one he loves." She smiled. "That's the luck of the draw, I guess."

"I don't understand you," Laura said. "I'll probably never understand you. I'd think one man would be enough. I'd think that you wouldn't want more, especially one who's married to another woman."

"One man would be enough if he were the right one. At least that's what I tell myself."

"You'd be wrong for Jeremy," Laura said. "I can see that now."

"Because I've known other men?"

Laura shook her head. "No, because he'd ask more of you than you could give him. He wouldn't want a wife who competed with him, who ran a merchandising establishment. Certainly not one who owned a place like this. Jeremy expects his wife to stay at home, to entertain, and to be a reflection of his good taste. Even I had a difficult time, at first, playing the part he expected me to play."

"I could give up the parlor house," Monique said, "but not the merchandising. And I'll never play a part for any man. Never, no matter how much I care for him."

"You'd be wrong for each other. I don't know whether I'm relieved or sad."

"Sad? Why should you be sad?"

She heard a knock. As Monique turned, Dr. Jamison bustled into the room. He stopped beside the bed, gasping for air, evidently winded from climbing the stairs.

"I never—expected—to find you here," he told Laura.

"You're no more surprised than I am."

Removing a stethoscope from his black bag, he went to the bed and held the instrument to Laura's chest. "Turn over," he told her after a few minutes. When he finished his examination, he said, "I don't think you've been following my advice."

"The cod-liver oil does no good."

"I'm going to recommend—phosphate of lime in milk. And a change—of climate."

"My husband and I are leaving for San Francisco in a few days."

"Excellent. And now—you should—go home and rest."

Monique saw Jess standing in the hall just outside the bedroom. She motioned him to come in.

"Wait," Laura told Jess. She went to Monique and took her in her arms. "I'm sad because I want Jeremy to be happy," she whispered in her ear.

"I still envy you," Monique murmured. "Not because of what you have, but because of what you are. You're the one who's brave, not me."

Laura stepped back, smiling. "Thank you," she said.

When Laura looked up at Jess and nodded to him, he lifted her into his arms and carried her from the room. After they and the doctor were gone, Monique went to the window and watched Jess place Laura on the seat of the buggy and then urge the horse away from the front of the house and up C Street. Even after the buggy was out of sight, she continued to stare into the night.

I would have liked her, she thought, if I'd known her at another time, in another place. Without Jeremy between us. And, she told herself, Laura might have liked me.

"You're not coming with me to the depot, Monique?" George asked the next morning.

"No, I'd rather say goodbye to you here."

"You won't change your mind? You won't sail with me?"

"I won't change my mind. I can't go, George. I'm flattered. I'm honored. But I can't go to England with you. Someday you'll thank me."

"Never."

He cradled her head in his hands and kissed her gently. The kiss of a friend, not a lover. When he stepped away she saw tears glistening in his eyes.

Noticing a flash of color near the door, she looked that way and saw Chai in her red gown.

"You no go?" Chai asked her.

"No, Chai, I'm going to stay here in Virginia City."

"This house is yours for as long as you want it," George said.

"Thank you, but I intend to move back to C Street after you're gone. I belong there, not here."

"Chai go."

Monique stared at the Chinese girl, not understanding her.

"She wants to go with me," George said. "She wants to sail to England."

"To England?" Surprised, Monique didn't know what to say.

"She talked to me about it early this morning," George said. "I told her it was up to you."

"Chai is free to go wherever she wishes," Monique said sharply.

"She'd work as a house servant at Guildford Hall. She understands that."

Monique looked from George to Chai. "Are you certain this is what you want to do?" she asked.

"Chai sure," the girl said.

Monique hugged her. "Then go with my blessing."

Chai bowed and left the room as silently as she'd entered.

"Take care of Chai," Monique told George. "Don't let anything happen to her."

"I wouldn't be surprised if she ended up taking care of me."

They stood looking at one another in silence. There seemed to be nothing more to say. For a moment Monique had an impulse to change her mind, to tell him she'd go with him, sail to England, and marry him. As quickly as it had come the notion fled, and she sighed for what might have been.

"I almost said I'd stay here," George told her, "and to hell with the Guildfords and the Guildford estate, to hell with the responsibility."

"But you didn't."

"No," he said, "I didn't." He walked from her, pausing at the door. "In two months I'll be riding on the Sussex meadows," he said.

"In a Confederate uniform?" She smiled through her tears.

"I've reluctantly resigned my commission. One can't manage an English estate and be an officer in the Confederate Army at one and the same time."

He looked at her for a long moment. "I'll ask you what you asked Chai," he said. "You're certain?"

"Yes," she said softly.

He nodded, raised his hand to his forehead in a last salute, and left the room. His steps went down the hall, and a few minutes later she heard the carriage rattle off in the direction of the stage depot.

As she had so often in the past, she felt her life was a succession of goodbyes. Nothing endured. Everything was of the moment. Fleeting. She thought of Laura. As all life was fleeting, she told herself.

"For heaven's sake, Astrid, what is it?" Monique asked several weeks later. Ever since she had moved back into the parlor house, the tall blond woman had hovered near her, always about to speak out, yet never saying what troubled her.

"How did you guess I had something on my mind?"

"It wasn't hard, the way you've been acting. Why don't you tell me and have done with it?"

"I don't know whether I ought to. I'm afraid no good will come of it."

"Just tell me, Astrid."

"You know Mike Renfell, don't you?"

"How could I help it? He's so taken with you that sometimes I think this is his second home."

"Mike used to work for Van Allen Reid, until six months ago when they had a falling-out. Last week he told me something you might want to hear. Remember how you told us a long time ago to keep our ears open?"

"About Philippe's murder. I'm sure I already know who killed him, though."

Astrid shook her head. "It was Russ, not Campbell, Mike said. But there's more. Mike told me the reason. At the beginning, when they were just starting to find silver here in the Comstock, Reid had a couple of the assayers in his hip pocket. Got them to tell the miners they'd come up dry when really they'd hit it big."

"And after awhile Reid went to the same spot and staked a claim himself?"

"More likely Alex Campbell did the actual claim-staikng, or one of Reid's other men."

"Are you sure? Can you trust Mike?"

"Yeah. The bastard spilled the beans because he was leaving for the East. He's long gone, headed back to where he came from. He wanted to get everything off his chest before he left."

"Philippe must have found out," Monique said. "He must have stumbled onto the secret through one of his gambling friends."

"That's what Mike thought. It makes sense. What can you do about it, that's the question."

Monique frowned. George Guildford was gone. Jeremy had taken Laura back to San Francisco. She could report the story—it was nothing more than hearsay, she realized—to Lester Harrington at the *Enterprise*. His response would undoubtedly be the same as it had been when she told him about Alex Campbell, a shrug of his shoulders.

She could have a showdown with Van Allen Reid. Face him, and make him tell her the truth. And when he did? She felt her heart pounding. She'd avenge Philippe, by God she would.

Should she go to Van? she wondered.

The decision was taken from her hands. Two days later Van Allen Reid came to her.

23

The Female of the Species

MONIQUE lay in bed listening to a loose shutter banging in the cold night wind. In the distance a violin played a sad, plaintive melody that told of a lost love and a home far away.

She finally slept, but fitfully, dreaming of hooded figures riding in the night, of horsemen carrying torches, and of weeping women kneeling at the entrance to a tomb. She sat up with a start. What had awakened her?

The knock came again. Monique slipped from the bed and stood shivering in the cold.

"Who's there?" she asked.

"Jeremy." The voice was muffled and indistinct.

She ran across the room, slid back the bolt, and opened the door. She gasped. Van Allen Reid stood in the dimly lighted hall. Before she had a chance to stop him, he pushed past her into the bedroom. When she turned to face him, he grabbed her arm and shoved her to one side. She heard the bolt slide home.

The derringer, she told herself. She kept the gun on the stand beside the bed. Staying out of the light from the windows, she hurried across the room. As she reached for the pistol, a hand closed over her wrist and Van yanked her away from the bed.

He pulled her against him and she smelled whiskey and cigar smoke. He slapped her, hard, and she staggered away from him, falling across the bed. She cried out.

A match flared and she saw Van, his pale face, his black hair. He was smiling at her, a cruel smile.

The light blinked out. She rolled over and sprawled across the bed to reach for the pistol on the stand. Where was it? Her fingers searched in vain. It was gone.

She saw the flare of another match, then saw Van replacing the chimney of the glowing lamp.

"Is this what you're looking for?" He showed her the derringer in his palm before he dropped the gun into a pocket of his frock coat.

Monique pushed herself off the bed. Her jaw hurt; she was breathing rapidly. She heard the thudding of her heart. Undaunted, she watched Van closely, waiting for a chance to elude him, unbolt the door, and escape.

The lamp. She recalled throwing a lamp at Alex Campbell. She glanced at the windows. What could she use to shatter the glass? Even if she did, would anyone notice?

Van stepped toward her. She drew in her breath, standing her ground.

"Remember the first time I came here?" he asked. The lamp was behind him,, his face in shadow.

She said nothing. How can I help but remember? she asked herself.

"I paid you a thousand dollars." He paused, his face inches from hers. "Do you know what you're worth to me now?"

He reached into his pocket, took out a coin and threw it on the bedside stand. It was a quarter.

Despite herself, color flooded Monique's face.

"You killed Philippe." Her voice was low, almost a whisper.

Van shrugged.

"You're a brave son-of-a-bitch, aren't you?" she asked. "Killing a gentle man who never harmed you."

He reached to his belt, and when he held up his hand the lamplight glinted on the blade of a knife. He held the knife beneath her chin, so close that the tip pricked her flesh.

"You were only a thorn in my side at first," Van said. "Lately you've become a festering sore."

"I'm glad." Her lips hurt when she tried to smile defiantly at him.

"Do you know what they do with festering sores? They lance them."

She shivered, a tremor of fear. This wasn't the Van Allen Reid she remembered. He'd killed Philippe. He'd lied and cheated his way to power in Virginia City. Is that where this arrogance came from? Did he imagine that no-one would dare challenge him? Did he think that he was untouchable?

"You're afraid," he whispered, "and you have reason to be. When I'm through with you, you won't be able to sell yourself for even two bits. You'll have to give yourself away."

He slid the knife into a sheath on his belt, reached into his pocket and took out a kerchief. Holding one end of the cloth in each hand, he twirled it into a gag. Or a garrot? With the kerchief stretched between his hands, he advanced on her. Monique drew away. She felt the bed against the backs of her legs. Van reached for her and she screamed.

He shoved her backwards onto the bed, forcing the gag into her mouth and quickly tying it at the back of her head.

She heard a sound from the hall. Van froze. Monique's heart leaped with hope.

"Miss Monique!" It was Jess.

She tried to call to him, to warn him, but the gag muffled her cries. She pulled at the knot.

There was a thud. She pictured Jess in the hall, slamming his powerful body against the door. The thud came again. Wood cracked. Again Jess hurled himself at the door. Wood splintered, the bolt gave, and the door burst open. Jess stumbled into the room just as Monique pulled off the gag and threw it aside.

Van, a pistol in his hand, faced the doorway where Jess' huge figure was outlined in the light from the hall.

"Get out of here, nigger," Van ordered.

"Go to hell, white man," Jess told him.

The black dodged to one side as Van's gun roared. Monique grabbed Van's arm and pulled it down, but he shook her off and she staggered away from him. Van swung down with the pistol, the barrel striking her shoulder. She moaned with pain.

Jess picked up the table and the lamp crashed to the floor, throwing the room into darkness. Monique saw the dark outline of Jess with the table held high over his head. She dropped to her knees, grasping Van's leg and pulling as Jess hurled the table. Van's gun roared once more, the sound hurting her eardrums, the gunsmoke choking her.

Van threw himself to one side, yanking his leg from her grasp just as the table struck his left arm. He grunted. She couldn't see Jess. Was he hit? From the corner of her eye she caught a flick of motion in the doorway. She saw Astrid peering into the room, a derringer in her hand.

"No!" Monique shouted to her. "Stay back!"

Two shots rang out in quick succession, two flashes of light. Monique heard a sharp cry. A moan was followed by the thud of a blow. A man cursed. There were sounds of running footsteps and shouts from downstairs. Then silence was broken by a whimper of pain.

She struggled to her feet.

"Jess?" she called into the darkness. "Jess, are you all right? Astrid?"

"The bastard knocked the wind out of me," Jess said.

She heard the black man getting slowly to his feet. The figure of a man appeared in the doorway with a lamp in his hand. She recognized Hal Stuart, the ringleader of the miners who had brought Sir George to the parlor house.

"What the hell . . ?" Hal stared down at the floor. "Good God." Turning to someone behind him, he shouted, "Get Doc Jamison. She's hurt." He knelt on the floor. "She's hurt bad."

Monique ran to his side. Astrid, her face ashen, lay sprawled on her back in the hall just outside the bedroom. Her eyes were closed and she was moaning. A bloodstain was spreading on the black satin of her gown just below her right breast.

There was no sign of Reid.

"Astrid, Astrid," Monique cried.

"We got to stop the bleeding," Hal said.

"Bring her in here." One of the miners had opened the door to Astrid's room.

Jess stooped beside the blond woman, lifted her into his arms, and carried her into the room, where he laid her gently on the bed. Monique ran to her

own room, returned with a pair of scissors, and cut
the cloth away from the wound, baring Astrid's bloodied flesh. The small hole, red and raw, bled freely.

Hal handed her white pads fashioned from a torn
sheet and Monique pressed the cloth to the wound.

"I'll tie it," Hal said.

"I'm going to die," Astrid whimpered. "My God,
I'm going to die."

"No," Monique told her, "you're not. The doctor's
on his way. You'll be all right."

"I'm going to die," Astrid said again, repeating the
words over and over like a litany.

"Here's Doc Jamison."

The doctor pushed his way through the crowd in
the hall and came into the bedroom. He knelt at Astrid's side, removing the impromptu bandage and
examining her wound. When he stood up, he shook
his head.

He opened his bag and laid a scalpel and forceps
on the bedside stand. "Clear that bureau," he told
the men, nodding to a long low chest of drawers covered with knick-knacks. "Get some towels," he said
to Monique.

Monique ran along the hall to the linen closet.
Astrid was trying to help me, she told herself. It's
my fault she was shot. When Monique returned with
a stack of towels, Astrid lay on the cleared top of
the chest, her eyes still closed.

"Get her to take a little whiskey if you can," Doc
Jamison told Monique as he took the towels from
her. He wiped off the scalpel and forceps, then laid
a towel across Astrid's stomach.

"She isn't swallowing the whiskey," Monique said.

"Never mind then." Jamison fumbled for the scalpel.

Monique handed him the small straight knife.

"Hold her down, boys," he told the two miners

standing on either side of Astrid. They grasped her shoulders.

The doctor bent over the wounded woman, scalpel in hand. He hesitated. Monique drew in her breath. The room was hushed.

Dr. Jamison hunched his shoulders, then stepped back. "Cover her over," he said. "She's dead."

"No!" Monique pushed past the doctor and knelt beside the blond woman. Astrid's face was serene.

"Do something," Monique told the doctor.

"There's naught to be done. She's dead."

Monique lowered her face into her hands and turned away, stunned. She felt a touch on her arm. Looking up she saw Jess standing beside her with tears in his dark eyes.

"She's done gone to a better place than this," Jess said.

Hal yanked a satin sheet from Astrid's bed and drew it up over her body. The room was still quiet, the only sounds the doctor's wheezing and the ticking of a clock on the mantel.

The funeral was held on Monday afternoon two days later. The service was conducted at Virginia City Engine House No. 1 on B Street by the Reverend William M. Martin. His remarks were brief and, the miners agreed, eloquent. Afterwards, the procession made its way to C Street with the hearse, drawn by four black horses, in the lead, followed by the Metropolitan Brass Band playing a dirge. Next came the members of the volunteer fire companies in full regalia, and sixteen carriages of mourners, friends of Astrid and members of the sisterhood of the deceased and, finally, groups of miners who trudged through the dust to Astrid's last resting place, the Flowery Hill Cemetery.

"That was far and away the biggest funeral this

town's ever seen," Lester Harrington told Monique as they rode back from the cemetery.

Monique, who was dressed in black with a black veil over her face, said nothing.

"I didn't see any of the churchwomen," Lester went on. "Lots of their husbands were there, though. I won't be a bit surprised if they find trouble waiting for them when they get home tonight. Probably they'll be locked out of their bedrooms for the next month."

Still Monique said nothing. As they approached the city, she drew the veil from her face.

"What's wrong with the men of Virginia City?" she asked him. "They know who killed Astrid. Yet will they do anything? No, they won't. They're afraid. They let Van Allen Reid strut around town as though he owned the place."

"He pretty much does." Harrington shook his head. "It's going to take more than Miss Astrid getting killed to rouse the miners. Reid claims he acted in self-defense."

"Self-defense? That's ridiculous."

"Astrid did have a gun. They found her derringer on the floor in the hall with one shot fired."

"She was trying to protect me. I don't understand these men. They all liked Astrid. She didn't have an enemy to her name. Yet they let her murderer walk the streets free and clear."

"That's the way of it," Harrington said. "If you've got money, you're above the law. At least you are in Virginia City."

"It's up to me, then." Monique raised her chin. "The miners might be afraid of Reid, but I'm not."

"Don't be foolhardy. Look at what happened when you tried the last time. Astrid got herself killed." When Monique drew in her breath, he hastened on. "It wasn't your fault, Miss Monique, nobody blames

you. But it's what happened, there's no denying that.
"You've got to outsmart Van Allen Reid, not try to
outshoot him."

"But how? He must have ten hired gunmen guarding that mine of his. And, as you say, he has money
and power. What can I do?"

"I have to admit that I don't know."

The carriage pulled up in front of the parlor house,
and Harrington helped her to the ground. Two miners
watched her from the top of the steps as she took
the front door key from her bag.

"You opening up today?" one of the men asked.
When she glared at him, he hung his head.

"Tomorrow?" he persisted.

Without answering, she unlocked the door and
went inside. Men are animals, she told herself. Have
they no respect for the dead, no sense of decency?
She walked into the parlor and sat in an overstuffed
chair, rested her head back and stared at the ceiling.

I'll leave Virginia City, she told herself. I'll close
the parlor house, shut down the store, and cancel my
plans to expand into mining supplies. I've had enough.
Philippe's dead, Astrid's dead. Jeremy's gone. Sir
George has sailed for England.

I've had enough of Nevada's winter cold and wind,
the summer heat, enough of drunken miners and hyp-
ocritical churchwomen. I've had enough of lust and
greed, of hate, of despair. Where will I go? she asked
herself. Anywhere. Anywhere would be better than
the Comstock.

She heard a plaintive cry. As she looked down,
Guinevere leaped into her lap and tried to lick her
face. Monique took the cat in her arms and hugged
her. You're all I've got, she thought, the only friend
I have in the world.

How could she possibly outsmart Van Allen Reid,
as Lester Harrington had suggested? Something else

the reporter had said on the ride from the cemetery nagged at her. What was it? She couldn't remember. She had a notion that his words, if she could only recall them, might suggest a way out of her dilemma.

Putting the cat on the floor, she stood and walked to the fireplace where she looked down at the burnt logs in the grate. She tried to bring back Harrington's words. He had said this was the largest funeral Virginia City had ever seen. He'd commented on the men who had attended the funeral without their wives. He had said that the women would . . . Of course!

"Ah Sing!" she called. Monique went to the hall and stood with her hand on the newel post. "Mariana! Gabrielle! Bertha! Rosie!"

The women appeared one by one at the head of the stairs.

"Come down to the parlor," Monique told them. "I have an idea. I want to know what you think."

It was eight o'clock. The night outside was dark and cold. Monique warmed her hands at the crackling fire, while the other five girls sat behind her, Mariana reading a thin volume of Spanish love poems, Rosie knitting, Gabrielle playing with the cat. Ah Sing and Bertha dozed in their chairs.

A fist pounded on the front door.

"They's back," Jess said from the hallway. "Shall I pay them no mind like I done the last time?"

"No," Monique said, "I'll see what they want. Come with me, Jess."

"If one of them so much as lays a finger on you . . ."

"They won't. Open the door."

Jess slid the bolt back and unlocked the door. A group of miners pushed forward, barred from entering by his outstretched arms.

"Miss Monique," a red-bearded miner from the Ophir called to her.

"What's the matter, Hank?" she asked.

Hearing the rustle of skirts behind her, she knew the other women had gathered to watch and listen.

"That's what we'd like to know," Hank said. "We been here to your place twice now. Closed. We been to Miss Belle's down on D Street. Closed. We been to Chinatown. Only the fan-tan parlors and the laundries are doing business. Even Miss Julia's locked her door. It ain't right. There ain't a whorehouse open in all of Virginia City."

"That's right, Hank," Monique agreed. "Not a single solitary one."

"You gotta do something to help us, Miss Monique. You was always on our side. Is it them damn church-women? Have you closed you all down?"

Monique shook her head. "Astrid's dead, Hank," she said. "I've closed out of respect, and I imagine the other women have done the same."

"Because of what happened to Miss Astrid?"

"That's right, Hank. She's dead, and her murderer hasn't been caught yet."

"But everybody knows it was Van Allen Reid that done it."

"They know it but they aren't doing anything about it."

Hank raised his eyebrows. "You—you mean," he stammered, "that you'll be closed until . . . That as long as Reid's walking around . . . Is that what you mean, Miss Monique?"

"That's exactly what I mean." She turned to Jess. "Lock up," she told him.

Hank and two of the miners near him started forward, but Jess shut the door in their faces. Monique heard a murmur of talk outside and then the sound of footsteps crossing the porch and receding down the street.

"What they meaning to do?" Jess asked.

"I don't know. We'll just have to wait and see." &

24

Showdown

"WE gotta do something."

"We can't go on like this. We got all the booze we can drink but what else have we got? Nothing."

Hal Stuart climbed onto the top of a poker table. "We've gone long enough without women," he told the miners who gathered around him. "Let's show the gals we ain't afeared of nothing. How many of you bastards are with me?"

The men cheered.

"We'll march on the Reid Building, then to the Reid mine."

"They say Reid's got more than ten hired guns at the mine."

"Are we scared of hired guns?" Hal asked.

"Hell no!" the miners shouted back.

"Then follow me."

Hal leaped from the table and led the miners out of the Silver Dollar to the dark street. More men joined the throng as they marched, miners from the

El Dorado, from Hahn's Hurdy-Gurdy Palace, and from the other saloons and gambling halls. They were armed with pistols and knives, rifles and shotguns. A few carried picks.

The miners shouted and laughed until they reached the Reid Building. They stopped across the street, suddenly quiet. Hal stepped out from the crowd.

"Reid," he shouted, "if you're in there, you'd best come out. If you don't, we're coming in after you."

The two-story office building remained dark and quiet.

"All right, boys," Hal called. "Follow me."

They charged in a ragged line across the street, over the sidewalk and up the steps. When they found the door chained, men in the rear passed a log forward to those in front. Using it as a ram, the miners battered the door until it crashed open amidst a shattering of glass and wood. Hal darted inside, followed by the others.

"There ain't nobody here." The miner's voice echoed his relief.

"They've cleared out."

"Must all be holed up at the mine."

With Hal in the lead, they marched back along C Street, up a low hill and down into a gully. They halted when they saw the huddled buildings of the Reid mine in front of them.

A miner picked up and threw it. They heard a tinkle of breaking glass.

A shot cracked from the window of the first building. One of the miners grunted in pain, his hand clutching his arm. The attackers scattered, taking shelter behind abandoned equipment, mounds of slag, and sheds. A fusillade of shots rattled from the gunmen hiding in the buildings. The miners answered with a scattered, ineffectual volley.

"Surround them," Hal said. "We're gonna have to starve the bastards out."

After posting men on all sides of the entrance to the mine, the attackers lit a campfire and gathered around it for a council of war.

"It'll take weeks, maybe months, to starve them out," Hank said.

"He's right."

They all looked at a curly-haired miner who had just joined them. "I was on the last shift in the Reid," he told them. "The mine's shut down tighter than a drum, but they got enough grub to last a good six months."

"We ain't about to starve them out then."

"Might be we could come on them from below," an older miner suggested. "The Mexican connects with the Ophir and the Ophir links up with the Reid. If we can locate the right stopes, we can give them a hell of a surprise."

"Won't work," the newcomer said, "cause they already thought of that. Reid himself is down below, getting set to blow up the connecting tunnels."

"He wouldn't do that," Hank said. "Not a mining man like Reid."

A muffled explosion shook the ground, followed by another and another, all from deep within the earth.

"He's doing it."

"God," one of the recruits from the El Dorado said, "I sure as hell wish I had a drink."

"There'll be no boozing," Hal told him, "till we get this thing sorted out. There must be some way to pry them gunmen out of there."

"I got me an idea." Lester Harrington pushed his way through the crowd and squatted in the circle of light from the fire. "I suggest we send them boys at the mine a present."

"What kind of present you got in mind?" Hal asked.

"A wagonload of black powder that'll blow them all to smithereens?"

"If we tried that," Harrington said, "like as not we'd send ourselves to kingdom come in the bargain. No, I got a notion to send them boys something they'll welcome with open arms. Her'es what I got in mind . . ."

The hours passed. The night was cold and dark. There was no moon. The besiegers sat around bonfires, talking and warming their hands at the flames, while the gunmen in the buildings at the mine entrance watched and waited, confident that their attackers would soon tire of the game and drift back to the saloons of Virginia City only a quarter of a mile away.

A wagon rattled out of the night and stopped fifty feet from the first of the mine buildings.

"Don't come no closer," the gunman on guard at the door warned.

"I ain't with them," the driver whispered hoarsely. "Joe Goodman of the *Enterprise* sent me. He's a friend of Van Allen Reid. Everybody knows that."

"You alone?"

"I swear to God."

"Get down off the wagon and walk over here with your hands in the air. If you're lying about being alone, you're dead."

The driver climbed to the ground and approached the guard with his hands raised.

"I swear to God," he said again. "It's just me."

"Pike," the guard said to a man posted at a window to his right. "Put a couple of rounds through the back of that there wagon."

"Go ahead, it don't matter to me," the driver said. "But you'll regret it."

"Why so?"

"The wagon's loaded with kegs of whiskey."

"You're lying through your teeth."

"Joe reckoned you men might be getting a mite thirsty down here, knowing how Reid feels about drinking and all. So he sent along a little something to quench your thirst and warm you up at the same time. If you want to put bullet holes in them kegs, go right ahead, it don't make no difference to me." He sighed. "Sure would be a waste of mighty good whiskey though."

"Go take a gander, Pike," the guard said.

Pike, his rifle in one hand, cautiously approached the wagon from the rear. He climbed up on the backboard and looked inside. Satisfied, he swung his leg over the side and clambered aboard. A few minutes later he was back inside the building.

"It's the God's honest truth he's telling us," Pike said. "There's naught in that there wagon 'cept five barrels of whiskey." He wiped his mouth with the back of his hand. "And mighty good whiskey at that."

It was dawn. The men posted around the Reid mine looked up at the mountains silhouetted darkly against a pale yellow sky. From the buildings below them came the sounds of laughter and singing.

"We'd best get us a move on," Hank suggested, "before old Reid gets wind of what's going on."

"What can he do if he does? Practically all his men are in them buildings."

"Let's move," Hal said. He raised his rifle above his head. From the crest of the hill on the far side of the mine another rifle was raised in answer to the signal.

Crouching, the men ran in relays across the rock-littered yard, dark shadows in the dim light of early morning. When they reached the first of the buildings, Hal put his heel to the door and kicked it open. He jumped back.

The men inside were singing "Dixie."

"All right boys," Hal shouted. "Let's go in there and get 'em."

The miners charged, crowding through the door, their pistols and rifles ready. Inside they found three gunmen passed out on the floor. The others looked up with foolish grins on their faces. One by one they staggered to their feet and raised their hands.

The siege of the Reid mine was over.

"There wasn't any trace of Van Allen Reid," Lester Harrington told Monique later that morning at the parlor house. "We went down into the mine and rounded up a few more of his gunmen, but by that time Reid had vamoosed. He's probably halfway to San Francisco by now."

"Will you drive me to see where the fighting was?" Monique asked. "I want to go to the mine and the Reid Building."

"Be glad to, though there's not much worth looking at. I expect that ten years from now this'll be remembered as a wild and woolly shootout, but actually only one shot was fired this morning. That was when Hank Streib shot himself in the foot. He lost his big toe."

"I'd like to go anyway." Turning to Mariana, she said, "It's all right to open up, even though they haven't caught Van. You can take care of that."

The Spanish girl nodded.

"Want me to come along?" Jess asked.

Monique shook her head. "There's no need, Jess. Keep an eye on things here. I expect the boys will be in a celebrating mood."

As Harrington drove her to the mine, he was strangely silent, as though he had something on his mind. After stopping briefly at the mine, they rode through Virginia City to Reid's office building. The street outside was empty; the building's battered door hung ajar.

Harrington helped Monique out of the buggy. As they climbed the steps, she hesitated.

"I just remembered something," she said. "Van told me there was an entrance to the mines from the cellar of his building. You don't think. . ?"

"That he came back here instead of hightailing it out of town? That's not likely. Why would he?"

"I don't know." Shaking her head, she continued into the building.

Their footsteps echoed in the long dark hallways. In the deserted offices papers were scattered on desks and floors. In one room the door to a small safe gaped open.

When Monique opened a door at the rear of a corridor on the first floor, she found herself staring into the musty gloom of the cellar.

"Let's go down," she said.

Harrington brought a lamp from one of the offices, lit it, and led the way into the cellar. When they reached the bottom of the steps he held the lamp above his head. The large room, whose beamed ceiling was supported by huge wooden timbers, smelled of dampness and decay.

"No sign of any tunnel here," Harrington said. "You must of misheard him."

"She didn't mishear me."

Van Allen Reid stepped from behind one of the posts, his face darkened by a growth of black beard, his head hatless, his hair covered with dust, and his black clothes streaked and rumpled. In one hand he held a pistol, in the other he carried a leather satchel.

"I—" Harrington began.

Van fired. Harrington cried out, dropping the lantern and stumbling back to sprawl on the steps. Monique, too startled to speak, put her hand to her mouth.

Van crossed the cellar and stared down at the reporter in the light from the still-glowing lantern. Blood stained the leg of Harrington's pants. Van put the muzzle of his pistol against Harrington's forehead.

"No," Monique said. "Don't."

"I won't kill him if you come with me," Van told her. "Without making a fuss." He saw her hesitate. "It's up to you," he said.

"All right," she whispered.

"Take this." The brown satchel, she found, was surprisingly heavy. Van, after retrieving the lantern from the floor, led her to the far wall of the cellar, where he shifted an empty storage closet to one side. She saw the black gaping entrance to a tunnel.

Van ducked his head to enter. Monique followed. The floor of the tunnel slanted downward in front of them, the earth overhead supported by great timbers almost within reach of their hands. As they hurried into the darkness, she saw other timbers spaced some six feet apart on the sides of a tunnel that steadily widened until she could see only the near side in the light from the lantern.

As they descended, the air grew hotter. She quickly realized that they were in one of the old mines, abandoned long ago to darkness and decay. The passages and chambers were ghastly, crumbling ruins, and the tunnel floors were littered with fallen rocks and dirt. Supporting timbers had been twisted into strange shapes, with some crushed down to half their original length by the weight of the mountain overhead. The air was foul and musty. Gigantic fungi grew from the moist and slimy walls and, at times, phosphorescent lights glowed in long-abandoned stopes leading off to their right and left.

All at once Van stopped, holding out his hand. Listening, she heard steps far behind them, hurrying steps echoing in the tunnel.

"It can't be Harrington," Van said. "Not with that leg wound."

Still the echoing steps came on, nearer now, and far back along the slanting tunnel they saw the faint hint of a light.

"Give me that." Van took the satchel from her.

He knelt in the rubble on the side of the tunnel floor and opened the satchel. Inside she saw coin pouches—no wonder it was so heavy, she thought— as well as fuses and cylinders of what she guessed were explosives. Van carried a fuse and several of the cylinders to the tunnel wall. A match flared in his hand and a moment later she heard a deadly hiss.

"We've got five minutes before she blows," he told her.

As soon as Van Allen Reid and Monique had left, Lester Harrington crawled up the cellar stairs to summon help. When he reached the door at the top, he stood, wincing from the pain of the wound in his right thigh. He staggered along the hall, leaning on one wall for support.

The front door opened, and he saw Jeremy Johnston blinking his eyes to accustom them to the hall's dim light. A moment later Jeremy was at Harrington's side.

"They told me at the house you might be here," he said. "What happened? Where's Monique?"

"In the mine," Harrington said. "Reid took her down into the mine. The entrance is in the far wall of the cellar."

Jeremy started past him.

"I'm going with you," Harrington said.

"It's not your concern."

"You're wrong. It's more my concern than yours. I'm her father."

"Her father?" Jeremy stared in disbelief at the grizzled reporter.

"That's right. At first I didn't say anything to her because I thought she'd be a hindrance to me. Then, when I saw she wasn't that kind, I didn't speak up because I thought I'd be a hindrance to her. I'd gotten sort of fond of her and I was afraid of disappointing her again. Better to let her have her dream of a father than be saddled with the real thing. Specially when the real thing was me."

"You underestimate her," Jeremy said.

Harrington shrugged. He pushed himself away from the wall and limped after Jeremy. At the top of the cellar stairs, he stopped and said, "I can't keep up. I'll be a drag on you."

"Go for help," Jeremy told him. "That's the best thing you can do."

Harrington nodded. "You're armed?" he asked.

Jeremy patted a pistol in his belt.

"There's lanterns in the cellar," Harrington called after him. "You'll need one to follow them."

"Bring the satchel," Van told Monique.

She snapped it shut as Van, lantern in hand, started down the tunnel. Monique picked up the satchel, followed him for a few steps, then dropped the satchel, turned and ran back the way they had come.

With a curse, Van ran after her. She raced ahead of him up the gradual slope. She saw the swaying light from his lantern and heard his footsteps pounding behind her, coming closer and closer. His hand grabbed her dress and she felt it tear. He seized her arm and yanked her back toward him. Glancing ahead along the tunnel, she saw the approaching light of the other lantern still more than a hundred yards away.

Van shoved her aside, and she fell in the dirt and rocks on the floor of the tunnel. When she saw Van's gun, she screamed. The gun's roar seemed to shake the mine, the flash momentarily lighting walls and ceiling with an eerie glow. Dirt cascaded down onto her hair and face.

She looked up along the tunnel, but could no longer see the other lantern. Van glanced from his lantern on the tunnel floor to Monique and then back into the tunnel. She knew he must be calculating how much time he had before the burning fuse ignited the explosives. How many minutes had gone by since he lit it? Two? Three?

Van picked up the lantern and ran down the tunnel. Picking up the satchel, he raced past the lighted fuse. Monique pushed herself to her feet. She was light-headed from the heat, from the dank odors of the mine, from her fall. She made her way up the pitch-black slope. She thought she heard a sound to one side. A hand touched her face and she screamed.

"Monique." It was Jeremy.

"Jeremy, Jeremy." She threw herself into his arms. After a moment she drew away.

"He's lit a fuse," she told him. "He'll blow up the tunnel."

Jeremy unshielded his lantern, gazed at her for a second, then grasped her hand, and together they ran up the slope. They had gone no more than fifty feet when an explosion rocked the earth, the concussion slamming them to the ground. Dust filled the dark tunnel and, a moment later, Monique heard a gurgling behind them.

"Are you all right?" Jeremy asked.

"Yes."

He pulled her to her feet. She felt water on her shoes, around her ankles, rising up her leg. Warm water. The lantern was gone.

"Hurry!" Jeremy took her hand.

They ran, stumbling and falling in the dark, then getting up to run again. At last Monique, able to run

no farther, dropped to her knees. The tunnel floor was
dry.

Looking ahead, she saw that the gloom had lessened,
so she knew they were near the opening into the
cellar.

"Van?" she asked.

"He must have drowned," Jeremy said, "when the
water flooded the mine."

Van was dead. Philippe was avenged. She had
looked forward to this moment, planned for it,
dreamed of it. She had expected to be exultant, at
least satisfied, but she felt nothing.

Jeremy took her hand gently in his and led her to
the tunnel entrance.

"How is Laura?" she asked.

"She died last week."

She sighed when she heard the inexpressible sadness in his voice. She wanted to comfort him without
knowing how.

They crawled through the opening into the cellar,
and Jeremy led her up the stairs to the dimly-lit corridor on the first floor.

"I had to come back to Virginia City," Jeremy said.
"I find I can't live without you."

She felt a rush of joy. Perversely, she said, "Just as
you can't live with me."

"Someday," he told her, "later, after time has passed,
I'd like to try. I've found that money isn't as important
as I thought. It's not more important than those you
love. I'm willing to try to change some, not completely,
if you are, Mary. Will you? Can you?"

"I'm not Mary," she said stubbornly. "I'm Monique."

"To me you'll always be Mary."

"But . . ." She paused, then smiled. "As a matter of
fact," she said, "I've been thinking of changing my
name again. Back to Mary Vere."

"I'd like that very much. But it's up to you."

She looked at him. She'd wait for Jeremy, she knew. Hadn't she been waiting all this time? She loved him and that was the beginning and the end of it. No matter what he said or what he did, she loved him, and always would.

They walked hand in hand to the door, leaving the darkness to go out into the sunlight of a Virginia City morning.

Lester Harrington, his leg bandaged, limped toward them, followed by a crowd of armed miners.

Seeing Harrington, Jeremy said to Monique, "I have a surprise for you."

"After these last few days, nothing can surprise me."

"I think Philippe Manigault would have laid odds of five-to-one that this will surprise you."

Jeremy, with Mary beside him, walked up to Harrington and put his arm around his shoulders. They stood talking in the middle of C Street, the two men and the woman, with the miners staring curiously at them from the sidewalks.

A Washoe zephyr sent a dust devil twisting past them up the street toward the brown thrusting slopes of the Nevada mountains. Mary, between the two men, her arms linked with theirs, looked past the whirling dust to Mount Davidson, to the flag unfurling in the wind on the peak, to the blue sky beyond.

This is where I belong, she told herself. I'm home at last. ✒︎

First in the Series

WOMEN WHO WON THE WEST

VOLUME
1

Tempest of Tombstone

by Lee Davis Willoughby

Sally Sewell was stranded in Tombstone, a wide-eyed slip
of a girl, abandoned by a ragtag troupe of touring players.
Rescued—and seduced—by the most powerful man in
Tombstone, she learned to fight for her rights in this, the
rowdiest, hell-roaringest of all frontier boomtowns. Sally
became the most powerful woman in Tombstone, and the
prize in the explosive struggle between Wyatt Earp and
John Behan—the man some called the Devil incarnate—
the struggle that tore the town apart and led to the bloody
Battle of the OK Corral.

ON SALE NOW FROM DELL/BRYANS

Dodge City Darling

by Lee Davis Willoughby

Bold and beautiful, a penniless Lucia Bone sells her body at a Dodge City bordello rather than give up the search for the mother she has never known.

Dubbed "Dodge City Darling", Lucia softens the heart of the legendary gunslinger, Bat Masterson. A tough private detective named Brooker and a hardened Dodge City madam also succumb to Lucia's fatal charm.

The stakes are high, the dangers great, but the determined young beauty stops at nothing in her relentless search for the truth. But a terrible secret may mark Lucia as the daughter of a murderess—and as the next victim of a ruthless killer. . . .

ON SALE NOW FROM DELL/BRYANS

THIRD IN THE
❧*WOMEN WHO WON THE WEST*❧
SERIES

Duchess of Denver

by Lee Davis Willoughby

She came from the river towns of the East
and crossed the wide open plains to the rich
land of California. Posing as the beardless
"E.J.", Elsa Jane toils and sweats to lead a stub-
born breed of sailors and pioneers.

Her beauty and bravery makes the young
widow the "Duchess of Denver" when she tames
the wild heart of an English Duke.

Despite the hazards of the land, Elsa strug-
gles to survive. She must fight the jealous Daris
Jamieson, who seeks to destroy the woman he
cannot possess.

ON SALE NOW FROM DELL/BRYANS

Ð SIGNET

GREAT MILITARY FICTION
BY DON BENDELL

CHIEF OF SCOUTS Rich with the passion and adventure of real history, this novel of the U.S. Cavalry brings forth a hero, worthy of the finest military fiction, who had to work above the law to uphold justice.   (176901—$4.50)

COLT Christopher Columbus Colt, legendary chief of cavalry scouts, was in for the biggest fight of his life—forced to lead an all-black U.S. Cavalry unit on a suicide mission. And even if the Chief of Scouts could conquer his own doubts, he would still have to reckon with two names that struck fear into the hearts of every frontier man: Victorio and Geronimo, renegade Apache chiefs who led their warriors on a bloody trail.   (178300—$4.50)

HORSE SOLDIERS In the embattled Oregon territory, Christopher Columbus Colt was a wanted man. General O.O. "One-Armed" Howard, commanding the U.S. Cavalry, wanted this legendary scout to guide his forces in his campaign to break the power and take the lands of the proud Nez Perce. The tactical genius, Nez Perce Chief Joseph needed Colt as an ally in this last ditch face-off. And only Colt can decide which side to fight on ...   (177207—$4.50)

*Prices slightly higher in Canada

Buy them at your local bookstore or use this convenient coupon for ordering.

PENGUIN USA
P.O. Box 999 — Dept. #17109
Bergenfield, New Jersey 07621

Please send me the books I have checked above.
I am enclosing $_____ (please add $2.00 to cover postage and handling). Send check or money order (no cash or C.O.D.'s) or charge by Mastercard or VISA (with a $15.00 minimum). Prices and numbers are subject to change without notice.

Card #_____ Exp. Date _____
Signature_____
Name_____
Address_____
City _____ State _____ Zip Code _____

For faster service when ordering by credit card call **1-800-253-6476**

Allow a minimum of 4-6 weeks for delivery. This offer is subject to change without notice.

⊘ **SIGNET**   (045

THE TRAILSMAN—
HAS GUN, WILL TRAVEL

☐ **THE TRAILSMAN #142: GOLDEN BULLETS by Jon Sharpe.** Skye Fargo goes on a Bla⋯
Hills, South Dakota sleigh ride where he will have to do a lot of digging to uncover th⋯
truth about who killed who and why—and a lot of shooting to keep him from bein⋯
buried with it.   (177533—$3.5⋯

☐ **THE TRAILSMAN #143: DEATHBLOW TRAIL by Jon Sharpe.** Skye Fargo has a gunhan⋯
full of trouble when an Arizona gold vein gushes blood.   (177541—$3.5⋯

☐ **THE TRAILSMAN #144: ABILENE AMBUSH by Jon Sharpe.** Skye Fargo was looking f⋯
rest and relaxation in Abilene, Kansas. What he found was five toothsome females wh⋯
wanted to lead them over the plains in a couple of creaking wagons.... Skye said n⋯
but the trouble was these lovely women wouldn't take no for an answer ... and the⋯
were willing to do anything short of telling the truth about the danger they were runnin⋯
from.   (177568—$3.5⋯

☐ **THE TRAILSMAN #145: CHEYENNE CROSSFIRE by Jon Sharpe.** Skye Fargo ... in th⋯
tightest spot in his life ... playing his most dangerous role ... a man who everyon⋯
thought was a monstrous murderer ... with his life riding on his trigger finger and ⋯
woman's trust ... Skye Fargo fights a Wyoming frame-up with flaming fury and blazin⋯
firepower.   (177576—$3.5⋯

☐ **THE TRAILSMAN #146: NEBRASKA NIGHTMARE by Jon Sharpe.** The settlers thought the⋯
had found a piece of paradise in the Nebraska Territory near the River Platte. But th⋯
trouble was ... a cougar named Nightmare, who killed without warning ... and ⋯
gang led by Rascomb.... What the farmers needed was a man who could kill a kill⋯
cat and outgun ... marauding murderers.... They got what they needed and more⋯
Skye Fargo.   (17876—$3.5⋯

Prices slightly higher in Canada

Buy them at your local bookstore or use this convenient coupon for ordering.

PENGUIN USA
P.O. Box 999 — Dept. #17109
Bergenfield, New Jersey 07621

Please send me the books I have checked above.
I am enclosing $＿＿＿＿＿＿ (please add $2.00 to cover postage and handling⋯
Send check or money order (no cash or C.O.D.'s) or charge by Mastercard⋯
VISA (with a $15.00 minimum). Prices and numbers are subject to change witho⋯
notice.

Card #＿＿＿＿＿＿＿＿＿＿＿＿ Exp. Date ＿＿＿＿＿＿＿＿
Signature＿＿＿＿＿＿＿＿＿＿＿＿＿＿＿＿＿＿＿＿＿＿＿＿
Name＿＿＿＿＿＿＿＿＿＿＿＿＿＿＿＿＿＿＿＿＿＿＿＿＿＿
Address＿＿＿＿＿＿＿＿＿＿＿＿＿＿＿＿＿＿＿＿＿＿＿＿＿
City ＿＿＿＿＿＿＿＿＿＿＿ State ＿＿＿＿＿＿＿ Zip Code ＿＿＿＿＿＿

For faster service when ordering by credit card call **1-800-253-6476**

Allow a minimum of 4-6 weeks for delivery. This offer is subject to change without notic⋯

⊘ **SIGNET** (0451)

BLAZING ACTION FROM THE TRAILSMAN SERIES!

] **THE TRAILSMAN #139: BUFFALO GUNS by Jon Sharpe.** Can Skye Fargo rip apart the veil of mystery and stand up to a titan of terror in a stampede of slaughter on a Kansas killing ground? (176669—$3.50)

] **THE TRAILSMAN #140: THE KILLING CORRIDOR by Jon Sharpe.** Skye Fargo shoots south through a Missouri maze of mystery and murder! (177517—$3.50)

] **THE TRAILSMAN #141: TOMAHAWK JUSTICE by Jon Sharpe.** In a sacred valley swarming with the most bloodthirsty redskins in the West, Fargo finds himself in the middle of a tug-of-want between two young Shoshone sisters who give him no rest, and in the line of fire of Indians who give no quarter and take no prisoners. (177525—$3.50)

Prices slightly higher in Canada

Buy them at your local bookstore or use this convenient coupon for ordering.

PENGUIN USA
P.O. Box 999 – Dept. #17109
Bergenfield, New Jersey 07621

Please send me the books I have checked above.
I am enclosing $_____ (please add $2.00 to cover postage and handling).
Send check or money order (no cash or C.O.D.'s) or charge by Mastercard or
VISA (with a $15.00 minimum). Prices and numbers are subject to change without
notice.

Card #_____ Exp. Date _____
Signature_____
Name_____
Address_____
City _____ State _____ Zip Code _____

For faster service when ordering by credit card call **1-800-253-6476**

Allow a minimum of 4-6 weeks for delivery. This offer is subject to change without notice.

① SIGNET

JON SHARPE'S WILD WEST

☐ **THE TRAILSMAN #147: DEATH TRAILS.** Skye Fargo was riding into double-barrele
danger when he hit the trail in Texas teeming with murderous Mescalero Apache
and brutal *banditos*. He was out to settle the score with a trio of bushwhacker
who had bashed in his head and stolen his roll. The only thing that the Trailsma
could trust was his trigger finger in a crossfire where lies flew as thick as bullet
and treachery was the name of the game.   (178823—$3.50

☐ **THE TRAILSMAN #148: CALIFORNIA QUARRY.** Sky Fargo had gone as far west an
as deep into trouble as he could get on San Francisco's Barbary Coast. Now h
was heading back east with a cargo of dead animals, a dodo of a professor,
stowaway pickpocket, and a beautiful fallen dove fleeing her gilded cage. Huntin
them was Barbary Coast bully boy Deke Johnson and his gang of killers.

(178831—$3.50

☐ **THE TRAILSMAN #149: SPRINGFIELD SHARPSHOOTERS.** Skye Fargo could win mos
shoot-outs gun hands down—but this one was different. He was roped into
contest against the best in the West for a pile of cash that made the top gu
worth its weight in gold. But when guns in the night started aiming at liv
targets, Fargo realized he had to do more than shoot to win, he had to shoot t
kill ...   (178858—$3.50

☐ **THE TRAILSMAN #150: SAVAGE GUNS.** Skye Fargo is caught in a wild Wyomin
war in which he must fight for his life in a crossfire of female fury, redskin rage
and the demented designs of a military madman who made war against th
innocent and smeared his flag with bloody guilt.   (178866—$3.50

*Prices slightly higher in Canada

Buy them at your local bookstore or use this convenient coupon for ordering.

PENGUIN USA
P.O. Box 999 — Dept. #17109
Bergenfield, New Jersey 07621

Please send me the books I have checked above.
I am enclosing $_____ (please add $2.00 to cover postage and handling). Sen
check or money order (no cash or C.O.D.'s) or charge by Mastercard or VISA (with a $15.0
minimum). Prices and numbers are subject to change without notice.

Card #_____ Exp. Date _____
Signature_____
Name_____
Address_____
City _____ State _____ Zip Code _____

For faster service when ordering by credit card call **1-800-253-6476**

Allow a minimum of 4-6 weeks for delivery. This offer is subject to change without notice.